TWELVE CLASSIC CHRISTMAS STORIES

EDITED BY **TIMOTHY LARSEN**

TWELVE CLASSIC CHRISTMAS STORIES

A FEAST OF YULETIDE TALES

MOODY PUBLISHERS
CHICAGO

All Scripture quotations, unless otherwise noted, are taken from the Holy Bible, New International Version, NIV. Copyright ©1973, 1978, 1984, 2011 by Biblica, Inc.™ Used by permission of Zondervan. All rights reserved worldwide. www.zondervan.com The "NIV" and "New International Version" are trademarks registered in the United States Patent and Trademark Office by Biblica, Inc.™

Scripture quotations marked KJV are taken from the King James Version.

Compiled and edited by Timothy Larsen
Interior design: Puckett Smartt
Cover and interior illustrations and cover design: Kaylee Lockenour Dunn

ISBN: 978-0-8024-3279-7

Originally delivered by fleets of horse-drawn wagons, the affordable paperbacks from D. L. Moody's publishing house resourced the church and served everyday people. Now, after more than 125 years of publishing and ministry, Moody Publishers' mission remains the same—even if our delivery systems have changed a bit. For more information on other books (and resources) created from a biblical perspective, go to www.moodypublishers.com or write to:

Moody Publishers
820 N. LaSalle Boulevard
Chicago, IL 60610

1 3 5 7 9 10 8 6 4 2

Printed in China

For families that love to read

and especially our daughter,

Lucia Holly

who reads to our family,
and who is our favorite Christmas gift.

CONTENTS

INTRODUCTION

The witness of the Gospels to the birth, ministry, death, and resurrection of Jesus of Nazareth has rightly been called "the greatest story ever told." Throughout history, even many doubters and skeptics have eventually come to realize that this story is so wonderful that no one could have made it up. Only someone who had witnessed true holiness could share it with others. Only someone who was themselves wise beyond our imagining could write a character who said things wise beyond our imagining. The Gospels are too good not to be true.

The narrative begins with the nativity. What a wondrous story! A young, holy woman named Mary; the angel Gabriel; the carpenter Joseph; the Roman Empire; Caesar Augustus demanding that more taxes be collected; the royal city of Bethlehem; the inn that had no room available; the shepherds keeping watch over their flocks by night; the heavenly host proclaiming peace and goodwill; the birth of a boy who is to be named Jesus because He is the long-awaited Savior; the manger and the swaddling clothes; the magi from the East; a star that is a sign in the heavens; the murderous Herod the Great; the gifts of gold, frankincense, and myrrh.

Every year when we celebrate Christmas, we tell this story again. In fact, we do many things over again every year during the holiday season. Many people have an ideal of celebrating an "old-fashioned Christmas." One of the stories in this collection, "Old Christmas at Bracebridge Hall" by Washington Irving, is over two hundred years old, yet it is a story about a man who wants to celebrate an old-fashioned Christmas! Christmas is a time for continuity. As adults we like to reexperience the delightful things we remember fondly from our childhood—and to share them with our own children. In the metropolitan area where I live, there is a radio station that most of the year round plays the latest contemporary pop songs, but during December you can tune in and hear, for instance, a recording made in the 1940s of a carol that goes back to the Middle Ages. There is an enchanting succession of song passed down the generations that goes back and back through the ages all the way to Mary's Magnificat. Do you hear what I hear? During the holidays, many people will watch much older films than they normally would, maybe going all the way back to the black-and-white era for a classic such as *It's a Wonderful Life* (1946). When the festive lights are up, the tree has been decorated, and the big day is on its way, you might find yourself eating and drinking treats that have been savored by generations past and would probably never occur to you to have at any other time of the year: eggnog, chestnuts, cranberry sauce, sage stuffing, mince pies, candy canes, gingerbread, and so on. The ghost of Christmas past can be a warm and welcoming presence.

And not only do we tell and retell the gospel story of Christ's nativity every December, we also tell and retell lots of other Christmas stories. This, too, can be part of keeping an old-fashioned Christmas. My father read Christmas stories aloud to our family when I was young, and so I did the same with our children. If and when they have children, I hope they will carry on the tradition—maybe even by reading aloud from this very book. Sometimes the stories I read to my children were even the very same ones that my father had read to me. Along with the carols and the cookies from recipes passed down the generations, we can also enjoy great literary classics from past ages. I have read Christmas stories avidly my entire life—and I read heaps and heaps more in order to make the selection for this collection. My hope is that some families will choose to read some of them aloud together as part of their yuletide celebrations. I also hope that schools will find ways to make use of this collection. And circles of friends as well. There are twelve stories in this book as a festive way of nodding at the twelve days of Christmas, the twelve days of feasting our merry-making ancestors would keep.

I have sought out some of the most celebrated and beloved writers of fiction for this collection: Charles Dickens, Louisa May Alcott, O. Henry, Sir Arthur Conan Doyle, Lucy Maud Montgomery, G. K. Chesterton, George MacDonald, and more. There is a one-paragraph introduction before the beginning of each story. Those introductions have been carefully written so that there are no plot spoilers. They are intended to serve as a guide so that you can see if it is the story you want to select to read at that particular time. Readers are therefore told if it is long or short, particularly happy or mingled with sadness, and so on. There is also a recommendation for what you might want to read next from the same author. The stories are annotated to help explain some historical and cultural contexts that are no longer familiar to us today, as well as words and phrases that are no longer in use or that have changed their meaning over time.

I have tried to create a Christmas variety pack so that there is something here for everyone. There is a ghost story (two, if you count the goblins!); there is a romance (two again actually, but only one is a romantic comedy—maybe even three, in fact, if you are broad-minded enough to believe that a romance can be a story about a husband and wife); there is a detective story; there are stories about children and their hopes and annoyances and schemes; there are stories with surprising plot twists.

When you read stacks of holiday fiction all in a row, as I have done in order to make this collection, you learn that the Christmas story is a true, literary genre and therefore yuletide tales often have a lot in common with each other. Given our culture's emphasis upon Christmas joy and jolliness—it's the most wonderful time of the year!—one perhaps somewhat surprising element is suffering. There is poverty and illness, there are widows and orphans. Children sometimes die. (I did not include in this collection one of the most famous Christmas stories, which is a well-known case in point, "The Little Match Girl" by Hans Christian Andersen. And we remember that even the nativity story itself includes Herod's slaughter of the innocents.) The word *myrrh* means "bitter." It speaks of sorrow and death. Myrrh was used to prepare Christ's body for burial (John 19:39). Every Christmas story does not bring the glitter of gold or the sweetness of frankincense. Some Christmas stories bring myrrh. Many of these "myrrh" tales that carry some of the sadness of the world inside them, however, end not with the sorrow of death, but with the triumph of resurrection life. At Christmas, we remember that Jesus came to give us life.

I think that all this suffering that runs so persistently through the genre of Christmas literature serves two purposes. First, it is there to remind us that part of the way we ought to keep Christmas is by helping those in need. These stories do not allow us to look away; they demand that we see those who are hungry or poor, ill or dying, desperate or lonely. They are a reminder that, even though it is a season of good cheer, there are people who are suffering. We must remember that they are there, even in this holiday season, and reach out to do something to help them. Christmas is a time for giving. This is the lesson that Ebenezer Scrooge needed to learn in the most famous yuletide tale of them all, "A Christmas Carol" by Charles Dickens.

The second purpose is to remind us to be grateful for our lives, for the good things that we enjoy and, most of all, for the people that we love and who love us. The real, secret message of a death in a holiday story is: how wonderful it is that there are people in your life whom you love and who are still alive! Stop taking them for granted or squabbling with them, and start being thankful and making the most of their company. Go find them and hug them and tell them that you love them. Give them a present as an expression of your Christmas joy. Read aloud to them a splendid tale about a basket or a burglar or a blue carbuncle or a gaggle of goblins. Make some memories with them this holiday season that you will cherish the rest of your life.

The deepest, truest theme in Christmas stories is therefore reconciliation in relationships. This is fitting, of course, because that is also the theme of the gospel, the greatest story ever told: "She will give birth to a son, and you are to give him the name Jesus, because he will save his people from their sins" (Matt. 1:21). Christmas is a time for forgiveness. It is the season for the estranged to become reconciled. It is a time for prodigals to come home—and to be rejoiced over with great feasting. Twelve days of feasting is not too much. It is a time for old grudges to be set aside; for long-simmering feuds to come to an end. You have hardened your heart against that person for too long; it is time for bygones to be bygones and for the love submerged underneath it all to be allowed to flow freely once again. It is a time for peace and goodwill. It is a time to give and receive love. It is a time for joy. Good Christian men, women, and children, rejoice!

In order to prepare this collection, I read every one of these stories many times. At first, I worried that after I knew the ending—especially for the stories that are built around a clever plot twist—there would be diminishing pleasure in reading them again. But I was wrong! These Christmas stories are true classics that one can revisit with delight again and again. It has long been thought that the very best Christmas gifts are the ones that we make ourselves. I have been quietly laboring on this project for a long time now—during the spring, summer, autumn, and winter. It is a labor of love. It is my Christmas gift for you and your family and friends.

TILLY'S CHRISTMAS

LOUISA MAY ALCOTT

This story is a quick read and should satisfy the desires of anyone hoping for a thoroughly happy story and, most especially, a happy ending. Indeed, the tone is so bright that it is easy to lose clear sight of the fact that this is despite truly difficult circumstances. In reality, it is a story about a poor, hardworking, single mother and her young daughter, without enough food to eat and fuel to keep warm. It also includes a robin and, for mysterious reasons (there are charming legends that attempt to explain why), robins are a symbol of Christmas. It is common, especially in Britain, for Christmas cards to have a picture that includes this red-breasted bird. When reading or listening to "Tilly's Christmas," it might be fun to see if you can notice the quotations from the Bible that are hiding in it. Though this one is not quoted, the story also reminds us that God's eyes are on even the common, little birds and therefore we can have faith that He is watching over people in need as well. "Tilly's Christmas" was first published in the children's magazine **Merry's Museum** in 1868. Its author, Louisa May Alcott (1832–1888), was also the magazine's editor—or about to become so. During that same year, Alcott was also busy writing her masterpiece, **Little Women** (1869). Its very first word is "Christmas." That great American novel begins: "'Christmas won't be Christmas without presents,' grumbled Jo." Therefore, the holiday season is also a perfect time to read or reread **Little Women**.

°°°

TILLY'S CHRISTMAS

LOUISA MAY ALCOTT

"I'm so glad tomorrow is Christmas, because I'm going to have lots of presents."

"So am I glad, though I don't expect any presents but a pair of mittens."

"And so am I; but I shan't have any presents at all."

As the three little girls trudged home from school they said these things, and as Tilly spoke, both the others looked at her with pity and some surprise, for she spoke cheerfully, and they wondered how she could be happy when she was so poor she could have no presents on Christmas.

"Don't you wish you could find a purse full of money right here in the path?" said Kate, the child who was going to have "lots of presents."

"Oh, don't I, if I could keep it honestly!" and Tilly's eyes shone at the very thought.

"What would you buy?" asked Bessy, rubbing her cold hands, and longing for her mittens.

"I'd buy a pair of large, warm blankets, a load of wood, a shawl for mother, and a pair of shoes for me; and if there was enough left, I'd give Bessy a new hat, and then she needn't wear Ben's old felt one," answered Tilly.

The girls laughed at that; but Bessy pulled the funny hat over her ears, and said she was much obliged but she'd rather have candy.

"Let's look, and maybe we *can* find a purse. People are always going about with money at Christmas time, and someone may lose it here," said Kate.

So, as they went along the snowy road, they looked about them, half in earnest, half in fun. Suddenly Tilly sprang forward, exclaiming—

"I see it! I've found it!"

The others followed, but all stopped disappointed; for it wasn't a purse, it was only a little bird. It lay upon the snow with its wings spread and feebly fluttering, as if too weak to fly. Its little feet were benumbed with cold; its once bright eyes were dull with pain, and instead of a blithe song, it could only utter a faint chirp, now and then, as if crying for help.

"Nothing but a stupid old robin; how provoking!" cried Kate, sitting down to rest.

"I shan't touch it. I found one once, and took care of it, and the ungrateful thing flew away the minute it was well," said Bessy, creeping under Kate's shawl, and putting her hands under her chin to warm them.

"Poor little birdie! How pitiful he looks, and how glad he must be to see someone coming to help him! I'll take him up gently, and carry him home to mother. Don't be frightened, dear, I'm your friend," and Tilly knelt down in the snow, stretching her hand to the bird, with the tenderest pity in her face.

Kate and Bessy laughed.

"Don't stop for that thing; it's getting late and cold: let's go on and look for the purse," they said moving away.

"You wouldn't leave it to die!" cried Tilly. "I'd rather have the bird than the money, so I shan't look any more. The purse wouldn't be mine, and I should only be tempted to keep it; but this poor thing will thank and love me, and I'm *so* glad I came in time."

Gently lifting the bird, Tilly felt its tiny, cold claws cling to her hand, and saw its dim eyes brighten as it nestled down with a grateful chirp.

"Now I've got a Christmas present after all," she said, smiling, as they walked on. "I always wanted a bird, and this one will be such a pretty pet for me."

"He'll fly away the first chance he gets, and die anyhow; so you'd better not waste your time over him," said Bessy.

"He can't pay you for taking care of him, and my mother says it isn't worth while to help folks that can't help us," added Kate.

"My mother says, 'Do as you'd be done by;' and I'm sure I'd like any one to help me if I was dying of cold and hunger. 'Love your neighbour as yourself,' is another of her sayings. This bird is my little neighbour, and I'll love him and care for him, as I often wish our rich neighbour would love and care for us," answered Tilly, breathing her warm breath over the benumbed bird, who looked up at her with confiding eyes, quick to feel and know a friend.

"What a funny girl you are," said Kate; "caring for that silly bird, and talking about loving your neighbour in that sober way. Mr. King don't care a bit for you, and never will, though he knows how poor you are; so I don't think your plan amounts to much."

"I believe it, though; and shall do my part, any way. Good-night. I hope you'll have a merry Christmas, and lots of pretty things," answered Tilly, as they parted.

Her eyes were full, and she felt so poor as she went on alone toward the little old house where she lived. It would have been so pleasant to know that she was going to have some of the pretty things all children love to find in their full stockings on Christmas morning. And pleasanter still to have been able to give her mother something nice. So many comforts were needed, and there was no hope of getting them; for they could barely get food and fire.

"Never mind, birdie, we'll make the best of what we have, and be merry in spite of every thing. *You* shall have a happy Christmas, any way;

and I know God won't forget us if every one else does."

She stopped a minute to wipe her eyes, and lean her cheek against the bird's soft breast, finding great comfort in the little creature, though it could only love her, nothing more.

"See, mother, what a nice present I've found," she cried, going in with a cheery face that was like sunshine in the dark room.

"I'm glad of that, dearie; for I haven't been able to get my little girl anything but a rosy apple. Poor bird! Give it some of your warm bread and milk."

"Why, mother, what a big bowlful! I'm afraid you gave me all the milk," said Tilly, smiling over the nice, steaming supper that stood ready for her.

"I've had plenty, dear. Sit down and dry your wet feet, and put the bird in my basket on this warm flannel."

Tilly peeped into the closet and saw nothing there but dry bread.

"Mother's given me all the milk, and is going without her tea,[1] 'cause she knows I'm hungry. Now I'll surprise her, and she shall have a good supper too. She is going to split wood, and I'll fix it while she's gone."

So Tilly put down the old tea-pot, carefully poured out a part of the milk, and from her pocket produced a great, plummy bun, that one of the school-children had given her, and she had saved for her mother. A slice of the dry bread was nicely toasted, and the bit of butter set by for her put on it. When her mother came in there was the table drawn up in a warm place, a hot cup of tea ready, and Tilly and birdie waiting for her.

Such a poor little supper, and yet such a happy one; for love, charity, and contentment were guests there, and that Christmas eve was a blither[2] one than that up at the great house, where lights shone, fires blazed, a

---

1. The "tea" is being used here to mean a meal. While Americans do not speak this way anymore, this usage is still common in Britain.
2. More joyful.

great tree glittered, and music sounded, as the children danced and played.

"We must go to bed early, for we've only wood enough to last over to-morrow. I shall be paid for my work the day after, and then we can get some," said Tilly's mother, as they sat by the fire.

"If my bird was only a fairy bird, and would give us three wishes, how nice it would be! Poor dear, he can't give me any thing; but it's no matter," answered Tilly, looking at the robin, who lay in the basket with his head under his wing, a mere little feathery bunch.

"He can give you one thing, Tilly—the pleasure of doing good. That is one of the sweetest things in life; and the poor can enjoy it as well as the rich."

As her mother spoke, with her tired hand softly stroking her little daughter's hair, Tilly suddenly started and pointed to the window, saying, in a frightened whisper—

"I saw a face—a man's face, looking in! It's gone now; but I truly saw it."

"Some traveller attracted by the light perhaps. I'll go and see." And Tilly's mother went to the door.

No one was there. The wind blew cold, the stars shone, the snow lay white on field and wood, and the Christmas moon was glittering in the sky.

"What sort of a face was it?" asked Tilly's mother, coming back.

"A pleasant sort of face, I think; but I was so startled I don't quite know what it was like. I wish we had a curtain there," said Tilly.

"I like to have our light shine out in the evening, for the road is dark and lonely just here, and the twinkle of our lamp is pleasant to people's eyes as they go by. We can do so little for our neighbours, I am glad to cheer the way for them. Now put these poor old shoes to dry, and go to bed, dearie; I'll come soon."

Tilly went, taking her bird with her to sleep in his basket near by, lest he should be lonely in the night.

Soon the little house was dark and still, and no one saw the Christmas spirits at their work that night.

When Tilly opened the door next morning, she gave a loud cry, clapped her hands, and then stood still; quite speechless with wonder and delight. There, before the door, lay a great pile of wood, all ready to burn, a big bundle and a basket, with a lovely nosegay[3] of winter roses, holly, and evergreen tied to the handle.

"Oh, mother! did the fairies do it?" cried Tilly, pale with her happiness, as she seized the basket, while her mother took in the bundle.

"Yes, dear, the best and dearest fairy in the world, called 'Charity.' She walks abroad at Christmas time, does beautiful deeds like this, and does not stay to be thanked," answered her mother with full eyes, as she undid the parcel.

There they were—the warm, thick blankets, the comfortable shawls, the new shoes, and, best of all, a pretty winter hat for Bessy. The basket was full of good things to eat, and on the flowers lay a paper, saying—

"For the little girl who loves her neighbour as herself."

"Mother, I really think my bird is a fairy bird, and all these splendid things come from him," said Tilly, laughing and crying with joy.

It really did seem so, for as she spoke, the robin flew to the table, hopped to the nosegay, and perching among the roses, began to chirp with all his little might. The sun streamed in on flowers, bird, and happy child, and no one saw a shadow glide away from the window; no one ever knew that Mr. King had seen and heard the little girls the night before, or dreamed that the rich neighbour had learned a lesson from the poor neighbour.

And Tilly's bird *was* a fairy bird; for by her love and tenderness to the helpless thing, she brought good gifts to herself, happiness to the unknown giver of them, and a faithful little friend who did not fly away, but stayed with her till the snow was gone, making summer for her in the winter-time.

---

3. A bouquet (an arrangement of a bunch of flowers).

THE ADVENTURE OF
THE BLUE CARBUNCLE

SIR ARTHUR CONAN DOYLE

No one ever did more to establish detective stories as a popular genre than Sir Arthur Conan Doyle (1859–1930). His celebrated sleuth, Sherlock Holmes, is one of the most famous and recognizable characters in all of literature. "The Adventure of the Blue Carbuncle" (1892) is a Christmas mystery. A "carbuncle" is a gemstone cut in a particular style, and the Countess of Morcar's dazzling, rare diamond has gone missing. There is mischief afoot, and before it's all over someone's goose is going to get cooked. We can count on Holmes to observe what everyone else has failed to see and to grasp what it all must mean. "The Adventure of the Blue Carbuncle" was published in the Strand magazine, and then included in the first collection of these short stories, The Adventures of Sherlock Holmes (1892). Doyle also wrote four novels featuring Sherlock Holmes and his partner in crime detection, Dr. Watson, the first of which is A Study in Scarlet (1887).

THE ADVENTURE OF THE BLUE CARBUNCLE

SIR ARTHUR CONAN DOYLE

I had called upon my friend Sherlock Holmes upon the second morning after Christmas, with the intention of wishing him the compliments of the season. He was lounging upon the sofa in a purple dressing-gown,[1] a pipe-rack within his reach upon the right, and a pile of crumpled morning papers, evidently newly studied, near at hand. Beside the couch was a wooden chair, and on the angle of the back hung a very seedy and disreputable hard-felt hat, much the worse for wear, and cracked in several places. A lens and a forceps lying upon the seat of the chair suggested that the hat had been suspended in this manner for the purpose of examination.

"You are engaged," said I; "perhaps I interrupt you."

"Not at all. I am glad to have a friend with whom I can discuss my results. The matter is a perfectly trivial one"—he jerked his thumb in the direction of the old hat—"but there are points in connection with it which are not entirely devoid of interest and even of instruction."

I seated myself in his armchair and warmed my hands before his crackling fire, for a sharp frost had set in, and the windows were thick with the

---

1. Similar to a bathrobe. Worn to be comfortable and informal at home.

ice crystals. "I suppose," I remarked, "that, homely as it looks, this thing has some deadly story linked on to it—that it is the clue which will guide you in the solution of some mystery and the punishment of some crime."

"No, no. No crime," said Sherlock Holmes, laughing. "Only one of those whimsical little incidents which will happen when you have four million human beings all jostling each other within the space of a few square miles. Amid the action and reaction of so dense a swarm of humanity, every possible combination of events may be expected to take place, and many a little problem will be presented which may be striking and bizarre without being criminal. We have already had experience of such."

"So much so," I remarked, "that of the last six cases which I have added to my notes, three have been entirely free of any legal crime."

"Precisely. You allude to my attempt to recover the Irene Adler papers, to the singular case of Miss Mary Sutherland, and to the adventure of the man with the twisted lip. Well, I have no doubt that this small matter will fall into the same innocent category. You know Peterson, the commissionaire?"[2]

"Yes."

"It is to him that this trophy belongs."

"It is his hat."

"No, no; he found it. Its owner is unknown. I beg that you will look upon it not as a battered billycock[3] but as an intellectual problem. And, first, as to how it came here. It arrived upon Christmas morning, in company with a good fat goose, which is, I have no doubt, roasting at this moment in front of Peterson's fire. The facts are these: about four o'clock on Christmas morning, Peterson, who, as you know, is a very honest fellow, was returning from some small jollification and was making his way

2. A commissionaire is a porter or messenger, such as someone working at a hotel desk who is helping customers with their requests.
3. A round style of hat like a bowler.

homeward down Tottenham Court Road.[4] In front of him he saw, in the gaslight, a tallish man, walking with a slight stagger, and carrying a white goose slung over his shoulder. As he reached the corner of Goodge Street, a row broke out between this stranger and a little knot of roughs.[5] One of the latter knocked off the man's hat, on which he raised his stick to defend himself and, swinging it over his head, smashed the shop window behind him. Peterson had rushed forward to protect the stranger from his assailants; but the man, shocked at having broken the window, and seeing an official-looking person in uniform rushing towards him, dropped his goose, took to his heels, and vanished amid the labyrinth of small streets which lie at the back of Tottenham Court Road. The roughs had also fled at the appearance of Peterson, so that he was left in possession of the field of battle, and also of the spoils of victory in the shape of this battered hat and a most unimpeachable Christmas goose."

"Which surely he restored to their owner?"

"My dear fellow, there lies the problem. It is true that 'For Mrs. Henry Baker' was printed upon a small card which was tied to the bird's left leg, and it is also true that the initials 'H. B.' are legible upon the lining of this hat; but as there are some thousands of Bakers, and some hundreds of Henry Bakers in this city of ours, it is not easy to restore lost property to any one of them."

"What, then, did Peterson do?"

"He brought round both hat and goose to me on Christmas morning, knowing that even the smallest problems are of interest to me. The goose we retained until this morning, when there were signs that, in spite of the slight frost, it would be well that it should be eaten without unnecessary delay. Its finder has carried it off, therefore, to fulfil the ultimate destiny of a goose, while I continue to retain the hat of the unknown gentleman who lost his Christmas dinner."

---

4. A major road in central London, England. This whole story is set in London.
5. People who are prone to be violent, unruly, or up to no good.

"Did he not advertise?"

"No."

"Then, what clue could you have as to his identity?"

"Only as much as we can deduce."

"From his hat?"

"Precisely."

"But you are joking. What can you gather from this old battered felt?"

"Here is my lens. You know my methods. What can you gather yourself as to the individuality of the man who has worn this article?"

I took the tattered object in my hands and turned it over rather ruefully. It was a very ordinary black hat of the usual round shape, hard and much the worse for wear. The lining had been of red silk, but was a good deal discoloured. There was no maker's name; but, as Holmes had remarked, the initials "H. B." were scrawled upon one side. It was pierced in the brim for a hat-securer, but the elastic was missing. For the rest, it was cracked, exceedingly dusty, and spotted in several places, although there seemed to have been some attempt to hide the discoloured patches by smearing them with ink.

"I can see nothing," said I, handing it back to my friend.

"On the contrary, Watson, you can see everything. You fail, however, to reason from what you see. You are too timid in drawing your inferences."

"Then, pray tell me what it is that you can infer from this hat?"

He picked it up and gazed at it in the peculiar introspective fashion which was characteristic of him. "It is perhaps less suggestive than it might have been," he remarked, "and yet there are a few inferences which are very distinct, and a few others which represent at least a strong balance of probability. That the man was highly intellectual is of course obvious upon the face of it, and also that he was fairly well-to-do within the last three years, although he has now fallen upon evil days. He had foresight, but has less now than formerly, pointing to a moral retrogression, which, when taken with the decline of his fortunes, seems to indicate some evil influence, probably drink, at work upon him. This may account also for the obvious fact that his wife has ceased to love him."

"My dear Holmes!"

"He has, however, retained some degree of self-respect," he continued, disregarding my remonstrance. "He is a man who leads a sedentary life, goes out little, is out of training entirely, is middle-aged, has grizzled hair which he has had cut within the last few days, and which he anoints with lime-cream. These are the more patent facts which are to be deduced from his hat. Also, by the way, that it is extremely improbable that he has gas laid on in his house."[6]

"You are certainly joking, Holmes."

"Not in the least. Is it possible that even now, when I give you these results, you are unable to see how they are attained?"

"I have no doubt that I am very stupid, but I must confess that I am unable to follow you. For example, how did you deduce that this man was intellectual?"

For answer Holmes clapped the hat upon his head. It came right over the forehead and settled upon the bridge of his nose. "It is a question of cubic capacity," said he; "a man with so large a brain must have something in it."

"The decline of his fortunes, then?"

"This hat is three years old. These flat brims curled at the edge came in then. It is a hat of the very best quality. Look at the band of ribbed silk and the excellent lining. If this man could afford to buy so expensive a hat three years ago, and has had no hat since, then he has assuredly gone down in the world."

---

6. A then-modern improvement over the old way of using candles for lighting. Lamps connected to a gas supply were much more convenient.

"Well, that is clear enough, certainly. But how about the foresight and the moral retrogression?"

Sherlock Holmes laughed. "Here is the foresight," said he, putting his finger upon the little disc and loop of the hat-securer. "They are never sold upon hats. If this man ordered one, it is a sign of a certain amount of foresight, since he went out of his way to take this precaution against the wind. But since we see that he has broken the elastic and has not troubled to replace it, it is obvious that he has less foresight now than formerly, which is a distinct proof of a weakening nature. On the other hand, he has endeavoured to conceal some of these stains upon the felt by daubing them with ink, which is a sign that he has not entirely lost his self-respect."

"Your reasoning is certainly plausible."

"The further points, that he is middle-aged, that his hair is grizzled, that it has been recently cut, and that he uses lime-cream, are all to be gathered from a close examination of the lower part of the lining. The lens discloses a large number of hair-ends, clean cut by the scissors of the barber. They all appear to be adhesive, and there is a distinct odour of lime-cream. This dust, you will observe, is not the gritty, gray dust of the street but the fluffy brown dust of the house, showing that it has been hung up indoors most of the time; while the marks of moisture upon the inside are proof positive that the wearer perspired very freely, and could therefore hardly be in the best of training."

"But his wife—you said that she had ceased to love him."

"This hat has not been brushed for weeks. When I see you, my dear Watson, with a week's accumulation of dust upon your hat, and when your wife allows you to go out in such a state, I shall fear that you also have been unfortunate enough to lose your wife's affection."

"But he might be a bachelor."

"Nay, he was bringing home the goose as a peace-offering to his wife. Remember the card upon the bird's leg."

"You have an answer to everything. But how on earth do you deduce that the gas is not laid on in his house?"

"One tallow[7] stain, or even two, might come by chance; but when I see no less than five, I think that there can be little doubt that the individual must be brought into frequent contact with burning tallow—walks upstairs at night probably with his hat in one hand and a guttering candle in the other. Anyhow, he never got tallow-stains from a gas-jet. Are you satisfied?"

"Well, it is very ingenious," said I, laughing; "but since, as you said just now, there has been no crime committed, and no harm done save the loss of a goose, all this seems to be rather a waste of energy."

Sherlock Holmes had opened his mouth to reply, when the door flew open, and Peterson, the commissionaire, rushed into the apartment with flushed cheeks and the face of a man who is dazed with astonishment.

"The goose, Mr. Holmes! The goose, sir!" he gasped.

"Eh? What of it, then? Has it returned to life and flapped off through the kitchen window?" Holmes twisted himself round upon the sofa to get a fairer view of the man's excited face.

"See here, sir! See what my wife found in its crop!"[8] He held out his hand and displayed upon the centre of the palm a brilliantly scintillating blue stone, rather smaller than a bean in size, but of such purity and radiance that it twinkled like an electric point in the dark hollow of his hand.

Sherlock Holmes sat up with a whistle. "By Jove, Peterson!" said he, "this is treasure trove indeed. I suppose you know what you have got?"

"A diamond, sir? A precious stone. It cuts into glass as though it were putty."

"It's more than a precious stone. It is *the* precious stone."

---

7. The candle wax.
8. A pouch that a goose has in its neck.

"Not the Countess of Morcar's blue carbuncle!"[9] I ejaculated.

"Precisely so. I ought to know its size and shape, seeing that I have read the advertisement about it in *The Times* every day lately. It is absolutely unique, and its value can only be conjectured, but the reward offered of £1000[10] is certainly not within a twentieth part of the market price."

"A thousand pounds! Great Lord of mercy!" The commissionaire plumped down into a chair and stared from one to the other of us.

"That is the reward, and I have reason to know that there are sentimental considerations in the background which would induce the Countess to part with half her fortune if she could but recover the gem."

"It was lost, if I remember aright, at the Hotel Cosmopolitan," I remarked.

"Precisely so, on December 22d, just five days ago. John Horner, a plumber, was accused of having abstracted it from the lady's jewel-case. The evidence against him was so strong that the case has been referred to the Assizes.[11] I have some account of the matter here, I believe." He rummaged amid his newspapers, glancing over the dates, until at last he smoothed one out, doubled it over, and read the following paragraph:

> Hotel Cosmopolitan Jewel Robbery. John Horner, 26, plumber, was brought up upon the charge of having upon the 22d inst., abstracted from the jewel-case of the Countess of Morcar the valuable gem known as the blue carbuncle. James Ryder, upper-attendant at the hotel, gave his evidence to the effect that he had shown Horner up to the dressing-room of the Countess of Morcar upon the day of the robbery in order that he might solder the second bar of the grate, which was loose. He had remained with Horner some little

---

9. A gemstone. As Holmes later describes it as "crystallized charcoal," Peterson is correct that it is a diamond. The word "carbuncle" indicates that it has been cut in a particular style.
10. An average worker in England at this time earned about £50 a year.
11. A court of law.

time, but had finally been called away. On returning, he found that Horner had disappeared, that the bureau had been forced open, and that the small morocco casket in which, as it afterwards transpired, the Countess was accustomed to keep her jewel, was lying empty upon the dressing-table. Ryder instantly gave the alarm, and Horner was arrested the same evening; but the stone could not be found either upon his person or in his rooms. Catherine Cusack, maid to the Countess, deposed to having heard Ryder's cry of dismay on discovering the robbery, and to having rushed into the room, where she found matters as described by the last witness. Inspector Bradstreet, B division, gave evidence as to the arrest of Horner, who struggled frantically, and protested his innocence in the strongest terms. Evidence of a previous conviction for robbery having been given against the prisoner, the magistrate refused to deal summarily with the offence, but referred it to the Assizes. Horner, who had shown signs of intense emotion during the proceedings, fainted away at the conclusion and was carried out of court.

"Hum! So much for the police-court," said Holmes thoughtfully, tossing aside the paper. "The question for us now to solve is the sequence of events leading from a rifled jewel-case at one end to the crop of a goose in Tottenham Court Road at the other. You see, Watson, our little deductions have suddenly assumed a much more important and less innocent aspect. Here is the stone; the stone came from the goose, and the goose came from Mr. Henry Baker, the gentleman with the bad hat and all the other characteristics with which I have bored you. So now we must set ourselves very seriously to finding this gentleman and ascertaining what part he has played in this little mystery. To do this, we must try the simplest means first, and these lie undoubtedly in an advertisement in all the evening papers. If this fails, I shall have recourse to other methods."

"What will you say?"

"Give me a pencil and that slip of paper. Now, then:

"Found at the corner of Goodge Street, a goose and a black felt hat. Mr. Henry Baker can have the same by applying at 6:30 this evening at 221B, Baker Street.

"That is clear and concise."

"Very. But will he see it?"

"Well, he is sure to keep an eye on the papers, since, to a poor man, the loss was a heavy one. He was clearly so scared by his mischance in breaking the window and by the approach of Peterson that he thought of nothing but flight, but since then he must have bitterly regretted the impulse which caused him to drop his bird. Then, again, the introduction of his name will cause him to see it, for everyone who knows him will direct his attention to it. Here you are, Peterson, run down to the advertising agency and have this put in the evening papers."

"In which, sir?"

"Oh, in the *Globe, Star, Pall Mall, St. James's, Evening News Standard, Echo*, and any others that occur to you."

"Very well, sir. And this stone?"

"Ah, yes, I shall keep the stone. Thank you. And, I say, Peterson, just buy a goose on your way back and leave it here with me, for we must have one to give to this gentleman in place of the one which your family is now devouring."

When the commissionaire had gone, Holmes took up the stone and held it against the light. "It's a bonny[12] thing," said he. "Just see how it glints and sparkles. Of course it is a nucleus and focus of crime. Every good stone is. They are the devil's pet baits. In the larger and older jewels every facet may stand for a bloody deed. This stone is not yet twenty

---

12. Good-looking.

years old. It was found in the banks of the Amoy River in southern China and is remarkable in having every characteristic of the carbuncle, save that it is blue in shade instead of ruby red. In spite of its youth, it has already a sinister history. There have been two murders, a vitriol-throwing,[13] a suicide, and several robberies brought about for the sake of this forty-grain weight of crystallized charcoal. Who would think that so pretty a toy would be a purveyor to the gallows[14] and the prison? I'll lock it up in my strong box now and drop a line to the Countess to say that we have it."

"Do you think that this man Horner is innocent?"

"I cannot tell."

"Well, then, do you imagine that this other one, Henry Baker, had anything to do with the matter?"

"It is, I think, much more likely that Henry Baker is an absolutely innocent man, who had no idea that the bird which he was carrying was of considerably more value than if it were made of solid gold. That, however, I shall determine by a very simple test if we have an answer to our advertisement."

"And you can do nothing until then?"

"Nothing."

"In that case I shall continue my professional round. But I shall come back in the evening at the hour you have mentioned, for I should like to see the solution of so tangled a business."

"Very glad to see you. I dine at seven. There is a woodcock,[15] I believe. By the way, in view of recent occurrences, perhaps I ought to ask Mrs. Hudson to examine its crop."

I had been delayed at a case, and it was a little after half-past six when I found myself in Baker Street once more. As I approached the house I

---

13. To attack someone by throwing acid at them.
14. A structure for hanging someone. The method of capital punishment in use at that time.
15. A type of bird. Holmes is informing Watson what the meal is going to be.

saw a tall man in a Scotch bonnet[16] with a coat which was buttoned up to his chin waiting outside in the bright semicircle which was thrown from the fanlight. Just as I arrived the door was opened, and we were shown up together to Holmes's room.

"Mr. Henry Baker, I believe," said he, rising from his armchair and greeting his visitor with the easy air of geniality which he could so read-ily assume. "Pray take this chair by the fire, Mr. Baker. It is a cold night, and I observe that your circulation is more adapted for summer than for winter. Ah, Watson, you have just come at the right time. Is that your hat, Mr. Baker?"

"Yes, sir, that is undoubtedly my hat."

He was a large man with rounded shoulders, a massive head, and a broad, intelligent face, sloping down to a pointed beard of grizzled brown. A touch of red in nose and cheeks, with a slight tremor of his extended hand, recalled Holmes's surmise as to his habits. His rusty black frock-coat[17] was buttoned right up in front, with the collar turned up, and his lank wrists protruded from his sleeves without a sign of cuff or shirt. He spoke in a slow staccato fashion, choosing his words with care, and gave the impression generally of a man of learning and letters who had had ill-usage at the hands of fortune.

"We have retained these things for some days," said Holmes, "because we expected to see an advertisement from you giving your address. I am at a loss to know now why you did not advertise."

Our visitor gave a rather shamefaced laugh. "Shillings[18] have not been so plentiful with me as they once were," he remarked. "I had no doubt that

---

16. It was considered respectable for a man to have his head covered whenever he went out in public and, besides, the weather is cold. Baker has lost his proper hat and thus has been reduced to wearing something that seems rather silly-looking for a man in London at that time. It looks something like a beret and was probably left over from his schoolboy days.
17. An informal kind of coat. A more prosperous man would have worn a more dignified coat.
18. A coin worth twelve pence (pennies). He is saying that he has not had much money of late.

the gang of roughs who assaulted me had carried off both my hat and the bird. I did not care to spend more money in a hopeless attempt at recovering them."

"Very naturally. By the way, about the bird, we were compelled to eat it."

"To eat it!" Our visitor half rose from his chair in his excitement.

"Yes, it would have been of no use to anyone had we not done so. But I presume that this other goose upon the sideboard, which is about the same weight and perfectly fresh, will answer your purpose equally well?"

"Oh, certainly, certainly," answered Mr. Baker with a sigh of relief.

"Of course, we still have the feathers, legs, crop, and so on of your own bird, so if you wish—"

The man burst into a hearty laugh. "They might be useful to me as relics of my adventure," said he, "but beyond that I can hardly see what use the disjecta membra[19] of my late acquaintance are going to be to me. No, sir, I think that, with your permission, I will confine my attentions to the excellent bird which I perceive upon the sideboard."

Sherlock Holmes glanced sharply across at me with a slight shrug of his shoulders.

"There is your hat, then, and there your bird," said he. "By the way, would it bore you to tell me where you got the other one from? I am somewhat of a fowl fancier, and I have seldom seen a better grown goose."

"Certainly, sir," said Baker, who had risen and tucked his newly gained property under his arm. "There are a few of us who frequent the Alpha Inn, near the Museum—we are to be found in the Museum itself during the day, you understand. This year our good host, Windigate by name, instituted a goose club, by which, on consideration of some few pence every week, we were each to receive a bird at Christmas. My pence

---

19. A Latin phrase that means scattered fragments.

were duly paid, and the rest is familiar to you. I am much indebted to you, sir, for a Scotch bonnet is fitted neither to my years nor my gravity." With a comical pomposity of manner he bowed solemnly to both of us and strode off upon his way.

"So much for Mr. Henry Baker," said Holmes when he had closed the door behind him. "It is quite certain that he knows nothing whatever about the matter. Are you hungry, Watson?"

"Not particularly."

"Then I suggest that we turn our dinner into a supper and follow up this clue while it is still hot."

"By all means."

It was a bitter night, so we drew on our ulsters and wrapped cravats[20] about our throats. Outside, the stars were shining coldly in a cloudless sky, and the breath of the passers-by blew out into smoke like so many pistol shots. Our footfalls rang out crisply and loudly as we swung through the doctors' quarter, Wimpole Street, Harley Street, and so through Wigmore Street into Oxford Street. In a quarter of an hour we were in Blooms-bury at the Alpha Inn, which is a small public-house at the corner of one of the streets which runs down into Holborn. Holmes pushed open the door of the private bar and ordered two glasses of beer from the ruddy-faced, white-aproned landlord. "Your beer should be excellent if it is as good as your geese," said he.

"My geese!" The man seemed surprised.

"Yes. I was speaking only half an hour ago to Mr. Henry Baker, who was a member of your goose club."

"Ah! yes, I see. But you see, sir, them's not our geese."

"Indeed! Whose, then?"

"Well, I got the two dozen from a salesman in Covent Garden."

---

20. An ulster is an overcoat, and cravat is being used here to mean a scarf.

"Indeed? I know some of them. Which was it?"

"Breckinridge is his name."

"Ah! I don't know him. Well, here's your good health, landlord, and prosperity to your house. Good-night.

"Now for Mr. Breckinridge," he continued, buttoning up his coat as we came out into the frosty air. "Remember, Watson, that though we have so homely a thing as a goose at one end of this chain, we have at the other a man who will certainly get seven years' penal servitude[21] unless we can establish his innocence. It is possible that our inquiry may but confirm his guilt; but, in any case, we have a line of investigation which has been missed by the police, and which a singular chance has placed in our hands. Let us follow it out to the bitter end. Faces to the south, then, and quick march!"

We passed across Holborn, down Endell Street, and so through a zigzag of slums to Covent Garden Market. One of the largest stalls bore the name of Breckinridge upon it, and the proprietor, a horsy-looking man, with a sharp face and trim side-whiskers, was helping a boy to put up the shutters.

"Good-evening. It's a cold night," said Holmes.

The salesman nodded and shot a questioning glance at my companion.

"Sold out of geese, I see," continued Holmes, pointing at the bare slabs of marble.

"Let you have five hundred to-morrow morning."

"That's no good."

"Well, there are some on the stall with the gas-flare."

"Ah, but I was recommended to you."

"Who by?"

"The landlord of the Alpha."

---

21. Prison with hard labor.

"Oh, yes; I sent him a couple of dozen."

"Fine birds they were, too. Now where did you get them from?"

To my surprise the question provoked a burst of anger from the salesman.

"Now, then, mister," said he, with his head cocked and his arms akimbo,[22] "what are you driving at? Let's have it straight, now."

"It is straight enough. I should like to know who sold you the geese which you supplied to the Alpha."

"Well, then, I shan't tell you. So now!"

"Oh, it is a matter of no importance; but I don't know why you should be so warm over such a trifle."

"Warm! You'd be as warm, maybe, if you were as pestered as I am. When I pay good money for a good article there should be an end of the business; but it's 'Where are the geese?' and 'Who did you sell the geese to?' and 'What will you take for the geese?' One would think they were the only geese in the world, to hear the fuss that is made over them."

"Well, I have no connection with any other people who have been making inquiries," said Holmes carelessly. "If you won't tell us, the bet is off, that is all. But I'm always ready to back my opinion on a matter of fowls, and I have a fiver on it that the bird I ate is country bred."

"Well, then, you've lost your fiver, for it's town bred," snapped the salesman.

"It's nothing of the kind."

"I say it is."

"I don't believe it."

"D'you think you know more about fowls than I, who have handled them ever since I was a nipper?[23] I tell you, all those birds that went to the Alpha were town bred."

---

22. He has his hands on his hips and his elbows sticking out in a stance of defiance.
23. A small boy.

"You'll never persuade me to believe that."

"Will you bet, then?"

"It's merely taking your money, for I know that I am right. But I'll have a sovereign[24] on with you, just to teach you not to be obstinate."

The salesman chuckled grimly. "Bring me the books, Bill," said he.

The small boy brought round a small thin volume and a great greasy-backed one, laying them out together beneath the hanging lamp.

"Now then, Mr. Cocksure,"[25] said the salesman, "I thought that I was out of geese, but before I finish you'll find that there is still one left in my shop. You see this little book?"

"Well?"

"That's the list of the folk from whom I buy. D'you see? Well, then, here on this page are the country folk, and the numbers after their names are where their accounts are in the big ledger. Now, then! You see this other page in red ink? Well, that is a list of my town suppliers. Now, look at that third name. Just read it out to me."

"Mrs. Oakshott, 117, Brixton Road—249," read Holmes.

"Quite so. Now turn that up in the ledger."

Holmes turned to the page indicated. "Here you are, 'Mrs. Oakshott, 117, Brixton Road, egg and poultry supplier.'"

"Now, then, what's the last entry?"

"'December 22d. Twenty-four geese at 7*s*. 6*d*.'"[26]

"Quite so. There you are. And underneath?"

"'Sold to Mr. Windigate of the Alpha, at 12*s*.'"

"What have you to say now?"

Sherlock Holmes looked deeply chagrined. He drew a sovereign from

---

24. A £1 coin.

25. He is giving him a teasing nickname to indicate that Holmes is someone who is overconfident or too certain that he is right.

26. The price is being given with "s." for shillings and "d." for pence. The "d." stands for the Latin word "denarius," a coin used in the Roman Empire.

his pocket and threw it down upon the slab, turning away with the air of a man whose disgust is too deep for words. A few yards off he stopped under a lamppost and laughed in the hearty, noiseless fashion which was peculiar to him.

"When you see a man with whiskers of that cut and the 'Pink 'un'[27] protruding out of his pocket, you can always draw him by a bet," said he. "I daresay that if I had put £100 down in front of him, that man would not have given me such complete information as was drawn from him by the idea that he was doing me on a wager. Well, Watson, we are, I fancy, nearing the end of our quest, and the only point which remains to be determined is whether we should go on to this Mrs. Oakshott to-night, or whether we should reserve it for to-morrow. It is clear from what that surly fellow said that there are others besides ourselves who are anxious about the matter, and I should—"

His remarks were suddenly cut short by a loud hubbub which broke out from the stall which we had just left. Turning round we saw a little rat-faced fellow standing in the centre of the circle of yellow light which was thrown by the swinging lamp, while Breckinridge, the salesman, framed in the door of his stall, was shaking his fists fiercely at the cringing figure.

"I've had enough of you and your geese," he shouted. "I wish you were all at the devil together. If you come pestering me any more with your silly talk I'll set the dog at you. You bring Mrs. Oakshott here and I'll answer her, but what have you to do with it? Did I buy the geese off you?"

"No; but one of them was mine all the same," whined the little man.

"Well, then, ask Mrs. Oakshott for it."

"She told me to ask you."

"Well, you can ask the King of Proosia, for all I care. I've had enough

---

27. The "Pink 'un" was a popular way to refer to a newspaper special edition that reported on the football results. It was printed on pink paper so that buyers would not confuse it for the regular edition.

of it. Get out of this!" He rushed fiercely forward, and the inquirer flitted away into the darkness.

"Ha! this may save us a visit to Brixton Road," whispered Holmes. "Come with me, and we will see what is to be made of this fellow." Striding through the scattered knots of people who lounged round the flaring stalls, my companion speedily overtook the little man and touched him upon the shoulder. He sprang round, and I could see in the gas-light that every vestige of colour had been driven from his face.

"Who are you, then? What do you want?" he asked in a quavering voice.

"You will excuse me," said Holmes blandly, "but I could not help overhearing the questions which you put to the salesman just now. I think that I could be of assistance to you."

"You? Who are you? How could you know anything of the matter?"

"My name is Sherlock Holmes. It is my business to know what other people don't know."

"But you can know nothing of this?"

"Excuse me, I know everything of it. You are endeavouring to trace some geese which were sold by Mrs. Oakshott, of Brixton Road, to a salesman named Breckinridge, by him in turn to Mr. Windigate, of the Alpha, and by him to his club, of which Mr. Henry Baker is a member."

"Oh, sir, you are the very man whom I have longed to meet," cried the little fellow with outstretched hands and quivering fingers. "I can hardly explain to you how interested I am in this matter."

Sherlock Holmes hailed a four-wheeler[28] which was passing. "In that case we had better discuss it in a cosy room rather than in this wind-swept market-place," said he. "But pray tell me, before we go farther, who it is that I have the pleasure of assisting."

---

28. A horse-drawn carriage serving as a taxi.

The man hesitated for an instant. "My name is John Robinson," he answered with a sidelong glance.

"No, no; the real name," said Holmes sweetly. "It is always awkward doing business with an alias."

A flush sprang to the white cheeks of the stranger. "Well, then," said he, "my real name is James Ryder."

"Precisely so. Head attendant at the Hotel Cosmopolitan. Pray step into the cab, and I shall soon be able to tell you everything which you would wish to know."

The little man stood glancing from one to the other of us with half-frightened, half-hopeful eyes, as one who is not sure whether he is on the verge of a windfall or of a catastrophe. Then he stepped into the cab, and in half an hour we were back in the sitting-room at Baker Street. Nothing had been said during our drive, but the high, thin breathing of our new companion, and the claspings and unclaspings of his hands, spoke of the nervous tension within him.

"Here we are!" said Holmes cheerily as we filed into the room. "The fire looks very seasonable in this weather. You look cold, Mr. Ryder. Pray take the basket-chair. I will just put on my slippers before we settle this little matter of yours. Now, then! You want to know what became of those geese?"

"Yes, sir."

"Or rather, I fancy, of that goose. It was one bird, I imagine, in which you were interested—white, with a black bar across the tail."

Ryder quivered with emotion. "Oh, sir," he cried, "can you tell me where it went to?"

"It came here."

"Here?"

"Yes, and a most remarkable bird it proved. I don't wonder that you should take an interest in it. It laid an egg after it was dead—the bonniest, brightest little blue egg that ever was seen. I have it here in my museum."

Our visitor staggered to his feet and clutched the mantelpiece with his right hand. Holmes unlocked his strong-box and held up the blue carbuncle, which shone out like a star, with a cold, brilliant, many-pointed radiance. Ryder stood glaring with a drawn face, uncertain whether to claim or to disown it.

"The game's up, Ryder," said Holmes quietly. "Hold up, man, or you'll be into the fire! Give him an arm back into his chair, Watson. He's not got blood enough to go in for felony with impunity. Give him a dash of brandy. So! Now he looks a little more human. What a shrimp it is, to be sure!"

For a moment he had staggered and nearly fallen, but the brandy brought a tinge of colour into his cheeks, and he sat staring with frightened eyes at his accuser.

"I have almost every link in my hands, and all the proofs which I could possibly need, so there is little which you need tell me. Still, that little may as well be cleared up to make the case complete. You had heard, Ryder, of this blue stone of the Countess of Morcar's?"

"It was Catherine Cusack who told me of it," said he in a crackling voice.

"I see—her ladyship's waiting-maid. Well, the temptation of sudden wealth so easily acquired was too much for you, as it has been for better men before you; but you were not very scrupulous in the means you used. It seems to me, Ryder, that there is the making of a very pretty villain in you. You knew that this man Horner, the plumber, had been concerned in some such matter before, and that suspicion would rest the more readily upon him. What did you do, then? You made some small job in my lady's room—you and your confederate Cusack—and you managed that he should be the man sent for. Then, when he had left, you rifled the jewel-case, raised the alarm, and had this unfortunate man arrested. You then—"

Ryder threw himself down suddenly upon the rug and clutched at my companion's knees. "For goodness' sake, have mercy!" he shrieked. "Think of my father! of my mother! It would break their hearts. I never went wrong before! I never will again. I swear it. I'll swear it on a Bible. Oh, don't bring it into court! For mercy's sake, don't!"

"Get back into your chair!" said Holmes sternly. "It is very well to cringe and crawl now, but you thought little enough of this poor Horner in the dock[29] for a crime of which he knew nothing."

"I will fly, Mr. Holmes. I will leave the country, sir. Then the charge against him will break down."

"Hum! We will talk about that. And now let us hear a true account of the next act. How came the stone into the goose, and how came the goose into the open market? Tell us the truth, for there lies your only hope of safety."

Ryder passed his tongue over his parched lips. "I will tell you it just as it happened, sir," said he. "When Horner had been arrested, it seemed to me that it would be best for me to get away with the stone at once, for I did not know at what moment the police might not take it into their heads to search me and my room. There was no place about the hotel where it would be safe. I went out, as if on some commission, and I made for my sister's house. She had married a man named Oakshott, and lived in Brixton Road, where she fattened fowls for the market. All the way there every man I met seemed to me to be a policeman or a detective; and, for all that it was a cold night, the sweat was pouring down my face before I came to the Brixton Road. My sister asked me what was the matter, and why I was so pale; but I told her that I had been upset by the jewel robbery at the hotel. Then I went into the back yard and smoked a pipe, and wondered what it would be best to do.

"I had a friend once called Maudsley, who went to the bad, and has

---

29. An enclosed place in a courtroom where the accused is confined during his or her trial.

just been serving his time in Pentonville.[30] One day he had met me, and fell into talk about the ways of thieves, and how they could get rid of what they stole. I knew that he would be true to me, for I knew one or two things about him; so I made up my mind to go right on to Kilburn, where he lived, and take him into my confidence. He would show me how to turn the stone into money. But how to get to him in safety? I thought of the agonies I had gone through in coming from the hotel. I might at any moment be seized and searched, and there would be the stone in my waistcoat pocket. I was leaning against the wall at the time and looking at the geese which were waddling about round my feet, and suddenly an idea came into my head which showed me how I could beat the best detective that ever lived.

"My sister had told me some weeks before that I might have the pick of her geese for a Christmas present, and I knew that she was always as good as her word. I would take my goose now, and in it I would carry my stone to Kilburn. There was a little shed in the yard, and behind this I drove one of the birds—a fine big one, white, with a barred tail. I caught it, and, prying its bill open, I thrust the stone down its throat as far as my finger could reach. The bird gave a gulp, and I felt the stone pass along its gullet and down into its crop. But the creature flapped and struggled, and out came my sister to know what was the matter. As I turned to speak to her the brute broke loose and fluttered off among the others.

"'Whatever were you doing with that bird, Jem?' says she.

"'Well,' said I, 'you said you'd give me one for Christmas, and I was feeling which was the fattest.'

"'Oh,' says she, 'we've set yours aside for you—Jem's bird, we call it. It's the big white one over yonder. There's twenty-six of them, which makes one for you, and one for us, and two dozen for the market.'

"'Thank you, Maggie,' says I; 'but if it is all the same to you, I'd rather have that one I was handling just now.'

---

30. A prison in north London.

"'The other is a good three pound heavier,' said she, 'and we fattened it expressly for you.'

"'Never mind. I'll have the other, and I'll take it now,' said I.

"'Oh, just as you like,' said she, a little huffed. 'Which is it you want, then?'

"'That white one with the barred tail, right in the middle of the flock.'

"'Oh, very well. Kill it and take it with you.'

"Well, I did what she said, Mr. Holmes, and I carried the bird all the way to Kilburn. I told my pal what I had done, for he was a man that it was easy to tell a thing like that to. He laughed until he choked, and we got a knife and opened the goose. My heart turned to water, for there was no sign of the stone, and I knew that some terrible mistake had occurred. I left the bird, rushed back to my sister's, and hurried into the back yard. There was not a bird to be seen there.

"'Where are they all, Maggie?' I cried.

"'Gone to the dealer's, Jem.'

"'Which dealer's?'

"'Breckinridge, of Covent Garden.'

"'But was there another with a barred tail?' I asked, 'The same as the one I chose?'

"'Yes, Jem; there were two barred-tailed ones, and I could never tell them apart.'

"Well, then, of course I saw it all, and I ran off as hard as my feet would carry me to this man Breckinridge; but he had sold the lot at once, and not one word would he tell me as to where they had gone. You heard him yourselves to-night. Well, he has always answered me like that. My sister thinks that I am going mad. Sometimes I think that I am myself. And now—and now I am myself a branded thief, without ever having touched the wealth for which I sold my character. God help me! God help me!" He burst into convulsive sobbing, with his face buried in his hands.

There was a long silence, broken only by his heavy breathing, and by the measured tapping of Sherlock Holmes's finger-tips upon the edge of the table. Then my friend rose and threw open the door.

"Get out!" said he.

"What, sir! Oh, Heaven bless you!"

"No more words. Get out!"

And no more words were needed. There was a rush, a clatter upon the stairs, the bang of a door, and the crisp rattle of running footfalls from the street.

"After all, Watson," said Holmes, reaching up his hand for his clay pipe, "I am not retained by the police to supply their deficiencies. If Horner were in danger it would be another thing; but this fellow will not appear against him, and the case must collapse. I suppose that I am commuting a felony,[31] but it is just possible that I am saving a soul. This fellow will not go wrong again; he is too terribly frightened. Send him to jail now, and you make him a jail-bird for life. Besides, it is the season of forgiveness. Chance has put in our way a most singular and whimsical problem, and its solution is its own reward. If you will have the goodness to touch the bell, Doctor, we will begin another investigation, in which, also a bird will be the chief feature."

---

31. To reduce someone's punishment to something less severe. Holmes is taking it upon himself to enable this man to receive a punishment that is less than what the law requires.

CHRISTMAS DAY AT KIRKBY COTTAGE
ANTHONY TROLLOPE

"Christmas Day at Kirkby Cottage" is a classic romantic comedy. As with all romantic comedies, part of the fun is that the reader can see that two people belong together before they are willing to admit it to themselves. (Benedick and Beatrice in Shakespeare's Much Ado About Nothing and Miss Bennet and Mr. Darcy in Jane Austen's Pride and Prejudice are prime examples.) Older people look on kindly as they remember when they, too, were young and assumed dramatically that things had gone so badly that they had better move to Africa. As the holiday season is a time for reconciliation, it is an ideal setting for a romantic comedy. "Christmas Day at Kirkby Cottage" was first published in Routledge's Christmas Annual for 1870. It is a longer reading that is divided into chapters. The English writer Anthony Trollope (1815–1882) might be the greatest Victorian novelist you have never read. He had a genius for portraying the ordinary ways of the human heart—the small but absorbing hopes, temptations, misunderstandings, vanities, sacrifices, and schemes that make up our lives. Trollope's series of six novels, The Chronicles of Baretshire, is especially beloved. The first one is The Warden (1855).

CHRISTMAS DAY AT KIRKBY COTTAGE

Anthony Trollope

CHAPTER I

What Maurice Archer Said About Christmas

"After all, Christmas is a bore!"

"Even though you should think so, Mr. Archer, pray do not say so here."

"But it is."

"I am very sorry that you should feel like that; but pray do not say anything so very horrible."

"Why not? and why is it horrible? You know very well what I mean."

"I do not want to know what you mean; and it would make papa very unhappy if he were to hear you."

"A great deal of beef is roasted, and a great deal of pudding is boiled, and then people try to be jolly by eating more than usual. The consequence is, they get very sleepy, and want to go to bed an hour before the proper time. That's Christmas."

He who made this speech was a young man about twenty-three years old, and the other personage in the dialogue was a young lady, who might be, perhaps, three years his junior. The "papa" to whom the lady had alluded was the Rev. John Lownd, parson[1] of Kirkby Cliffe, in Craven, and the scene was the parsonage[2] library, as pleasant a little room as you would wish to see, in which the young man who thought Christmas to be a bore was at present sitting over the fire, in the parson's armchair, with a novel in his hand, which he had been reading till he was interrupted by the parson's daughter. It was nearly time for him to dress for dinner,[3] and the young lady was already dressed. She had entered the room on the pretext of looking for some book or paper, but perhaps her main object may have been to ask for some assistance from Maurice Archer in the work of dec‑ orating the parish church. The necessary ivy and holly branches had been collected, and the work was to be performed on the morrow. The day following would be Christmas Day. It must be acknowledged, that Mr. Archer had not accepted the proposition made to him very graciously.

Maurice Archer was a young man as to whose future career in life many of his elder friends shook their heads and expressed much fear. It was not that his conduct was dangerously bad, or that he spent his money too fast, but that he was abominably conceited, so said these elder friends; and then there was the unfortunate fact of his being altogether beyond control. He had neither father, nor mother, nor uncle, nor guardian. He was the owner of a small property not far from Kirkby Cliffe, which gave him an income of some six or seven hundred a year, and he had altogether declined any of the professions which had been suggested to him. He had, in the course of the year now coming to a close, taken his degree at Oxford, with some academical honours, which were not high enough to confer distinction, and had already positively refused to be ordained,

---

1. Minister.
2. A house provided by the church for the minister and his family to live in.
3. It is a traditional custom that one can wear casual clothes during the day, but should dress more formally for the evening meal.

although, would he do so, a small living would be at his disposal on the death of a septuagenarian cousin.[4] He intended, he said, to farm a portion of his own land, and had already begun to make amicable arrangements for buying up the interest of one of his two tenants. The rector[5] of Kirkby Cliffe, the Rev. John Lownd, had been among his father's dearest friends, and he was now the parson's guest for Christmas.

There had been many doubts in the parsonage before the young man had been invited. Mrs. Lownd had considered that the visit would be dangerous. Their family consisted of two daughters, the youngest of whom was still a child; but Isabel was turned twenty, and if a young man were brought into the house, would it not follow, as a matter of course, that she should fall in love with him? That was the mother's first argument.

"Young people don't always fall in love," said the father.

"But people will say that he is brought here on purpose," said the mother, using her second argument.

The parson, who in family matters generally had his own way, expressed an opinion that if they were to be governed by what other people might choose to say, their course of action would be very limited indeed. As for his girl, he did not think she would ever give her heart to any man before it had been asked; and as for the young man—whose father had been for over thirty years his dearest friend—if he chose to fall in love, he must run his chance, like other young men. Mr. Lownd declared he knew nothing against him, except that he was, perhaps, a little self-willed; and so Maurice Archer came to Kirkby Cliffe, intending to spend two months in the same house with Isabel Lownd.

Hitherto, as far as the parents or the neighbours saw—and in their

---

4. The "living" is a position as a minister with an income which one can live on. At this time, you could own the right to appoint a parish minister. Someone in his family owns this right for a particular parish and thus Maurice knows that, if he sought ordination, he would be guaranteed a full-time position once his elderly cousin died.
5. Another way to refer to the parson. "Rector" indicates that he is the parish minister.

endeavours to see, the neighbours were very diligent—there had been no love-making. Between Mabel, the young daughter, and Maurice, there had grown up a violent[6] friendship—so much so, that Mabel, who was fourteen, declared that Maurice Archer was "the jolliest person" in the world. She called him Maurice, as did Mr. and Mrs. Lownd; and to Maurice, of course, she was Mabel. But between Isabel and Maurice it was always Miss Lownd and Mr. Archer, as was proper. It was so, at least, with this difference, that each of them had got into a way of dropping, when possible, the other's name.

It was acknowledged throughout Craven—which my readers of course know to be a district in the northern portion of the West Riding of Yorkshire,[7] of which Skipton is the capital—that Isabel Lownd was a very pretty girl. There were those who thought that Mary Manniwick, of Barden, excelled her; and others, again, expressed a preference for Fanny Grange, the pink-cheeked daughter of the surgeon at Giggleswick. No attempt shall here be made to award the palm of superior merit; but it shall be asserted boldly, that no man need desire a prettier girl with whom to fall in love than was Isabel Lownd. She was tall, active, fair, the very picture of feminine health, with bright grey eyes, a perfectly beautiful nose—as is common to almost all girls belonging to Craven—a mouth by no means delicately small, but eager, eloquent, and full of spirit, a well-formed short chin, with a dimple, and light brown hair, which was worn plainly smoothed over her brows, and fell in short curls behind her head. Of Maurice Archer it cannot be said that he was handsome. He had a snub nose; and a man so visaged can hardly be good-looking, though a girl with a snub nose may be very pretty. But he was a well-made young fellow, having a look of power about him, with dark-brown hair, cut very

---

6. Strong.
7. Yorkshire is a large county in the north of England. It was divided into three sections called "ridings."

short, close shorn, with clear but rather small blue eyes, and an expression of countenance which allowed no one for a moment to think that he was weak in character, or a fool. His own place, called Hundlewick Hall, was about five miles from the parsonage. He had been there four or five times a week since his arrival at Kirkby Cliffe, and had already made arrange' ments for his own entrance upon the land in the following September. If a marriage were to come of it, the arrangement would be one very comfort' able for the father and mother at Kirkby Cliffe. Mrs. Lownd had already admitted as much as that to herself, though she still trembled for her girl. Girls are so prone to lose their hearts, whereas the young men of these days are so very cautious and hard! That, at least, was Mrs. Lownd's idea of girls and young men; and even at this present moment she was hardly happy about her child. Maurice, she was sure, had spoken never a word that might not have been proclaimed from the church tower; but her girl, she thought, was not quite the same as she had been before the young man had come among them. She was somewhat less easy in her manner, more preoccupied, and seemed to labour under a conviction that the presence in the house of Maurice Archer must alter the nature of her life. Of course it had altered the nature of her life, and of course she thought a great deal of Maurice Archer.

It had been chiefly at Mabel's instigation that Isabel had invited the co-operation of her father's visitor in the adornment of the church for Christmas Day. Isabel had expressed her opinion that Mr. Archer didn't care a bit about such things, but Mabel declared that she had already extracted a promise from him. "He'll do anything I ask him," said Mabel proudly. Isabel, however, had not cared to undertake the work in such company, simply under her sister's management, and had proffered the request herself. Maurice had not declined the task—had indeed prom' ised his assistance in some indifferent fashion—but had accompanied his promise by a suggestion that Christmas was a bore! Isabel had rebuked him, and then he had explained. But his explanation, in Isabel's view of the case, only made the matter worse. Christmas to her was a very great affair indeed—a festival to which the roast beef and the plum pudding were, no doubt, very necessary; but not by any means the essence, as he had chosen to consider them. Christmas a bore! No; a man who thought Christmas to be a bore should never be more to her than a mere acquaintance. She listened to his explanation, and then left the room, almost indignantly. Maurice, when she had gone, looked after her, and then read a page of his novel; but he was thinking of Isabel, and not of the book. It was quite true that he had never said a word to her that might not have been declared from the church tower; but, nevertheless, he had thought about her a good deal. Those were days on which he was sure that he was in love with her, and would make her his wife. Then there came days on which he ridiculed himself for the idea. And now and then there was a day on which he asked himself whether he was sure that she would take him were he to ask her. There was sometimes an air with her, some little trick of the body, a manner of carrying her head when in his presence, which he was not physiognomist[8] enough to investigate, but which in some way suggested doubts to him. It was on such occasions as this that he was most in love with her; and now she had left the room with that particular motion of her head which seemed almost to betoken contempt.

"If you mean to do anything before dinner you'd better do it at once," said the parson, opening the door. Maurice jumped up, and in ten minutes was dressed and down in the dining-room. Isabel was there, but did not greet him.

"You'll come and help us to-morrow," said Mabel, taking him by the arm and whispering to him.

"Of course I will," said Maurice.

---

8. An expert in reading people's faces.

"And you won't go to Hundlewick again till after Christmas?"

"It won't take up the whole day to put up the holly."

"Yes, it will—to do it nicely—and nobody ever does any work the day before Christmas."

"Except the cook," suggested Maurice. Isabel, who heard the words, assumed that look of which he was already afraid, but said not a word. Then dinner was announced, and he gave his arm to the parson's wife.[9]

Not a word was said about Christmas that evening. Isabel had threatened the young man with her father's displeasure on account of his expressed opinion as to the festival being a bore, but Mr. Lownd was not himself one who talked a great deal about any Church festival. Indeed, it may be doubted whether his more enthusiastic daughter did not in her heart think him almost too indifferent on the subject. In the decorations of the church he, being an elderly man, and one with other duties to perform, would of course take no part. When the day came he would preach, no doubt, an appropriate sermon, would then eat his own roast beef and pudding with his ordinary appetite, would afterwards, if allowed to do so, sink into his armchair behind his book—and then, for him, Christmas would be over. In all this there was no disrespect for the day, but it was hardly an enthusiastic observance. Isabel desired to greet the morning of her Saviour's birth with some special demonstration of joy. Perhaps from year to year she was somewhat disappointed—but never before had it been hinted to her that Christmas was a bore.

On the following morning the work was to be commenced immediately after breakfast. The same thing had been done so often at Kirkby Cliffe, that the rector was quite used to it. David Drum, the clerk,[10] who was also schoolmaster, and Barty Crossgrain, the parsonage gardener, would devote their services to the work in hand throughout the whole

9. A traditional custom in which a gentleman escorts a lady to her place at the dinner table.
10. A layman who assists the minister.

day, under the direction of Isabel. Mabel would of course be there assisting, as would also two daughters of a neighbouring farmer. Mrs. Lownd
would go down to the church about eleven, and stay till one, when the
whole party would come up to the parsonage for refreshment. Mrs.
Lownd would not return to the work, but the others would remain there
till it was finished, which finishing was never accomplished till candles
had been burned in the church for a couple of hours. Then there would
be more refreshments; but on this special day the parsonage dinner was
never comfortable and orderly. The rector bore it all with good humour,
but no one could say that he was enthusiastic in the matter. Mabel, who
delighted in going up ladders, and leaning over the pulpit, and finding herself in all those odd parts of the church to which her imagination would
stray during her father's sermons, but which were ordinarily inaccessible
to her, took great delight in the work. And perhaps Isabel's delight had
commenced with similar feelings. Immediately after breakfast, which was
much hurried on the occasion, she put on her hat and hurried down to the
church, without a word to Maurice on the subject. There was another
whisper from Mabel, which was answered also with a whisper, and then
Mabel also went. Maurice took up his novel, and seated himself comfortably by the parlour fire.

But again he did not read a word. Why had Isabel made herself so
disagreeable, and why had she perked up her head as she left the room
in that self-sufficient way, as though she was determined to show him
that she did not want his assistance? Of course, she had understood well
enough that he had not intended to say that the ceremonial observance of
the day was a bore. He had spoken of the beef and the pudding, and she
had chosen to pretend to misunderstand him. He would not go near the
church. And as for his love, and his half-formed resolution to make her his
wife, he would get over it altogether. If there were one thing more fixed
with him than another, it was that on no consideration would he marry

a girl who should give herself airs. Among them they might decorate the church as they pleased, and when he should see their handywork—as he would do, of course, during the service of Christmas Day—he would pass it by without a remark. So resolving, he again turned over a page or two of his novel, and then remembered that he was bound, at any rate, to keep his promise to his friend Mabel. Assuring himself that it was on that plea that he went, and on no other, he sauntered down to the church.

Chapter II
Kirkby Cliffe Church

Kirkby Cliffe Church stands close upon the River Wharfe, about a quarter of a mile from the parsonage, which is on a steep hillside running down from the moors to the stream. A prettier little church or graveyard you shall hardly find in England. Here, no large influx of population has necessitated the removal of the last home of the parishioners from beneath the shelter of the parish church. Every inhabitant of Kirkby Cliffe has, when dead, the privilege of rest among those green hillocks. Within the building is still room for tablets commemorative of the rectors and their wives and families, for there are none others in the parish to whom such honour is accorded. Without the walls, here and there, stand the tombstones of the farmers; while the undistinguished graves of the peasants lie about in clusters which, solemn though they be, are still picturesque. The church itself is old, and may probably be doomed before long to that kind of destruction which is called restoration; but hitherto, it has been allowed to stand beneath all its weight of ivy, and has known but little change during the last two hundred years. Its old oak pews and ancient exalted reading-desk[11] and pulpit are offensive to many who come to see the spot; but

---

11. For reading passages from the Bible aloud as part of the church service.

Isabel Lownd is of the opinion that neither the one nor the other could be touched, in the way of change, without profanation.

In the very porch Maurice Archer met Mabel, with her arms full of ivy branches, attended by David Drum. "So you have come at last, Master Maurice?" she said.

"Come at last! Is that all the thanks I get? Now let me see what it is you're going to do. Is your sister here?"

"Of course she is. Barty is up in the pulpit, sticking holly branches round the sounding-board,[12] and she is with him."

"T' boorde's that rotten an' maaky, it'll be doon on Miss Is'bel's heede, an' Barty Crossgrain ain't more than or'nary saft-handed," said the clerk.[13]

They entered the church, and there it was, just as Mabel had said. The old gardener was standing on the rail of the pulpit, and Isabel was beneath, handing up to him nails and boughs, and giving him directions as to their disposal. "Naa, miss, naa; it wonot do that a-way," said Barty. "Thou'll ha' me on to t' stanes—thou wilt, that a-gait. Lard-a-mussy, miss, thou munnot clim' up, or thou't be doon, and brek thee banes, thee ull!"[14] So saying, Barty Crossgrain, who had contented himself with remonstrating when called upon by his young mistress[15] to imperil his own neck, jumped on to the floor of the pulpit and took hold of the young lady by both her ankles. As he did so, he looked up at her with anxious eyes, and steadied himself on his own feet, as though it might become necessary for him to perform some great feat of activity. All this Maurice Archer saw, and Isabel saw that he saw it. She was not well pleased at knowing that

---

12. A board suspended above the pulpit. In the days before microphones, it was a way to help the voice of the preacher to carry more effectively.

13. Both David Drum and Barty Crossgrain speak with the accent and distinctive phrases of the common folk of Yorkshire. Drum warns that the board is rotten and fears it will come down and Barty won't be able to keep it from hitting Isabel on the head.

14. Barty now warns that if Isabel insists on trying to climb up herself the result will be that she will get her bones broken.

15. The lady he is serving.

he should see her in that position, held by the legs by the old gardener, and from which she could only extricate herself by putting her hand on the old man's neck as she jumped down from her perch. But she did jump down, and then began to scold Crossgrain, as though the awkwardness had come from fault of his.

"I've come to help, in spite of the hard words you said to me yesterday, Miss Lownd," said Maurice, standing on the lower steps of the pulpit. "Couldn't I get up and do the things at the top?" But Isabel thought that Mr. Archer could not get up and "do the things at the top." The wood was so far decayed that they must abandon the idea of ornamenting the sounding-board, and so both Crossgrain and Isabel descended into the body of the church.

Things did not go comfortably with them for the next hour. Isabel had certainly invited his co-operation, and therefore could not tell him to go away; and yet, such was her present feeling towards him, she could not employ him profitably, and with ease to herself. She was somewhat angry with him, and more angry with herself. It was not only that she had spoken hard words to him, as he had accused her of doing, but that, after the speaking of the last words, she had been distant and cold in her manner to him. And yet he was so much to her! She liked him so well!— and though she had never dreamed of admitting to herself that she was in love with him, yet—yet it would be pleasant to have the opportunity of asking herself whether she could not love him, should he ever give her a fair and open opportunity of searching her own heart on the matter. There had now sprung up some half-quarrel between them, and it was impossible that it could be set aside by any action on her part. She could not be otherwise than cold and haughty in her demeanour to him. Any attempt at reconciliation must come from him, and the longer she continued to be cold and haughty, the less chance there was that it would come. And yet she knew that she had been right to rebuke him for what he had said. "Christmas a bore!" She would rather lose his friendship for ever than hear such words from his mouth, without letting him know what she thought of them. Now he was there with her, and his coming could not but be taken as a sign of repentance. Yet she could not soften her manners to him, and become intimate with him, and playful, as had been her wont. He was allowed to pull about the masses of ivy, and to stick up branches of holly here and there at discretion; but what he did was done under Mabel's direction, and not under hers—with the aid of one of the farmer's daughters, and not with her aid. In silence, she continued to work round the chancel and communion-table, with Crossgrain, while Archer, Mabel, and David Drum used their taste and diligence in the nave and aisles of the little church.[16] Then Mrs. Lownd came among them, and things went more easily; but hardly a word had been spoken between Isabel and Maurice when, after sundry hints from David Drum as to the lateness of the hour, they left the church and went up to the parsonage for their luncheon.

Isabel stoutly walked on first, as though determined to show that she had no other idea in her head but that of reaching the parsonage as quickly as possible. Perhaps Maurice Archer had the same idea, for he followed her. Then he soon found that he was so far in advance of Mrs. Lownd and the old gardener as to be sure of three minutes' uninterrupted conversation; for Mabel remained with her mother, making earnest supplication as to the expenditure of certain yards of green silk tape, which she declared to be necessary for the due performance of the work which they had in hand. "Miss Lownd," said Maurice, "I think you are a little hard upon me."

"In what way, Mr. Archer?"

"You asked me to come down to the church, and you haven't spoken to me all the time I was there."

"I asked you to come and work, not to talk," she said.

---

16. The chancel is the part of the church where the minister officiates, and the nave is the part where the congregation is.

"You asked me to come and work with you."

"I don't think that I said any such thing; and you came at Mabel's request, and not at mine. When I asked you, you told me it was all—a bore. Indeed you said much worse than that. I certainly did not mean to ask you again. Mabel asked you, and you came to oblige her. She talked to you, for I heard her; and I was half disposed to tell her not to laugh so much, and to remember that she was in church."

"I did not laugh, Miss Lownd."

"I was not listening especially to you."

"Confess, now," he said, after a pause; "don't you know that you misinterpreted me yesterday, and that you took what I said in a different spirit from my own."

"No; I do not know it."

"But you did. I was speaking of the holiday part of Christmas, which consists of pudding and beef, and is surely subject to ridicule, if one chooses to ridicule pudding and beef. You answered me as though I had spoken slightingly of the religious feeling which belongs to the day."

"You said that the whole thing was—I won't repeat the word. Why should pudding and beef be a bore to you, when it is prepared as a sign that there shall be plenty on that day for people who perhaps don't have plenty on any other day of the year? The meaning of it is, that you don't like it all, because that which gives unusual enjoyment to poor people, who very seldom have any pleasure, is tedious to you. I don't like you for feeling it to be tedious. There! that's the truth. I don't mean to be uncivil, but—"

"You are very uncivil."

"What am I to say, when you come and ask me?"

"I do not well know how you could be more uncivil, Miss Lownd. Of course it is the commonest thing in the world, that one person should dislike another. It occurs every day, and people know it of each other. I can perceive very well that you dislike me, and I have no reason to be angry with you for disliking me. You have a right to dislike me, if your mind runs that way. But it is very unusual for one person to tell another so to his face—and more unusual to say so to a guest." Maurice Archer, as he said this, spoke with a degree of solemnity to which she was not at all accustomed, so that she became frightened at what she had said. And not only was she frightened, but very unhappy also. She did not quite know whether she had or had not told him plainly that she disliked him, but she was quite sure that she had not intended to do so. She had been determined to scold him—to let him see that, however much of real friendship there might be between them, she would speak her mind plainly, if he offended her; but she certainly had no desire to give him cause for lasting wrath against her. "However," continued Maurice, "perhaps the truth is best after all, though it is so very unusual to hear such truths spoken."

"I didn't mean to be uncivil," stammered Isabel.

"But you meant to be true?"

"I mean to say what I felt about Christmas Day." Then she paused a moment. "If I have offended you, I beg your pardon."

He looked at her and saw that her eyes were full of tears, and his heart was at once softened towards her. Should he say a word to her, to let her know that there was—or, at any rate, that henceforth there should be no offence? But it occurred to him that if he did so, that word would mean so much, and would lead perhaps to the saying of other words, which ought not to be shown without forethought. And now, too, they were within the parsonage gate, and there was no time for speaking. "You will go down again after lunch?" he asked.

"I don't know—not if I can help it. Here's papa." She had begged his pardon—had humbled herself before him. And he had not said a word in acknowledgement of the grace she had done him. She almost thought that she did dislike him—really dislike him. Of course he had known what she meant, and he had chosen to misunderstand her and to take her, as it were, at an advantage. In her difficulty she had abjectly apologized to him, and he had not even deigned to express himself as satisfied with what she had done. She had known him to be conceited and masterful; but that, she had thought, she could forgive, believing it to be the common way with men—imagining, perhaps, that a man was only the more worthy of love on account of such fault; but now she found that he was ungenerous also, and deficient in that chivalry without which a man can hardly appear at advantage in a woman's eyes. She went on into the house, merely touching her father's arm, as she passed him, and hurried up to her own room. "Is there anything wrong with Isabel?" asked Mr. Lownd.

"She has worked too hard, I think, and is tired," said Maurice.

Within ten minutes they were all assembled in the dining-room, and Mabel was loud in her narrative of the doings of the morning. Barty Crossgrain and David Drum had both declared the sounding-board to be so old that it mustn't even be touched, and she was greatly afraid that it would tumble down some day and "squash papa" in the pulpit. The rector ridiculed the idea of any such disaster; and then there came a full description of the morning's scene, and of Barty's fears lest Isabel should "brek her banes."[17]

"His own wig was almost off," said Mabel, "and he gave Isabel such a lug by the leg that she very nearly had to jump into his arms."

"I didn't do anything of the kind," said Isabel.

"You had better leave the sounding-board alone," said the parson.

"We have left it alone, papa," said Isabel, with great dignity. "There are some other things that can't be done this year." For Isabel was becoming tired of her task, and would not have returned to the church at all could she have avoided it.

"What other things?" demanded Mabel, who was as enthusiastic as ever. "We can finish all the rest. Why shouldn't we finish it? We are ever

---

17. Break her bones.

so much more forward than we were last year, when David and Barty went to dinner. We've finished the Granby-Moor pew,[18] and we never used to get to that till after luncheon." But Mabel on this occasion had all the enthusiasm to herself. The two farmer's daughters, who had been brought up to the parsonage as usual, never on such occasions uttered a word. Mrs. Lownd had completed her part of the work; Maurice could not trust himself to speak on the subject; and Isabel was dumb. Luncheon, however, was soon over, and something must be done. The four girls of course returned to their labours, but Maurice did not go with them, nor did he make any excuse for not doing so.

"I shall walk over to Hundlewick before dinner," he said, as soon as they were all moving. The rector suggested that he would hardly be back in time. "Oh, yes; ten miles—two hours and a half; and I shall have two hours there besides. I must see what they are doing with our own church, and how they mean to keep Christmas there. I'm not quite sure that I shan't go over there again to-morrow." Even Mabel felt that there was something wrong, and said not a word in opposition to this wicked desertion.

He did walk to Hundlewick and back again, and when at Hundlewick he visited the church, though the church was a mile beyond his own farm. And he added something to the store provided for the beef and pudding of those who lived upon his own land; but of this he said nothing on his return to Kirkby Cliffe. He walked his dozen miles, and saw what was being done about the place, and visited the cottages of some who knew him, and yet was back at the parsonage in time for dinner. And during his walk he turned many things over in his thoughts, and endeavoured to make up his mind on one or two points. Isabel had never looked so pretty as when she jumped down into the pulpit, unless it was when she was begging his pardon for her want of courtesy to him. And though she had been, as he

18. As a way of raising money for the church, families would pay to have a particular pew reserved for their use.

described it to himself, "rather down upon him," in regard to what he had said of Christmas, did he not like her the better for having an opinion of her own? And then, as he had stood for a few minutes leaning on his own gate, and looking at his own house at Hundlewick, it had occurred to him that he could hardly live there without a companion. After that he had walked back again, and was dressed for dinner, and in the drawing-room before any one of the family.

With poor Isabel the afternoon had gone much less satisfactorily. She found that she almost hated her work, that she really had a headache, and that she could put no heart into what she was doing. She was cross to Mabel, and almost surly to David Drum and Barty Crossgain. The two farmer's daughters were allowed to do almost what they pleased with the holly branches—a state of things which was most unusual—and then Isabel, on her return to the parsonage, declared her intention of going to bed! Mrs. Lownd, who had never before known her to do such a thing, was perfectly shocked. Go to bed, and not come down the whole of Christmas Eve! But Isabel was resolute. With a bad headache she would be better in bed than up. Were she to attempt to shake it off, she would be ill the next day. She did not want anything to eat, and would not take anything. No; she would not have any tea, but would go to bed at once. And to bed she went.

She was thoroughly discontented with herself, and felt that Maurice had, as it were, made up his mind against her for ever. She hardly knew whether to be angry with herself or with him; but she did know very well that she had not intended really to quarrel with him. Of course she had been in earnest in what she had said; but he had taken her words as signifying so much more than she had intended! If he chose to quarrel with her, of course he must; but a friend could not, she was sure, care for her a great deal who would really be angry with her for such a trifle. Of course this friend did not care for her at all—not the least, or he would not treat her so savagely. He had been quite savage to her, and she hated him for it.

And yet she hated herself almost more. What right could she have had first to scold him, and then to tell him to his face that she disliked him? Of course he had gone away to Hundlewick. She would not have been a bit surprised if he had stayed there and never come back again. But he did come back, and she hated herself as she heard their voices as they all went in to dinner without her. It seemed to her that his voice was more cheery than ever. Last night and all the morning he had been silent and almost sullen, but now, the moment that she was away, he could talk and be full of spirits. She heard Mabel's ringing laughter downstairs, and she almost hated Mabel. It seemed to her that everybody was gay[19] and happy because she was upstairs in her bed, and ill. Then there came a peal of laughter. She was glad that she was upstairs in bed, and ill. Nobody would have laughed, nobody would have been gay, had she been there. Maurice Archer liked them all, except her—she was sure of that. And what could be more natural after her conduct to him? She had taken upon herself to lecture him, and of course he had not chosen to endure it. But of one thing she was quite sure, as she lay there, wretched in her solitude—that now she would never alter her demeanour to him. He had chosen to be cold to her, and she would be like frozen ice to him. Again and again she heard their voices, and then, sobbing on her pillow, she fell asleep.

Chapter III

Showing How Isabel Lownd Told a Lie

On the following morning—Christmas morning—when she woke, her headache was gone, and she was able as she dressed, to make some stern resolutions. The ecstasy of her sorrow was over, and she could see how foolish she had been to grieve as she had grieved. After all, what had she lost, or what harm had she done? She had never fancied that the young

---

19. Cheerful.

man was her lover, and she had never wished—so she now told herself—that he should become her lover. If one thing was plainer to her than another, it was this—that they two were not fitted for each other. She had sometimes whispered to herself, that if she were to marry at all, she would fain marry a clergyman. Now, no man could be more unlike a clergyman than Maurice Archer. He was, she thought, irreverent, and at no pains to keep his want of reverence out of sight, even in that house. He had said that Christmas was a bore, which, to her thinking, was abominable. Was she so poor a creature as to go to bed and cry for a man who had given her no sign that he even liked her, and of whose ways she disapproved so greatly, that even were he to offer her his hand she would certainly refuse it? She consoled herself for the folly of the preceding evening by assuring herself that she had really worked in the church till she was ill, and that she would have gone to bed, and must have gone to bed, had Maurice Archer never been seen or heard of at the parsonage. Other people went to bed when they had headaches, and why should not she? Then she resolved, as she dressed, that there should be no sign of illness, no bit of ill-humour on her, on this sacred day. She would appear among them all full of mirth and happiness, and would laugh at the attack brought upon her by Barty Crossgrain's sudden fear in the pulpit; and she would greet Maurice Archer with all possible cordiality, wishing him a merry Christmas as she gave him her hand, and would make him understand in a moment that she had altogether forgotten their mutual bickerings. He should understand that, or should, at least, understand that she willed that it should all be regarded as forgotten. What was he to her, that any thought of him should be allowed to perplex her mind on such a day as this?

She went downstairs, knowing that she was the first up in the house—the first, excepting the servants. She went into Mabel's room, and kissing her sister, who was only half awake, wished her many, many, many happy Christmases.

"Oh, Bell," said Mabel, "I do so hope you are better!"

"Of course I am better. Of course I am well. There is nothing for a headache like having twelve hours round of sleep. I don't know what made me so tired and so bad."

"I thought it was something Maurice said," suggested Mabel.

"Oh, dear, no. I think Barty had more to do with it than Mr. Archer. The old fellow frightened me so when he made me think I was falling down. But get up, dear. Papa is in his room, and he'll be ready for prayers before you."[20]

Then she descended to the kitchen, and offered her good wishes to all the servants. To Barty, who always breakfasted there on Christmas mornings, she was especially kind, and said something civil about his work in the church.

"She'll 'bout brek her little heart for t'young mon there, an' he's naa true t'her,"[21] said Barty, as soon as Miss Lownd had closed the kitchen door; showing, perhaps, that he knew more of the matter concerning herself than she did.

She then went into the parlour to prepare the breakfast, and to put a little present, which she had made for her father, on his place—when, whom should she see but Maurice Archer!

It was a fact known to all the household, and a fact that had not recommended him at all to Isabel, that Maurice never did come downstairs in time for morning prayers. He was always the last; and, though in most respects a very active man, seemed to be almost a sluggard in regard to lying in bed late. As far as she could remember at the moment, he had never been present at prayers a single morning since the first after his arrival at the parsonage, when shame, and a natural feeling of strangeness

---

20. Following a traditional practice, the household gathers for family devotions in the morning. This would typically involve prayers and a Scripture reading.
21. Barty observes that Isabel will be heartbroken because Maurice does not love her.

in the house, had brought him out of his bed. Now he was there half an hour before the appointed time, and during that half-hour she was doomed to be alone with him. But her courage did not for a moment desert her.

"This is a wonder!" she said, as she took his hand. "You will have a long Christmas Day, but I sincerely hope that it may be a happy one."

"That depends on you," said he.

"I'll do everything I can," she answered. "You shall only have a very little bit of roast beef, and the unfortunate pudding shan't be brought near you." Then she looked in his face, and saw that his manner was very serious—almost solemn—and quite unlike his usual ways. "Is anything wrong?" she asked.

"I don't know; I hope not. There are things which one has to say which seem to be so very difficult when the time comes. Miss Lownd, I want you to love me."

"What!" She started back as she made the exclamation, as though some terrible proposition had wounded her ears. If she had ever dreamed of his asking for her love, she had dreamed of it as a thing that future days might possible produce—when he should be altogether settled at Hundlewick, and when they should have got to know each other intimately by the association of years.

"Yes, I want you to love me, and to be my wife. I don't know how to tell you; but I love you better than anything and everything in the world— better than all the world put together. I have done so from the first moment that I saw you; I have. I knew how it would be the very first instant I saw your dear face, and every word you have spoken, and every look out of your eyes, has made me love you more and more. If I offended you yesterday, I will beg your pardon."

"Oh, no," she said.

"I wish I had bitten my tongue out before I had said what I did about Christmas Day. I do, indeed. I only meant, in a half-joking way, to—to—to—But I ought to have known you wouldn't like it, and I beg your pardon. Tell me, Isabel, do you think that you can love me?"

Not half an hour since she had made up her mind that, even were he to propose to her—which she then knew to be absolutely impossible— she would certainly refuse him. He was not the sort of man for whom she would be a fitting wife; and she had made up her mind also, at the same time, that she did not at all care for him, and that he certainly did not in the least care for her. And now the offer had absolutely been made to her! Then came across her mind an idea that he ought in the first place to have gone to her father; but as to that she was not quite sure. Be that as it might, there he was, and she must give him some answer. As for thinking about it, that was altogether beyond her. The shock to her was too great to allow of her thinking. After some fashion, which afterwards was quite unintelli-gible to herself, it seemed to her, at that moment, that duty, and maidenly reserve, and filial obedience, all required her to reject him instantly. Indeed, to have accepted him would have been quite beyond her power.

"Dear Isabel," said he, "may I hope that some day you will love me?"

"Oh! Mr. Archer, don't," she said. "Do not ask me."

"Why should I not ask you?"

"It can never be." This she said quite plainly, and in a voice that seemed to him to settle his fate for ever; and yet at the moment her heart was full of love towards him. Though she could not think, she could feel. Of course she loved him. At the very moment in which she was telling him that it could never be, she was elated by an almost ecstatic triumph, as she remembered all her fears, and now knew that the man was at her feet.

When a girl first receives the homage of a man's love, and receives it from one whom, whether she loves him or not, she thoroughly respects, her earliest feeling is one of victory—such a feeling as warmed the heart of a conqueror in the Olympian games. He is the spoil of her spear, the fruit of her prowess, the quarry brought down by her own bow and arrow.

She, too, by some power of her own which she is hitherto quite unable to analyse, has stricken a man to the very heart, so as to compel him for the moment to follow wherever she may lead him. So it was with Isabel Lownd as she stood there, conscious of the eager gaze which was fixed upon her face, and fully alive to the anxious tones of her lover's voice. And yet she could only deny him. Afterwards, when she thought of it, she could not imagine why it had been so with her; but, in spite of her great love, she continued to tell herself that there was some obstacle which could never be overcome—or was it that a maidenly reserve sat so strong within her bosom that she could not bring herself to own to him that he was dear to her?

"Never!" exclaimed Maurice, despondently.

"Oh, no!"

"But why not? I will be very frank with you, dear. I did think you liked me a little before that affair in the study." Like him a little! Oh, how she had loved him! She knew it now, and yet not for worlds could she tell him so. "You are not still angry with me, Isabel?"

"No; not angry."

"Why should you say never? Dear Isabel, cannot you try to love me?" Then he attempted to take her hand, but she recoiled at once from his touch, and did feel something of anger against him in that he should thus refuse to take her word. She knew not what it was that she desired of him, but certainly he should not attempt to take her hand, when she told him plainly that she could not love him. A red spot rose to each of her cheeks as again he pressed her. "Do you really mean that you can never, never love me?" She muttered some answer, she knew not what, and then he turned from her, and stood looking out upon the snow which had fallen during the night. She kept her ground for a few seconds, and then escaped through the door, and up to her own bedroom. When once there, she burst out into tears. Could it be possible that she had thrown away for ever her own happiness, because she had been too silly to give a true answer to an honest question? And was this the enjoyment and content which she had promised herself for Christmas Day? But surely, surely he would come to her again. If he really loved her as he had declared, if it was true that ever since his arrival at Kirkby Cliffe he had thought of her as his wife, he would not abandon her because in the first tumult of her surprise she had lacked courage to own to him the truth; and then in the midst of her tears there came upon her that delicious recognition of a triumph which, whatever be the victory won, causes such elation to the heart! Nothing, at any rate, could rob her of this—that he had loved her. Then, as a thought suddenly struck her, she ran quickly across the passage, and in a moment was upstairs, telling her tale with her mother's arm close folded round her waist.

In the meantime Mr. Lownd had gone down to the parlour, and had found Maurice still looking out upon the snow. He, too, with some gentle sarcasm, had congratulated the young man on his early rising, as he expressed the ordinary wish of the day. "Yes," said Maurice, "I had something special to do. Many happy Christmases, sir! I don't know much about its being happy to me."

"Why, what ails you?"

"It's a nasty sort of day, isn't it?" said Maurice.

"Does that trouble you? I rather like a little snow on Christmas Day. It has a pleasant, old-fashioned look. And there isn't enough to keep even an old woman at home."

"I dare say not," said Maurice, who was still beating about the bush, having something to tell, but not knowing how to tell it. "Mr. Lownd, I should have come to you first, if it hadn't been for an accident."

"Come to me first! What accident?"

"Yes; only I found Miss Lownd down here this morning, and I asked her to be my wife. You needn't be unhappy about it, sir. She refused me point blank."

76

"You must have startled her, Maurice. You have startled me, at any rate."

"There was nothing of that sort, Mr. Lownd. She took it all very easily. I think she does take things easily." Poor Isabel! "She just told me plainly that it never could be so, and then she walked out of the room."

"I don't think she expected it, Maurice."

"Oh, dear no! I'm quite sure she didn't. She hadn't thought about me any more than if I were an old dog. I suppose men do make fools of themselves sometimes. I shall get over it, sir."

"Oh, I hope so."

"I shall give up the idea of living here. I couldn't do that. I shall probably sell out the property, and go to Africa. "

"Go to Africa!"

"Well, yes. It's as good a place as any other, I suppose. It's wild, and a long way off, and all that kind of thing. As this is Christmas, I had better stay here to-day, I suppose."

"Of course you will."

"If you don't mind, I'll be off early to-morrow, sir. It's a kind of thing, you know, that does flurry a man. And then my being here may be disagreeable to her—not that I suppose she thinks about me any more than if I were an old cow."

It need hardly be remarked that the rector was a much older man than Maurice Archer, and that he therefore knew the world much better. Nor was he in love. And he had, moreover, the advantage of a much closer knowledge of the young lady's character than could be possessed by the lover. And, as it happened, during the last week, he had been fretted by fears expressed by his wife—fears which were altogether opposed to Archer's present despondency and African resolutions. Mrs. Lownd had been uneasy—almost more than uneasy—lest poor dear Isabel should be stricken at her heart; whereas, in regard to that young man, she didn't believe that he cared a bit for her girl. He ought not to have been brought into the house. But he was there, and what could they do? The rector was of the opinion that things would come straight—that they would be straightened not by any lover's propensities on the part of his guest, as to which he protested himself to be altogether indifferent, but by his girl's good sense. His Isabel would never allow herself to be seriously affected by a regard for a young man who had made no overtures to her. That was the rector's argument; and perhaps, within his own mind, it was backed by a feeling that, were she so weak, she must stand the consequence. To him it seemed to be an absurd degree of caution that two young people should not be brought together in the same house lest one should fall in love with the other. And he had seen no symptoms of such love. Nevertheless his wife had fretted him, and he had been uneasy. Now the shoe was altogether on the other foot. The young man was the despondent lover, and was asserting that he must go instantly to Africa, because the young lady treated him like an old dog, and thought no more about him than of an old cow.

A father in such a position can hardly venture to hold out hopes to a lover, even though he may approve of the man as a suitor for his daughter's hand. He cannot answer for his girl, nor can he very well urge upon a lover the expediency of renewing his suit. In this case Mr. Lownd did think, that in spite of the cruel, determined obduracy which his daughter was said to have displayed, she might probably be softened by constancy and perseverance. But he knew nothing of the circumstances, and could only suggest that Maurice should not take his place for the first stage on his way to Africa quite at once. "I do not think you need hurry away because of Isabel," he said, with a gentle smile.

"I couldn't stand it—I couldn't indeed," said Maurice, impetuously. "I hope I didn't do wrong in speaking to her when I found her here this morning. If you had come first I should have told you."

"I could only have referred you to her, my dear boy. Come—here they are; and now we will have prayers." As he spoke, Mrs. Lownd entered the room, followed closely by Mabel, and then at a little distance by Isabel. The three maid-servants were standing behind in a line, ready to come in for prayers. Maurice could not but feel that Mrs. Lownd's manner to him was especially affectionate; for, in truth, hitherto she had kept somewhat aloof from him, as though he had been a ravening wolf. Now she held him by the hand, and had a spark of motherly affection in her eyes, as she, too, repeated her Christmas greeting. It might well be so, thought Maurice. Of course she would be more kind to him than ordinary, if she knew that he was a poor blighted individual. It was a thing of course that Isabel should have told her mother; equally a thing of course that he should be pitied and treated tenderly. But on the next day he would be off. Such tenderness as that would kill him.

As they sat at breakfast, they all tried to be very gracious to each other. Mabel was sharp enough to know that something special had happened, but could not quite be sure what it was. Isabel struggled very hard to make little speeches about the day, but cannot be said to have succeeded well. Her mother, who had known at once how it was with her child, and had required no positive answers to direct questions to enable her to assume that Isabel was now devoted to her lover, had told her girl that if the man's love were worth having, he would surely ask her again. "I don't think he will, mamma," Isabel had whispered, with her face half-hidden on her mother's arm. "He must be very unlike other men if he does not," Mrs. Lownd had said, resolving that the opportunity should not be wanting. Now she was very gracious to Maurice, speaking before him as though he were quite one of the family. Her trembling maternal heart had feared him, while she thought that he might be a ravening wolf, who would steal away her daughter's heart, leaving nothing in return; but now that he had proved himself willing to enter the fold as a useful domestic sheep, nothing could be too good for him. The parson himself, seeing all this, understanding every turn in his wife's mind, and painfully anxious that no word might be spoken which should seem to entrap his guest, strove diligently to talk as though nothing was amiss. He spoke of his sermon, and of David Drum, and of the allowance of pudding that was to be given to the inmates of the neighbouring poorhouse. There had been a subscription, so as to relieve the rates[22] from the burden of the plum pudding, and Mrs. Lownd thought that the farmers had not been sufficiently liberal.

"There's Furness, at Loversloup, gave us half a crown.[23] I told him he ought to be ashamed of himself. He declared to me to my face that if he could find puddings for his own bairns,[24] that was enough for him."

"The richest farmer in these parts, Maurice," said Mrs. Lownd.

"He holds above three hundred acres of land, and could stock double as many, if he had them," said the would-be indignant rector, who was thinking a great deal more of his daughter than of the poorhouse festival. Maurice answered him with a word or two, but found it very hard to assume any interest in the question of the pudding. Isabel was more hard-hearted, he thought, than even Farmer Furness of Loversloup. And why should he trouble himself about these people—he, who intended to sell his acres, and go away to Africa? But he smiled and made some reply, and buttered his toast, and struggled hard to seem as though nothing ailed him.

The parson went down to church before his wife, and Mabel went with him. "Is anything wrong with Maurice Archer?" she asked her father.

"Nothing, I hope," said he.

"Because he doesn't seem to be able to talk this morning."

"Everybody isn't a chatter-box like you, Mab."

"I don't think I chatter more than Mamma, or Bell. Do you know, Papa, I think Bell has quarrelled with Maurice Archer."

---

22. The subscription refers to an effort to get people to make donations so that there is not a need to raise the money by taxation (the rates).
23. A coin in British money at that time. The British unit of currency is the pound (the American equivalent is the dollar) and a half crown was worth 1/8 of a pound.
24. Children.

"I hope not. I should be very sorry that there should be any quar-
relling at all—particularly on this day. Well, I think you've done it very
nicely; and it is none the worse because you've left the sounding-board
alone." Then Mabel went over to David Drum's cottage, and asked after
the condition of Mrs. Drum's plum pudding.

No one had ventured to ask Maurice Archer whether he would
stay in church for the sacrament,[25] but he did. Let us hope that no undue
motive of pleasing Isabel Lownd had any effect upon him at such a time.
But it did please her. Let us hope also that, as she knelt beside her lover at
the low railing, her young heart was not too full of her love. That she had
been thinking of him throughout her father's sermon—thinking of him,
then resolving that she would think of him no more, and then thinking of
him more than ever—must be admitted. When her mother had told her
that he would come again to her, she had not attempted to assert that,
were he to do so, she would again reject him. Her mother knew all her
secret, and, should he not come again, her mother would know that she
was heartbroken. She had told him positively that she would never love
him. She had so told him, knowing well that at the very moment he was
dearer to her than all the world beside. Why had she been so wicked as
to lie to him? And if now she were punished for her lie by his silence,
would she not be served properly? Her mind ran much more on the subject of this great sin which she had committed on that very morning—
that sin against one who loved her so well, and who desired to do good
to her—that on those general arguments in favour of Christian kindness
and forbearance which the preacher drew form the texts applicable to
Christmas Day. All her father's eloquence was nothing to her. On ordinary occasions he had no more devoted listener; but, on this morning, she
could only exercise her spirit by repenting her own unchristian conduct.

---

25. The full church service has two halves. The second half was when Holy Communion was
administered, and at this time often only especially devout people stayed for it.

And then he came and knelt beside her at that sacred moment! It was impossible that he should forgive her, because he could not know that she had sinned against him.

There were certain visits to her poorer friends in the immediate village which, according to custom, she would make after church. When Maurice and Mrs. Lownd went up to the parsonage, she and Mabel made their usual round. They all welcomed her, but they felt that she was not quite herself with them, and even Mabel asked her what ailed her.

"Why should anything ail me?—only I don't like walking in the snow."

Then Mabel took courage. "If there is a secret, Bell, pray tell me. I would tell you any secret."

"I don't know what you mean," said Isabel, almost crossly.

"Is there a secret, Bell? I'm sure there is a secret about Maurice."

"Don't—don't," said Isabel.

"I do like Maurice so much. Don't you like him?"

"Pray do not talk about him, Mabel."

"I believe he is in love with you, Bell; and, if he is, I think you ought to be in love with him. I don't know how you could have anybody nicer. And he is going to live at Hundlewick, which would be such great fun. Would not Papa like it?"

"I don't know. Oh, dear!—oh, dear!" Then she burst out into tears, and, walking out of the village, told Mabel the whole truth. Mabel heard it with consternation, and expressed her opinion that, in these circumstances Maurice would never ask again to make her his wife.

"Then I shall die," said Isabel frankly.

CHAPTER IV

Showing How Isabel Lownd Repented Her Fault

In spite of her piteous condition and near prospect of death, Isabel Lownd completed her round of visits among her old friends. That Christmas should be kept in some way by every inhabitant of Kirkby Cliffe, was a thing of course. The district is not poor, and plenty on that day was rarely wanting. But Parson Lownd was not what we call a rich man; and there was no resident squire[26] in the parish. The farmers, comprehending well their own privileges, and aware that the obligation of gentle living did not lie on them, were inclined to be close-fisted; and thus there was sometimes a difficulty in providing for the old and the infirm. There was a certain ancient widow in the village, of the name of Mucklewort, who was troubled with three orphan grandchildren and a lame daughter; and Isabel had, some days since, expressed a fear up at the parsonage that the good things of this world might be scarce in the old widow's cottage. Something had, of course, been done for the old woman, but not enough, as Isabel had thought.

"My dear," her mother had said, "it is no use trying to make very poor people think that they are not poor."

"It is only one day in the year," Isabel had pleaded.

"What you give in excess to one, you take from another," replied Mrs. Lownd, with the stern wisdom which experience teaches. Poor Isabel could say nothing further, but had feared greatly that the rations in Mrs. Mucklewort's abode would be deficient. She now entered the cottage, and found the whole family at that moment preparing themselves for the consumption of a great Christmas banquet. Mrs. Mucklewort, whose temper

---

26. The squire is a gentleman from an ancient family recognized as the leading figure in that part of the country. With this honor also came a sense of responsibility that it was especially his duty to help the needy. As there is no squire, however, people look all the more to the minister to take care of those in need.

was not always the best in the world, was radiant. The children were silent, open-eyed, expectant, and solemn. The lame aunt was in the act of
transferring a large lump of beef, which seemed to be commingled in a most
inartistic way with potatoes and cabbage, out of a pot on to the family dish.
At any rate there was plenty; for no five appetites—had the five all been
masculine, adult, and yet youthful—could, by any feats of strength, have
emptied that dish at a sitting. And Isabel knew well that there had been
pudding. She herself had sent the pudding; but that, as she was well aware,
had not been allowed to abide its fate till this late hour of the day.[27]

"I'm glad you're all so well employed," said Isabel. "I thought you had
done dinner long ago. I won't stop a minute now."

The old woman got up from her chair, and nodded her head, and held
out her withered old hand to be shaken. The children opened their mouths
wider than ever, and hoped there might be no great delay. The lame aunt
curtseyed and explained the circumstances. "Beef, Miss Isabel, do take a
mortal time t' boil; and it ain't no wise good for t' bairns to have it any
ways raw."[28] To this opinion Isabel gave her full assent, and expressed
her gratification that the amount of beef should be sufficient to require so
much cooking. Then the truth came out. "Muster Archer just sent us over
from Rowdy's a meal's meat with a vengeance; God bless him!" crooned
out the old woman, and the children muttered some unintelligible sound,
as though aware that duty required them to express some Amen to the
prayer of their elders. Now Rowdy was the butcher living at Grassington,
some six miles away—for at Kirkby Cliffe there was no butcher. Isabel
smiled all round upon them sweetly, with her eyes full of tears, and then
left the cottage without a word.

He had done this because she had expressed a wish that these people

---

27. They ate dessert while waiting for the meal to cook.
28. It takes a long time for it to cook by boiling and it is important that the children are not
eating raw meat.

should be kindly treated—had done it without a syllable spoken to her or to any one—had taken trouble, sending all the way to Grassington for Mrs. Mucklewort's beef! No doubt he had given other people beef, and had whispered no word of his kindness to any one at the rectory. And yet she had taken upon herself to rebuke him, because he had not cared for Christmas Day. As she walked along, silent, holding Mabel's hand, it seemed to her that of all men he was the most perfect. She had rebuked him, and had then told him—with incredible falseness—that she did not like him; and after that, when he had proposed to her in the kindest, noblest manner, she had rejected him—almost as though he had not been good enough for her! She felt now as though she would like to bite the tongue out of her head for such misbehaviour.

"Was not that nice of him?" said Mabel. But Isabel could not answer the question.

"I always thought he was like that," continued the younger sister. "If he were my lover, I'd do anything he asked me, because he is so good-natured."

"Don't talk to me," said Isabel. And, Mabel, who comprehended something of the condition of her sister's mind, did not say another word on their way back to the parsonage.

It was the rule of the house that on Christmas Day they should dine at four o'clock—a rule which almost justified the very strong expression with which Maurice first offended the young lady whom he loved. To dine at one or two o'clock is a practice which has its recommendations. It suits the appetite, is healthy, and divides the day into two equal halves, so that no man so dining fancies that his dinner should bring to him an end of his usual occupations. And to dine at six, seven, or eight is well adapted to serve several purposes of life. It is convenient, as inducing that gentle lethargy which will sometimes follow the pleasant act of eating at a time when the work of the day is done; and it is both fashionable and comfortable. But to dine at four is almost worse than not to dine at all. The rule, however, existed at Kirkby Cliffe parsonage in regard to this one special day in the year, and was always obeyed.

On this occasion Isabel did not see her lover from the moment in which he left her at the church door till they met at table. She had been with her mother, but her mother had not said a word to her about Maurice. Isabel knew very well that they two had walked home together from the church, and she had thought that her best chance lay in the possibility that he would have spoken of what had occurred during the walk. Had this been so, surely her mother would have told her; but not a word had been said; and even with her mother Isabel had been too shamefaced to ask a question. In truth, Isabel's name had not been mentioned between them, nor had any allusion been made to what had taken place during the morning. Mrs. Lownd had been too wise and too wary—too well aware of what was really due to her daughter—to bring up the subject herself; and he had been silent, subdued, and almost sullen. If he could not get an acknowledgement of affection from the girl herself, he certainly would not endeavour to extract a cold compliance by the mother's aid. Africa, and a disruption of all the plans of his life, would be better to him than that. But Mrs. Lownd knew very well how it was with him; knew how it was with them both; and was aware that in such a condition things should be allowed to arrange themselves. At dinner, both she and the rector were full of mirth and good humour, and Mabel, with great glee, told the story of Mrs. Mucklewort's dinner. "I don't want to destroy your pleasure," she said, bobbing her head at Maurice; "but it did look so nasty! Beef should always be roast beef on Christmas Day."

"I told the butcher it was to be roast beef," said Maurice, sadly.

"I dare say the little Muckleworts would just as soon have it boiled," said Mrs. Lownd. "Beef is beef to them, and a pot for boiling is an easy apparatus."

"If you had beef, Miss Mab, only once or twice a year," said her father,

86

"you would not care whether it were roast or boiled." But Isabel spoke not a word. She was most anxious to join the conversation about Mrs. Mucklewort, and would have liked much to give testimony to the generosity displayed in regard to quantity; but she found that she could not do it. She was absolutely dumb. Maurice Archer did speak, making, every now and then, a terrible effort to be jocose;[29] but Isabel from first to last was silent. Only by silence could she refrain from a renewed deluge of tears.

In the evening two or three girls came in with their younger brothers, the children of farmers of the better class in the neighbourhood, and the usual attempts were made at jollity. Games were set on foot, in which even the rector joined, instead of going to sleep behind his book, and Mabel, still conscious of her sister's wounds, did her very best to promote the sports. There was blindman's-buff, and hide and seek, and snapdragon,[30] and forfeits,[31] and a certain game with music and chairs—very prejudicial to the chairs—in which it was everybody's object to sit down as quickly as possible when the music stopped. In the game Isabel insisted on playing, because she could do that alone. But even to do this was too much for her. The sudden pause could hardly be made without a certain hilarity of spirit, and her spirits were unequal to any exertion. Maurice went through his work like a man, was blinded, did his forfeits, and jostled for the chairs with the greatest diligence; but in the midst of it all he, too, was as solemn as a judge, and never once spoke a single word to Isabel. Mrs. Lownd, who usually was not herself much given to the playing of games, did on this occasion make an effort, and absolutely consented to cry the forfeits; but Mabel was wonderfully quiet, so that the farmers' daughters hardly perceived that there was anything amiss.

It came to pass, after a while, that Isabel had retreated to her

---

29. Full of jokes.
30. Raisins are put in a bowl of brandy that is then set alight. The game is to show your daring by grabbing a raisin from the flames and eating it.
31. Forfeits is a game in which people are set dares of silly things to do.

room—not for the night as it was as yet hardly eight o'clock—and she certainly would not disappear till the visitors had taken their departure—a ceremony which was sure to take place with the greatest punctuality at ten, after an early supper. But she had escaped for a while, and in the meantime some frolic was going on which demanded the absence of one of the party from the room, in order that mysteries might be arranged of which the absent one should remain in ignorance. Maurice was thus banished, and desired to remain in desolation for the space of five minutes; but, just as he had taken up his position, Isabel descended with slow, solemn steps, and found him standing at her father's study door. She was passing on, and had almost entered the drawing-room when he called her. "Miss Lownd," he said. Isabel stopped, but did not speak; she was absolutely beyond speaking. The excitement of the day had been so great, that she was almost overcome by it, and doubted, herself, whether she would be able to keep up appearances till the supper should be over, and she should be relieved for the night. "Would you let me say one word to you?" said Maurice. She bowed her head and went with him into the study.

Five minutes had been allowed for the arrangement of the mysteries, and at the end of the five minutes Maurice was authorized, by the rules of the game, to return to the room. But he did not come, and upon Mabel's suggesting that possibly he might not be able to see his watch in the dark, she was sent to fetch him. She burst into the study, and there she found the truant and her sister, very close, standing together on the hearthrug. "I didn't know you were here, Bell," she exclaimed. Whereupon Maurice, as she declared afterwards, jumped round the table after her, and took her in his arms and kissed her. "But you must come," said Mabel, who accepted the embrace with perfect goodwill.

"Of course you must. Do go, pray, and I'll follow—almost immediately." Mabel perceived at once that her sister had altogether recovered her voice.

"I'll tell 'em you're coming," said Mabel, vanishing.

"You must go now," said Isabel. "They'll all be away soon, and then you can talk about it." As she spoke, he was standing with his arm round her waist, and Isabel Lownd was the happiest girl in all Craven.

Mrs. Lownd knew all about it from the moment in which Maurice Archer's prolonged absence had become cause of complaint among the players. Her mind had been intent upon the matter, and she had become well aware that it was only necessary that the two young people should be alone together for a few moments. Mabel had entertained great hopes, thinking, however, that perhaps three or four years must be passed in melancholy gloomy doubts before the path of true love could be made to run smooth; but the light had shone upon her as soon as she saw them standing together. The parson knew nothing about it till the supper was over. Then, when the front door was open, and the farmers' daughters had been cautioned not to get themselves more wet than they could help in the falling snow, Maurice said a word to his future father-in-law. "She has consented at last, sir. I hope you have nothing to say against it."

"Not a word," said the parson, grasping the young man's hand, and remembering, as he did so, the extension of the time over which that phrase "at last" was supposed to spread itself.

Maurice had been promised some further opportunity of "talking about it," and of course claimed a fulfillment of the promise. There was a difficulty about it, as Isabel, having now been assured of her happiness, was anxious to talk about it all to her mother rather than to him; but he was imperative, and there came at last for him a quarter of an hour of delicious triumph in that very spot on which he had been so scolded for saying that Christmas was a bore. "You were so very sudden," said Isabel, excusing herself for her conduct in the morning.

"But you did love me?"

"If I do now, that ought to be enough for you. But I did, and I've been so unhappy since; and I thought that, perhaps, you would never speak to me again. But it was all your fault; you were so sudden. And then you ought to have asked Papa first—you know you ought. But, Maurice, you will promise me one thing. You won't ever again say that Christmas Day is a bore!"

The End

THE BURGLAR'S CHRISTMAS

WILLA CATHER

This is the happiest of stories. To have a happy ending, however, there first must be trouble to overcome. William ran away from his good and prosperous family to live a life free from restraint. He thought he could make a living by his wits, but now he has come to his wit's end. Hungry, alone, and in despair, he is in need of a Christmas miracle. Rather than wait for one, however, William decides to take matters into his own hands and become a thief. "The Burglar's Christmas" was first published in the December 1896 issue of the Home Monthly. Willa Cather (1873–1947) is one of America's great novelists. Many of her books offer poignant accounts of life out West. Novels such as O Pioneers! (1913) and My Ántonia (1918) hauntingly immortalize obscure, humble, and poor immigrant families struggling to establish farms on the Great Plains.

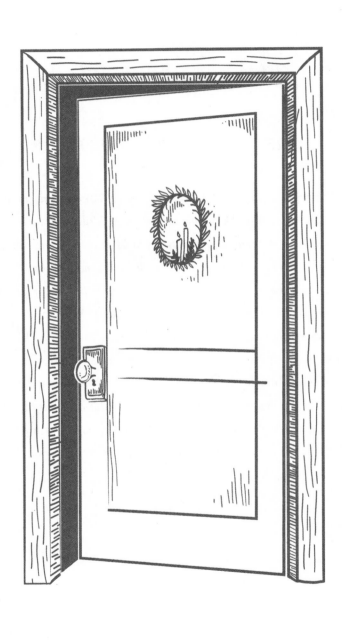

THE BURGLAR'S CHRISTMAS

WILLA CATHER

Two very shabby looking young men stood at the corner of Prairie avenue and Eightieth street, looking despondently at the carriages that whirled by. It was Christmas Eve, and the streets were full of vehicles; florists' wagons, grocers' carts, and carriages. The streets were in that half-liquid, half-congealed condition peculiar to the streets of Chicago at that season of the year. The swift wheels that spun by sometimes threw the slush of mud and snow over the two young men who were talking on the corner.

"Well," remarked the elder of the two, "I guess we are at our rope's end, sure enough. How do you feel?"

"Pretty shaky. The wind's sharp to-night. If I had had anything to eat I mightn't mind it so much. There is simply no show. I'm sick of the whole business. Looks like there's nothing for it but the lake."

"O, nonsense, I thought you had more grit. Got anything left you can hoc?"[1]

---

1. Something that a pawnbroker would give you money in exchange for such as a ring or watch (written today as "hock").

"Nothing but my beard, and I am afraid they wouldn't find it worth a pawn ticket," said the younger man ruefully, rubbing the week's growth of stubble on his face.

"Got any folks anywhere? Now's your time to strike 'em if you have."

"Never mind if I have, they're out of the question."

"Well, you'll be out of it before many hours if you don't make a move of some sort. A man's got to eat. See here, I am going down to Longtin's saloon. I used to play the banjo in there, and I'll bone[2] him for some of his free lunch stuff. You'd better come along, perhaps they'll fill an order for two."

"How far down is it?"

"Well, it's clear down town, of course, way down on Michigan avenue."

"Thanks, I guess I'll loaf around here. I don't feel equal to the walk, and the cars—well, the cars are crowded." His features drew themselves into what might have been a smile under happier circumstances.

"No, you never did like street cars, you're too aristocratic.[3] See here, Crawford, I don't like leaving you here. You ain't good company for yourself to-night."

"Crawford? O, yes, that's the last one. There have been so many I forget them."

"Have you got a real name, anyway?"

"O, yes, but it's one of the ones I've forgotten. Don't you worry about me. You go along and get your free lunch. I think I had a row in Longtin's place once. I'd better not show myself there again." As he spoke the young man nodded and turned slowly up the avenue.

He was miserable enough to want to be quite alone. Even the crowd that jostled by him annoyed him. He wanted to think about himself. He

---

2. Accost.
3. He was raised in a well-to-do family that viewed public transportation as only for the lower classes.

had avoided this final reckoning with himself for a year now. He had laughed it off and drunk it off. But now, when all those artificial devices which are employed to turn our thoughts into other channels and shield us from ourselves had failed him, it must come. Hunger is a powerful incentive to introspection.

It is a tragic hour, that hour when we are finally driven to reckon with ourselves, when every avenue of mental distraction has been cut off and our own life and all its ineffaceable failures closes about us like the walls of that old torture chamber of the Inquisition. To-night, as this man stood stranded in the streets of the city, his hour came. It was not the first time he had been hungry and desperate and alone. But always before there had been some outlook, some chance ahead, some pleasure yet untasted that seemed worth the effort, some face that he fancied was, or would be, dear. But it was not so to-night. The unyielding conviction was upon him that he had failed in everything, had outlived everything. It had been near him for a long time, that Pale Spectre. He had caught its shadow at the bottom of his glass many a time, at the head of his bed when he was sleep-less at night, in the twilight shadows when some great sunset broke upon him. It had made life hateful to him when he awoke in the morning before now. But now it settled slowly over him, like night, the endless Northern nights that bid the sun a long farewell. It rose up before him like granite. From this brilliant city with its glad bustle of Yule-tide he was shut off as completely as though he were a creature of another species. His days seemed numbered and done, sealed over like the little coral cells at the bottom of the sea. Involuntarily he drew that cold air through his lungs slowly, as though he were tasting it for the last time.

Yet he was but four and twenty, this man—he looked even younger— and he had a father some place down East who had been very proud of him once. Well, he had taken his life into his own hands, and this was what he had made of it. That was all there was to be said. He could remember the hopeful things they used to say about him at college in the old days, before he had cut away and begun to live by his wits, and he found courage to smile at them now. They had read him wrongly. He knew now that he never had the essentials of success, only the superficial agility that is often mistaken for it. He was tow without the tinder,[4] and he had burnt himself out at other people's fires. He had helped other people to make it win, but he himself—he had never touched an enterprise that had not failed eventu-ally. Or, if it survived his connection with it, it left him behind.

His last venture had been with some ten-cent specialty company,[5] a little lower than all the others, that had gone to pieces in Buffalo, and he had worked his way to Chicago by boat. When the boat made up its crew for the outward voyage, he was dispensed with as usual. He was used to that. The reason for it? O, there are so many reasons for failure! His was a very common one.

As he stood there in the wet under the street light he drew up his reckoning with the world and decided that it had treated him as well as he deserved. He had overdrawn his account[6] once too often. There had been a day when he thought otherwise; when he had said he was unjustly handled, that his failure was merely the lack of proper adjustment between himself and other men, that some day he would be recognized and it would all come right. But he knew better than that now, and he was still man enough to bear no grudge against any one—man or woman.

To-night was his birthday, too. There seemed something particularly amusing in that. He turned up a limp little coat collar to try to keep a little of the wet chill from his throat, and instinctively began to remember all

---

4. This phrase means that he would be easily burnt up, but there is nothing to set him alight. "Tow" literally means a thread, but came to be used to evoke highly flammable material. It recurs in the King James Version. For instance, "And the strong shall be as tow, and the maker of it as a spark, and they shall both burn together" (Isa. 1:31).

5. In the past there were "dime stores." The name was meant to entice customers with the thought that a lot of items only cost ten cents. The equivalent today is a "dollar store."

6. Written a check when he did not actually have the money in his bank account.

the birthday parties he used to have. He was so cold and empty that his mind seemed unable to grapple with any serious question. He kept thinking about ginger bread and frosted cakes like a child. He could remember the splendid birthday parties his mother used to give him, when all the other little boys in the block came in their Sunday clothes and creaking shoes, with their ears still red from their mother's towel, and the pink and white birthday cake, and the stuffed olives and all the dishes of which he had been particularly fond, and how he would eat and eat and then go to bed and dream of Santa Claus. And in the morning he would awaken and eat again, until by night the family doctor arrived with his castor oil, and poor William used to dolefully say that it was altogether too much to have your birthday and Christmas all at once. He could remember, too, the royal birthday suppers he had given at college, and the stag dinners,[7] and the toasts, and the music, and the good fellows who had wished him happiness and really meant what they said.

And since then there were other birthday suppers that he could not remember so clearly; the memory of them was heavy and flat, like cigarette smoke that has been shut in a room all night, like champagne that has been a day opened, a song that has been too often sung, an acute sensation that has been overstrained. They seemed tawdry and garish, discordant to him now. He rather wished he could forget them altogether.

Whichever way his mind now turned there was one thought that it could not escape, and that was the idea of food. He caught the scent of a cigar suddenly, and felt a sharp pain in the pit of his abdomen and a sudden moisture in his mouth. His cold hands clenched angrily, and for a moment he felt that bitter hatred of wealth, of ease, of everything that is well-fed and well-housed that is common to starving men. At any rate he had a right to eat! He had demanded great things from the world once:

---

7. A bachelor party or a celebration to which only men are invited.

fame and wealth and admiration. Now it was simply bread—and he would have it! He looked about him quickly and felt the blood begin to stir in his veins. In all his straits he had never stolen anything, his tastes were above it. But to-night there would be no to-morrow. He was amused at the way in which the idea excited him. Was it possible there was yet one more experience that would distract him, one thing that had power to excite his jaded interest? Good! he had failed at everything else, now he would see what his chances would be as a common thief. It would be amusing to watch the beautiful consistency of his destiny work itself out even in that role. It would be interesting to add another study to his gallery of futile attempts, and then label them all: "the failure as a journalist," "the failure as a lecturer," "the failure as a business man," "the failure as a thief," and so on, like the titles under the pictures of the Dance of Death.[8] It was time that Childe Roland came to the dark tower.[9]

A girl hastened by him with her arms full of packages. She walked quickly and nervously, keeping well within the shadow, as if she were not accustomed to carrying bundles and did not care to meet any of her friends. As she crossed the muddy street, she made an effort to lift her skirt a little, and as she did so one of the packages slipped unnoticed from beneath her arm. He caught it up and overtook her. "Excuse me, but I think you dropped something."

She started, "O, yes, thank you, I would rather have lost anything than that."

The young man turned angrily upon himself. The package must have contained something of value. Why had he not kept it? Was this the sort

---

8. A series of images often made in the medieval period showing Death personified (sometimes called the Grim Reaper) coming for different kinds of people. A famous series was done by the artist Hans Holbein the Younger (1497–1543). The titles identify who is dying in each scene and include the Miser, the Old Man, and the Ploughman.
9. A reference to a poem by Robert Browning, "Childe Roland to the Dark Tower Came." Childe Roland finds himself in a depressing wasteland and thinks back on the good times he used to have in the past. To come to the tower is for the ordeal finally to be over.

of thief he would make? He ground his teeth together. There is nothing more maddening than to have morally consented to crime and then lack the nerve force to carry it out.

A carriage drove up to the house before which he stood. Several richly dressed women alighted and went in. It was a new house, and must have been built since he was in Chicago last. The front door was open and he could see down the hall-way and up the staircase. The servant had left the door and gone with the guests. The first floor was brilliantly lighted, but the windows upstairs were dark. It looked very easy, just to slip upstairs to the darkened chambers where the jewels and trinkets of the fashion-able occupants were kept.

Still burning with impatience against himself he entered quickly. Instinctively he removed his mud-stained hat as he passed quickly and qui-etly up the staircase. It struck him as being a rather superfluous courtesy in a burglar, but he had done it before he had thought. His way was clear enough, he met no one on the stairway or in the upper hall. The gas was lit in the upper hall.[10] He passed the first chamber door through sheer cow-ardice. The second he entered quickly, thinking of something else lest his courage should fail him, and closed the door behind him. The light from the hall shone into the room through the transom.[11] The apartment was furnished richly enough to justify his expectations. He went at once to the dressing case. A number of rings and small trinkets lay in a silver tray. These he put hastily in his pocket. He opened the upper drawer and found, as he expected, several leather cases. In the first he opened was a lady's watch, in the second a pair of old-fashioned bracelets; he seemed to dimly remember having seen bracelets like them before, somewhere. The third case was heavier, the spring was much worn, and it opened easily. It held a cup of some kind. He held it up to the light and then his strained

---

10. In other words, the lights are on.
11. There is a glass panel above the door.

nerves gave way and he uttered a sharp exclamation. It was the silver mug he used to drink from when he was a little boy.

The door opened, and a woman stood in the doorway facing him. She was a tall woman, with white hair, in evening dress. The light from the hall streamed in upon him, but she was not afraid. She stood looking at him a moment, then she threw out her hand and went quickly toward him.

"Willie, Willie! Is it you!"

He struggled to loose her arms from him, to keep her lips from his cheek. "Mother—you must not! You do not understand! O, my God, this is worst of all!" Hunger, weakness, cold, shame, all came back to him, and shook his self-control completely. Physically he was too weak to stand a shock like this. Why could it not have been an ordinary discovery, arrest, the station house[12] and all the rest of it. Anything but this! A hard dry sob broke from him. Again he strove to disengage himself.

"Who is it says I shall not kiss my son? O, my boy, we have waited so long for this! You have been so long in coming, even I almost gave you up."

Her lips upon his cheek burnt him like fire. He put his hand to his throat, and spoke thickly and incoherently: "You do not understand. I did not know you were here. I came here to rob—it is the first time—I swear it—but I am a common thief. My pockets are full of your jewels now. Can't you hear me? I am a common thief!"

"Hush, my boy, those are ugly words. How could you rob your own house? How could you take what is your own? They are all yours, my son, as wholly yours as my great love—and you can't doubt that, Will, do you?"

That soft voice, the warmth and fragrance of her person stole through his chill, empty veins like a gentle stimulant. He felt as though all his strength were leaving him and even consciousness. He held fast to her and bowed his head on her strong shoulder, and groaned aloud.

---

12. The police station.

"O, mother, life is hard, hard!"

She said nothing, but held him closer. And O, the strength of those white arms that held him! O, the assurance of safety in that warm bosom that rose and fell under his cheek! For a moment they stood so, silently. Then they heard a heavy step upon the stair. She led him to a chair and went out and closed the door. At the top of the staircase she met a tall, broad-shouldered man, with iron gray hair, and a face alert and stern. Her eyes were shining and her cheeks on fire, her whole face was one expression of intense determination.

"James, it is William in there, come home. You must keep him at any cost. If he goes this time, I go with him. O, James, be easy with him, he has suffered so." She broke from a command to an entreaty, and laid her hand on his shoulder. He looked questioningly at her a moment, then went in the room and quietly shut the door.

She stood leaning against the wall, clasping her temples with her hands and listening to the low indistinct sound of the voices within. Her own lips moved silently. She waited a long time, scarcely breathing. At last the door opened, and her husband came out. He stopped to say in a shaken voice,

"You go to him now, he will stay. I will go to my room. I will see him again in the morning."

She put her arm about his neck, "O, James, I thank you, I thank you! This is the night he came so long ago, you remember? I gave him to you then, and now you give him back to me!"

"Don't, Helen," he muttered. "He is my son, I have never forgotten that. I failed with him. I don't like to fail, it cuts my pride. Take him and make a man of him." He passed on down the hall.

She flew into the room where the young man sat with his head bowed upon his knee. She dropped upon her knees beside him. Ah, it was so good to him to feel those arms again!

"He is so glad, Willie, so glad! He may not show it, but he is as happy as I. He never was demonstrative with either of us, you know."

"O, my God, he was good enough," groaned the man. "I told him everything, and he was good enough. I don't see how either of you can look at me, speak to me, touch me." He shivered under her clasp again as when she had first touched him, and tried weakly to throw her off.

But she whispered softly,

"This is my right, my son."

Presently, when he was calmer, she rose. "Now, come with me into the library, and I will have your dinner brought there."

As they went down stairs she remarked apologetically, "I will not call Ellen to-night; she has a number of guests to attend to. She is a big girl now, you know, and came out[13] last winter. Besides, I want you all to myself to-night."

When the dinner came, and it came very soon, he fell upon it savagely. As he ate she told him all that had transpired during the years of his absence, and how his father's business had brought them there. "I was glad when we came. I thought you would drift West. I seemed a good deal nearer to you here."

There was a gentle unobtrusive sadness in her tone that was too soft for a reproach.

"Have you everything you want? It is a comfort to see you eat."

He smiled grimly. "It is certainly a comfort to me. I have not indulged in this frivolous habit for some thirty-five hours."

She caught his hand and pressed it sharply, uttering a quick remonstrance.

"Don't say that! I know, but I can't hear you say it—it's too terrible! My boy, food has choked me many a time when I have thought of the

---

13. She was a debutante. There was a society gathering to announce officially that she was no longer a girl but now a young woman.

possibility of that. Now take the old lounging chair by the fire, and if you are too tired to talk, we will just sit and rest together."

He sank into the depths of the big leather chair with the lion's heads on the arms, where he had sat so often in the days when his feet did not touch the floor and he was half afraid of the grim monsters cut in the polished wood. That chair seemed to speak to him of things long forgotten. It was like the touch of an old familiar friend. He felt a sudden yearning tenderness for the happy little boy who had sat there and dreamed of the big world so long ago. Alas, he had been dead many a summer, that little boy!

He sat looking up at the magnificent woman beside him. He had almost forgotten how handsome she was; how lustrous and sad were the eyes that were set under that serene brow, how impetuous and wayward the mouth even now, how superb the white throat and shoulders! Ah, the wit and grace and fineness of this woman! He remembered how proud he had been of her as a boy when she came to see him at school. Then in the deep red coals of the grate he saw the faces of other women who had come since then into his vexed, disordered life. Laughing faces, with eyes artificially bright, eyes without depth or meaning, features without the stamp of high sensibilities. And he had left this face for such as those!

He sighed restlessly and laid his hand on hers. There seemed refuge and protection in the touch of her, as in the old days when he was afraid of the dark. He had been in the dark so long now, his confidence was so thoroughly shaken, and he was bitterly afraid of the night and of himself.

"Ah, mother, you make other things seem so false. You must feel that I owe you an explanation, but I can't make any, even to myself. Ah, but we make poor exchanges in life. I can't make out the riddle of it all. Yet there are things I ought to tell you before I accept your confidence like this."

"I'd rather you wouldn't, Will. Listen: Between you and me there can be no secrets. We are more alike than other people. Dear boy, I know all about it. I am a woman, and circumstances were different with me, but we are of one blood. I have lived all your life before you. You have never had an impulse that I have not known, you have never touched a brink that my feet have not trod. This is your birthday night. Twenty-four years ago I foresaw all this. I was a young woman then and I had hot battles of my own, and I felt your likeness to me. You were not like other babies. From the hour you were born you were restless and discontented, as I had been before you. You used to brace your strong little limbs against mine and try to throw me off as you did to-night. To-night you have come back to me, just as you always did after you ran away to swim in the river that was forbidden you, the river you loved because it was forbidden. You are tired and sleepy, just as you used to be then, only a little older and a little paler and a little more foolish. I never asked you where you had been then, nor will I now. You have come back to me, that's all in all to me. I know your every possibility and limitation, as a composer knows his instrument."

He found no answer that was worthy to give to talk like this. He had not found life easy since he had lived by his wits. He had come to know poverty at close quarters. He had known what it was to be gay[14] with an empty pocket, to wear violets in his button hole when he had not break-fasted, and all the hateful shams of the poverty of idleness. He had been a reporter on a big metropolitan daily, where men grind out their brains on paper until they have not one idea left—and still grind on. He had worked in a real estate office, where ignorant men were swindled. He had sung in a comic opera chorus and played Harris in an Uncle Tom's Cabin Company,[15] and edited a Socialist weekly. He had been dogged by debt and hunger and grinding poverty, until to sit here by a warm fire without concern as to how it would be paid for seemed unnatural.

---

14. Cheerful. He was putting on a brave face and acting like he was happy even though he wasn't.
15. Harriet Beecher Stowe's popular anti-slavery novel, *Uncle Tom's Cabin* (1852), was often staged as a play.

He looked up at her questioningly. "I wonder if you know how much you pardon?"

"O, my poor boy, much or little, what does it matter? Have you wan-dered so far and paid such a bitter price for knowledge and not yet learned that love has nothing to do with pardon or forgiveness, that it only loves, and loves—and loves? They have not taught you well, the women of your world." She leaned over and kissed him, as no woman had kissed him since he left her.

He drew a long sigh of rich content. The old life, with all its bitterness and useless antagonism and flimsy sophistries, its brief delights that were always tinged with fear and distrust and unfaith, that whole miserable, futile, swindled world of Bohemia[16] seemed immeasurably distant and far away, like a dream that is over and done. And as the chimes rang joyfully outside and sleep pressed heavily upon his eyelids, he wondered dimly if the Author of this sad little riddle of ours were not able to solve it after all, and if the Potter would not finally mete out his all comprehensive justice, such as none but he could have, to his Things of Clay,[17] which are made in his own patterns, weak or strong, for his own ends; and if some day we will not awaken and find that all evil is a dream, a mental distortion that will pass when the dawn shall break.

---

16. "Bohemians" is a way to refer to people who defy the conventions of respectable society, often living in ways that others find improper.
17. He is starting to have faith in God and God's providential overseeing of his life. Hebrews 12:2 says that Jesus is "the author and finisher of our faith (KJV)," and Isaiah 64:8 declares: "But now, O LORD, thou are our father; we are the clay, and thou our potter; and we all are the work of thy hand (KJV)."

OLD CHRISTMAS
AT BRACEBRIDGE HALL
WASHINGTON IRVING

While readers are not likely to understand all the words and phrases used in this reading, it is, nevertheless, quite an easy story to follow along with and to delight in. "Old Christmas at Bracebridge Hall" revels in the customs of an old-fashioned Christmas, and thus while you might not always grasp precisely what something is, you will understand that you are being treated to a high-hearted description of foods or clothes or games from the olden days of legend and romance. The author himself, Washington Irving (1783–1859), elucidated some of these obscure references in the endnotes, and additional explanations are provided in the footnotes. The squire is determined to celebrate Christmas in the exuberant, festive way of "Merrie Olde England." His jolly efforts are endearing, but sometimes they slide toward the ridiculous. Part of the fun is to see aristocratic England through American eyes. Irving was the first fiction writer from the United States to gain an international reputation. "Old Christmas at Bracebridge Hall" is really three consecutive chapters from his book The Sketch Book of Geoffrey Crayon, Gentleman (1820). This is therefore a longer reading, but the chapter titles and divisions have been kept so it is easy to spread it out over multiple days if you wish. The Sketch Book is a series of short stories that have been stitched together. It contains some of the most famous tales in all of American literature, including "Rip Van Winkle" and "The Legend of Sleepy Hollow."

OLD CHRISTMAS AT BRACEBRIDGE HALL

WASHINGTON IRVING

Christmas Eve

Saint Francis and Saint Benedight
Blesse this house from wicked wight;
From the night-mare and the goblin,
That is hight good fellow Robin;
Keep it from all evil spirits,
Fairies, weezels, rats, and ferrets:
From curfew time
To the next prime.
CARTWRIGHT.

I t was a brilliant moonlight night, but extremely cold; our chaise[1] whirled rapidly over the frozen ground; the postboy smacked his whip incessantly, and a part of the time his horses were on a gallop. "He knows where he is going," said my companion, laughing, "and is eager to arrive in time for some of the merriment and good cheer of the servants'

---

1. A type of carriage.

hall. My father, you must know, is a bigoted devotee of the old school, and prides himself upon keeping up something of old English hospitality. He is a tolerable specimen of what you will rarely meet with nowadays in its purity, the old English country gentleman; for our men of fortune spend so much of their time in town, and fashion is carried so much into the country, that the strong rich peculiarities of ancient rural life are almost polished away. My father, however, from early years, took honest Peacham[i] for his textbook, instead of Chesterfield;[2] he determined in his own mind that there was no condition more truly honorable and enviable than that of a country gentleman on his paternal lands, and therefore passes the whole of his time on his estate. He is a strenuous advocate for the revival of the old rural games and holiday observances, and is deeply read in the writers, ancient and modern, who have treated on the subject. Indeed, his favorite range of reading is among the authors who flourished at least two centuries since, who, he insists, wrote and thought more like true Englishmen than any of their successors. He even regrets sometimes that he had not been born a few centuries earlier, when England was itself and had its peculiar manners and customs. As he lives at some distance from the main road, in rather a lonely part of the country, without any rival gentry[3] near him, he has that most enviable of all blessings to an Englishman—an opportunity of indulging the bent of his own humor without molestation. Being representative of the oldest family in the neighborhood, and a great part of the peasantry being his tenants, he is much looked up to, and in general is known simply by the appellation of 'The Squire'[4]—a title which

---

2. The Earl of Chesterfield, *Letters to His Son on the Art of Becoming a Man of the World and a Gentleman* (1774). The point is that though his father lives in the nineteenth century, even an eighteenth-century guide to proper conduct is too modern for him, and thus he prefers a seventeenth-century one.
3. The families of a higher social class even if they do not have aristocratic titles.
4. A title going back to the days of knighthood which came to be used for the most prominent gentleman in a particular part of the country, usually someone from an old, respectable family who is also a significant landowner.

has been accorded to the head of the family since time immemorial. I think it best to give you these hints about my worthy old father, to prepare you for any eccentricities that might otherwise appear absurd."

We had passed for some time along the wall of a park, and at length the chaise stopped at the gate. It was in a heavy, magnificent old style, of iron bars fancifully wrought at the top into flourishes and flowers. The huge square columns that supported the gate were surmounted by the family crest. Close adjoining was the porter's lodge, sheltered under dark fir trees and almost buried in shrubbery.

The postboy rang a large porter's bell, which resounded through the still frosty air, and was answered by the distant barking of dogs, with which the mansion-house seemed garrisoned. An old woman immediately appeared at the gate. As the moonlight fell strongly upon her, I had a full view of a little primitive dame, dressed very much in the antique taste, with a neat kerchief and stomacher,[5] and her silver hair peeping from under a cap of snowy whiteness. She came curtseying forth, with many expressions of simple joy at seeing her young master. Her husband, it seemed, was up at the house keeping Christmas Eve in the servants' hall; they could not do without him, as he was the best hand at a song and story in the household.

My friend proposed that we should alight and walk through the park to the hall, which was at no great distance, while the chaise should follow on. Our road wound through a noble avenue of trees, among the naked branches of which the moon glittered as she rolled through the deep vault of a cloudless sky. The lawn beyond was sheeted with a slight covering of snow, which here and there sparkled as the moonbeams caught a frosty crystal, and at a distance might be seen a thin transparent vapor stealing up from the low grounds and threatening gradually to shroud the landscape.

---

5. An ornamental vest.

My companion looked around him with transport. "How often," said he, "have I scampered up this avenue on returning home on school vacations! How often have I played under these trees when a boy! I feel a degree of filial reverence for them, as we look up to those who have cherished us in childhood. My father was always scrupulous in exacting our holidays and having us around him on family festivals. He used to direct and superintend our games with the strictness that some parents do the studies of their children. He was very particular that we should play the old English games according to their original form, and consulted old books for precedent and authority for every 'merrie disport;' yet I assure you there never was pedantry so delightful. It was the policy of the good old gentleman to make his children feel that home was the happiest place in the world; and I value this delicious home-feeling as one of the choicest gifts a parent could bestow."

We were interrupted by the clamor of a troop of dogs of all sorts and sizes, "mongrel, puppy, whelp, and hound, and curs of lower degree," that disturbed by the ring of the porter's bell and the rattling of the chaise, came bounding, open-mouthed, across the lawn.

"'The little dogs and all,
Tray, Blanch, and Sweetheart, see, they bark at me!'"[6]

cried Bracebridge, laughing. At the sound of his voice the bark was changed into a yelp of delight, and in a moment he was surrounded and almost overpowered by the caresses of the faithful animals.

We had now come in full view of the old family mansion, partly thrown in deep shadow and partly lit up by the cold moonshine. It was an irregular building of some magnitude, and seemed to be of the architecture of different periods. One wing was evidently very ancient, with heavy

---

6. Quoting from Shakespeare's *King Lear*, Act 3, scene 6.

stone-shafted bow windows jutting out and overrun with ivy, from among the foliage of which the small diamond-shaped panes of glass glittered with the moonbeams. The rest of the house was in the French taste of Charles the Second's time, having been repaired and altered, as my friend told me, by one of his ancestors who returned with that monarch at the Restoration.[7] The grounds about the house were laid out in the old formal manner of artificial flower-beds, clipped shrubberies, raised terraces, and heavy stone balustrades,[8] ornamented with urns, a leaden statue or two, and a jet of water. The old gentleman, I was told, was extremely careful to preserve this obsolete finery in all its original state. He admired this fashion in gardening; it had an air of magnificence, was courtly and noble, and befitting good old family style. The boasted imitation of Nature in modern gardening had sprung up with modern republican notions, but did not suit a monarchical government; it smacked of the leveling system.[9] I could not help smiling at this introduction of politics into gardening, though I expressed some apprehension that I should find the old gentleman rather intolerant in his creed. Frank assured me, however, that it was almost the only instance in which he had ever heard his father meddle with politics; and he believed that he had got this notion from a member of Parliament who once passed a few weeks with him. The squire was glad of any argument to defend his clipped yew trees and formal terraces, which had been occasionally attacked by modern landscape gardeners.

As we approached the house we heard the sound of music, and now and then a burst of laughter from one end of the building. This, Bracebridge said, must proceed from the servants' hall, where a great deal of

---

7. The monarchy had been abolished during the English Civil War. The Restoration was when this political experiment came to an end in 1660 and King Charles II (1630–1685) came to the throne.
8. Pillars.
9. To try to eradicate class distinctions and put everyone on the same level.

revelry was permitted, and even encouraged, by the squire throughout the twelve days of Christmas, provided everything was done conformably to ancient usage. Here were kept up the old games of hoodman blind, shoe the wild mare, hot cockles, steal the white loaf, bob apple, and snap dragon; the Yule-clog and Christmas candle were regularly burnt, and the mistletoe with its white berries hung up, to the imminent peril of all the pretty housemaids.[ii]

So intent were the servants upon their sports that we had to ring repeatedly before we could make ourselves heard. On our arrival being announced the squire came out to receive us, accompanied by his two other sons—one a young officer in the army, home on a leave of absence; the other an Oxonian,[10] just from the university. The squire was a fine healthy-looking old gentleman, with silver hair curling lightly round an open florid countenance, in which the physiognomist,[11] with the advantage, like myself, of a previous hint or two, might discover a singular mixture of whim and benevolence.

The family meeting was warm and affectionate; as the evening was far advanced, the squire would not permit us to change our travelling dresses, but ushered us at once to the company, which was assembled in a large old-fashioned hall. It was composed of different branches of a numerous family connection, where there were the usual proportion of old uncles and aunts, comfortable married dames, superannuated spinsters,[12] blooming country cousins, half-fledged striplings, and bright-eyed boarding-school hoydens.[13] They were variously occupied—some at a round game of cards; others conversing around the fireplace; at one end of the hall was a group of the young folks, some nearly grown up, others of a more tender and

---

10. Someone from the University of Oxford.
11. Someone who studies people's faces, often claiming to be able to discern their character from their facial features.
12. Women who have never married and have not found or been given a role in life.
13. They are not well behaved, a bit rowdy.

budding age, fully engrossed by a merry game; and a profusion of wooden horses, penny trumpets, and tattered dolls about the floor showed traces of a troop of little fairy beings who, having frolicked through a happy day, had been carried off to slumber through a peaceful night.

While the mutual greetings were going on between young Brace-bridge and his relatives I had time to scan the apartment. I have called it a hall, for so it had certainly been in old times, and the squire had evidently endeavored to restore it to something of its primitive state. Over the heavy projecting fireplace was suspended a picture of a warrior in armor, stand-ing by a white horse, and on the opposite wall hung a helmet, buckler, and lance. At one end an enormous pair of antlers were inserted in the wall, the branches serving as hooks on which to suspend hats, whips, and spurs, and in the corners of the apartment were fowling-pieces,[14] fishing-rods, and other sporting implements. The furniture was of the cumbrous workman-ship of former days, though some articles of modern convenience had been added and the oaken floor had been carpeted, so that the whole presented an odd mixture of parlor and hall.

The grate had been removed from the wide overwhelming fireplace to make way for a fire of wood, in the midst of which was an enormous log glowing and blazing, and sending forth a vast volume of light and heat: this, I understood, was the Yule-clog, which the squire was particular in having brought in and illumined on a Christmas Eve, according to ancient custom.[iii]

Herrick mentions it in one of his songs:[15]

Come, bring with a noise,

    My metric, merrie boys,

The Christmas Log to the firing;

---

14. Guns used for hunting birds.
15. The English poet, Robert Herrick (1591–1674). Again, the general point is the squire's preference for the seventeenth century.

> While my good dame, she
> Bids ye all be free,
> And drink to your hearts' desiring.

The Yule-clog is still burnt in many farm-houses and kitchens in England, particularly in the north, and there are several superstitions connected with it among the peasantry. If a squinting person come to the house while it is burning, or a person barefooted, it is considered an ill omen. The brand remaining from the Yule-clog is carefully put away to light the next year's Christmas fire.

It was really delightful to see the old squire seated in his hereditary elbow-chair by the hospitable fireside of his ancestors, and looking around him like the sun of a system, beaming warmth and gladness to every heart. Even the very dog that lay stretched at his feet, as he lazily shifted his position and yawned would look fondly up in his master's face, wag his tail against the floor, and stretch himself again to sleep, confident of kindness and protection. There is an emanation from the heart in genuine hospitality which cannot be described, but is immediately felt and puts the stranger at once at his ease. I had not been seated many minutes by the comfortable hearth of the worthy old cavalier[16] before I found myself as much at home as if I had been one of the family.

Supper was announced shortly after our arrival. It was served up in a spacious oaken chamber, the panels of which shone with wax, and around which were several family portraits decorated with holly and ivy. Besides the accustomed lights, two great wax tapers, called Christmas candles, wreathed with greens, were placed on a highly polished beaufet[17]

---

16. Literally someone who took the Royalist side in the English Civil War of the seventeenth century. In the squire's case, of course, it merely means that he knows which side he would have taken had he been alive back then. More generally, "cavalier" can simply mean someone who is courtly or gentlemanly in their manners.
17. Buffet table.

among the family plate. The table was abundantly spread with substantial fare; but the squire made his supper of frumenty, a dish made of wheat cakes boiled in milk with rich spices, being a standing dish in old times for Christmas Eve. I was happy to find my old friend, minced pie, in the retinue of the feast and, finding him to be perfectly orthodox, and that I need not be ashamed of my predilection, I greeted him with all the warmth wherewith we usually greet an old and very genteel acquaintance.

The mirth of the company was greatly promoted by the humors of an eccentric personage whom Mr. Bracebridge always addressed with the quaint appellation of Master Simon. He was a tight brisk little man, with the air of an arrant[18] old bachelor. His nose was shaped like the bill of a parrot; his face slightly pitted with the small-pox, with a dry perpetual bloom on it, like a frostbitten leaf in autumn. He had an eye of great quickness and vivacity, with a drollery and lurking waggery[19] of expression that was irresistible. He was evidently the wit of the family, dealing very much in sly jokes and innuendoes with the ladies, and making infinite merriment by harping upon old themes, which, unfortunately, my ignorance of the family chronicles did not permit me to enjoy. It seemed to be his great delight during supper to keep a young girl next to him in a continual agony of stifled laughter, in spite of her awe of the reproving looks of her mother, who sat opposite. Indeed, he was the idol of the younger part of the company, who laughed at everything he said or did and at every turn of his countenance. I could not wonder at it; for he must have been a miracle of accomplishments in their eyes. He could imitate Punch and Judy;[20] make an old woman of his hand, with the assistance of a burnt cork and pocket-handkerchief; and cut an orange into such a ludicrous caricature that the young folks were ready to die with laughing.

---

18. One who travels about rather than living a settled life in one place.
19. Drollery means humorous and waggery means mischievous.
20. Standard characters in a traditional puppet show.

I was let briefly into his history by Frank Bracebridge. He was an old bachelor, of a small independent income, which by careful management was sufficient for all his wants. He revolved through the family system like a vagrant comet in its orbit, sometimes visiting one branch, and sometimes another quite remote, as is often the case with gentlemen of extensive connections and small fortunes in England. He had a chirping, buoyant disposition, always enjoying the present moment; and his frequent change of scene and company prevented his acquiring those rusty, unaccommodating habits with which old bachelors are so uncharitably charged. He was a complete family chronicle, being versed in the genealogy, history, and intermarriages of the whole house of Bracebridge, which made him a great favorite with the old folks; he was a beau[21] of all the elder ladies and superannuated spinsters, among whom he was habitually considered rather a young fellow; and he was master of the revels among the children, so that there was not a more popular being in the sphere in which he moved than Mr. Simon Bracebridge. Of late years he had resided almost entirely with the squire, to whom he had become a factotum,[22] and whom he particularly delighted by jumping with his humor in respect to old times and by having a scrap of an old song to suit every occasion. We had presently a specimen of his last-mentioned talent, for no sooner was supper removed and spiced wines and other beverages peculiar to the season introduced, than Master Simon was called on for a good old Christmas song. He bethought himself for a moment, and then, with a sparkle of the eye and a voice that was by no means bad, excepting that it ran occasionally into a falsetto like the notes of a split reed, he quavered forth a quaint old ditty:

---

21. The darling.
22. He runs errands for him and generally does whatever little jobs he can for him that might arise in the moment.

Now Christmas is come,

    Let us beat up the drum,

And call all our neighbors together;

    And when they appear,

    Let us make them such cheer,

As will keep out the wind and the weather, &c.

The supper had disposed every one to gayety,[23] and an old harper was summoned from the servants' hall, where he had been strumming all the evening, and to all appearance comforting himself with some of the squire's home-brewed. He was a kind of hanger-on, I was told, of the establishment, and, though ostensibly a resident of the village, was oftener to be found in the squire's kitchen than his own home, the old gentleman being fond of the sound of "harp in hall."

The dance, like most dances after supper, was a merry one: some of the older folks joined in it, and the squire himself figured down several couple with a partner with whom he affirmed he had danced at every Christmas for nearly half a century. Master Simon, who seemed to be a kind of connecting link between the old times and the new, and to be withal a little antiquated in the taste of his accomplishments, evidently piqued himself on his dancing, and was endeavoring to gain credit by the heel and toe, rigadoon,[24] and other graces of the ancient school; but he had unluckily assorted himself with a little romping girl from boarding-school, who by her wild vivacity kept him continually on the stretch and defeated all his sober attempts at elegance: such are the ill-sorted matches to which antique gentlemen are unfortunately prone.

The young Oxonian, on the contrary, had led out one of his maiden aunts, on whom the rogue played a thousand little knaveries with

---

23. Jollity—put them in a playful, happy mood.
24. A type of dance or dance move from the seventeenth century.

impunity: he was full of practical jokes, and his delight was to tease his aunts and cousins, yet, like all madcap youngsters, he was a universal favorite among the women. The most interesting couple in the dance was the young officer and a ward of the squire's, a beautiful blushing girl of seventeen. From several shy glances which I had noticed in the course of the evening I suspected there was a little kindness growing up between them; and indeed the young soldier was just the hero to captivate a romantic girl. He was tall, slender, and handsome, and, like most young British officers of late years, had picked up various small accomplishments on the Continent: he could talk French and Italian, draw landscapes, sing very tolerably, dance divinely, but, above all, he had been wounded at Waterloo.[25] What girl of seventeen, well read in poetry and romance, could resist such a mirror of chivalry and perfection?

The moment the dance was over he caught up a guitar, and, lolling against the old marble fireplace in an attitude which I am half inclined to suspect was studied, began the little French air of the Troubadour.[26] The squire, however, exclaimed against having anything on Christmas Eve but good old English; upon which the young minstrel,[27] casting up his eye for a moment as if in an effort of memory, struck into another strain, and with a charming air of gallantry gave Herrick's "Night-Piece to Julia":

Her eyes the glow-worm lend thee,
The shooting stars attend thee,
    And the elves also,
    Whose little eyes glow
Like the sparks of fire, befriend thee.
No Will-o'-the-Wisp mislight thee;

---

25. The Battle of Waterloo (1815), at which Napoleon was defeated, is one of the most celebrated military victories in British history.
26. A kind of singer who were known for their songs about chivalry.
27. Entertainer, especially by singing.

Nor snake nor slow-worm bite thee;

    But on thy way,

    Not making a stay,

Since ghost there is none to affright thee,

Then let not the dark thee cumber;

What though the moon does slumber,

    The stars of the night

    Will lend thee their light,

Like tapers clear without number.

Then, Julia, let me woo thee,

Thus, thus to come unto me,

    And when I shall meet

    Thy silvery feet,

My soul I'll pour into thee.

The song might or might not have been intended in compliment to the fair Julia, for so I found his partner was called; she, however, was certainly unconscious of any such application, for she never looked at the singer, but kept her eyes cast upon the floor. Her face was suffused, it is true, with a beautiful blush, and there was a gentle heaving of the bosom, but all that was doubtless caused by the exercise of the dance; indeed, so great was her indifference that she amused herself with plucking to pieces a choice bouquet of hot-house flowers, and by the time the song was concluded the nosegay[28] lay in ruins on the floor.

The party now broke up for the night with the kind-hearted old custom of shaking hands. As I passed through the hall on my way to my chamber, the dying embers of the Yule-clog still sent forth a dusky glow, and had it not been the season when "no spirit dares stir abroad," I should have been half tempted to steal from my room at midnight and peep

---

28. Flower arrangement.

whether the fairies might not be at their revels about the hearth.

My chamber was in the old part of the mansion, the ponderous furniture of which might have been fabricated in the days of the giants. The room was panelled, with cornices[29] of heavy carved work, in which flowers and grotesque faces were strangely intermingled, and a row of black-looking portraits stared mournfully at me from the walls. The bed was of rich though faded damask,[30] with a lofty tester,[31] and stood in a niche opposite a bow window. I had scarcely got into bed when a strain of music seemed to break forth in the air just below the window. I listened, and found it proceeded from a band which I concluded to be the Waits[32] from some neighboring village. They went round the house, playing under the windows. I drew aside the curtains to hear them more distinctly. The moonbeams fell through the upper part of the casement; partially lighting up the antiquated apartment. The sounds, as they receded, became more soft and aerial, and seemed to accord with the quiet and moonlight. I listened and listened—they became more and more tender and remote, and, as they gradually died away, my head sunk upon the pillow and I fell asleep.

CHRISTMAS DAY

Dark and dull night, flie hence away,
And give the honor to this day
That sees December turn'd to May.

. . . . .

Why does the chilling winter's morne
Smile like a field beset with corn?
Or smell like to a meade new-shorne,

---

29. There is a decorative design running around the top of the room.
30. It has an artistic pattern and is made of silk.
31. There is a canopy above the bed.
32. An ensemble of Christmas Eve carolers and musicians.

Thus on the sudden?—come and see
The cause why things thus fragrant be.
HERRICK.

When I woke the next morning it seemed as if all the events of the preceding evening had been a dream, and nothing but the identity of the ancient chamber convinced me of their reality. While I lay musing on my pillow I heard the sound of little feet pattering outside of the door, and a whispering consultation. Presently a choir of small voices chanted forth an old Christmas carol, the burden of which was—

Rejoice! our Saviour, he was born
On Christmas day in the morning.[33]

I rose softly, slipt on my clothes, opened the door suddenly, and beheld one of the most beautiful little fairy groups that a painter could imagine. It consisted of a boy and two girls, the eldest not more than six, and lovely as seraphs. They were going the rounds of the house and singing at every chamber door, but my sudden appearance frightened them into mute bash-fulness. They remained for a moment playing on their lips with their fingers, and now and then stealing a shy glance from under their eyebrows, until, as if by one impulse, they scampered away, and as they turned an angle of the gallery I heard them laughing in triumph at their escape.

Everything conspired to produce kind and happy feelings in this stronghold of old-fashioned hospitality. The window of my chamber looked out upon what in summer would have been a beautiful landscape. There was a sloping lawn, a fine stream winding at the foot of it, and a tract of park beyond, with noble clumps of trees and herds of deer. At a distance was a neat hamlet,[34] with the smoke from the cottage chimneys

---

33. From the traditional carol *Good Christians, Rise, This Is the Morn.*
34. A small village.

hanging over it, and a church with its dark spire in strong relief against the clear cold sky. The house was surrounded with evergreens, according to the English custom, which would have given almost an appearance of summer; but the morning was extremely frosty; the light vapor of the preceding evening had been precipitated by the cold, and covered all the trees and every blade of grass with its fine crystalizations. The rays of a bright morning sun had a dazzling effect among the glittering foliage. A robin, perched upon the top of a mountain-ash that hung its clusters of red berries just before my window, was basking himself in the sunshine and piping a few querulous notes, and a peacock was displaying all the glories of his train and strutting with the pride and gravity of a Spanish grandee on the terrace walk below.

I had scarcely dressed myself when a servant appeared to invite me to family prayers. He showed me the way to a small chapel in the old wing of the house, where I found the principal part of the family already assembled in a kind of gallery furnished with cushions, hassocks,[35] and large prayer-books; the servants were seated on benches below. The old gentleman read prayers from a desk in front of the gallery, and Master Simon acted as clerk[36] and made the responses; and I must do him the justice to say that he acquitted himself with great gravity and decorum.

The service was followed by a Christmas carol, which Mr. Bracebridge himself had constructed from a poem of his favorite author, Herrick, and it had been adapted to an old church melody by Master Simon. As there were several good voices among the household, the effect was extremely pleasing, but I was particularly gratified by the exaltation of heart and sudden sally of grateful feeling with which the worthy squire delivered one stanza, his eye glistening and his voice rambling out of all the bounds of time and tune:

---

35. A different cushion for kneeling on during the part of the service when they are praying.
36. Someone designated to play an official part in a worship service.

"'Tis Thou that crown'st my glittering hearth
With guiltless mirth,
And givest me Wassaile bowles to drink
    Spiced to the brink;
Lord, 'tis Thy plenty-dropping hand
    That soiles my land:
And giv'st me for my bushell sowne,
    Twice ten for one."

I afterwards understood that early morning service was read on every Sunday and saint's day throughout the year, either by Mr. Bracebridge or by some member of the family. It was once almost universally the case at the seats of the nobility and gentry of England, and it is much to be regretted that the custom is falling into neglect; for the dullest observer must be sensible of the order and serenity prevalent in those households where the occasional exercise of a beautiful form of worship in the morning gives, as it were, the keynote to every temper for the day and attunes every spirit to harmony.

Our breakfast consisted of what the squire denominated true old English fare. He indulged in some bitter lamentations over modern breakfasts of tea and toast, which he censured as among the causes of modern effeminacy and weak nerves and the decline of old English heartiness; and, though he admitted them to his table to suit the palates of his guests, yet there was a brave display of cold meats, wine, and ale on the sideboard.

After breakfast I walked about the grounds with Frank Bracebridge and Master Simon, or Mr. Simon, as he was called by everybody but the squire. We were escorted by a number of gentlemanlike dogs, that seemed loungers about the establishment, from the frisking spaniel to the steady old stag-hound, the last of which was of a race that had been in the family time out of mind; they were all obedient to a dog-whistle which hung to Master Simon's buttonhole, and in the midst of their gambols[37] would glance an eye occasionally upon a small switch he carried in his hand.

The old mansion had a still more venerable look in the yellow sun-shine than by pale moonlight; and I could not but feel the force of the squire's idea that the formal terraces, heavily moulded balustrades, and clipped yew trees carried with them an air of proud aristocracy. There appeared to be an unusual number of peacocks about the place, and I was making some remarks upon what I termed a flock of them that were bask-ing under a sunny wall, when I was gently corrected in my phraseology by Master Simon, who told me that according to the most ancient and approved treatise on hunting I must say a muster of peacocks. "In the same way," added he, with a slight air of pedantry, "we say a flight of doves or swallows, a bevy of quails, a herd of deer, of wrens, or cranes, a skulk of foxes, or a building of rooks." He went on to inform me that, accord-ing to Sir Anthony Fitzherbert,[38] we ought to ascribe to this bird "both understanding and glory; for, being praised, he will presently set up his tail, chiefly against the sun, to the intent you may the better behold the beauty thereof. But at the fall of the leaf, when his tail falleth, he will mourn and hide himself in corners till his tail come again as it was."

I could not help smiling at this display of small erudition on so whim-sical a subject; but I found that the peacocks were birds of some conse-quence at the hall, for Frank Bracebridge informed me that they were great favorites with his father, who was extremely careful to keep up the breed; partly because they belonged to chivalry, and were in great request at the stately banquets of the olden time, and partly because they had a pomp and magnificence about them highly becoming an old family man-sion. Nothing, he was accustomed to say, had an air of greater state and

---

37. Moving about playfully.
38. Sir Anthony Fitzherbert (1470–1538) was a judge who also wrote about agriculture and therefore nature and life in the country.

dignity than a peacock perched upon an antique stone balustrade.

Master Simon had now to hurry off, having an appointment at the parish church with the village choristers, who were to perform some music of his selection. There was something extremely agreeable in the cheerful flow of animal spirits of the little man; and I confess I had been somewhat surprised at his apt quotations from authors who certainly were not in the range of every-day reading. I mentioned this last circumstance to Frank Bracebridge, who told me with a smile that Master Simon's whole stock of erudition was confined to some half a dozen old authors, which the squire had put into his hands, and which he read over and over whenever he had a studious fit, as he sometimes had on a rainy day or a long winter evening. Sir Anthony Fitzherbert's *Book of Husbandry*, Markham's *Country Contentments*, the *Tretyse of Hunting*, by Sir Thomas Cockayne, Knight, Isaac Walton's *Angler*,[39] and two or three more such ancient worthies of the pen were his standard authorities; and, like all men who know but a few books, he looked up to them with a kind of idolatry and quoted them on all occasions. As to his songs, they were chiefly picked out of old books in the squire's library, and adapted to tunes that were popular among the choice spirits of the last century. His practical application of scraps of literature, however, had caused him to be looked upon as a prodigy of book-knowledge by all the grooms, huntsmen, and small sportsmen of the neighborhood.

While we were talking we heard the distant toll of the village bell, and I was told that the squire was a little particular in having his household at church on a Christmas morning, considering it a day of pouring out of thanks and rejoicing; for, as old Tusser[40] observed—

---

39. His love of old books about country life, here mentioning ones by Gervase Markham (d. 1637) and Sir Thomas Cokayne (1520–1592). Izaak Walton's (1593–1683) book on fishing is a celebrated work: *The Complete Angler* (1653).
40. A sixteenth-century author on country life, Thomas Tusser (d. 1580).

"At Christmas be merry, and thankful withal,
And feast thy poor neighbors, the great with the small."

"If you are disposed to go to church," said Frank Bracebridge, "I can promise you a specimen of my cousin Simon's musical achievements. As the church is destitute of an organ, he has formed a band from the village amateurs, and established a musical club for their improvement; he has also sorted a choir, as he sorted my father's pack of hounds, according to the directions of Jervaise Markham in his *Country Contentments*: for the bass he has sought out all the 'deep, solemn mouths,' and for the tenor the 'loud-ringing mouths,' among the country bumpkins,[41] and for 'sweet-mouths,' he has culled with curious taste among the prettiest lasses in the neighborhood; though these last, he affirms, are the most difficult to keep in tune, your pretty female singer being exceedingly wayward and capricious, and very liable to accident."

As the morning, though frosty, was remarkably fine and clear, the most of the family walked to the church, which was a very old building of gray stone, and stood near a village about half a mile from the park gate. Adjoining it was a low snug parsonage which seemed coeval with the church. The front of it was perfectly matted with a yew tree that had been trained against its walls, through the dense foliage of which apertures had been formed to admit light into the small antique lattices.[42] As we passed this sheltered nest the parson issued forth and preceded us.

I had expected to see a sleek well-conditioned pastor, such as is often found in a snug living in the vicinity of a rich patron's table, but I was disappointed. The parson was a little, meagre, black-looking man, with a grizzled wig that was too wide and stood off from each ear; so that his head seemed to have shrunk away within it, like a dried filbert[43] in its shell. He

---

41. Unsophisticated folk.
42. Windows with cross bars.
43. Hazelnut.

wore a rusty coat, with great skirts and pockets that would have held the church Bible and prayer-book: and his small legs seemed still smaller from being planted in large shoes decorated with enormous buckles.

I was informed by Frank Bracebridge that the parson had been a chum of his father's at Oxford, and had received this living[44] shortly after the latter had come to his estate. He was a complete black-letter hunter, and would scarcely read a work printed in the Roman character.[45] The editions of Caxton and Wynkyn de Worde[46] were his delight, and he was indefatigable in his researches after such old English writers as have fallen into oblivion from their worthlessness. In deference, perhaps, to the notions of Mr. Bracebridge he had made diligent investigations into the festive rites and holiday customs of former times, and had been as zealous in the inquiry as if he had been a boon[47] companion; but it was merely with that plodding spirit with which men of adust[48] temperament follow up any track of study, merely because it is denominated learning; indifferent to its intrinsic nature, whether it be the illustration of the wisdom or of the ribaldry and obscenity of antiquity. He had pored over these old volumes so intensely that they seemed to have been reflected into his countenance; which, if the face be indeed an index of the mind, might be compared to a title-page of black-letter.

On reaching the church-porch we found the parson rebuking the gray-headed sexton[49] for having used mistletoe among the greens with which the church was decorated. It was, he observed, an unholy plant,

---

44. A way to say a paid, full-time appointment and thus a position by which one can make a living.
45. Black-letter is another term for the Gothic script which is to be found in older books before the more modern Roman type replaced it.
46. He likes the books printed by these partners who were among the first users of the printing press in England: William Caxton (who died around 1491) and Wynkyn de Worde (who died around 1534).
47. Gift—so much an ideal companion as to feel like a gift.
48. Dry.
49. The person in charge of taking care of the church building and its grounds.

profaned by having been used by the Druids in their mystic ceremonies; and, though it might be innocently employed in the festive ornamenting of halls and kitchens, yet it had been deemed by the Fathers of the Church as unhallowed and totally unfit for sacred purposes. So tenacious was he on this point that the poor sexton was obliged to strip down a great part of the humble trophies of his taste before the parson would consent to enter upon the service of the day.

The interior of the church was venerable, but simple; on the walls were several mural monuments of the Bracebridges, and just beside the altar was a tomb of ancient workmanship, on which lay the effigy[50] of a warrior in armor with his legs crossed, a sign of his having been a crusader. I was told it was one of the family who had signalized[51] himself in the Holy Land, and the same whose picture hung over the fireplace in the hall.

During service Master Simon stood up in the pew and repeated the responses very audibly, evincing that kind of ceremonious devotion punctually observed by a gentleman of the old school and a man of old family connections. I observed too that he turned over the leaves of a folio prayer-book with something of a flourish; possibly to show off an enormous seal-ring which enriched one of his fingers and which had the look of a family relic. But he was evidently most solicitous about the musical part of the service, keeping his eye fixed intently on the choir, and beating time with much gesticulation and emphasis.

The orchestra was in a small gallery, and presented a most whimsical grouping of heads piled one above the other, among which I particularly noticed that of the village tailor, a pale fellow with a retreating forehead and chin, who played on the clarinet, and seemed to have blown his face to a point; and there was another, a short pursy[52] man, stooping and laboring

---

50. Something made to look like a particular person. In this case it is a life-size statue.
51. Distinguished.
52. Short of breath.

at a bass-viol, so as to show nothing but the top of a round bald head, like the egg of an ostrich. There were two or three pretty faces among the female singers, to which the keen air of a frosty morning had given a bright rosy tint; but the gentlemen choristers had evidently been chosen, like old Cremona fiddles,[53] more for tone than looks; and as several had to sing from the same book, there were clusterings of odd physiognomies[54] not unlike those groups of cherubs we sometimes see on country tombstones.

The usual services of the choir were managed tolerably well, the vocal parts generally lagging a little behind the instrumental, and some loitering fiddler now and then making up for lost time by travelling over a passage with prodigious celerity[55] and clearing more bars than the keenest fox-hunter to be in at the death. But the great trial was an anthem that had been prepared and arranged by Master Simon, and on which he had founded great expectation. Unluckily, there was a blunder at the very outset: the musicians became flurried; Master Simon was in a fever; everything went on lamely and irregularly until they came to a chorus beginning, "Now let us sing with one accord," which seemed to be a signal for parting company: all became discord and confusion: each shifted for himself, and got to the end as well—or, rather, as soon—as he could, excepting one old chorister in a pair of horn spectacles bestriding and pinching a long sonorous nose, who happened to stand a little apart, and, being wrapped up in his own melody, kept on a quavering course, wriggling his head, ogling his book, and winding all up by a nasal solo of at least three bars' duration.

The parson gave us a most erudite sermon on the rites and ceremonies of Christmas, and the propriety of observing it not merely as a day of thanksgiving but of rejoicing, supporting the correctness of his opinions

---

53. Made at—or in the style of those used at—the Italian city of Cremona.
54. Faces.
55. Speed.

by the earliest usages of the Church, and enforcing them by the authorities of Theophilus of Caesarea, St. Cyprian, St. Chrysostom, St. Augustine,[56] and a cloud more of saints and fathers, from whom he made copious quotations. I was a little at a loss to perceive the necessity of such a mighty array of forces to maintain a point which no one present seemed inclined to dispute; but I soon found that the good man had a legion of ideal adversaries to contend with, having in the course of his researches on the subject of Christmas got completely embroiled in the sectarian controversies of the Revolution,[57] when the Puritans made such a fierce assault upon the ceremonies of the Church, and poor old Christmas was driven out of the land by proclamation of Parliament.[iv] The worthy parson lived but with times past, and knew but little of the present.

Shut up among worm-eaten tomes in the retirement of his antiquated little study, the pages of old times were to him as the gazettes[58] of the day, while the era of the Revolution was mere modern history. He forgot that nearly two centuries had elapsed since the fiery persecution of poor mince-pie throughout the land; when plum porridge was denounced as "mere popery,"[59] and roast beef as anti-christian, and that Christmas had been brought in again triumphantly with the merry court of King Charles at the Restoration. He kindled into warmth with the ardor of his contest and the host of imaginary foes with whom he had to combat; he had a stubborn conflict with old Prynne and two or three other forgotten champions of the Roundheads[60] on the subject of Christmas festivity; and con-

---

56. These are all church fathers—bishops and theologians from the first five centuries of church history.
57. The English Revolution is another term for the English Civil War (which began in 1642) and the Commonwealth period that followed it before the monarchy was restored in 1660.
58. Journals or newspapers.
59. In other words, the ways of the Pope, Roman Catholicism.
60. The Roundheads were the side opposed to the Royalists (the Cavaliers) in the English Civil War. William Prynne (1600–1669) was a prominent polemicist on the side of the Roundheads.

cluded by urging his hearers, in the most solemn and affecting manner, to stand to the traditional customs of their fathers and feast and make merry on this joyful anniversary of the Church.

I have seldom known a sermon attended apparently with more immediate effects, for on leaving the church the congregation seemed one and all possessed with the gayety of spirit so earnestly enjoined by their pastor. The elder folks gathered in knots in the churchyard, greeting and shaking hands, and the children ran about crying Ule! Ule![61] and repeating some uncouth rhymes,[v] which the parson, who had joined us, informed me had been handed down from days of yore. The villagers doffed their hats to the squire as he passed, giving him the good wishes of the season with every appearance of heartfelt sincerity, and were invited by him to the hall to take something to keep out the cold of the weather; and I heard blessings uttered by several of the poor, which convinced me that, in the midst of his enjoyments, the worthy old cavalier had not forgotten the true Christmas virtue of charity.

On our way homeward his heart seemed overflowed with generous and happy feelings. As we passed over a rising ground which commanded something of a prospect, the sounds of rustic merriment now and then reached our ears: the squire paused for a few moments and looked around with an air of inexpressible benignity. The beauty of the day was of itself sufficient to inspire philanthropy. Notwithstanding the frostiness of the morning the sun in his cloudless journey had acquired sufficient power to melt away the thin covering of snow from every southern declivity, and to bring out the living green which adorns an English landscape even in mid-winter. Large tracts of smiling verdure contrasted with the dazzling whiteness of the shaded slopes and hollows. Every sheltered bank on which the broad rays rested yielded its silver rill of cold and limpid

---

61. That is, "yule"—another word for Christmas.

water, glittering through the dripping grass, and sent up slight exhalations to contribute to the thin haze that hung just above the surface of the earth. There was something truly cheering in this triumph of warmth and verdure over the frosty thraldom of winter; it was, as the squire observed, an emblem of Christmas hospitality breaking through the chills of ceremony and selfishness and thawing every heart into a flow. He pointed with pleasure to the indications of good cheer reeking from the chimneys of the comfortable farm-houses and low thatched cottages. "I love," said he, "to see this day well kept by rich and poor; it is a great thing to have one day in the year, at least, when you are sure of being welcome wherever you go, and of having, as it were, the world all thrown open to you; and I am almost disposed to join with Poor Robin[62] in his malediction on every churlish enemy to this honest festival:

> "'Those who at Christmas do repine,
>   And would fain hence dispatch him,
> May they with old Duke Humphry dine,
>   Or else may Squire Ketch catch 'em.'"

The squire went on to lament the deplorable decay of the games and amusements which were once prevalent at this season among the lower orders and countenanced by the higher, when the old halls of castles and manor-houses were thrown open at daylight; when the tables were covered with brawn[63] and beef and humming ale; when the harp and the carol resounded all day long; and when rich and poor were alike welcome to enter and make merry.[vi] "Our old games and local customs," said he, "had a great effect in making the peasant fond of his home, and the promotion of them by the gentry made him fond of his lord. They made the times merrier

---

62. *Poor Robin's Almanack.* An annual that was popular in the seventeenth and eighteenth centuries.
63. Meat from a pig.

and kinder and better, and I can truly say, with one of our old poets,

> "'I like them well: the curious preciseness
>   And all-pretended gravity of those
>   That seek to banish hence these harmless sports,
>   Have thrust away much ancient honesty.'"

"The nation," continued he, "is altered; we have almost lost our simple true-hearted peasantry. They have broken asunder from the higher classes, and seem to think their interests are separate. They have become too knowing, and begin to read newspapers, listen to ale-house politicians, and talk of reform. I think one mode to keep them in good-humor in these hard times would be for the nobility and gentry to pass more time on their estates, mingle more among the country-people, and set the merry old English games going again."

Such was the good squire's project for mitigating public discontent: and, indeed, he had once attempted to put his doctrine in practice, and a few years before had kept open house during the holidays in the old style. The country-people, however, did not understand how to play their parts in the scene of hospitality; many uncouth circumstances occurred; the manor was overrun by all the vagrants of the country, and more beggars drawn into the neighborhood in one week than the parish officers could get rid of in a year. Since then he had contented himself with inviting the decent part of the neighboring peasantry to call at the hall on Christmas Day, and with distributing beef, and bread, and ale among the poor, that they might make merry in their own dwellings.

We had not been long home when the sound of music was heard from a distance. A band of country lads, without coats, their shirt-sleeves fancifully tied with ribbons, their hats decorated with greens, and clubs in their hands, was seen advancing up the avenue, followed by a large number of villagers and peasantry. They stopped before the hall door, where the music struck up a peculiar air, and the lads performed a curious and intri-cate dance, advancing, retreating, and striking their clubs together, keeping exact time to the music; while one, whimsically crowned with a fox's skin, the tail of which flaunted down his back, kept capering round the skirts of the dance and rattling a Christmas box[64] with many antic gesticulations.

The squire eyed this fanciful exhibition with great interest and delight, and gave me a full account of its origin, which he traced to the times when the Romans held possession of the island, plainly proving that this was a lineal descendant of the sword dance of the ancients. "It was now," he said, "nearly extinct, but he had accidentally met with traces of it in the neighborhood, and had encouraged its revival; though, to tell the truth, it was too apt to be followed up by the rough cudgel[65] play and broken heads in the evening."

After the dance was concluded the whole party was entertained with brawn and beef and stout home-brewed. The squire himself mingled among the rustics, and was received with awkward demonstrations of deference and regard. It is true I perceived two or three of the younger peasants, as they were raising their tankards to their mouths, when the squire's back was turned making something of a grimace, and giving each other the wink; but the moment they caught my eye they pulled grave faces and were exceedingly demure. With Master Simon, however, they all seemed more at their ease. His varied occupations and amusements had made him well known throughout the neighborhood. He was a visitor at every farmhouse and cottage, gossiped with the farmers and their wives, romped with their daughters, and, like that type of a vagrant bachelor, the bumblebee, tolled the sweets from all the rosy lips of the country round.

The bashfulness of the guests soon gave way before good cheer and affability. There is something genuine and affectionate in the gayety of

---

64. For taking donations.
65. A club; a thick stick that could be used as a weapon.

the lower orders when it is excited by the bounty and familiarity of those above them; the warm glow of gratitude enters into their mirth, and a kind word or a small pleasantry frankly uttered by a patron gladdens the heart of the dependent more than oil and wine. When the squire had retired the merriment increased, and there was much joking and laughter, particularly between Master Simon and a hale, ruddy-faced, white-headed farmer who appeared to be the wit of the village; for I observed all his companions to wait with open months for his retorts, and burst into a gratuitous laugh before they could well understand them.

The whole house indeed seemed abandoned to merriment: as I passed to my room to dress for dinner, I heard the sound of music in a small court, and, looking through a window that commanded it, I perceived a band of wandering musicians with pandean pipes[66] and tambourine; a pretty coquettish housemaid was dancing a jig with a smart country lad, while several of the other servants were looking on. In the midst of her sport the girl caught a glimpse of my face at the window, and, coloring up, ran off with an air of roguish affected confusion.

The Christmas Dinner

Lo, now is come our joyful'st feast!
    Let every man be jolly.
Eache roome with yvie leaves is drest,
    And every post with holly.
Now all our neighbours' chimneys smoke,
    And Christmas blocks are burning;
Their ovens they with bak't meats choke
    And all their spits are turning.
    Without the door let sorrow lie,

---

66. A simple wind instrument sort of like a primitive harmonica.

And if, for cold, it hap to die,

Wee'l bury 't in a Christmas pye,

And evermore be merry.

WITHERS, *Juvenilia.*

I had finished my toilet,[67] and was loitering with Frank Bracebridge in the library, when we heard a distant thwacking sound, which he informed me was a signal for the serving up of the dinner. The squire kept up old customs in kitchen as well as hall, and the rolling-pin, struck upon the dresser by the cook, summoned the servants to carry in the meats.

Just in this nick the cook knock'd thrice,

And all the waiters in a trice

His summons did obey;

Each serving-man, with dish in hand,

March'd boldly up, like our train-band,

Presented and away.[vii]

The dinner was served up in the great hall, where the squire always held his Christmas banquet. A blazing crackling fire of logs had been heaped on to warm the spacious apartment, and the flame went sparkling and wreathing up the wide-mouthed chimney. The great picture of the crusader and his white horse had been profusely decorated with greens for the occasion, and holly and ivy had like-wise been wreathed round the helmet and weapons on the opposite wall, which I understood were the arms of the same warrior. I must own, by the by, I had strong doubts about the authenticity of the painting and armor as having belonged to the crusader, they certainly having the stamp of more recent days; but I was told that the painting had been so considered time out of mind; and that

---

67. Preparing his personal appearance with actions such as washing his face and combing his hair.

as to the armor, it had been found in a lumber-room[68] and elevated to its present situation by the squire, who at once determined it to be the armor of the family hero; and as he was absolute authority on all such subjects in his own household, the matter had passed into current acceptation. A sideboard was set out just under this chivalric trophy, on which was a display of plate that might have vied (at least in variety) with Belshazzar's parade of the vessels of the temple: "flagons, cans, cups, beakers, goblets, basins, and ewers,"[69] the gorgeous utensils of good companionship that had gradually accumulated through many generations of jovial housekeepers. Before these stood the two Yule candles, beaming like two stars of the first magnitude; other lights were distributed in branches, and the whole array glittered like a firmament of silver.

We were ushered into this banqueting scene with the sound of minstrelsy, the old harper being seated on a stool beside the fireplace and twanging, his instrument with a vast deal more power than melody. Never did Christmas board display a more goodly and gracious assemblage of countenances; those who were not handsome were at least happy, and happiness is a rare improver of your hard-favored visage. I always consider an old English family as well worth studying as a collection of Holbein's portraits or Albert Durer's prints.[70] There is much antiquarian lore to be acquired, much knowledge of the physiognomies of former times. Perhaps it may be from having continually before their eyes those rows of old family portraits, with which the mansions of this country are stocked; certain it is that the quaint features of antiquity are often most faithfully perpetuated in these ancient lines, and I have traced an old family nose through a whole picture-gallery, legitimately handed down from generation to

---

68. Storage room.
69. Belshazzar's parade is a reference to the story in Daniel chapter 5. The quotation is from a seventeenth-century play by George Chapman, *May Day: A Comedy* (1611).
70. Famous artists from the past, Hans Holbein the Younger (d. 1543) and Albrecht Dürer (1471–1528).

generation almost from the time of the Conquest.[71] Something of the kind was to be observed in the worthy company around me. Many of their faces had evidently originated in a Gothic age, and been merely copied by succeeding generations; and there was one little girl in particular, of staid demeanor, with a high Roman nose and an antique vinegar aspect, who was a great favorite of the squire's, being, as he said, a Bracebridge all over, and the very counterpart of one of his ancestors who figured in the court of Henry VIII.[72]

The parson said grace, which was not a short familiar one, such as is commonly addressed to the Deity in these unceremonious days, but a long, courtly, well-worded one of the ancient school. There was now a pause, as if something was expected, when suddenly the butler entered the hall with some degree of bustle: he was attended by a servant on each side with a large wax-light, and bore a silver dish on which was an enormous pig's head decorated with rosemary, with a lemon in its mouth, which was placed with great formality at the head of the table. The moment this pageant made its appearance the harper struck up a flourish; at the conclusion of which the young Oxonian, on receiving a hint from the squire, gave, with an air of the most comic gravity, an old carol, the first verse of which was as follows

> Caput apri defero
> > Reddens laudes Domino.
> The boar's head in hand bring I,
> With garlands gay and rosemary.
> I pray you all synge merily
> > Qui estis in convivio.[73]

---

71. When the Normans invaded England in the eleventh century.
72. Henry VIII (1491–1547), King of England.
73. The first two lines and the last one are in Latin. They translate: "The boar's head I bear / Rendering praises to the Lord," and "As many as are at the feast."

Though prepared to witness many of these little eccentricities, from being apprised of the peculiar hobby of mine host, yet I confess the parade with which so odd a dish was introduced somewhat perplexed me, until I gathered from the conversation of the squire and the parson that it was meant to represent the bringing in of the boar's head, a dish formerly served up with much ceremony and the sound of minstrelsy and song at great tables on Christmas Day. "I like the old custom," said the squire, "not merely because it is stately and pleasing in itself, but because it was observed at the college at Oxford at which I was educated. When I hear the old song chanted it brings to mind the time when I was young and gamesome,[74] and the noble old college hall, and my fellow-students loitering about in their black gowns; many of whom, poor lads! are now in their graves."

The parson, however, whose mind was not haunted by such associations, and who was always more taken up with the text than the sentiment, objected to the Oxonian's version of the carol, which he affirmed was different from that sung at college. He went on, with the dry perseverance of a commentator, to give the college reading, accompanied by sundry annotations, addressing himself at first to the company at large; but, finding their attention gradually diverted to other talk and other objects, he lowered his tone as his number of auditors diminished, until he concluded his remarks in an under voice to a fat-headed old gentleman next him who was silently engaged in the discussion of a huge plateful of turkey.[viii]

The table was literally loaded with good cheer, and presented an epitome of country abundance in this season of overflowing larders.[75] A distinguished post was allotted to "ancient sirloin," as mine host termed it, being, as he added, "the standard of old English hospitality, and a joint of goodly presence, and full of expectation." There were several dishes quaintly decorated, and which had evidently something traditional in their

---

74. Playful.
75. Food storage rooms.

141

embellishments, but about which, as I did not like to appear overcurious, I asked no questions.

I could not, however, but notice a pie magnificently decorated with peacock's feathers, in imitation of the tail of that bird, which overshadowed a considerable tract of the table. This, the squire confessed with some little hesitation, was a pheasant pie, though a peacock pie was certainly the most authentical; but there had been such a mortality among the peacocks this season that he could not prevail upon himself to have one killed.[ix]

The peacock was also an important dish for the Christmas feast; and Massinger, in his "City Madam,"[76] gives some idea of the extravagance with which this, as well as other dishes, was prepared for the gorgeous revels of the olden times:

> Men may talk of Country Christmasses, their thirty pound butter'd eggs, their pies of carps' tongues; Their pheasants drench'd with ambergris: the carcases of three fat wethers bruised for gravy to make sauce for a single peacock!

It would be tedious, perhaps, to my wiser readers, who may not have that foolish fondness for odd and obsolete things to which I am a little given, were I to mention the other makeshifts or this worthy old humorist, by which he was endeavoring to follow up, though at humble distance, the quaint customs of antiquity. I was pleased, however, to see the respect shown to his whims by his children and relatives; who, indeed, entered readily into the full spirit of them, and seemed all well versed in their parts, having doubtless been present at many a rehearsal. I was amused, too, at the air of profound gravity with which the butler and other servants executed the duties assigned them, however eccentric. They had an old-fashioned look, having, for the most part, been brought up in the

---

76. Another reference to a seventeenth-century play: Philip Massinger's *The City Madam* (1632).

household and grown into keeping with the antiquated mansion and the humors of its lord, and most probably looked upon all his whimsical regulations as the established laws of honorable housekeeping.

When the cloth was removed the butler brought in a huge silver vessel of rare and curious workmanship, which he placed before the squire. Its appearance was hailed with acclamation, being the Wassail Bowl,[77] so renowned in Christmas festivity. The contents had been prepared by the squire himself; for it was a beverage in the skilful mixture of which he particularly prided himself, alleging that it was too abstruse and complex for the comprehension of an ordinary servant. It was a potation,[78] indeed, that might well make the heart of a toper leap within him, being composed of the richest and raciest wines, highly spiced and sweetened, with roasted apples bobbing about the surface.[x]

The old gentleman's whole countenance beamed with a serene look of indwelling delight as he stirred this mighty bowl. Having raised it to his lips, with a hearty wish of a merry Christmas to all present, he sent it brimming round the board, for every one to follow his example, according to the primitive style, pronouncing it "the ancient fountain of good feeling, where all hearts met together."[xi]

There was much laughing and rallying as the honest emblem of Christmas joviality circulated and was kissed rather coyly by the ladies. When it reached Master Simon, he raised it in both hands, and with the air of a boon companion struck up an old Wassail Chanson:[79]

The brown bowle,

The merry brown bowle,

As it goes round-about-a,

---

77. A wassail is a special, ceremonial drink used for toasting each other's health—or it can mean the toast itself.
78. Concoction.
79. A chanson is a kind of French song.

Fill

Still,

Let the world say what it will,

And drink your fill all out-a.

The deep canne,

The merry deep canne,

As thou dost freely quaff-a,

Sing

Fling,

Be as merry as a king,

And sound a lusty laugh-a.[xii]

Much of the conversation during dinner turned upon family topics, to which I was a stranger. There was, however, a great deal of rallying[80] of Master Simon about some gay[81] widow with whom he was accused of having a flirtation. This attack was commenced by the ladies, but it was continued throughout the dinner by the fat-headed old gentleman next the parson with the persevering assiduity of a slow hound, being one of those long-winded jokers who, though rather dull at starting game, are unrivalled for their talents in hunting it down. At every pause in the general conversation he renewed his bantering in pretty much the same terms, winking hard at me with both eyes whenever he gave Master Simon what he considered a home thrust. The latter, indeed, seemed fond of being teased on the subject, as old bachelors are apt to be, and he took occasion to inform me, in an undertone, that the lady in question was a prodigiously fine woman and drove her own curricle.[82]

The dinner-time passed away in this flow of innocent hilarity, and, though the old hall may have resounded in its time with many a scene

---

80. Teasing.
81. Jolly.
82. A type of small carriage.

of broader rout and revel, yet I doubt whether it ever witnessed more honest and genuine enjoyment. How easy it is for one benevolent being to diffuse pleasure around him! and how truly is a kind heart a fountain of gladness, making everything in its vicinity to freshen into smiles! The joyous disposition of the worthy squire was perfectly contagious; he was happy himself, and disposed to make all the world happy, and the little eccentricities of his humor did but season, in a manner, the sweetness of his philanthropy.

When the ladies had retired,[83] the conversation, as usual, became still more animated; many good things were broached which had been thought of during dinner, but which would not exactly do for a lady's ear; and, though I cannot positively affirm that there was much wit uttered, yet I have certainly heard many contests of rare wit produce much less laughter. Wit, after all, is a mighty tart, pungent ingredient, and much too acid for some stomachs; but honest good-humor is the oil and wine of a merry meeting, and there is no jovial companionship equal to that where the jokes are rather small and the laughter abundant.

The squire told several long stories of early college pranks and adventures, in some of which the parson had been a sharer, though in looking at the latter it required some effort of imagination to figure such a little dark anatomy of a man into the perpetrator of a madcap gambol.[84] Indeed, the two college chums presented pictures of what men may be made by their different lots in life. The squire had left the university to live lustily[85] on his paternal domains in the vigorous enjoyment of prosperity and sunshine, and had flourished on to a hearty and florid old age; whilst the poor parson, on the contrary, had dried and withered away among dusty tomes in the

---

83. As was the custom, the women have gone together to another room to talk among themselves for a while.
84. Game, stunt, or adventure.
85. Energetically.

silence and shadows of his study. Still, there seemed to be a spark of almost extinguished fire feebly glimmering in the bottom of his soul; and as the squire hinted at a sly story of the parson and a pretty milkmaid whom they once met on the banks of the Isis,[86] the old gentleman made an "alphabet of faces," which, as far as I could decipher his physiognomy, I verily believe was indicative of laughter; indeed, I have rarely met with an old gentleman that took absolute offence at the imputed gallantries of his youth.

I found the tide of wine and wassail fast gaining on the dry land of sober judgment. The company grew merrier and louder as their jokes grew duller. Master Simon was in as chirping a humor as a grasshopper filled with dew; his old songs grew of a warmer complexion, and he began to talk maudlin about the widow. He even gave a long song about the woo-ing[87] of a widow which he informed me he had gathered from an excellent black-letter work entitled Cupid's Solicitor for Love, containing store of good advice for bachelors, and which he promised to lend me; the first verse was to effect.

> He that will woo a widow must not dally
>> He must make hay while the sun doth shine;
> He must not stand with her, shall I, shall I,
>> But boldly say, Widow, thou must be mine.

This song inspired the fat-headed old gentleman, who made several attempts to tell a rather broad story out of Joe Miller, that was pat to the purpose; but he always stuck in the middle, everybody recollecting the latter part excepting himself. The parson, too, began to show the effects of good cheer, having gradually settled down into a doze and his wig sitting most suspiciously on one side. Just at this juncture we were summoned to

---

86. The river Thames flows through Oxford on its way to London and it is traditional in Oxford to refer to it as "the Isis."
87. To pursue with the hopes of a romantic relationship developing.

the drawing room, and I suspect, at the private instigation of mine host, whose joviality seemed always tempered with a proper love of decorum.

After the dinner-table was removed the hall was given up to the younger members of the family, who, prompted to all kind of noisy mirth by the Oxonian and Master Simon, made its old walls ring with their merriment as they played at romping[88] games. I delight in witnessing the gambols of children, and particularly at this happy holiday season, and could not help stealing out of the drawing-room on hearing one of their peals of laughter. I found them at the game of blindman's-buff. Master Simon, who was the leader of their revels, and seemed on all occasions to fulfill the office of that ancient potentate, the Lord of Misrule,[xiii] was blinded in the midst of the hall. The little beings were as busy about him as the mock fairies about Falstaff, pinching him, plucking at the skirts of his coat, and tickling him with straws.[89] One fine blue-eyed girl of about thirteen, with her flaxen hair all in beautiful confusion, her frolic face in a glow, her frock half torn off her shoulders, a complete picture of a romp, was the chief tormentor; and, from the slyness with which Master Simon avoided the smaller game and hemmed this wild little nymph in corners, and obliged her to jump shrieking over chairs, I suspected the rogue of being not a whit more blinded than was convenient.

When I returned to the drawing-room I found the company seated round the fire listening to the parson, who was deeply ensconced in a high-backed oaken chair, the work of some cunning artificer of yore, which had been brought from the library for his particular accommoda-tion. From this venerable piece of furniture, with which his shadowy figure and dark weazen[90] face so admirably accorded, he was dealing out strange accounts of the popular superstitions and legends of the

---

88. Rowdy—involving a lot of energetic moving about.
89. Falstaff is a fictitious character in several Shakespeare plays. This is a reference to a scene in one of them, *The Merry Wives of Windsor*.
90. Shriveled up and wrinkled from old age (written today as "wizen").

surrounding country, with which he had become acquainted in the course of his antiquarian researches. I am half inclined to think that the old gentleman was himself somewhat tinctured with superstition, as men are very apt to be who live a recluse and studious life in a sequestered part of the country and pore over black-letter tracts, so often filled with the marvelous and supernatural. He gave us several anecdotes of the fancies of the neighboring peasantry concerning the effigy of the crusader which lay on the tomb by the church altar. As it was the only monument of the kind in that part of the country, it had always been regarded with feelings of superstition by the good wives of the village. It was said to get up from the tomb and walk the rounds of the churchyard in stormy nights, particularly when it thundered; and one old woman, whose cottage bordered on the churchyard, had seen it through the windows of the church, when the moon shone, slowly pacing up and down the aisles. It was the belief that some wrong had been left unredressed by the deceased, or some treasure hidden, which kept the spirit in a state of trouble and restlessness. Some talked of gold and jewels buried in the tomb, over which the spectre kept watch; and there was a story current of a sexton in old times who endeavored to break his way to the coffin at night, but just as he reached it received a violent blow from the marble hand of the effigy, which stretched him senseless on the pavement. These tales were often laughed at by some of the sturdier among the rustics, yet when night came on there were many of the stoutest unbelievers that were shy of venturing alone in the footpath that led across the churchyard.

From these and other anecdotes that followed the crusader appeared to be the favorite hero of ghost-stories throughout the vicinity. His picture, which hung up in the hall, was thought by the servants to have something supernatural about it; for they remarked that in whatever part of the hall you went the eyes of the warrior were still fixed on you. The old porter's wife, too, at the lodge, who had been born and brought up in the family, and was a great gossip among the maid-servants, affirmed that in her young days she had often heard say that on Midsummer Eve, when it was well known all kinds of ghosts, goblins, and fairies become visible and walk abroad, the crusader used to mount his horse, come down from his picture, ride about the house, down the avenue, and so to the church to visit the tomb; on which occasion the church-door most civilly swung open of itself; not that he needed it, for he rode through closed gates, and even stone walls, and had been seen by one of the dairymaids to pass between two bars of the great park gate, making himself as thin as a sheet of paper.

All these superstitions I found had been very much countenanced by the squire, who, though not superstitious himself, was very fond of seeing others so. He listened to every goblin tale of the neighboring gossips with infinite gravity, and held the porter's wife in high favor on account of her talent for the marvellous. He was himself a great reader of old legends and romances, and often lamented that he could not believe in them; for a superstitious person, he thought, must live in a kind of fairy-land.

Whilst we were all attention to the parson's stories, our ears were suddenly assailed by a burst of heterogeneous sounds from the hall, in which were mingled something like the clang of rude minstrelsy with the uproar of many small voices and girlish laughter. The door suddenly flew open, and a train came trooping into the room that might almost have been mistaken for the breaking up of the court of Faery.[91] That indefatigable spirit, Master Simon, in the faithful discharge of his duties as lord of misrule, had conceived the idea of a Christmas mummery or masking;[92] and having called in to his assistance the Oxonian and the young officer, who were equally ripe for anything that should occasion romping and merriment, they had carried it into instant effect. The old housekeeper had been consulted; the antique clothespresses and wardrobes rummaged and made

91. An old-fashioned spelling of "fairy"—the fairy court.
92. A costume party or masquerade.

to yield up the relics of finery that had not seen the light for several generations; the younger part of the company had been privately convened from the parlor and hall, and the whole had been bedizened[93] out into a burlesque[94] imitation of an antique mask.[xiv]

Master Simon led the van,[95] as "Ancient Christmas," quaintly apparelled in a ruff, a short cloak, which had very much the aspect of one of the old housekeeper's petticoats, and a hat that might have served for a village steeple, and must indubitably have figured in the days of the Covenanters.[96] From under this his nose curved boldly forth, flushed with a frost-bitten bloom that seemed the very trophy of a December blast. He was accompanied by the blue-eyed romp, dished up, as "Dame Mince Pie," in the venerable magnificence of a faded brocade,[97] long stomacher, peaked hat, and high-heeled shoes. The young officer appeared as Robin Hood, in a sporting dress of Kendal green[98] and a foraging cap with a gold tassel.

The costume, to be sure, did not bear testimony to deep research, and there was an evident eye to the picturesque, natural to a young gallant in the presence of his mistress.[99] The fair Julia hung on his arm in a pretty rustic dress as "Maid Marian." The rest of the train had been metamorphosed in various ways; the girls trussed up in the finery of the ancient belles of the Bracebridge line, and the striplings bewhiskered with burnt cork,[100] and gravely clad in broad skirts, hanging sleeves, and full-bottomed wigs, to represent the character of Roast Beef, Plum Pudding, and other worthies celebrated in ancient maskings. The whole was under the control of

---

93. Dressed up, decorated.
94. Comic.
95. The group at the front.
96. In the seventeenth century, the Covenanters were Scots who stood up against political and religious impositions being made by the kings of those days.
97. A fabric with a raised pattern on it.
98. A green woolen cloth.
99. Like a knight-errant with the lady he serves.
100. They have burnt a cork to make a black ash that can be rubbed on as makeup to represent a mustache.

the Oxonian in the appropriate character of Misrule; and I observed that he exercised rather a mischievous sway with his wand over the smaller personages of the pageant.

The irruption of this motley crew with beat of drum, according to ancient custom, was the consummation of uproar and merriment. Master Simon covered himself with glory by the stateliness with which, as Ancient Christmas, he walked a minuet with the peerless though giggling Dame Mince Pie. It was followed by a dance of all the characters, which from its medley of costumes seemed as though the old family portraits had skipped down from their frames to join in the sport. Different centuries were figuring at cross hands and right and left; the Dark Ages were cutting pirouettes and rigadoons;[101] and the days of Queen Bess[102] jigging merrily down the middle through a line of succeeding generations.

The worthy squire contemplated these fantastic sports and this resurrection of his old wardrobe with the simple relish of childish delight. He stood chuckling and rubbing his hands, and scarcely hearing a word the parson said, notwithstanding that the latter was discoursing most authentically on the ancient and stately dance of the Pavon, or peacock, from which he conceived the minuet to be derived.[xv] For my part, I was in a continual excitement from the varied scenes of whim and innocent gayety passing before me. It was inspiring to see wild-eyed frolic and warm-hearted hospitality breaking out from among the chills and glooms of winter, and old age throwing off his apathy and catching once more the freshness of youthful enjoyment. I felt also an interest in the scene from the consideration that these fleeting customs were posting fast into oblivion, and that this was perhaps the only family in England in which the whole of them was still punctiliously observed. There was a quaintness, too, mingled with all this revelry that gave it a peculiar zest: it was suited

---

101. These are both dance steps.
102. An informal way to refer to Elizabeth I (1533–1603), Queen of England.

to the time and place; and as the old manor-house almost reeled with mirth and wassail, it seemed echoing back the joviality of long departed years.[xvi]

But enough of Christmas and its gambols; it is time for me to pause in this garrulity.[103] Methinks I hear the questions asked by my graver readers, "To what purpose is all this? How is the world to be made wiser by this talk?" Alas! Is there not wisdom enough extant for the instruction of the world? And if not, are there not thousands of abler pens laboring for its improvement? It is so much pleasanter to please than to instruct—to play the companion rather than the preceptor.[104]

What, after all, is the mite of wisdom that I could throw into the mass of knowledge! or how am I sure that my sagest deductions may be safe guides for the opinions of others? But in writing to amuse, if I fail the only evil is in my own disappointment. If, however, I can by any lucky chance, in these days of evil, rub out one wrinkle from the brow of care or beguile the heavy heart of one moment of sorrow; if I can now and then penetrate through the gathering film of misanthropy, prompt a benevolent view of human nature, and make my reader more in good-humor with his fellow-beings and himself—surely, surely, I shall not then have written entirely in vain.

---

103. Talkativeness—he has been going on and go and now will pause to consider what it means.
104. Instructor.

i. Peacham's Complete Gentleman, 1622.

ii. The mistletoe is still hung up in farm-houses and kitchens at Christmas, and the young men have the privilege of kissing the girls under it, plucking each time a berry from the bush. When the berries are all plucked the privilege ceases.

iii. The Yule-clog is a great log of wood, sometimes the root of a tree, brought into the house with great ceremony on Christmas Eve, laid in the fireplace, and lighted with the brand of last year's clog. While it lasted there was great drinking, singing, and telling of tales. Sometimes it was accompanied by Christmas candles; but in the cottages the only light was from the ruddy blaze of the great wood fire. The Yule-clog was to burn all night; if it went out, it was considered a sign of ill luck.

iv. From the "*Flying Eagle*," a small gazette, published December 24, 1652: "The House spent much time this day about the business of the Navy, for settling the affairs at sea, and before they rose, were presented with a terrible remonstrance against Christmas day, grounded upon divine Scriptures, 2 Cor. v. 16; I Cor. xv. 14, 17; and in honor of the Lord's Day, grounded upon these Scriptures, John xx. I; Rev. i. 10; Psalms cxviii. 24; Lev. xxiii. 7, 11; Mark xv. 8; Psalms lxxxiv. 10, in which Christmas is called Anti-christ's masse, and those Masse-mongers and Papists who observe it, etc. In consequence of which parliament spent some time in consultation about the abolition of Christmas day, passed orders to that effect, and resolved to sit on the following day, which was commonly called Christmas day."

v. "Ule! Ule!
   Three puddings in a pule;
   Crack nuts and cry ule!"

vi. "An English gentleman, at the opening of the great day—i.e., on Christmas Day in the morning—had all his tenants and neighbors enter his hall by daybreak. The strong beer was broached, and the black-jacks went plentifully about, with toast, sugar and nutmeg, and good Cheshire cheese. The Hackin (the great sausage) must be boiled by daybreak, or else two young men must take the maiden (i.e., the cook) by the arms and run her round the market-place till she is shamed of her laziness."—Round about our Sea-Coal Fire.

vii. Sir John Suckling.

viii. The old ceremony of serving up the boar's head on Christmas Day is still observed in the hall of Queen's College, Oxford. I was favored by the parson with a copy of the carol as now sung, and as it may be acceptable to such of my readers as are curious in these grave and learned matters, I give it entire:

   The boar's head in hand bear I,
   Bodeck'd with bays and rosemary
   And I pray you, my masters, be merry
      Quot estis in convivio

Caput apri defero,
Reddens laudes domino.

The boar's head, as I understand,
Is the rarest dish in all this land,
Which thus bedeck'd with a gay garland
      Let us servire cantico.
      Caput apri defero, etc.

Our steward hath provided this
In honor of the King of Bliss,
Which on this day to be served is
      In Reginensi Atrio.
      Caput apri defero, etc., etc., etc.

ix. The peacock was anciently in great demand for stately entertainments. Sometimes it was made into a pie, at one end of which the head appeared above the crust in all its plumage, with the beak richly gilt; at the other end the tail was displayed. Such pies were served up at the solemn banquets of chivalry, when knights-errant pledged themselves to undertake any perilous enterprise, whence came the ancient oath, used by Justice Shallow [a character from *Shakespeare's Henry IV, Part 2*], "by cock and pie."

x. The Wassail Bowl was sometimes composed of ale instead of wine, with nutmeg, sugar, toast, ginger, and roasted crabs; in this way the nut-brown beverage is still prepared in some old families and round the hearths of substantial farmers at Christmas. It is also called Lamb's Wool, and is celebrated by Herrick in his "Twelfth Night":

Next crowne the bowle full
      With gentle Lamb's Wool;
Add sugar, nutmeg, and ginger,
      With store of ale too,
      And thus ye must doe
To make the Wassaile a swinger.

xi. "The custom of drinking out of the same cup gave place to each having his cup. When the steward came to the doore with the Wassel, he was to cry three times, Wassel, Wassel, Wassel, and then the chappell (chaplain) was to answer with a song."—Archaeologia.

xii. From Poor Robin's Almanack.

xiii. "At Christmasse there was in the Kinges house, wheresoever hee was lodged, a lorde of misrule or mayster of merie disportes, and the like had ye in the house of every nobleman of honor, or good worshipper were he spirituall or temporall."—STOW.

xiv. Maskings or mummeries were favorite sports at Christmas in old times, and the wardrobes at halls and manor-houses were often laid under contribution to furnish dresses and fantastic disguisings. I strongly suspect Master Simon to have taken the idea of his from Ben Jonson's "Masque of Christmas."

xv. Sir John Hawkins, speaking of the dance called the Pavon, from pavo, a peacock, says, "It is a grave and majestic dance; the method of dancing it anciently was by gentlemen dressed with caps and swords, by those of the long robe in their gowns, by the peers in their mantles, and by the ladies in gowns with long trains, the motion whereof, in dancing, resembled that of a peacock."—History of Music.

xvi. At the time of the first publication of this paper the picture of an old-fashioned Christmas in the country was pronounced by some as out of date. The author had afterwards an opportunity of witnessing almost all the customs above described, existing in unexpected vigor in the skirts of Derbyshire and York-shire, where he passed the Christmas holidays. The reader will find some notice of them in the author's account of his sojourn at Newstead Abbey.

THE SHOP OF GHOSTS

G. K. CHESTERTON

Christmas is traditionally a time for ghost stories, and "The Shop of Ghosts" is one in the sense that famous people from the past who have long been dead come back to make a visit. It is quite a short story in length, but it puts more demands on the reader than most. Chesterton is having fun with the notion that Christmas—or at least the true spirit of Christmas—is somehow now being cancelled, dying out, or going away. It was originally published in the 22 December 1906 issue of the Daily News. Delightfully, this newspaper had been founded by Charles Dickens, the author of A Christmas Carol (1843). G. K. Chesterton (1874–1936) was a compelling and witty defender of the Christian faith, not least in books such as Orthodoxy (1908) and The Everlasting Man (1925). His works of fiction include his detective short stories in which the investigations are pursued by his celebrated literary creation, Father Brown. These stories have also inspired a popular TV series. The first book in the series is The Innocence of Father Brown (1911).

THE SHOP OF GHOSTS

G. K. CHESTERTON

Nearly all the best and most precious things in the universe you can get for a halfpenny.[1] I make an exception, of course, of the sun, the moon, the earth, people, stars, thunderstorms, and such trifles. You can get them for nothing. Also I make an exception of another thing, which I am not allowed to mention in this paper, and of which the lowest price is a penny halfpenny.[2] But the general principle will be at once apparent. In the street behind me, for instance, you can now get a ride on an electric tram[3] for a halfpenny. To be on an electric tram is to be on a flying castle in a fairy tale. You can get quite a large number of brightly coloured sweets for a halfpenny. Also you can get the chance of reading this article for a halfpenny; along, of course, with other and irrelevant matter.[4]

---

1. The halfpenny (commonly referred to as a "ha'penny") was the smallest coin in British currency until it was eliminated in 1969. It is mentioned in the traditional Christmas song, "Christmas Is Coming (the Geese Are Getting Fat)": *"If you haven't got a penny, a ha'penny will do / If you haven't got a ha'penny, then God bless you!"*
2. A postage stamp cost a penny and a half at this time. It is not clear what is behind the teasing nature of this comment, but the Chesterton scholar, Dale Ahlquist, suggests that it was probably in reference to some political or policy differences that the *Daily News* was having with the Postmaster General, a cabinet-level, partisan, political appointment in the British government.
3. A streetcar—that is, something like a public bus, only it runs on a track and is connected to electric wires.
4. In other words, you could buy a copy of the *Daily News* for a halfpenny.

But if you want to see what a vast and bewildering array of valuable things you can get at a halfpenny each you should do as I was doing last night. I was gluing my nose against the glass of a very small and dimly lit toy shop in one of the greyest and leanest of the streets of Battersea.[5] But dim as was that square of light, it was filled (as a child once said to me) with all the colours God ever made. Those toys of the poor were like the children who buy them; they were all dirty;[6] but they were all bright. For my part, I think brightness more important than cleanliness; since the first is of the soul, and the second of the body. You must excuse me; I am a democrat;[7] I know I am out of fashion in the modern world.

❍ ❍ ❧

As I looked at that palace of pigmy[8] wonders, at small green omnibuses,[9] at small blue elephants, at small black dolls, and small red Noah's arks, I must have fallen into some sort of unnatural trance. That lit shop-window became like the brilliantly lit stage when one is watching some highly coloured comedy. I forgot the grey houses and the grimy people behind me as one forgets the dark galleries and the dim crowds at a theatre. It seemed as if the little objects behind the glass were small, not because they were toys, but because they were objects far away. The green omnibus was really a green omnibus, a green Bayswater[10] omnibus, passing across some huge desert on its ordinary way to Bayswater. The blue elephant was no longer blue with paint; he was blue with distance. The red Noah's ark was really the enormous ship of earthly salvation riding on the rain-swollen sea, red in the first morning of hope.

---

5. A district in south London, England.
6. At this time most poor people in London did not have indoor plumbing or running water at home and thus were not able to stay clean the way that those from better-off homes could.
7. A believer in democracy and thus a believer in the dignity and worth even of the less well-off.
8. Miniature.
9. Like saying "telephone" rather than just "phone," "omnibus" is the full, old-fashioned way to refer to a bus.
10. Another district in London. It is a public bus running in that part of the city.

Every one, I suppose, knows such stunning instants of abstraction, such brilliant blanks in the mind. In such moments one can see the face of one's own best friend as an unmeaning pattern of spectacles or moustaches. They are commonly marked by the two signs of the slowness of their growth and the suddenness of their termination. The return to real thinking is often as abrupt as bumping into a man. Very often indeed (in my case) it is bumping into a man. But in any case the awakening is always emphatic and, generally speaking, it is always complete. Now, in this case, I did come back with a shock of sanity to the consciousness that I was, after all, only staring into a dingy little toy-shop; but in some strange way the mental cure did not seem to be final. There was still in my mind an unmanageable something that told me that I had strayed into some odd atmosphere, or that I had already done some odd thing. I felt as if I had worked a miracle or committed a sin. It was as if I had at any rate, stepped across some border in the soul.

To shake off this dangerous and dreamy sense I went into the shop and tried to buy wooden soldiers. The man in the shop was very old and broken, with confused white hair covering his head and half his face, hair so startlingly white that it looked almost artificial. Yet though he was senile and even sick, there was nothing of suffering in his eyes; he looked rather as if he were gradually falling asleep in a not unkindly decay. He gave me the wooden soldiers, but when I put down the money he did not at first seem to see it; then he blinked at it feebly, and then he pushed it feebly away.

"No, no," he said vaguely. "I never have. I never have. We are rather old-fashioned here."

"Not taking money," I replied, "seems to me more like an uncommonly new fashion than an old one."

"I never have," said the old man, blinking and blowing his nose; "I've always given presents. I'm too old to stop."

"Good heavens!" I said. "What can you mean? Why, you might be Father Christmas."[11]

"I am Father Christmas," he said apologetically, and blew his nose again.

The lamps could not have been lighted yet in the street outside. At any rate, I could see nothing against the darkness but the shining shop-window. There were no sounds of steps or voices in the street; I might have strayed into some new and sunless world. But something had cut the chords of common sense, and I could not feel even surprise except sleepily. Something made me say, "You look ill, Father Christmas."

"I am dying," he said.

I did not speak, and it was he who spoke again.

"All the new people have left my shop. I cannot understand it. They seem to object to me on such curious and inconsistent sort of grounds, these scientific men, and these innovators. They say that I give people superstitions and make them too visionary; they say I give people sausages and make them too coarse. They say my heavenly parts are too heavenly; they say my earthly parts are too earthly; I don't know what they want, I'm sure. How can heavenly things be too heavenly, or earthly things too earthly? How can one be too good, or too jolly? I don't understand. But I understand one thing well enough. These modern people are living and I am dead."

"You may be dead," I replied. "You ought to know. But as for what they are doing, do not call it living."

o o ?

A silence fell suddenly between us which I somehow expected to be unbroken. But it had not fallen for more than a few seconds when, in the utter stillness, I distinctly heard a very rapid step coming nearer and nearer along the street. The next moment a figure flung itself into the

---

11. In Britain today, "Father Christmas" is often used as a synonym for "Santa Claus," but it is a much older term which simply meant the spirit of Christmas personified.

shop and stood framed in the doorway. He wore a large white hat tilted back as if in impatience; he had tight black old-fashioned pantaloons,[12] a gaudy old-fashioned stock and waistcoat,[13] and an old fantastic coat. He had large, wide-open, luminous eyes like those of an arresting actor; he had a pale, nervous face, and a fringe of beard. He took in the shop and the old man in a look that seemed literally a flash and uttered the exclamation of a man utterly staggered.

"Good lord!" he cried out; "it can't be you! It isn't you! I came to ask where your grave was."

"I'm not dead yet, Mr. Dickens,"[14] said the old gentleman, with a feeble smile; "but I'm dying," he hastened to add reassuringly.

"But, dash it all, you were dying in my time," said Mr. Charles Dickens with animation; "and you don't look a day older."

"I've felt like this for a long time," said Father Christmas.

Mr. Dickens turned his back and put his head out of the door into the darkness.

"Dick," he roared at the top of his voice; "he's still alive."

○ ● ◗

Another shadow darkened the doorway, and a much larger and more full-blooded gentleman in an enormous periwig[15] came in, fanning his flushed face with a military hat of the cut of Queen Anne.[16] He carried his head well back like a soldier, and his hot face had even a look of arrogance, which was suddenly contradicted by his eyes, which were literally as humble as a dog's. His sword made a great clatter, as if the shop were too small for it.

"Indeed," said Sir Richard Steele, "'tis a most prodigious matter, for

---

12. Trousers.
13. A stock is a necktie like an ascot or cravat and a waistcoat is a vest.
14. Charles Dickens (1812–1870), author of *A Christmas Carol* (1843).
15. A wig (artificial hair).
16. Queen Anne (1665–1714), sovereign of Great Britain.

the man was dying when I wrote about Sir Roger de Coverley and his Christmas Day."[17]

My senses were growing dimmer and the room darker. It seemed to be filled with newcomers.

"It hath ever been understood," said a burly man, who carried his head humorously and obstinately a little on one side—I think he was Ben Johnson[18]—"It hath ever been understood, consule Jacobo,[19] under our King James[20] and her late Majesty, that such good and hearty customs were fallen sick, and like to pass from the world. This grey beard most surely was no lustier when I knew him than now."

And I also thought I heard a green-clad man, like Robin Hood,[21] say in some mixed Norman French, "But I saw the man dying."

"I have felt like this a long time," said Father Christmas, in his feeble way again.

Mr. Charles Dickens suddenly leant across to him.

"Since when?" he asked. "Since you were born?"

"Yes," said the old man, and sank shaking into a chair. "I have been always dying."

Mr. Dickens took off his hat with a flourish like a man calling a mob to rise.

"I understand it now," he cried, "you will never die."

---

17. Sir Richard Steele (1672–1729) founded a short-lived newspaper, the *Spectator*, in which he included his stories about the fictitious Sir Roger de Coverley.
18. Benjamin Johnson (1572–1637), playwright and author of *Christmas, His Masque* (1616).
19. This is Latin for "consult James," that is, consider the time of King James.
20. King James I of England and Scotland (1566–1625). He commissioned a translation of the Bible into English and thus it is known as the King James Bible (KJV).
21. A legendary English folk hero—stories about him are usually set during the time of King Richard the Lionhearted (1157–1199).

THE GIFTS OF THE CHILD CHRIST
GEORGE MACDONALD

"*The Gifts of the Child Christ*" *is one of the greatest Christmas stories ever written. It is not as well-known as it should be, however, because publishers have usually preferred tales focused on the cultural aspects of the holiday, while this story jingles with Christian hope. There are sad events in it which might not make it a preferred reading for someone who has high demands for a thoroughly happy story. It is also longer—and a bit more difficult to understand—than some of the other stories in this collection. Little Sophy is so young that she still sucks her thumb. Yet she is trying her best to understand and apply to herself what is being said in her church's weekly sermons. Her earnest confusions turn out to be a more excellent way than the downward paths being taken by the adults in her life. The Scottish author George MacDonald (1824–1905) was himself a preacher, and his writings are infused with faith.* The Gifts of the Christ Child, and other Tales *was published in 1882. MacDonald also wrote many celebrated fairytales and fantasy books. In* The Princess and the Goblin *(1872), eight-year-old Irene is in grave danger from a sinister plot.* At the Back of the North Wind *(1871) recounts the mysterious, nighttime adventures of a poor boy named Diamond.*

The Gifts of the Child Christ

George MacDonald

Chapter I.

"My hearers, we grow old," said the preacher. "Be it summer or be it spring with us now, autumn will soon settle down into winter, that winter whose snow melts only in the grave. The wind of the world sets for the tomb. Some of us rejoice to be swept along on its swift wings, and hear it bellowing in the hollows of earth and sky; but it will grow a terror to the man of trembling limb and withered brain, until at length he will long for the shelter of the tomb to escape its roaring and buffeting. Happy the man who shall then be able to believe that old age itself, with its pitiable decays and sad dreams of youth, is the chastening of the Lord,[1] a sure sign of his love and his fatherhood."

It was the first Sunday in Advent; but "the chastening of the Lord" came into almost every sermon that man preached.

"Eloquent! But after all, can this kind of thing be true?" said to himself

---

1. As will become clear, the preacher has been emphasizing the text: "For whom the Lord loveth he chasteneth" (Heb. 12:6 KJV). Modern translations often use the word "disciplines" for "chasteneth."

a man of about thirty, who sat decorously listening. For many years he had thought he believed this kind of thing—but of late he was not so sure.

Beside him sat his wife, in her new winter bonnet, her pretty face turned up toward the preacher; but her eyes—nothing else—revealed that she was not listening. She was much younger than her husband—hardly twenty, indeed.

In the upper corner of the pew sat a pale-faced child about five, sucking her thumb, and staring at the preacher.

The sermon over, they walked home in proximity.[2] The husband looked gloomy, and his eyes sought the ground. The wife looked more smiling than cheerful, and her pretty eyes went hither and thither. Behind them walked the child—steadily, "with level-fronting eyelids."[3]

It was a late-built region of large, common-place houses, and at one of them they stopped and entered. The door of the dining-room was open, showing the table laid for their Sunday dinner. The gentleman passed on to the library behind it, the lady went up to her bedroom, and the child a stage higher to the nursery.

It wanted half an hour to dinner. Mr. Greatorex sat down, drummed with his fingers on the arm of his easy-chair, took up a book of arctic exploration, threw it again on the table, got up, and went to the smoking-room. He had built it for his wife's sake, but was often glad of it for his own. Again he seated himself, took a cigar, and smoked gloomily.

Having reached her bedroom, Mrs. Greatorex took off her bonnet, and stood for ten minutes turning it round and round. Earnestly she regarded it—now gave a twist to the wire-stem of a flower, then spread wider the loop of a bow. She was meditating what it lacked of perfection rather than brooding over its merits: she was keen in bonnets.

---

2. Close to one another.
3. A quotation from "Lady Geraldine's Courtship" (1844), a poem by Elizabeth Barrett Browning.

Little Sophy—or, as she called herself by a transposition of consonant sounds common with children, Phosy—found her nurse Alice in the nursery. But she was lost in the pages of a certain London weekly, which had found her in a mood open to its influences, and did not even look up when the child entered. With some effort Phosy drew off her gloves, and with more difficulty untied her hat. Then she took off her jacket, smoothed her hair, and retreated to a corner. There a large shabby doll lay upon her little chair: she took it up, disposed it gently upon the bed, seated herself in its place, got a little book from where she had left it under the chair, smoothed down her skirts, and began simultaneously to read and suck her thumb. The book was an unhealthy one, a cup filled to the brim with a poverty-stricken and selfish religion: such are always breaking out like an eruption here and there over the body of the Church, doing their part, doubtless, in carrying off the evil humours generated by poverty of blood, or the congestion of self-preservation. It is wonderful out of what spoiled fruit some children will suck sweetness.

But she did not read far: her thoughts went back to a phrase which had haunted her ever since first she went to church: "Whom the Lord loveth, he chasteneth."

"I wish he would chasten me," she thought for the hundredth time.

The small Christian had no suspicion that her whole life had been a period of chastening—that few children indeed had to live in such a sunless atmosphere as hers.

Alice threw down the newspaper, gazed from the window into the back-yard of the next house, saw nothing but an elderly man-servant brushing a garment, and turned upon Sophy.

"Why don't you hang up your jacket, miss?" she said, sharply.

The little one rose, opened the wardrobe-door wide, carried a chair to it, fetched her jacket from the bed, clambered up on the chair, and, leaning far forward to reach a peg, tumbled right into the bottom of the wardrobe.

"You clumsy!" exclaimed the nurse angrily, and pulling her out by the arm, shook her.

Alice was not generally rough to her, but there were reasons to-day.

Phosy crept back to her seat, pale, frightened, and a little hurt. Alice hung up the jacket, closed the wardrobe, and, turning, contemplated her own pretty face and neat figure in the glass opposite. The dinner-bell rang.

"There, I declare!" she cried, and wheeled round on Phosy. "And your hair not brushed yet, miss! Will you ever learn to do a thing without being told it? Thank goodness, I shan't be plagued with you long! But I pity her as comes after me: I do!"

"If the Lord would but chasten me!" said the child to herself, as she rose and laid down her book with a sigh.

The maid seized her roughly by the arm, and brushed her hair with an angry haste that made the child's eyes water, and herself feel a little ashamed at the sight of them.

"How could anybody love such a troublesome chit?"[4] she said, seeking the comfort of justification from the child herself.

Another sigh was the poor little damsel's only answer. She looked very white and solemn as she entered the dining-room.

Mr. Greatorex was a merchant in the City. But he was more of a man than a merchant, which all merchants are not. Also, he was more scrupulous in his dealings than some merchants in the same line of business, who yet stood as well with the world as he; but, on the other hand, he had the meanness to pride himself upon it as if it had been something he might have done without and yet held up his head.

Some six years before, he had married to please his parents; and a year before, he had married to please himself. His first wife had intellect, education, and heart, but little individuality—not enough to reflect the

---

4. Chit means a small child and often has the connotation of their being a brat.

individuality of her husband. The consequence was, he found her uninter-esting. He was kind and indulgent however, and not even her best friend blamed him much for manifesting nothing beyond the average devotion of husbands. But in truth his wife had great capabilities, only they had never ripened, and when she died, a fortnight after giving birth to Sophy, her husband had not a suspicion of the large amount of undeveloped power that had passed away with her.

Her child was so like her both in countenance and manner that he was too constantly reminded of her unlamented mother; and he loved neither enough to discover that, in a sense as true as marvellous, the child was the very flower-bud of her mother's nature, in which her retarded[5] blossom had yet a chance of being slowly carried to perfection. Love alone gives insight, and the father took her merely for a miniature edition of the volume which he seemed to have laid aside for ever in the dust of the earth's lumber-room.[6] Instead, therefore, of watering the roots of his little human slip from the well of his affections, he had scarcely as yet perceived more in relation to her than that he was legally accountable for her existence, and bound to give her shelter and food. If he had questioned himself on the matter, he would have replied that love was not wanting, only waiting upon her growth, and the development of something to interest him.

Little right as he had had to expect anything from his first marriage, he had yet cherished some hopes therein—tolerably vague, it is true, yet hardly faint enough, it would seem, for he was disappointed in them. When its bonds fell from him, however, he flattered himself that he had not worn them in vain, but had through them arrived at a knowledge of women as rare as profound. But whatever the reach of this knowledge, it was not sufficient to prevent him from harbouring the presumptuous

---

5. Slow to develop.
6. Storage room.

hope of so choosing and so fashioning the heart and mind of a woman that they should be as concave mirrors to his own. I do not mean that he would have admitted the figure, but such was really the end he blindly sought. I wonder how many of those who have been disappointed in such an attempt have been thereby aroused to the perception of what a fright-ful failure their success would have been on both sides. It was bad enough that Augustus Greatorex's theories had cramped his own development; it would have been ten-fold worse had they been operative to the stunting of another soul.

Letty Merewether was the daughter of a bishop *in partibus*.[7] She had been born tolerably innocent, had grown up more than tolerably pretty, and was, when she came to England at the age of sixteen, as nearly a gen-uine example of Locke's sheet of white paper[8] as could well have fallen to the hand of such an experimenter as Greatorex would fain become.

In his suit he had prospered—perhaps too easily. He loved the girl, or at least loved the modified reflection of her in his own mind; while she, thoroughly admiring the dignity, good looks, and accomplishments of the man whose attentions flattered her self-opinion, accorded him deference enough to encourage his vainest hopes. Although she knew little, fluttering over the merest surfaces of existence, she had sense enough to know that he talked sense to her, and foolishness enough to put it down to her own credit, while for the sense itself she cared little or nothing. And Greatorex, without even knowing what she was rough-hewn for, would take upon him to shape her ends!—an ambition the Divinity never permits to succeed: he who fancies himself the carver finds himself but the chisel, or indeed perhaps only the mallet, in the hand of the true workman.

---

7. This means a bishop "in any country." It is a way for a church to give ministers the rank and title of a bishop even though they do not have a regular diocese.
8. A reference to the philosophy of John Locke (1632–1704). Often referred to by the Latin phrase *tabula rasa*, it is the idea that people begin as a "blank slate" rather than possessing any innate knowledge.

During the days of his courtship, then, Letty listened and smiled, or answered with what he took for a spiritual response, when it was merely a brain-echo. Looking down into the pond of her being, whose surface was not yet ruffled by any bubbling of springs from below, he saw the reflection of himself and was satisfied. An able man on his hobby looks a centaur[9] of wisdom and folly; but if he be at all a wise man, the beast will one day or other show him the jade's[10] favour of unseating him. Meantime Augustus Greatorex was fooled, not by poor little Letty, who was not capable of fooling him, but by himself. Letty had made no pretences; had been interested, and had shown her interest; had understood, or seemed to understand, what he said to her, and forgotten it the next moment—had no pocket to put it in, did not know what to do with it, and let it drop into the Limbo[11] of Vanity. They had not been married many days before the scouts of advancing disappointment were upon them. Augustus resisted manfully for a time. But the truth was each of the two had to become a great deal more than either was, before any approach to unity was possible. He tried to interest her in one subject after another—tried her first, I am ashamed to say, with political economy. In that instance, when he came home to dinner he found that she had not got beyond the first page of the book he had left with her. But she had the best of excuses, namely, that of that page she had not understood a sentence. He saw his mistake, and tried her with poetry. But Milton,[12] with whom unfortunately he commenced his approaches, was to her, if not equally unintelligible, equally uninteresting. He tried her next with the elements of science, but with no better success. He returned to poetry, and read some of the

---

9. Mixture—a centaur is a mythical creature that is part human and part horse.
10. An ill-tempered horse (and thus it will throw him off).
11. Oblivion.
12. John Milton (1608–1674).

Faerie Queene[13] with her: she was, or seemed to be, interested in all his talk about it, and inclined to go on with it in his absence, but found the first stanza she tried more than enough without him to give life to it. She could give it none, and therefore it gave her none. I believe she read a chapter of the Bible every day, but the only books she read with any real interest were novels of a sort that Augustus despised. It never occurred to him that he ought at once to have made friends of this Momus[14] of unrighteousness, for by them he might have found entrance to the sealed chamber. He ought to have read with her the books she did like, for by them only could he make her think, and from them alone could he lead her to better. It is but from the very step upon which one stands that one can move to the next. Besides these books, there was nothing in her scheme of the universe but fashion, dress, calls, the park, other-peopledom, concerts, plays, churchgoing—whatever could show itself on the frosted glass of her *camera obscura*[15]—make an interest of motion and colour in her darkened chamber. Without these, her bosom's mistress[16] would have found life unendurable, for not yet had she ascended her throne, but lay on the floor of her nursery, surrounded with toys that imitated life.

It was no wonder, therefore, that Augustus was at length compelled to allow himself disappointed. That it was the fault of his self-confidence made the thing no whit better.[17] He was too much of a man not to cherish a certain tenderness for her, but he soon found to his dismay that it had begun to be mingled with a shadow of contempt. Against this he struggled,

---

13. *The Faire Queene* (1590), by Edmund Spenser. The general point is that he has tried to start her education in poetry with difficult works that are made all the harder to understand because they are centuries old.
14. A person who is always finding fault. This is a confusing sentence, but the basic idea is that even though the things she read could be easily criticized, he should build upon them rather than disdain them.
15. A machine for reflecting images. The idea is that she does not have a rich, thoughtful inner life, but just responds to the external events that come her way.
16. Her inner self.
17. That is, not a bit better.

but with fluctuating success. He stopped later and later at business, and when he came home spent more and more of his time in the smoking-room, where by and by he had bookshelves put up. Occasionally he would accept an invitation to dinner and accompany his wife, but he detested evening parties, and when Letty, who never refused an invitation if she could help it, went to one, he remained at home with his books. But his power of reading began to diminish. He became restless and irritable. Something kept gnawing at his heart. There was a sore spot in it. The spot grew larger and larger, and by degrees the centre of his consciousness came to be a soreness: his cherished idea had been fooled; he had taken a silly girl for a woman of undeveloped wealth[18]—a bubble, a surface whereon fair colours chased each other, for a hearted crystal.

On her part, Letty too had her grief, which, unlike Augustus, she did not keep to herself, receiving in return from more than one of her friends the soothing assurance that Augustus was only like all other men; that women were but their toys, which they cast away when weary of them. Letty did not see that she was herself making a toy of her life, or that Augustus was right in refusing to play with such a costly and delicate thing. Neither did Augustus see that, having, by his own blunder, married a mere child, he was bound to deal with her as one, and not let the child suffer for his fault more than what could not be helped. It is not by pressing our insights upon them, but by bathing the sealed eyelids of the human kittens, that we can help them.[19]

And all the time poor little Phosy was left to the care of Alice, a clever, careless, good-hearted, self-satisfied damsel, who, although seldom so rough in her behaviour as we have just seen her, abandoned the child almost entirely to her own resources. It was often she sat alone in the

---

18. That is, undeveloped potential.
19. In other words, our goal should be to enable people to open their eyes and see for themselves rather than just telling them what we see.

nursery, wishing the Lord would chasten her—because then he would love her.

The first course was nearly over ere Augustus had brought himself to ask—

"What did you think of the sermon to-day, Letty?"

"Not much," answered Letty. "I am not fond of finery. I prefer simplicity."

Augustus held his peace bitterly. For it was just finery in a sermon, without knowing it, that Letty was fond of: what seemed to him a flimsy syllabub[20] of sacred things, beaten up with the whisk of composition, was charming to Letty; while, on the contrary, if a man such as they had been listening to was carried away by the thoughts that struggled in him for utterance, the result, to her judgment, was finery, and the object display. In excuse it must be remembered that she had been used to her father's style, which no one could have aspersed[21] with lack of sobriety. Presently she spoke again.

"Gus, dear, couldn't you make up your mind for once to go with me to Lady Ashdaile's to-morrow? I am getting quite ashamed of appearing so often without you."

"There is another way of avoiding that unpleasantness," remarked her husband drily.

"You cruel creature!" returned Letty playfully. "But I must go this once, for I promised Mrs. Holden."

"You know, Letty," said her husband, after a little pause, "it gets of more and more consequence that you should not fatigue yourself. By keeping such late hours in such stifling rooms you are endangering two lives—remember that, Letty. If you stay at home to-morrow, I will come home early, and read to you all the evening."

---

20. Frothy, vapid discourse.
21. Charged.

"Gussy, that would be charming. You know there is nothing in the world I should enjoy so much. But this time I really mustn't."

She launched into a list of all the great nobodies and small somebodies who were to be there, and whom she positively must see: it might be her only chance.

Those last words quenched a sarcasm on Augustus' lips. He was kinder than usual the rest of the evening, and read her to sleep with the *Pilgrim's Progress*.[22]

Phosy sat in a corner, listened, and understood. Or where she mis-understood, it was an honest misunderstanding, which never does much hurt. Neither father nor mother spoke to her till they bade her good night. Neither saw the hungry heart under the mask of the still face. The father never imagined her already fit for the modelling she was better without, and the stepmother had to become a mother before she could value her.

Phosy went to bed to dream of the Valley of Humiliation.[23]

CHAPTER II.

The next morning Alice gave her mistress warning.[24] It was quite unex-pected, and she looked at her aghast.

"Alice," she said at length, "you're never going to leave me at such a time!"

"I'm sorry it don't suit you, ma'am, but I must."

"Why, Alice? What is the matter? Has Sophy been troublesome?"

"No, ma'am; there's no harm in that child."

"Then what can it be, Alice? Perhaps you are going to be married sooner than you expected?"

---

22. John Bunyan, *The Pilgrim's Progress* (1678).
23. *Pilgrim's Progress* is an allegory, and the Valley of Humiliation is a place encountered in the pilgrimage it depicts.
24. That is, that she had given notice that she was quitting their employment.

Alice gave her chin a little toss, pressed her lips together, and was silent.

"I have always been kind to you," resumed her mistress.

"I'm sure, ma'am, I never made no complaints!" returned Alice, but as she spoke she drew herself up straighter than before.

"Then what is it?" said her mistress.

"The fact is, ma'am," answered the girl, almost fiercely, "I cannot any longer endure a state of domestic slavery."

"I don't understand you a bit better," said Mrs. Greatorex, trying, but in vain, to smile, and therefore looking angrier than she was.

"I mean, ma'am—an' I see no reason as I shouldn't say it, for it's the truth—there's a worm at the root of society where one yuman[25] bein''s got to do the dirty work of another. I don't mind sweepin' up my own dust, but I won't sweep up nobody else's. I ain't a goin' to demean myself no longer! There!"

"Leave the room, Alice," said Mrs. Greatorex; and when, with a toss and a flounce, the young woman had vanished, she burst into tears of anger and annoyance.

The day passed. The evening came. She dressed without Alice's usual help, and went to Lady Ashdaile's with her friend. There a reaction took place, and her spirits rose unnaturally. She even danced—to the disgust of one or two quick-eyed matrons[26] who sat by the wall.

When she came home she found her husband sitting up for her. He said next to nothing, and sat up an hour longer with his book.

In the night she was taken ill. Her husband called Alice, and ran himself to fetch the doctor. For some hours she seemed in danger, but by noon was much better. Only the greatest care was necessary.

---

25. "Human"—MacDonald often misspells words when he is recording dialogue to indicate the speaker's dialect and accent.
26. Older, dignified, married women.

As soon as she could speak, she told Augustus of Alice's warning, and he sent for her to the library.

She stood before him with flushed cheeks and flashing eyes.

"I understand, Alice, you have given your mistress warning," he said gently.

"Yes, sir."

"Your mistress is very ill, Alice."

"Yes, sir."

"Don't you think it would be ungrateful of you to leave her in her present condition? She's not likely to be strong for some time to come."

The use of the word "ungrateful" was an unfortunate one. Alice begged to know what she had to be grateful for. Was her work worth nothing? And her master, as every one must who claims that which can only be freely given, found himself in the wrong.

"Well, Alice," he said, "we won't dispute that point; and if you are really determined on going, you must do the best you can for your mistress for the rest of the month."

Alice's sense of injury was soothed by her master's forbearance. She had always rather approved of Mr. Greatorex, and she left the room more softly than she had entered it.

Letty had a fortnight in bed, during which she reflected a little.

The very day on which she left her room, Alice sought an interview with her master, and declared she could not stay out her month; she must go home at once.

She had been very attentive to her mistress during the fortnight: there must be something to account for her strange behaviour.

"Come now, Alice," said her master, "what's at the back of all this? You have been a good, well-behaved, obliging girl till now, and I am certain you would never be like this if there weren't something wrong somewhere."

"Something wrong, sir! No, indeed, sir! Except you call it wrong to have an old uncle 's dies and leaves ever so much money—thousands on thousands, the lawyers say."

"And does it come to you then, Alice?"

"I get my share, sir. He left it to be parted even between his nephews and nieces."

"Why, Alice, you are quite an heiress, then!" returned her master, scarcely however believing the thing so grand as Alice would have it. "But don't you think now it would be rather hard that your fortune should be Mrs. Greatorex's misfortune?"

"Well, I don't see as how it shouldn't," replied Alice. "It's mis'ess's fortun' as 'as been my misfortun'—ain't it now, sir? An' why shouldn't it be the other way next?"

"I don't quite see how your mistress's fortune can be said to be your misfortune, Alice."

"Anybody would see that, sir, as wasn't blinded by class-prejudices."

"Class-prejudices!" exclaimed Mr. Greatorex, in surprise at the word.

"It's a term they use, I believe, sir! But it's plain enough that if mis'ess hadn't 'a' been better off than me, she wouldn't ha' been able to secure my services—as you calls it."

"That is certainly plain enough," returned Mr. Greatorex. "But suppose nobody had been able to secure your services, what would have become of you?"

"By that time the people'd have rose to assert their rights."

"To what?—To fortunes like yours?"

"To bread and cheese at least, sir," returned Alice, pertly.

"Well, but you've had something better than bread and cheese."

"I don't make no complaints as to the style of livin' in the house, sir, but that's all one, so long as it's on the vile condition of domestic slavery—which it's nothing can justify."

"Then of course, although you are now a woman of property, you will never dream of having any one to wait on you," said her master, amused with the volume of human nature thus opened to him.

"All I say, sir, is—it's my turn now; and I ain't goin' to be sit upon by no one. I know my dooty to myself."

"I didn't know there was such a duty, Alice," said her master.

Something in his tone displeased her.

"Then you know now, sir," she said, and bounced out of the room.

The next moment, however, ashamed of her rudeness, she re-entered, saying, "I don't want to be unkind, sir, but I must go home. I've got a brother that's ill, too, and wants to see me. If you don't object to me goin' home for a month, I promise you to come back and see mis'ess through her trouble—as a friend, you know, sir."

"But just listen to me first, Alice," said Mr. Greatorex. "I've had something to do with wills in my time, and I can assure you it is not likely to be less than a year before you can touch the money. You had much better stay where you are till your uncle's affairs are settled. You don't know what may happen. There's many a slip between cup and lip, you know."

"Oh! it's all right, sir. Everybody knows the money's left to his nephews and nieces, and me and my brother's as good as any."

"I don't doubt it: still, if you'll take my advice, you'll keep a sound roof over your head till another's ready for you."

Alice only threw her chin in the air, and said almost threateningly, "Am I to go for the month, sir?"

"I'll talk to your mistress about it," answered Mr. Greatorex, not at all sure that such an arrangement would be for his wife's comfort.

But the next day Mrs. Greatorex had a long talk with Alice, and the result was that on the following Monday she was to go home for a month, and then return for two months more at least. What Mr. Greatorex had said about the legacy, had had its effect, and, besides, her mistress had spoken to her with pleasure in her good fortune. About Sophy no one felt any anxiety: she was no trouble to any one, and the housemaid would see to her.

Chapter III.

On the Sunday evening, Alice's lover, having heard, not from herself, but by a side wind, that she was going home the next day, made his appearance in Wimborne Square, somewhat perplexed—both at the move, and at her leaving him in ignorance of the same. He was a cabinet-maker in an honest shop in the neighbourhood, and in education, faculty, and general worth, considerably Alice's superior—a fact which had hitherto rather pleased her, but now gave zest to the change which she imagined had subverted their former relation. Full of the sense of her new superiority, she met him draped in an indescribable strangeness. John Jephson felt, at the very first word, as if her voice came from the other side of the English Channel. He wondered what he had done, or rather what Alice could imagine he had done or said, to put her in such tantrums.

"Alice, my dear," he said—for John was a man to go straight at the enemy, "what's amiss? What's come over you? You ain't altogether like your own self to-night! And here I find you're goin' away, and ne'er a word to me about it! What have I done?"

Alice's chin alone made reply. She waited the fitting moment, with splendour to astonish, and with grandeur to subdue her lover. To tell the sad truth, she was no longer sure that it would be well to encourage him on the old footing; was she not standing on tiptoe, her skirts in her hand, on the brink of the brook that parted serfdom from gentility,[27] on the point of stepping daintily across, and leaving domestic slavery, red hands, caps, and obedience behind her? How then was she to marry a man that

---

27. From being at the humble level of the servants to joining the higher social classes.

had black nails, and smelt of glue? It was incumbent on her at least, for propriety's sake, to render him at once aware that it was in condescension ineffable[28] she took any notice of him.

"Alice, my girl!" began John again, in expostulatory tone.

"Miss Cox, if you please, John Jephson," interposed Alice.

"What on 'arth's come over you?" exclaimed John, with the first throb of rousing indignation. "But if you ain't your own self no more, why, Miss Cox be it. 'T seems to me 's if I warn't my own self no more—'s if I'd got into some un else, or 't least hedn't got my own ears on m' own head—Never saw or heerd Alice like this afore!" he added, turning in gloomy bewilderment to the housemaid for a word of human sympathy.

The movement did not altogether please Alice, and she felt she must justify her behaviour.

"You see, John," she said, with dignity, keeping her back towards him, and pretending to dust the globe of a lamp, "there's things as no woman can help, and therefore as no man has no right to complain of them. It's not as if I'd gone an' done it, or changed myself, no more 'n if it 'ad took place in my cradle. What can I help it, if the world goes and changes itself? Am I to blame?—tell me that. It's not that. I make no complaint, but I tell you it ain't me, it's circumstances as is gone and changed theirselves, and bein' as circumstances is changed, things ain't the same as they was, and Miss is the properer term from you to me, John Jephson."

"Dang it if I know what you're a drivin' at, Alice!—Miss Cox!—and I beg yer pardon, miss, I'm sure—Dang me if I do!"

"Don't swear, John Jephson—leastways before a lady. It's not proper."

"It seems to me, Miss Cox, as if the wind was a settin' from Bedlam, or may be Colney Hatch,"[29] said John, who was considered a humourist among his comrades. "I wouldn't take no liberties with a lady, Miss Cox;

---

28. She has an inexplicably superior attitude to him.
29. Bedlam and Colney Hatch were both institutions for the mentally ill.

but if I might be so bold as to arst[30] the joke of the thing—"

"Joke, indeed!" cried Alice. "Do you call a dead uncle and ten thou-sand pounds a joke?"

"God bless me!" said John. "You don't mean it, Alice?"

"I do mean it, and that you'll find, John Jephson. I'm goin' to bid you good-bye to-morrer."

"Whoy, Alice!" exclaimed honest John, aghast.

"It's truth I tell ye," said Alice.

"And for how long?" gasped John, fore-feeling illimitable[31] misfortune.

"That depends," returned Alice, who did not care to lessen the effect of her communication by mentioning her promised return for a season. "—It ain't likely," she added, "as a heiress is a goin' to act the nuss-maid much longer."

"But Alice," said John, "you don't mean to say—it's not in your mind now—it can't be, Alice—you're only jokin' with me—"

"Indeed, and I'm not!" interjected Alice, with a sniff.

"I don't mean that way, you know. What I mean is, you don't mean as how this 'ere money—dang it all!—as how it's to be all over between you and me?—You can't mean that, Alice!" ended the poor fellow, with a choking in his throat.

It was very hard upon him! He must either look as if he wanted to share her money, or else as if he were ready to give her up.

"Arst yourself, John Jephson," answered Alice, "whether it's likely a young lady of fortun' would be keepin' company with a young man as didn't know how to take off his hat to her in the park?"

Alice did not above half mean what she said: she wished mainly to enhance her own importance. At the same time she did mean it half, and that would have been enough for Jephson. He rose, grievously wounded.

---

30. Ask.
31. Unlimited.

"Good-bye, Alice," he said, taking the hand she did not refuse. "Ye're throwin' from ye what all yer money won't buy."

She gave a scornful little laugh, and John walked out of the kitchen.

At the door he turned with one lingering look; but in Alice there was no sign of softening. She turned scornfully away, and no doubt enjoyed her triumph to the full.

The next morning she went away.

Chapter IV.

Mr. Greatorex had ceased to regard the advent of Christmas with much interest. Naturally gifted with a strong religious tendency, he had, since his first marriage, taken, not to denial, but to the side of objection, spending much energy in contempt for the foolish opinions of others, a self-indulgence which does less than little to further the growth of one's own spirit in truth and righteousness. The only person who stands excused—I do not say justified—in so doing, is the man who, having been taught the same opinions, has found them a legion of adversaries barring his way to the truth. But having got rid of them for himself, it is, I suspect, worse than useless to attack them again, save as the ally of those who are fighting their way through the same ranks to the truth. Greatorex had been indulging his intellect at the expense of his heart. A man may have light in the brain and darkness in the heart. It were better to be an owl than a strong-eyed apteryx.[32] He was on the path which naturally ends in blindness and unbelief. I fancy, if he had not been neglectful of his child, she would ere this time have relighted his Christmas-candles for him; but now his second disappointment in marriage had so dulled his heart that he had begun to regard life as a stupid affair, in which the most enviable fool was

---

32. An apteryx is a nocturnal bird native to New Zealand that does not rely on vision for navigation. Mr. Greatorex would be better off if he would continue to see.

the man who could still expect to realize an ideal. He had set out on a false track altogether, but had not yet discovered that there had been an immoral element at work in his mistake.

For what right had he to desire the fashioning of any woman after his ideas? Did not the angel of her eternal Ideal for ever behold the face of her Father in heaven? The best that can be said for him is, that, notwithstanding his disappointment and her faults, yea, notwithstanding his own faults, which were, with all his cultivation and strength of character, yet more serious than hers, he was still kind to her; yes, I may say for him, that, notwithstanding even her silliness, which is a sickening fault, and one which no supremacy of beauty can overshadow, he still loved her a little. Hence the care he showed for her in respect of the coming sorrow was genuine; it did not all belong to his desire for a son to whom he might be a father indeed—after his own fancies, however. Letty, on her part, was as full of expectation as the girl who has been promised a doll that can shut and open its eyes, and cry when it is pinched; her carelessness of its safe arrival came of ignorance and not indifference.

It cannot but seem strange that such a man should have been so careless of the child he had. But from the first she had painfully reminded him of her mother, with whom in truth he had never quarrelled, but with whom he had not found life the less irksome on that account. Add to this that he had been growing fonder of business—a fact which indicated, in a man of his endowment and development, an inclination downwards of the plane of his life. It was some time since he had given up reading poetry. History had almost followed: he now read little except politics, travels, and popular expositions of scientific progress.

That year Christmas Eve fell upon a Monday. The day before, Letty not feeling very well, her husband thought it better not to leave her, and gave up going to church. Phosy was utterly forgotten, but she dressed herself, and at the usual hour appeared with her prayer-book in her hand ready for church. When her father told her that he was not going, she looked so blank that he took pity upon her, and accompanied her to the church-door, promising to meet her as she came out. Phosy sighed from relief as she entered, for she had a vague idea that by going to church to pray for it she might move the Lord to chasten her. At least he would see her there, and might think of it. She had never had such an attention from her father before, never such dignity conferred upon her as to be allowed to appear in church alone, sitting in the pew by herself like a grown damsel. But I doubt if there was any pride in her stately step, or any vanity in the smile—no, not smile, but illuminated mist, the vapour of smiles, which haunted her sweet little solemn church-window of a face, as she walked up the aisle.

The preacher was one of whom she had never heard her father speak slighting word, in whom her unbounded trust had never been shaken. Also he was one who believed with his whole soul in the things that make Christmas precious. To him the birth of the wonderful baby hinted at hundreds of strange things in the economy of the planet. That a man could so thoroughly persuade himself that, he believed the old fable, was matter of marvel to some of his friends who held blind Nature the eternal mother, and Night the everlasting grandmother of all things. But the child Phosy, in her dreams or out of them, in church or nursery, with her book or her doll, was never out of the region of wonders, and would have believed, or tried to believe, anything that did not involve a moral impossibility.

What the preacher said I need not even partially repeat; it is enough to mention a certain metamorphosed deposit from the stream of his elo-quence carried home in her mind by Phosy: from some of his sayings about the birth of Jesus into the world, into the family, into the individual human bosom, she had got it into her head that Christmas Day was not a birthday like that she had herself last year, but that, in some wonderful way, to her requiring no explanation, the baby Jesus was born every Christmas Day afresh. What became of him afterwards she did not know, and indeed she had never yet thought to ask how it was that he could come to every house in London as well as No. 1, Wimborne Square. Little of a home as another might think it, that house was yet to her the centre of all houses, and the wonder had not yet widened rippling beyond it: into that spot of the pool the eternal gift would fall.

Her father forgot the time over his book, but so entranced was her heart with the expectation of the promised visit, now so near—the day after to-morrow—that, if she did not altogether forget to look for him as she stepped down the stair from the church door to the street, his absence caused her no uneasiness; and when, just as she reached it, he opened the house-door in tardy haste to redeem his promise, she looked up at him with a solemn, smileless repose, born of spiritual tension and speech-less anticipation, upon her face, and walking past him without change in the rhythm of her motion, marched stately up the stairs to the nursery. I believe the centre of her hope was that when the baby came she would beg him on her knees to ask the Lord to chasten her.

When dessert was over, her mother on the sofa in the drawing-room, and her father in an easy-chair, with a bottle of his favourite wine by his side, she crept out of the room and away again to the nursery. There she reached up to her little bookshelf, and, full of the sermon as spongy mists are full of the sunlight, took thence a volume of stories from the German, the re-reading of one of which, narrating the visit of the Christ-child, laden with gifts, to a certain household, and what he gave to each and all therein, she had, although sorely tempted, saved up until now, and sat down with it by the fire, the only light she had.[33] When the housemaid,

---

33. For many people in many different cultures, Christmas is a time for gifts brought by mysterious figures. The most famous of these is perhaps St. Nicholas, who has now come to be known by many, especially in America, under the guise of Santa Claus. Another, however, is *Christkind* (the Christ child). *Christkind* as a gift-bearer is popular in various countries, not least German-speaking ones. The title of this story, "The Gifts of the Child Christ," is evoking the tradition of the *Christkind* while also widening it to remind us that all true gifts come from Jesus, the Christ who became incarnate as a child on the first Christmas.

suddenly remembering she must put her to bed, and at the same time dis-covering it was a whole hour past her usual time, hurried to the nursery, she found her fast asleep in her little armchair, her book on her lap, and the fire self-consumed into a dark cave with a sombre glow in its deepest hollows. Dreams had doubtless come to deepen the impressions of sermon and *maehrchen*,[34] for as she slowly yielded to the hands of Polly putting her to bed, her lips, unconsciously moved of the slumbering but not sleeping spirit, more than once murmured the words Lord loveth and chasteneth. Right blessedly would I enter the dreams of such a child—revel in them, as a bee in the heavenly gulf of a cactus-flower.

Chapter V.

On Christmas Eve the church bells were ringing through the murky air of London, whose streets lay flaring and steaming below. The brightest of their constellations were the butchers' shops, with their shows of prize beef; around them, the eddies[35] of the human tides were most confused and knotted. But the toy-shops were brilliant also. To Phosy they would have been the treasure-caves of the Christ-child—all mysteries, all with insides to them—boxes, and desks, and windmills, and dove-cots,[36] and hens with chickens, and who could tell what all? In every one of those shops her eyes would have searched for the Christ-child, the giver of all their wealth. For to her he was everywhere that night—ubiquitous as the luminous mist that brooded all over London—of which, however, she saw nothing but the glow above the mews.[37] John Jephson was out in the mid-dle of all the show, drifting about in it: he saw nothing that had pleasure

---

34. Folktale or fairytale. (This German word is standardly written *märchen* today.)
35. Whirlpools—the waters are not flowing in the standard direction but in a backward or swirling way.
36. A house for doves or pigeons. This is, of course, a toy one to be used with stuffed animals or the like.
37. The row of houses.

189

in it, his heart was so heavy. He never thought once of the Christ-child, or even of the Christ-man, as the giver of anything. Birth is the one standing promise-hope for the race, but for poor John this Christmas held no promise. With all his humour, he was one of those people, generally dull and slow—God grant me and mine such dullness and such sloth—who having once loved, cannot cease. During the fortnight he had scarce had a moment's ease from the sting of his Alice's treatment. The honest fellow's feelings were no study to himself; he knew nothing but the pleasure and the pain of them; but, I believe it was not mainly for himself that he was sorry. Like Othello, "the pity of it"[38] haunted him: he had taken Alice for a downright[39] girl, about whom there was and could be no mistake; and the first hot blast of prosperity had swept her away like a hectic leaf. What were all the shops dressed out in holly and mistletoe, what were all the rushing flaming gas-jets,[40] what the fattest of prize-pigs to John, who could never more imagine a spare-rib on the table between Alice and him of a Sunday? His imagination ran on seeing her pass in her carriage, and drop him a nod of condescension as she swept noisily by him—trudging home weary from his work to his loveless fireside. He didn't want her money! Honestly, he would rather have her without than with money, for he now regarded it as an enemy, seeing what evil changes it could work. "There be some devil in it, sure!" he said to himself. True, he had never found any in his week's wages, but he did remember once finding the devil in a month's wages received in the lump.[41]

As he was thus thinking with himself, a carriage came suddenly from a side street into the crowd, and while he stared at it, thinking Alice might be sitting inside it while he was tramping the pavement alone, she

---

38. A line spoken by Othello himself in Shakespeare's tragedy *Othello*.
39. Straightforward, honest.
40. Bright lights.
41. In other words, receiving too much money all at once creates new temptations.

passed him on the other side on foot—was actually pushed against him: he looked round, and saw a young woman, carrying a small bag, disappearing in the crowd.

"There's an air of Alice about her," said John to himself, seeing her back only. But of course it couldn't be Alice; for her he must look in the carriages now! And what a fool he was: every young woman reminded him of the one he had lost! Perhaps if he was to call the next day—Polly was a good-natured creature—he might hear some news of her.

It had been a troubled fortnight with Mrs. Greatorex. She wished much that she could have talked to her husband more freely, but she had not learned to feel at home with him. Yet he had been kinder and more attentive than usual all the time, so much so that Letty thought with herself—if she gave him a boy, he would certainly return to his first devotion. She said boy, because any one might see he cared little for Phosy. She had never discovered that he was disappointed in herself, but, since her disregard of his wishes had brought evil upon her, she had begun to suspect that he had some ground for being dissatisfied with her. She never dreamed of his kindness as the effort of a conscientious nature to make the best of what could not now be otherwise helped. Her own poverty of spirit and lack of worth achieved, she knew as little of as she did of the riches of Michael the archangel. One must have begun to gather wisdom before he can see his own folly.

That evening she was seated alone in the drawing-room, her husband having left her to smoke his cigar, when the butler entered and informed her that Alice had returned, but was behaving so oddly that they did not know what to do with her. Asking wherein her oddness consisted, and learning that it was mostly in silence and tears, she was not sorry to gather that some disappointment had befallen her, and felt considerable curiosity to know what it was. She therefore told him to send her upstairs.

Meantime Polly, the housemaid, seeing plainly enough from her return in the middle of her holiday, and from her utter dejection, that Alice's expectations had been frustrated, and cherishing no little resentment against her because of her uppishness on the first news of her good fortune, had been ungenerous enough to take her revenge in a way as stinging in effect as bitter in intention; for she loudly protested that no amount of such luck as she pretended to suppose in Alice's possession, would have induced her to behave herself so that a handsome honest fellow like John Jephson should be driven to despise her, and take up with her betters. When her mistress's message came, Alice was only too glad to find refuge from the kitchen in the drawing-room.

The moment she entered, she fell on her knees at the foot of the couch on which her mistress lay, covered her face with her hands, and sobbed grievously.

Nor was the change more remarkable in her bearing than in her person. She was pale and worn, and had a hunted look—was in fact a mere shadow of what she had been. For a time her mistress found it impossible to quiet her so as to draw from her her story: tears and sobs combined with repugnance to hold her silent.

"Oh, ma'am!" she burst out at length, wringing her hands, "how ever can I tell you? You will never speak to me again. Little did I think such a disgrace was waiting me!"

"It was no fault of yours if you were misinformed," said her mistress, "or that your uncle was not the rich man you fancied."

"Oh, ma'am, there was no mistake there! He was more than twice as rich as I fancied. If he had only died a beggar, and left things as they was!"

"Then he didn't leave it to his nephews and nieces as they told you?—Well, there's no disgrace in that."

"Oh! but he did, ma'am: that was all right; no mistake there either, ma'am—And to think o' me behavin' as I did—to you and master as was so good to me! Who'll ever take any more notice of me now, after what has come out—as I'm sure I no more dreamed on than the child unborn!"

An agonized burst of fresh weeping followed, and it was with prolonged difficulty, and by incessant questioning, that Mrs. Greatorex at
length drew from her the following facts.

Before Alice and her brother could receive the legacy to which they
laid claim, it was necessary to produce certain documents, the absence of
which, as of any proof to take their place, led to the unavoidable publication of a fact previously known only to a living few—namely, that the
father and mother of Alice Hopwood had never been married, which fact
deprived them of the smallest claim on the legacy, and fell like a millstone
upon Alice and her pride.[42] From the height of her miserable arrogance she
fell prone—not merely hurled back into the lowly condition from which
she had raised her head only to despise it with base unrighteousness, and
to adopt and reassert the principles she had abhorred when they affected
herself—not merely this, but, in her own judgment at least, no longer the
respectable member of society she had hitherto been justified in suppos-
ing herself. The relation of her father and mother she felt overshadow her
with a disgrace unfathomable—the more overwhelming that it cast her
from the gates of the Paradise she had seemed on the point of entering:
her fall she measured by the height of the social ambition she had cherished, and had seemed on the point of attaining. But it is not an evil that
the devil's money, which this legacy had from the first proved to Alice,
should turn to a hot cinder in the hand. Rarely had a more haughty spirit
than hers gone before a fall,[43] and rarely has the fall been more sudden
or more abject. And the consciousness of the behaviour into which her
false riches had seduced her, changed the whip of her chastisement into

---

42. Because Alice's parents had never married, she was considered an "illegitimate" child. She
was therefore not a legal relative and thus could not inherit under the terms of the will.
Being "illegitimate" was also considered a social disgrace and usually would severely limit
someone's prospects in life.
43. "Pride goeth before destruction, and an haughty spirit before a fall" (Prov. 16:18 KJV).

scorpions.[44] Worst of all, she had insulted her lover as beneath her notice, and the next moment had found herself too vile for his. Judging by herself, in the injustice of bitter humiliation she imagined him scoffing with his mates at the base-born menial[45] who would set up for a fine lady. But had she been more worthy of honest John, she would have understood him better. As it was, no really good fortune could have befallen her but such as now seemed to her the depth of evil fortune. Without humiliation to prepare the way for humility, she must have become capable of more and more baseness, until she lost all that makes life worth having.

When Mrs. Greatorex had given her what consolation she found handy, and at length dismissed her, the girl, unable to endure her own company, sought the nursery, where she caught Sophy in her arms and embraced her with fervour. Never in her life having been the object of any such display of feeling, Phosy was much astonished: when Alice had set her down and she had resumed her seat by the fireside, she went on staring for a while—and then a strange sort of miming ensued.

It was Phosy's habit—one less rare with children than may by most be imagined—to do what she could to enter into any state of mind whose shows were sufficiently marked for her observation. She sought to lay hold of the feeling that produced the expression: less than the reproduction of a similar condition in her own imaginative sensorium,[46] subject to her leisurely examination, would in no case satisfy the little metaphysician.[47] But what was indeed very odd was the means she took for arriving at the sympathetic knowledge she desired. As if she had been the most earnest student of dramatic expression through the facial muscles, she would sit watching the countenance of the object of her solicitude, all the

---

44. "My father hath chastised you with whips, but I will chastise you with scorpions" (1 Kings 12:11 KJV).
45. Servant of lowly birth.
46. The place in your mind where sensations are received and interpreted.
47. Philosopher.

time, with full consciousness, fashioning her own as nearly as she could into the lines and forms of the other: in proportion as she succeeded, the small psychologist imagined she felt in herself the condition that produced the phenomenon she observed—as if the shape of her face cast inward its shadow upon her mind, and so revealed to it, through the two faces, what was moving and shaping in the mind of the other.

In the present instance, having at length, after modelling and remodelling her face like that of a gutta-percha[48] doll for some time, composed it finally into the best correspondence she could effect, she sat brooding for a while, with Alice's expression as it were frozen upon it. Gradually the forms assumed melted away, and allowed her still, solemn face to look out from behind them. The moment this evanishment[49] was complete, she rose and went to Alice, where she sat staring into the fire, unconscious of the scrutiny she had been undergoing, and, looking up in her face, took her thumb out of her mouth, and said, "Is the Lord chastening Alice? I wish he would chasten Phosy."

Her face was calm as that of the Sphinx;[50] there was no mist in the depth of her gray eyes, not a cloud on the wide heaven of her forehead.

Was the child crazed? What could the atom[51] mean, with her big eyes looking right into her? Alice never had understood her: it were indeed strange if the less should comprehend the greater! She was not yet, capable of recognising the word of the Lord in the mouth of babes and sucklings.[52] But there was a something in Phosy's face besides its calmness and unintelligibility. What it was Alice could never have told—yet it did her good. She lifted the child on her lap. There she soon fell asleep. Alice

---

48. Made of rubber.
49. To vanish.
50. A sphinx is a mythical creature that is part human and part lion. The Great Sphinx of Giza, a statue from ancient Egypt, is famous for its inscrutable, imperturbable appearance.
51. Little one.
52. Matthew 21:16 (quoting Ps. 8:2): "And Jesus saith unto them, Yea; have ye never read, Out of the mouth of babes and sucklings thou hast perfected praise?" (KJV).

undressed her, laid her in her crib, and went to bed herself.

But, weary as she was, she had to rise again before she got to sleep. Her mistress was again taken ill. Doctor and nurse were sent for in hot haste; hansom cabs[53] came and went throughout the night, like noisy moths to the one lighted house in the street; there were soft steps within, and doors were gently opened and shut. The waters of Mara had risen and filled the house.[54]

Towards morning they were ebbing slowly away. Letty did not know that her husband was watching by her bedside. The street was quiet now. So was the house. Most of its people had been up throughout the night, but now they had all gone to bed except the strange nurse and Mr. Greatorex.

It was the morning of Christmas Day, and little Phosy knew it in every cranny of her soul. She was not of those who had been up all night, and now she was awake, early and wide, and the moment she awoke she was speculating: He was coming to-day—how would he come? Where should she find the baby Jesus? And when would he come? In the morning, or the afternoon, or in the evening? Could such a grief be in store for her as that he would not appear until night, when she would be again in bed? But she would not sleep till all hope was gone. Would everybody be gathered to meet him, or would he show himself to one after another, each alone? Then her turn would be last, and oh, if he would come to the nursery! But perhaps he would not appear to her at all!—for was she not one whom the Lord did not care to chasten?

Expectation grew and wrought in her until she could lie in bed no longer. Alice was fast asleep. It must be early, but whether it was yet light or not she could not tell for the curtains. Anyhow she would get up and dress, and then she would be ready for Jesus whenever he should come.

---

53. A small cab (taxi).
54. The atmosphere in the house was dominated by a bitter reality (see Ex. 15:23).

True, she was not able to dress herself very well, but he would know, and would not mind. She made all the haste she could, consistently with taking pains,[55] and was soon attired after a fashion.

She crept out of the room and down the stair. The house was very still. What if Jesus should come and find nobody awake? Would he go again and give them no presents? She couldn't expect any herself—but might he not let her take theirs for the rest? Perhaps she ought to wake them all, but she dared not without being sure.

On the last landing above the first floor, she saw, by the low gaslight at the end of the corridor, an unknown figure pass the foot of the stair: could she have anything to do with the marvel of the day? The woman looked up, and Phosy dropped the question. Yet she might be a charwoman,[56] whose assistance the expected advent rendered necessary. When she reached the bottom of the stair she saw her disappearing in her step-mother's room. That she did not like. It was the one room into which she could not go. But, as the house was so still, she would search everywhere else, and if she did not find him, would then sit down in the hall and wait for him.

The room next the foot of the stair, and opposite her step-mother's, was the spare room, with which she associated ideas of state and grandeur: where better could she begin than at the guest-chamber?—There!— Could it be? Yes!—Through the chink of the scarce-closed door she saw light. Either he was already there or there they were expecting him. From that moment she felt as if lifted out of the body. Far exalted above all dread, she peeped modestly in, and then entered. Beyond the foot of the bed, a candle stood on a little low table, but nobody was to be seen. There was a stool near the table: she would sit on it by the candle, and wait for him. But ere she reached it, she caught sight of something upon the bed

---

55. Making an effort.
56. A woman hired to clean the house.

that drew her thither. She stood entranced—Could it be?—It might be. Perhaps he had left it there while he went into her mamma's room with something for her—The loveliest of dolls ever imagined! She drew nearer. The light was low, and the shadows were many: she could not be sure what it was. But when she had gone close up to it, she concluded with certainty that it was in very truth a doll—perhaps intended for her—but beyond doubt the most exquisite of dolls. She dragged a chair to the bed, got up, pushed her little arms softly under it, and drawing it gently to her, slid down with it. When she felt her feet firm on the floor, filled with the solemn composure of holy awe she carried the gift of the child Jesus to the candle, that she might the better admire its beauty and know its preciousness. But the light had no sooner fallen upon it than a strange undefinable doubt awoke within her. Whatever it was, it was the very essence of loveliness—the tiny darling with its alabaster[57] face, and its delicately modelled hands and fingers! A long night-gown covered all the rest—Was it possible?—Could it be?—Yes, indeed! it must be—it could be nothing else than a real baby! What a goose she had been! Of course it was baby Jesus himself!—for was not this his very own Christmas Day on which he was always born?—If she had felt awe of his gift before, what a grandeur of adoring love, what a divine dignity possessed her, holding in her arms the very child himself! One shudder of bliss passed through her, and in an agony of possession she clasped the baby to her great heart—then at once became still with the satisfaction of eternity, with the peace of God. She sat down on the stool, near the little table, with her back to the candle, that its rays should not fall on the eyes of the sleeping Jesus and wake him: there she sat, lost in the very majesty of bliss, at once the mother and the slave of the Lord Jesus.

She sat for a time still as marble waiting for marble to awake, heedful

---

57. Smooth like a polished stone.

as tenderest woman not to rouse him before his time, though her heart was swelling with the eager petition that he would ask his Father to be as good as chasten her. And as she sat, she began, after her wont, to model her face to the likeness of his, that she might understand his stillness—the absolute peace that dwelt on his countenance. But as she did so, again a sudden doubt invaded her: Jesus lay so very still—never moved, never opened his pale eye-lids! And now set thinking, she noted that he did not breathe. She had seen babies asleep, and their breath came and went— their little bosoms heaved up and down, and sometimes they would smile, and sometimes they would moan and sigh. But Jesus did none of all these things: was it not strange? And then he was cold—oh, so cold!

A blue silk coverlid lay on the bed: she half rose and dragged it off, and contrived to wind it around herself and the baby. Sad at heart, very sad, but undismayed, she sat and watched him on her lap.

CHAPTER VI.

Meantime the morning of Christmas Day grew. The light came and filled the house. The sleepers slept late, but at length they stirred. Alice awoke last—from a troubled sleep, in which the events of the night mingled with her own lost condition and destiny. After all Polly had been kind, she thought, and got Sophy up without disturbing her.

She had been but a few minutes down, when a strange and appalling rumour made itself—I cannot say audible, but—somehow known through the house, and every one hurried up in horrible dismay.

The nurse had gone into the spare room, and missed the little dead thing she had laid there. The bed was between her and Phosy, and she never saw her. The doctor had been sharp with her about something the night before: she now took her revenge in suspicion of him, and after a hasty and fruitless visit of inquiry to the kitchen, hurried to Mr. Greatorex.

The servants crowded to the spare room, and when their master, incredulous indeed, yet shocked at the tidings brought him, hastened to the spot, he found them all in the room, gathered at the foot of the bed. A little sunlight filtered through the red window-curtains, and gave a strange pallid expression to the flame of the candle, which had now burned very low. At first he saw nothing but the group of servants, silent, motionless, with heads leaning forward, intently gazing: he had come just in time: another moment and they would have ruined the lovely sight. He stepped forward, and saw Phosy, half shrouded in blue, the candle behind illuminating the hair she had found too rebellious to the brush, and making of it a faint aureole[58] about her head and white face, whence cold and sorrow had driven all the flush, rendering it colourless as that upon her arm which had never seen the light. She had pored on the little face until she knew death, and now she sat a speechless mother of sorrow, bending in the dim light of the tomb over the body of her holy infant.

How it was I cannot tell, but the moment her father saw her she looked up, and the spell of her dumbness broke.

"Jesus is dead," she said, slowly and sadly, but with perfect calmness. "He is dead," she repeated. "He came too early, and there was no one up to take care of him, and he's dead—dead—dead!"

But as she spoke the last words, the frozen lump of agony gave way; the well of her heart suddenly filled, swelled, overflowed; the last word was half sob, half shriek of utter despair and loss.

Alice darted forward and took the dead baby tenderly from her. The same moment her father raised the little mother and clasped her to his bosom. Her arms went round his neck, her head sank on his shoulder, and sobbing in grievous misery, yet already a little comforted, he bore her from the room.

---

58. Halo.

"No, no, Phosy!" they heard him say, "Jesus is not dead, thank God. It is only your little brother that hadn't life enough, and is gone back to God for more."

Weeping the women went down the stairs. Alice's tears were still flowing, when John Jephson entered. Her own troubles forgotten in the emotion of the scene she had just witnessed, she ran to his arms and wept on his bosom.

John stood as one astonished.

"O Lord! this is a Christmas!" he sighed at last.

"Oh John!" cried Alice, and tore herself from his embrace, "I forgot! You'll never speak to me again, John! Don't do it, John."

And with the words she gave a stifled cry, and fell a weeping again, behind her two shielding hands.

"Why, Alice!—you ain't married, are you?" gasped John, to whom that was the only possible evil.

"No, John, and never shall be: a respectable man like you would never think of looking twice at a poor girl like me!"

"Let's have one more look anyhow," said John, drawing her hands from her face. "Tell me what's the matter, and if there's anything can be done to right you, I'll work day and night to do it, Alice."

"There's nothing can be done, John," replied Alice, and would again have floated out on the ocean of her misery, but in spite of wind and tide, that is sobs and tears, she held on by the shore at his entreaty, and told her tale, not even omitting the fact that when she went to the eldest of the cousins, inheriting through the misfortune of her and her brother so much more than their expected share, and "demeaned herself" to beg a little help for her brother, who was dying of consumption,[59] he had all but ordered her out of the house, swearing he had nothing to do with her or

---

59. What the Victorians diagnosed with the general word "consumption" was often what we now call tuberculosis.

her brother, and saying she ought to be ashamed to show her face.

"And that when we used to make mud pies together!" concluded Alice with indignation. "There, John! you have it all," she added. "—And now?"

With the word she gave a deep, humbly questioning look into his honest eyes.

"Is that all, Alice?" he asked.

"Yes, John; ain't it enough?" she returned.

"More'n enough," answered John. "I swear to you, Alice, you're worth to me ten times what you would ha' been, even if you'd ha' had me, with ten thousand pounds in your ridicule. Why, my woman, I never saw you look one 'alf so 'an'some as you do now!"

"But the disgrace of it, John!" said Alice, hanging her head, and so hiding the pleasure that would dawn through all the mist of her misery.

"Let your father and mother settle that betwixt 'em, Alice. 'Tain't none o' my business. Please God, we'll do different—When shall it be, my girl?"

"When you like, John," answered Alice, without raising her head, thoughtfully.

When she had withdrawn herself from the too rigorous embrace with which he received her consent, she remarked—

"I do believe, John, money ain't a good thing! Sure as I live, with the very wind o' that money, the devil entered into me. Didn't you hate me, John? Speak the truth now."

"No, Alice. I did cry a bit over you, though. You was possessed like."

"I was possessed. I do believe if that money hadn't been took from me, I'd never ha' had you, John. Ain't it awful to think on?"

"Well, no. O' coorse! How could ye?" said Jephson—with reluctance.

"Now, John, don't ye talk like that, for I won't stand it. Don't you go for to set me up again with excusin' of me. I'm a nasty conceited cat, I am—and all for nothing but mean pride."

"Mind ye, ye're mine now, Alice; an' what's mine's mine, an' I won't have it abused. I knows you twice the woman you was afore, and all the world couldn't gi' me such another Christmas-box—no, not if it was all gold watches and roast beef."

When Mr. Greatorex returned to his wife's room, and thought to find her asleep as he had left her, he was dismayed to hear sounds of soft weeping from the bed. Some tone or stray word, never intended to reach her ear, had been enough to reveal the truth concerning her baby.

"Hush! hush!" he said, with more love in his heart than had moved there for many months, and therefore more in his tone than she had heard for as many—"if you cry you will be ill. Hush, my dear!"

In a moment, ere he could prevent her, she had flung her arms around his neck as he stooped over her.

"Husband! husband!" she cried, "is it my fault?"

"You behaved perfectly," he returned. "No woman could have been braver."

"Ah, but I wouldn't stay at home when you wanted me."

"Never mind that now, my child," he said.

At the word she pulled his face down to hers.

"I have you, and I don't care," he added.

"Do you care to have me?" she said, with a sob that ended in a loud cry. "Oh! I don't deserve it. But I will be good after this. I promise you I will."

"Then you must begin now, my darling. You must lie perfectly still, and not cry a bit, or you will go after the baby, and I shall be left alone."

She looked up at him with such a light in her face as he had never dreamed of there before. He had never seen her so lovely. Then she withdrew her arms, repressed her tears, smiled, and turned her face away. He put her hands under the clothes, and in a minute or two she was again fast asleep.

Chapter VII.

That day, when Phosy and her father had sat down to their Christmas dinner, he rose again, and taking her up as she sat, chair and all, set her down close to him, on the other side of the corner of the table. It was the first of a new covenant between them. The father's eyes having been suddenly opened to her character and preciousness, as well as to his own neglected duty in regard to her, it was as if a well of life had burst forth at his feet. And every day, as he looked in her face and talked to her, it was with more and more respect for what he found in her, with growing tenderness for her predilections,[60] and reverence for the divine idea enclosed in her ignorance, for her childish wisdom, and her calm seeking—until at length he would have been horrified at the thought of training her up in his way: had she not a way of her own to go—following—not the dead Jesus, but Him who liveth for evermore?[61] In the endeavour to help her, he had to find his own position towards the truth; and the results were weighty—Nor did the child's influence work forward merely. In his interactions with her he was so often reminded of his first wife, and that, with the gloss or comment of a childish reproduction, that his memories of her at length grew a little tender, and through the child he began to understand the nature and worth of the mother. In her child she had given him what she could not be herself. Unable to keep up with him, she had handed him her baby, and dropped on the path.

Nor was little Sophy his only comfort. Through their common loss and her husband's tenderness, Letty began to grow a woman. And her growth was the more rapid that, himself taught through Phosy, her husband no longer desired to make her adopt his tastes, and judge with his experiences, but, as became the elder and the tried, entered into her tastes

---

60. Preferences.
61. "I am he that liveth, and was dead; and, behold, I am alive for evermore" (Rev. 1:18 KJV).

and experiences—became, as it were, a child again with her, that, through the thing she was, he might help the thing she had to be.

As soon as she was able to bear it, he told her the story of the dead Jesus, and with the tale came to her heart love for Phosy. She had lost a son for a season, but she had gained a daughter for ever.

Such were the gifts the Christ-child brought to one household that Christmas. And the days of the mourning of that household were ended.[62]

---

62. "Thy sun shall no more go down; neither shall thy moon withdraw itself; for the LORD shall be thine everlasting light, and the days of thy mourning shall be ended" (Isa. 60:20 KJV).

CHRISTMAS EVE STORY

FANNY JACKSON COPPIN

This story is short and sweet. In fact, it is the shortest tale in this whole collection. Nevertheless, despite its brevity, it has a way of lingering with you and coming back to mind. Its message is one we need to hear again and again: what most people would think of as a burden might actually be a blessing, if only we could see it through eyes of faith and love. "Christmas Eve Story" was first published in the December 23, 1880, issue of the Christian Recorder, a publication of the African Methodist Episcopal Church (AME). Fanny Jackson Coppin (1837–1913) was born into slavery. Her intellectual gifts were apparent when she was young, and after emancipation she became one of the first Black women in the United States to earn a college degree, graduating from Oberlin College in 1865. She was an educator, a school principal, and the first African American to become the superintendent of a school district. Her husband was an AME bishop and they served for a time as missionaries in South Africa. Coppin also wrote a memoir, Reminiscences of School Life and Hints on Teaching (1913).

CHRISTMAS EVE STORY

FANNY JACKSON COPPIN

Once upon a time, there was a little girl named Maggie Devins, and she had a brother named Johnny, just one year older than she. Here they both are. Now if they could they would get up and make you a bow. But dear me! we all get so fastened down in pictures that we have to keep as quiet as mice, or we'd tear the paper all to pieces. I'm going to tell you something about this little boy and girl, and perhaps some little reader will remember it. You see how very clean and neat both of these look. Well, if you had seen them when Grandma Devins first found them you never would have thought that they could be made to look as nice as this. Now hear their story:

Last Christmas eve while Grandma Devins was sitting by her bright fire, there was a loud knock at the door, and upon opening it, she found a policeman who had in his arms two children that were nearly dead.

"I come, mum,"[1] he said, "to ask you if you will let these poor little young ones stay here to-night in your kitchen; their mother has just died from the fever. She lived in an old hovel around in Acorn Alley, and I'm afraid to leave the young ones there to-night, for they're half starved and half frozen to death now. God pity the poor, mum, God pity the poor, for it's hard upon them, such weather as this."

---

1. He is using "mum" as a title of respect for a woman similar to "ma'am."

Meanwhile, Grandma Devins had pulled her big sofa up to the fire and was standing looking down upon the dirty and pinched little faces before her. She didn't say anything, but she just kept looking at the children and wiping her eyes and blowing her nose. All at once she turned around as if she had been shot; she flew to the pantry and brought out some milk which she put on the fire to boil. And very soon she had two steaming cups of hot milk with a nice biscuit broken into it, and with this she fed the poor little creatures until a little color came into their faces, and she knew that she had given them enough for that time.

The policeman said he would call for the children in the morning and take them to the almshouse.[2] The fact is the policeman was a kind-hearted man, and he secretly hoped that he could get some one to take the children and be kind to them.

As soon as Maggie and Johnny had had their nice warm milk they began to talk. Johnny asked Grandma Devins if she had anybody to give her Christmas presents, and Grandma said, "no." But Maggie spoke up and said her mumma told her before she died that God always gave Christmas presents to those who had no one to give them any. And throwing her arms around Grandma's neck she said, "God will not forget you, dear lady, for you've been so good to us." Like a flash of light it passed through Grandma Devins' mind that God had sent her these children as her Christmas gift. So she said at once:

"Children, I made a mistake. I *have* had a Christmas present."

"There," said Maggie, "I knew you would get one; I knew it." When the policeman came in the morning his heart was overjoyed to see the "young ones," as he called them, nicely washed and sitting by the fire bundled up in some of Grandma Devins' dresses. She had burnt every stitch of the few dirty rags which they had on the night before. So that accounted for their being muffled up so.

---

2. An institution for the poor. (They would end up in an orphanage.)

"You can go right away, policeman; these children are my Christmas gift, and please God I'll be mother and father both, to the poor little orphans."

A year has passed since then, and she says that Johnny and Maggie are the best Christmas gifts that any old woman ever had. She has taught Maggie to darn[3] and sew neatly, and one of these days she will be able to earn money as a seamstress. Have you noticed her little needle-case hanging against the wall? Do you see the basket of apples on one side? Johnny was paring them when Maggie asked him to show her about her arithmetic, for Johnny goes to school, but Maggie stays at home and helps Grandma. Now as soon as Grandma comes back she is going to make them some mince pies for Christmas. Johnny will finish paring the apples while Maggie is stoning the raisins.[4] Oh! what a happy time they will have to-morrow. For I will whisper in your ear, little reader, that Grandma Devins is going to bring home something else with her than raisins. The same kind-hearted policeman that I told you about in the beginning, has made Johnny a beautiful sled, and painted the name "Hero" on it. Grandma has bought for Maggie the nicest little hood and cloak that ever you saw. Is not that nice? I guess if they knew what they're going to get they wouldn't sit so quietly as we see them; they'd jump up and dance about the floor, even if they tore the paper all to pieces. Oh I let every little boy and girl thank our loving heavenly Father for the blessed gift of His dear Son on the first Christmas day, eighteen hundred and eighty years ago.

---

3. To repair a hole in a piece of cloth.
4. To pare an apple is to cut its skin off and to stone a raisin is to remove the seeds from it.

AUNT CYRILLA'S CHRISTMAS BASKET

L. M. MONTGOMERY

This is a light and pleasant story. The holiday season calls us to rise above our embarrassments and annoyances and even disappointments. For one, there is no shame in being "countrified," as Aunt Cyrilla reminds us all. Even when life is not going as they would wish, Christmas can bring the best out of people if only they will let it. This edition of "Aunt Cyrilla's Christmas Basket" has been copied word for word from a clipping of the origin publication in a magazine that the author, Lucy Maud Montgomery (1874–1942), herself saved. It does not say on it when or where it was published, but scholars believe it was originally published in a journal called Young People in 1902 or 1903. Montgomery is a beloved Canadian author. She was a devout Christian, and her husband was a Presbyterian minister. L. M. Montgomery is most famous for her novels about her character Anne Shirley. There are six books in the series that are focused on Anne herself and five more related ones that are set in the same fictional world. Begin at the beginning with the celebrated Anne of Green Gables (1908), which starts telling Anne's story when she is eleven years old. It even includes a chapter (chapter 25, "Matthew Insists on Puffed Sleeves"), which is a humorous and charming Christmas story.

AUNT CYRILLA'S CHRISTMAS BASKET

L. M. MONTGOMERY

When Lucy Rose met Aunt Cyrilla coming downstairs, somewhat flushed and breathless from her ascent to the garret,[1] with a big, flat-covered basket hanging over her plump arm, she gave a little sigh of despair. Lucy Rose had done her brave best for some years—in fact, ever since she had put up her hair and lengthened her skirts—to break Aunt Cyrilla of the habit of carrying that basket with her every time she went to Pembroke;[2] but Aunt Cyrilla still insisted on taking it, and only laughed at what she called Lucy Rose's "finicky notions." Lucy Rose had a horrible, haunting idea that it was extremely provincial for her aunt always to take the big basket, packed full of country good things, whenever she went to visit Edward and Geraldine. Geraldine was so stylish, and might think it queer;[3] and then Aunt Cyrilla always would carry it on her arm and give cookies and apples and molasses taffy out of it to every child she encountered and, just as often as not, to older folks too. Lucy Rose, when she went to town with Aunt Cyrilla, felt chagrined

---

1. The attic.
2. Pembroke, Ontario, Canada.
3. Odd.

over this—all of which goes to prove that Lucy was as yet very young and had a great deal to learn in this world.

That troublesome worry over what Geraldine would think nerved her to make a protest in this instance.

"Now, Aunt C'rilla," she pleaded, "you're surely not going to take that funny old basket to Pembroke this time—Christmas Day and all."

"'Deed and 'deed I am," returned Aunt Cyrilla briskly, as she put it on the table and proceeded to dust it out. "I never went to see Edward and Geraldine since they were married that I didn't take a basket of good things along with me for them, and I'm not going to stop now. As for it's being Christmas, all the more reason. Edward is always real glad to get some of the old farmhouse goodies. He says they beat city cooking all hollow, and so they do."

'But it's so countrified," moaned Lucy Rose.

"Well, I am countrified," said Aunt Cyrilla firmly, "and so are you. And what's more, I don't see that it's anything to be ashamed of. You've got some real silly pride about you, Lucy Rose. You'll grow out of it in time, but just now it is giving you a lot of trouble."

"The basket is a lot of trouble," said Lucy Rose crossly. "You're always mislaying it or afraid you will. And it does look so funny to be walking through the streets with that big, bulgy basket hanging on your arm."

"I'm not a mite worried about its looks," returned Aunt Cyrilla calmly. "As for its being a trouble, why, maybe it is, but I have that, and other people have the pleasure of it. Edward and Geraldine don't need it—I know that—but there may be those that will. And if it hurts your feelings to walk 'longside of a countrified old lady with a countrified basket, why, you can just fall behind, as it were."

Aunt Cyrilla nodded and smiled good-humouredly, and Lucy Rose, though she privately held to her own opinion, had to smile too.

"Now, let me see," said Aunt Cyrilla reflectively, tapping the snowy kitchen table with the point of her plump, dimpled forefinger, "what shall I take? That big fruit cake for one thing—Edward does like my fruit cake; and that cold boiled tongue[4] for another. Those three mince pies too, they'd spoil before we got back or your uncle'd make himself sick eating them—mince pie is his besetting sin. And that little stone bottle full of cream—Geraldine may carry any amount of style, but I've yet to see her look down on real good country cream, Lucy Rose; and another bottle of my raspberry vinegar. That plate of jelly cookies and doughnuts will please the children and fill up the chinks,[5] and you can bring me that box of ice-cream candy out of the pantry, and that bag of striped candy sticks your uncle brought home from the corner last night. And apples, of course—three or four dozen of those good eaters—and a little pot of my greengage preserves[6]—Edward'll like that. And some sandwiches and pound cake for a snack for ourselves. Now, I guess that will do for eatables. The presents for the children can go in on top. There's a doll for Daisy and the little boat your uncle made for Ray and a tatted lace handkerchief apiece for the twins, and the crochet hood for the baby. Now, is that all?"

"There's a cold roast chicken in the pantry," said Lucy Rose wickedly, "and the pig Uncle Leo killed is hanging up in the porch. Couldn't you put them in too?"

Aunt Cyrilla smiled broadly. "Well, I guess we'll leave the pig alone; but since you have reminded me of it, the chicken may as well go in. I can make room."

Lucy Rose, in spite of her prejudices, helped with the packing and, not having been trained under Aunt Cyrilla's eye for nothing, did it very well too, with much clever economy of space. But when Aunt Cyrilla had

4. A cut of beef.
5. Gaps—yet more things to eat to make sure the children end up totally full.
6. Plum.

put in as a finishing touch a big bouquet of pink and white everlastings, and tied the bulging covers down with a firm hand, Lucy Rose stood over the basket and whispered vindictively:

"Some day I'm going to burn this basket—when I get courage enough. Then there'll be an end of lugging it everywhere we go like a—like an old market-woman."

Uncle Leopold came in just then, shaking his head dubiously. He was not going to spend Christmas with Edward and Geraldine, and perhaps the prospect of having to cook and eat his Christmas dinner all alone made him pessimistic.

"I mistrust you folks won't get to Pembroke tomorrow," he said sagely. "It's going to storm."

Aunt Cyrilla did not worry over this. She believed matters of this kind were fore-ordained, and she slept calmly. But Lucy Rose got up three times in the night to see if it were storming, and when she did sleep had horrible nightmares of struggling through blinding snowstorms dragging Aunt Cyrilla's Christmas basket along with her.

It was not snowing in the early morning, and Uncle Leopold drove Aunt Cyrilla and Lucy Rose and the basket to the station, four miles off. When they reached there the air was thick with flying flakes. The station-master sold them their tickets with a grim face.

"If there's any more snow comes, the trains might as well keep Christmas too," he said. "There's been so much snow already that traffic is blocked half the time, and now there ain't no place to shovel the snow off onto."

Aunt Cyrilla said that if the train were to get to Pembroke in time for Christmas, it would get there; and she opened her basket and gave the stationmaster and three small boys an apple apiece.

"That's the beginning," groaned Lucy Rose to herself.

When their train came along Aunt Cyrilla established herself in one seat and her basket in another, and looked beamingly around her at her fellow travellers.

These were few in number—a delicate little woman at the end of the car, with a baby and four other children, a young girl across the aisle with a pale, pretty face, a sunburned lad three seats ahead in a khaki uniform,[7] a very handsome, imposing old lady in a sealskin coat ahead of him, and a thin young man with spectacles opposite.

"A minister," reflected Aunt Cyrilla, beginning to classify, "who takes better care of other folks' souls than of his own body; and that woman in the sealskin is discontented and cross at something—got up too early to catch the train, maybe; and that young chap must be one of the boys not long out of the hospital. That woman's children look as if they hadn't enjoyed a square meal since they were born; and if that girl across from me has a mother, I'd like to know what the woman means, letting her daughter go from home in this weather in clothes like that."

Lucy Rose merely wondered uncomfortably what the others thought of Aunt Cyrilla's basket.

They expected to reach Pembroke that night, but as the day wore on the storm grew worse. Twice the train had to stop while the train hands[8] dug it out. The third time it could not go on. It was dusk when the conductor came through the train, replying brusquely to the questions of the anxious passengers.

"A nice lookout for Christmas—no, impossible to go on or back—track blocked for miles—what's that, madam?—no, no station near—woods for miles. We're here for the night. These storms of late have played the mischief with everything."

---

7. As will become clear, he is a soldier who, because Canada was part of the British Empire, has been fighting in the South Africa War (1899–1902). This conflict is also sometimes called the Boer War or the Second Boer War.
8. Employees.

"Oh, dear," groaned Lucy Rose.

Aunt Cyrilla looked at her basket complacently. "At any rate, we won't starve," she said.

The pale, pretty girl seemed indifferent. The sealskin lady looked crosser than ever. The khaki boy said, "Just my luck," and two of the children began to cry. Aunt Cyrilla took some apples and striped candy sticks from her basket and carried them to them. She lifted the oldest into her ample lap and soon had them all around her, laughing and contented.

The rest of the travellers straggled over to the corner and drifted into conversation. The khaki boy said it was hard lines not to get home for Christmas, after all.

"I was invalided from South Africa three months ago, and I've been in the hospital at Netley[9] ever since. Reached Halifax three days ago and telegraphed the old folks I'd eat my Christmas dinner with them, and to have an extra-big turkey because I didn't have any last year. They'll be badly disappointed."

He looked disappointed too. One khaki sleeve hung empty by his side. Aunt Cyrilla passed him an apple.

"We were all going down to Grandpa's for Christmas," said the little mother's oldest boy dolefully. "We've never been there before, and it's just too bad."

He looked as if he wanted to cry but thought better of it and bit off a mouthful of candy.

"Will there be any Santa Claus on the train?" demanded his small sister tearfully. "Jack says there won't."

"I guess he'll find you out," said Aunt Cyrilla reassuringly.

The pale, pretty girl came up and took the baby from the tired mother. "What a dear little fellow," she said softly.

---

9. Netley Royal Victoria Military Hospital, near Southampton, England.

"Are you going home for Christmas too?" asked Aunt Cyrilla.

The girl shook her head. "I haven't any home. I'm just a shop girl out of work at present, and I'm going to Pembroke to look for some."

Aunt Cyrilla went to her basket and took out her box of cream candy. "I guess we might as well enjoy ourselves. Let's eat it all up and have a good time. Maybe we'll get down to Pembroke in the morning."

The little group grew cheerful as they nibbled, and even the pale girl brightened up. The little mother told Aunt Cyrilla her story aside. She had been long estranged from her family, who had disapproved of her marriage. Her husband had died the previous summer, leaving her in poor circumstances.

"Father wrote to me last week and asked me to let bygones be by-gones and come home for Christmas. I was so glad. And the children's hearts were set on it. It seems too bad that we are not to get there. I have to be back at work the morning after Christmas."

The khaki boy came up again and shared the candy. He told amusing stories of campaigning in South Africa. The minister came too, and lis-tened, and even the sealskin lady turned her head over her shoulder.

By and by the children fell asleep, one on Aunt Cyrilla's lap and one on Lucy Rose's, and two on the seat. Aunt Cyrilla and the pale girl helped the mother make up beds for them. The minister gave his overcoat and the sealskin lady came forward with a shawl.

"This will do for the baby," she said.

"We must get up some Santa Claus for these youngsters," said the khaki boy. "Let's hang their stockings on the wall and fill 'em up as best we can. I've nothing about me but some hard cash and a jack-knife. I'll give each of 'em a quarter and the boy can have the knife."

"I've nothing but money either," said the sealskin lady regretfully.

Aunt Cyrilla glanced at the little mother. She had fallen asleep with her head against the seat-back.

"I've got a basket over there," said Aunt Cyrilla firmly, "and I've some presents in it that I was taking to my nephew's children. I'm going to give 'em to these. As for the money, I think the mother is the one for it to go to. She's been telling me her story, and a pitiful one it is. Let's make up a little purse[10] among us for a Christmas present."

The idea met with favour. The khaki boy passed his cap and everybody contributed. The sealskin lady put in a crumpled note. When Aunt Cyrilla straightened it out she saw that it was for twenty dollars.[11]

Meanwhile, Lucy Rose had brought the basket. She smiled at Aunt Cyrilla as she lugged it down the aisle and Aunt Cyrilla smiled back. Lucy Rose had never touched that basket of her own accord before.

Ray's boat went to Jacky, and Daisy's doll to his oldest sister, the twins' lace handkerchiefs to the two smaller girls and the hood to the baby. Then the stockings were filled up with doughnuts and jelly cookies and the money was put in an envelope and pinned to the little mother's jacket.

"That baby is such a dear little fellow," said the sealskin lady gently. "He looks something like my little son. He died eighteen Christmases ago."

Aunt Cyrilla put her hand over the lady's kid glove. "So did mine," she said. Then the two women smiled tenderly at each other. Afterwards they rested from their labours and all had what Aunt Cyrilla called a "snack" of sandwiches and pound cake. The khaki boy said he hadn't tasted anything half so good since he left home.

"They didn't give us pound cake in South Africa," he said.

When morning came the storm was still raging. The children wakened and went wild with delight over their stockings. The little mother found her envelope and tried to utter thanks and broke down; and nobody knew what to say or do, when the conductor fortunately came in and made a

---

10. That is, let's take up a collection for her.
11. A laborer in Canada at this time needed to work full-time for about a month to earn twenty dollars.

Aunt Cyrilla's Christmas Basket

diversion by telling them they might as well resign themselves to spending Christmas on the train.

"This is serious," said the khaki boy, "when you consider that we've no provisions. Don't mind for myself, used to half rations or no rations at all. But these kiddies will have tremendous appetites."

Then Aunt Cyrilla rose to the occasion.

"I've got some emergency rations here," she announced. "There's plenty for all and we'll have our Christmas dinner, although a cold one. Breakfast first thing. There's a sandwich apiece left and we must fill up on what is left of the cookies and doughnuts and save the rest for a real good spread at dinner time. The only thing is, I haven't any bread."

"I've a box of soda crackers," said the little mother eagerly.

Nobody in that car will ever forget that Christmas. To begin with, after breakfast they had a concert. The khaki boy gave two recitations, sang three songs, and gave a whistling solo. Lucy Rose gave three recitations and the minister a comic reading. The pale shop girl sang two songs. It was agreed that the khaki boy's whistling solo was the best number, and Aunt Cyrilla gave him the bouquet of everlastings as a reward of merit.

Then the conductor came in with the cheerful news that the storm was almost over and he thought the track would be cleared in a few hours.

"If we can get to the next station we'll be all right," he said. "The branch joins the main line there and the tracks will be clear."

At noon they had dinner. The train hands were invited in to share it. The minister carved the chicken with the brakeman's jack-knife and the khaki boy cut up the tongue and the mince pies, while the sealskin lady mixed the raspberry vinegar with its due proportion of water. Bits of paper served as plates. The train furnished a couple of glasses, a tin pint cup was discovered and given to the children, Aunt Cyrilla and Lucy Rose and the sealskin lady drank, turn about, from the latter's graduated medicine glass, the shop girl and the little mother shared one of the empty bottles, and the khaki boy, the minister, and the train men drank out of the other bottle.

Everybody declared they had never enjoyed a meal more in their lives. Certainly it was a merry one, and Aunt Cyrilla's cooking was never more appreciated; indeed, the bones of the chicken and the pot of preserves were all that was left. They could not eat the preserves because they had no spoons, so Aunt Cyrilla gave them to the little mother.

When all was over, a hearty vote of thanks was passed to Aunt Cyrilla and her basket. The sealskin lady wanted to know how she made her pound cake, and the khaki boy asked for her receipt for jelly cookies. And when two hours later the conductor came in and said the snowploughs had got along and they'd soon be starting, they all wondered if it could really be less than twenty-four hours since they met.

"I feel as if I'd been campaigning with you all my life," said the khaki boy.

At the next station they all parted. The little mother and the children had to take the next train back home. The minister stayed there, and the khaki boy and the sealskin lady changed trains. The sealskin lady shook Aunt Cyrilla's hand. She no longer looked discontented or cross.

"This has been the pleasantest Christmas I have ever spent," she said heartily. "I shall never forget that wonderful basket of yours. The little shop girl is going home with me. I've promised her a place in my husband's store."

When Aunt Cyrilla and Lucy Rose reached Pembroke there was nobody to meet them because everyone had given up expecting them. It was not far from the station to Edward's house and Aunt Cyrilla elected to walk.

"I'll carry the basket," said Lucy Rose.

Aunt Cyrilla relinquished it with a smile. Lucy Rose smiled too.

"It's a blessed old basket," said the latter, "and I love it. Please forget all the silly things I ever said about it, Aunt C'rilla."

THE GOBLINS WHO STOLE A SEXTON
CHARLES DICKENS

*C*harles Dickens (1812–1870) is the most celebrated novelist of
Victorian England. He also wrote the most famous Christmas
story of them all, the novella A Christmas Carol (1843). The holiday
season was traditionally a time for ghost stories. While that practice has
largely died out, the memory of it is kept alive in the Christmas song "It's
the Most Wonderful Time of the Year": "There'll be scary ghost stories
/ And tales of the glories of / Christmases long, long ago." And it is easy
to forget that A Christmas Carol is a ghost story. In fact, its subtitle
is "Being a Ghost Story of Christmas." It is also not well known that
A Christmas Carol is a reworking of another story that Dickens had
written years earlier, "The Goblins Who Stole a Sexton." This story
appeared in Dickens's first novel, The Pickwick Papers (published seri-
ally in 1836–37). When you read "The Goblins Who Stole a Sexton,"
you might want to see if you can identify parallels with Ebenezer Scrooge,
Tiny Tim, and the like. Dickens often got paid by the word and thus his
books can be quite long! In addition to reading or rereading A Christmas Carol, you could also begin by trying one of his shorter novels:
Hard Times (1854) includes a satire of schooling that does not foster
the imagination; and A Tale of Two Cities (1859) is an adventurous
story set during the dangerous times of the French Revolution.

THE GOBLINS WHO STOLE A SEXTON

CHARLES DICKENS

In an old abbey town,[1] down in this part of the country, a long, long while ago—so long, that the story must be a true one, because our great-grandfathers implicitly believed it—there officiated as sexton[2] and grave-digger in the churchyard, one Gabriel Grub. It by no means follows that because a man is a sexton, and constantly surrounded by the emblems of mortality, therefore he should be a morose and melancholy man; your undertakers are the merriest fellows in the world; and I once had the honour of being on intimate terms with a mute, who in private life, and off duty, was as comical and jocose a little fellow as ever chirped out a devil-may-care song, without a hitch in his memory, or drained off a good stiff glass without stopping for breath. But notwithstanding these precedents to the contrary, Gabriel Grub was an ill-conditioned, cross-grained, surly fellow—a morose and lonely man, who consorted with nobody but himself, and an old wicker bottle which fitted into his large deep waistcoat

1. A town in Britain where there had been a monastery before they had been disbanded in the sixteenth century as part of the Reformation.
2. The maintenance man responsible for taking care of the church building and surrounding property, which included a graveyard.

pocket—and who eyed each merry face, as it passed him by, with such a deep scowl of malice and ill-humour, as it was difficult to meet without feeling something the worse for.

A little before twilight, one Christmas Eve, Gabriel shouldered his spade, lighted his lantern, and betook himself towards the old churchyard; for he had got a grave to finish by next morning, and, feeling very low, he thought it might raise his spirits, perhaps, if he went on with his work at once. As he went his way, up the ancient street, he saw the cheerful light of the blazing fires gleam through the old casements,[3] and heard the loud laugh and the cheerful shouts of those who were assembled around them; he marked the bustling preparations for next day's cheer, and smelled the numerous savoury odours consequent thereupon, as they steamed up from the kitchen windows in clouds. All this was gall and wormwood[4] to the heart of Gabriel Grub; and when groups of children bounded out of the houses, tripped across the road, and were met, before they could knock at the opposite door, by half a dozen curly-headed little rascals who crowded round them as they flocked upstairs to spend the evening in their Christmas games, Gabriel smiled grimly, and clutched the handle of his spade with a firmer grasp, as he thought of measles, scarlet fever, thrush, whooping-cough, and a good many other sources of consolation besides.

In this happy frame of mind, Gabriel strode along, returning a short, sullen growl to the good-humoured greetings of such of his neighbours as now and then passed him, until he turned into the dark lane which led to the churchyard. Now, Gabriel had been looking forward to reaching the dark lane, because it was, generally speaking, a nice, gloomy, mournful place, into which the townspeople did not much care to go, except in broad daylight, and when the sun was shining; consequently, he was not a

---

3. Windows.
4. Bitterness. "Gall and wormwood" is an allusion to Deuteronomy 29:18 (KJV).

little indignant to hear a young urchin[5] roaring out some jolly song about a merry Christmas, in this very sanctuary which had been called Coffin Lane ever since the days of the old abbey, and the time of the shaven-headed monks. As Gabriel walked on, and the voice drew nearer, he found it proceeded from a small boy, who was hurrying along, to join one of the little parties in the old street, and who, partly to keep himself company, and partly to prepare himself for the occasion, was shouting out the song at the highest pitch of his lungs. So Gabriel waited until the boy came up, and then dodged him into a corner, and rapped him over the head with his lantern five or six times, just to teach him to modulate his voice. And as the boy hurried away with his hand to his head, singing quite a different sort of tune, Gabriel Grub chuckled very heartily to himself, and entered the churchyard, locking the gate behind him.

He took off his coat, set down his lantern, and getting into the unfinished grave, worked at it for an hour or so with right good will. But the earth was hardened with the frost, and it was no very easy matter to break it up, and shovel it out; and although there was a moon, it was a very young one, and shed little light upon the grave, which was in the shadow of the church. At any other time, these obstacles would have made Gabriel Grub very moody and miserable, but he was so well pleased with having stopped the small boy's singing, that he took little heed of the scanty progress he had made, and looked down into the grave, when he had finished work for the night, with grim satisfaction, murmuring as he gathered up his things—

Brave lodgings for one, brave lodgings for one,
A few feet of cold earth, when life is done;
A stone at the head, a stone at the feet,
A rich, juicy meal for the worms to eat;

5. A child who is poor and often ragged.

Rank grass overhead, and damp clay around,

Brave lodgings for one, these, in holy ground!

"Ho! ho!" laughed Gabriel Grub, as he sat himself down on a flat tombstone which was a favourite resting-place of his, and drew forth his wicker bottle. "A coffin at Christmas! A Christmas box![6] Ho! ho! ho!"

"Ho! ho! ho!" repeated a voice which sounded close behind him.

Gabriel paused, in some alarm, in the act of raising the wicker bottle to his lips, and looked round. The bottom of the oldest grave about him was not more still and quiet than the churchyard in the pale moonlight. The cold hoar[7] frost glistened on the tombstones, and sparkled like rows of gems, among the stone carvings of the old church. The snow lay hard and crisp upon the ground; and spread over the thickly-strewn mounds of earth, so white and smooth a cover that it seemed as if corpses lay there, hidden only by their winding sheets. Not the faintest rustle broke the profound tranquility of the solemn scene. Sound itself appeared to be frozen up, all was so cold and still.

"It was the echoes," said Gabriel Grub, raising the bottle to his lips again.

"It was *not*," said a deep voice.

Gabriel started up, and stood rooted to the spot with astonishment and terror; for his eyes rested on a form that made his blood run cold.

Seated on an upright tombstone, close to him, was a strange, unearthly figure, whom Gabriel felt at once, was no being of this world. His long, fantastic legs which might have reached the ground, were cocked up, and crossed after a quaint, fantastic fashion; his sinewy[8] arms were bare; and his hands rested on his knees. On his short, round body, he wore a close covering, ornamented with small slashes; a short cloak dangled

---

6. A Christmas box was a box to put money in as a collection for a Christmas tip or bonus for people who provided services throughout the year.
7. Gray-looking.
8. Muscular.

at his back; the collar was cut into curious peaks, which served the goblin in lieu of ruff or neckerchief; and his shoes curled up at his toes into long points. On his head, he wore a broad-brimmed sugar-loaf hat,[9] garnished with a single feather. The hat was covered with the white frost; and the goblin looked as if he had sat on the same tombstone very comfortably, for two or three hundred years. He was sitting perfectly still; his tongue was put out, as if in derision; and he was grinning at Gabriel Grub with such a grin as only a goblin could call up.

"It was *not* the echoes," said the goblin.

Gabriel Grub was paralysed, and could make no reply.

"What do you do here on Christmas Eve?" said the goblin sternly.

"I came to dig a grave, Sir," stammered Gabriel Grub.

"What man wanders among graves and churchyards on such a night as this?" cried the goblin.

"Gabriel Grub! Gabriel Grub!" screamed a wild chorus of voices that seemed to fill the churchyard. Gabriel looked fearfully round—nothing was to be seen.

"What have you got in that bottle?" said the goblin.

"Hollands, Sir," replied the sexton, trembling more than ever; for he had bought it of the smugglers, and he thought that perhaps his questioner might be in the excise department of the goblins.[10]

"Who drinks Hollands alone, and in a churchyard, on such a night as this?" said the goblin.

"Gabriel Grub! Gabriel Grub!" exclaimed the wild voices again.

The goblin leered maliciously at the terrified sexton, and then raising his voice, exclaimed—

---

9. A style of hat with a cone-shaped top.

10. "Hollands" is a type of gin so named because it is made in Holland. The excise department is a branch of the British government in charge of collecting duties or taxes. His drink is contraband; he has illegally evaded paying the required taxes.

"And who, then, is our fair and lawful prize?"

To this inquiry the invisible chorus replied, in a strain that sounded like the voices of many choristers singing to the mighty swell of the old church organ—a strain that seemed borne to the sexton's ears upon a wild wind, and to die away as it passed onward; but the burden of the reply was still the same, "Gabriel Grub! Gabriel Grub!"

The goblin grinned a broader grin than before, as he said, "Well, Gabriel, what do you say to this?"

The sexton gasped for breath.

"What do you think of this, Gabriel?" said the goblin, kicking up his feet in the air on either side of the tombstone, and looking at the turned-up points with as much complacency as if he had been contemplating the most fashionable pair of Wellingtons in all Bond Street.[11]

"It's—it's—very curious, Sir," replied the sexton, half dead with fright; "very curious, and very pretty, but I think I'll go back and finish my work, Sir, if you please."

"Work!" said the goblin, "what work?"

"The grave, Sir; making the grave," stammered the sexton.

"Oh, the grave, eh?" said the goblin; "who makes graves at a time when all other men are merry, and takes a pleasure in it?"

Again the mysterious voices replied, "Gabriel Grub! Gabriel Grub!"

"I am afraid my friends want you, Gabriel," said the goblin, thrusting his tongue farther into his cheek than ever—and a most astonishing tongue it was—"I'm afraid my friends want you, Gabriel," said the goblin.

"Under favour, Sir," replied the horror-stricken sexton, "I don't think they can, Sir; they don't know me, Sir; I don't think the gentlemen have ever seen me, Sir."

"Oh, yes, they have," replied the goblin; "we know the man with the

11. "Wellingtons" are a style of boots. Bond Street in the West End of London was where the wealthy did their clothes shopping.

sulky face and grim scowl, that came down the street to-night, throwing his evil looks at the children, and grasping his burying-spade the tighter. We know the man who struck the boy in the envious malice of his heart, because the boy could be merry, and he could not. We know him, we know him."

Here, the goblin gave a loud, shrill laugh, which the echoes returned twentyfold; and throwing his legs up in the air, stood upon his head, or rather upon the very point of his sugar-loaf hat, on the narrow edge of the tombstone, whence he threw a Somerset[12] with extraordinary agility, right to the sexton's feet, at which he planted himself in the attitude in which tailors generally sit upon the shop-board.

"I—I—am afraid I must leave you, Sir," said the sexton, making an effort to move.

"Leave us!" said the goblin, "Gabriel Grub going to leave us. Ho! ho! ho!"

As the goblin laughed, the sexton observed, for one instant, a brilliant illumination within the windows of the church, as if the whole building were lighted up; it disappeared, the organ pealed forth a lively air, and whole troops of goblins, the very counterpart of the first one, poured into the churchyard, and began playing at leap-frog with the tombstones, never stopping for an instant to take breath, but "overing" the highest among them, one after the other, with the most marvellous dexterity. The first goblin was a most astonishing leaper, and none of the others could come near him; even in the extremity of his terror the sexton could not help observing, that while his friends were content to leap over the common-sized gravestones, the first one took the family vaults, iron railings and all, with as much ease as if they had been so many street-posts.

At last the game reached to a most exciting pitch; the organ played

---

12. Somersault.

quicker and quicker, and the goblins leaped faster and faster, coiling them-selves up, rolling head over heels upon the ground, and bounding over the tombstones like footballs. The sexton's brain whirled round with the rapidity of the motion he beheld, and his legs reeled beneath him, as the spirits flew before his eyes; when the goblin king, suddenly darting towards him, laid his hand upon his collar, and sank with him through the earth.

When Gabriel Grub had had time to fetch his breath, which the rapidity of his descent had for the moment taken away, he found himself in what appeared to be a large cavern, surrounded on all sides by crowds of goblins, ugly and grim; in the centre of the room, on an elevated seat, was stationed his friend of the churchyard; and close behind him stood Gabriel Grub himself, without power of motion.

"Cold to-night," said the king of the goblins, "very cold. A glass of something warm here!"

At this command, half a dozen officious goblins, with a perpetual smile upon their faces, whom Gabriel Grub imagined to be courtiers, on that account, hastily disappeared, and presently returned with a goblet of liquid fire, which they presented to the king.

"Ah!" cried the goblin, whose cheeks and throat were transparent, as he tossed down the flame, "this warms one, indeed! Bring a bumper[13] of the same, for Mr. Grub."

It was in vain for the unfortunate sexton to protest that he was not in the habit of taking anything warm at night; one of the goblins held him while another poured the blazing liquid down his throat; the whole assembly screeched with laughter, as he coughed and choked, and wiped away the tears which gushed plentifully from his eyes, after swallowing the burning draught.

"And now," said the king, fantastically poking the taper[14] corner of

---

13. A full glass.
14. Pointed.

his sugar-loaf hat into the sexton's eye, and thereby occasioning him the most exquisite pain; "and now, show the man of misery and gloom, a few of the pictures from our own great storehouse!"

As the goblin said this, a thick cloud which obscured the remoter end of the cavern rolled gradually away, and disclosed, apparently at a great distance, a small and scantily furnished, but neat and clean apartment. A crowd of little children were gathered round a bright fire, clinging to their mother's gown, and gambolling[15] around her chair. The mother occasionally rose, and drew aside the window-curtain, as if to look for some expected object; a frugal meal was ready spread upon the table; and an elbow chair[16] was placed near the fire. A knock was heard at the door; the mother opened it, and the children crowded round her, and clapped their hands for joy, as their father entered. He was wet and weary, and shook the snow from his garments, as the children crowded round him, and seizing his cloak, hat, stick, and gloves, with busy zeal, ran with them from the room. Then, as he sat down to his meal before the fire, the children climbed about his knee, and the mother sat by his side, and all seemed happiness and comfort.

But a change came upon the view, almost imperceptibly. The scene was altered to a small bedroom, where the fairest and youngest child lay dying; the roses had fled from his cheek, and the light from his eye; and even as the sexton looked upon him with an interest he had never felt or known before, he died. His young brothers and sisters crowded round his little bed, and seized his tiny hand, so cold and heavy; but they shrank back from its touch, and looked with awe on his infant face; for calm and tranquil as it was, and sleeping in rest and peace as the beautiful child seemed to be, they saw that he was dead, and they knew that he

---

15. Running or moving playfully; jumping and dancing abound.
16. Armchair.

was an angel[17] looking down upon, and blessing them, from a bright and happy Heaven.

Again the light cloud passed across the picture, and again the subject changed. The father and mother were old and helpless now, and the number of those about them was diminished more than half; but content and cheerfulness sat on every face, and beamed in every eye, as they crowded round the fireside, and told and listened to old stories of earlier and bygone days. Slowly and peacefully, the father sank into the grave, and, soon after, the sharer of all his cares and troubles followed him to a place of rest. The few who yet survived them, kneeled by their tomb, and watered the green turf which covered it with their tears; then rose, and turned away, sadly and mournfully, but not with bitter cries, or despairing lamentations, for they knew that they should one day meet again; and once more they mixed with the busy world, and their content and cheerfulness were restored. The cloud settled upon the picture, and concealed it from the sexton's view.

"What do you think of *that*?" said the goblin, turning his large face towards Gabriel Grub.

Gabriel murmured out something about its being very pretty, and looked somewhat ashamed, as the goblin bent his fiery eyes upon him.

"You miserable man!" said the goblin, in a tone of excessive contempt. "You!" He appeared disposed to add more, but indignation choked his utterance, so he lifted up one of his very pliable legs, and, flourishing it above his head a little, to insure his aim, administered a good sound kick to Gabriel Grub; immediately after which, all the goblins in waiting crowded round the wretched sexton, and kicked him without mercy, according to the established and invariable custom of courtiers upon earth, who kick

---

17. Jesus taught that in the afterlife the redeemed will be "as the angels which are in heaven" (Mark 12:25 KJV), and Christmas stories sometimes over-read this to mean that God's people become angels when they die. (The film *It's a Wonderful Life* is a classic example.)

whom royalty kicks, and hug whom royalty hugs.

"Show him some more!" said the king of the goblins.

At these words, the cloud was dispelled, and a rich and beautiful landscape was disclosed to view—there is just such another, to this day, within half a mile of the old abbey town. The sun shone from out the clear blue sky, the water sparkled beneath his rays, and the trees looked greener, and the flowers more gay, beneath its cheering influence. The water rippled on with a pleasant sound, the trees rustled in the light wind that murmured among their leaves, the birds sang upon the boughs, and the lark carolled on high her welcome to the morning. Yes, it was morning; the bright, balmy morning of summer; the minutest leaf, the smallest blade of grass, was instinct with life. The ant crept forth to her daily toil, the butterfly fluttered and basked in the warm rays of the sun; myriads of insects spread their transparent wings, and revelled in their brief but happy existence. Man walked forth, elated with the scene; and all was brightness and splendour.

"*You* a miserable man!" said the king of the goblins, in a more contemptuous tone than before. And again the king of the goblins gave his leg a flourish; again it descended on the shoulders of the sexton; and again the attendant goblins imitated the example of their chief.

Many a time the cloud went and came, and many a lesson it taught to Gabriel Grub, who, although his shoulders smarted with pain from the frequent applications of the goblins' feet thereunto, looked on with an interest that nothing could diminish. He saw that men who worked hard, and earned their scanty bread with lives of labour, were cheerful and happy; and that to the most ignorant, the sweet face of Nature was a never-failing source of cheerfulness and joy. He saw those who had been delicately nurtured, and tenderly brought up, cheerful under privations, and superior to suffering, that would have crushed many of a rougher grain, because they bore within their own bosoms the materials of happiness, contentment, and peace. He saw that women, the tenderest and most fragile of all God's creatures, were the oftenest superior to sorrow, adversity, and distress; and he saw that it was because they bore, in their own hearts, an inexhaustible well-spring of affection and devotion. Above all, he saw that men like himself, who snarled at the mirth and cheerfulness of others, were the foulest weeds on the fair surface of the earth; and setting all the good of the world against the evil, he came to the conclusion that it was a very decent and respectable sort of world after all. No sooner had he formed it, than the cloud which had closed over the last picture, seemed to settle on his senses, and lull him to repose. One by one, the goblins faded from his sight; and, as the last one disappeared, he sank to sleep.

The day had broken when Gabriel Grub awoke, and found himself lying at full length on the flat gravestone in the churchyard, with the wicker bottle lying empty by his side, and his coat, spade, and lantern, all well whitened by the last night's frost, scattered on the ground. The stone on which he had first seen the goblin seated, stood bolt upright before him, and the grave at which he had worked, the night before, was not far off. At first, he began to doubt the reality of his adventures, but the acute pain in his shoulders when he attempted to rise assured him that the kicking of the goblins was certainly not ideal. He was staggered again, by observing no traces of footsteps in the snow on which the goblins had played at leap-frog with the gravestones, but he speedily accounted for this circumstance when he remembered that, being spirits, they would leave no visible impression behind them. So, Gabriel Grub got on his feet as well as he could, for the pain in his back; and, brushing the frost off his coat, put it on, and turned his face towards the town.

But he was an altered man, and he could not bear the thought of returning to a place where his repentance would be scoffed at, and his reformation disbelieved. He hesitated for a few moments; and then turned away to wander where he might, and seek his bread elsewhere.

The lantern, the spade, and the wicker bottle were found, that day, in the churchyard. There were a great many speculations about the sexton's fate, at first, but it was speedily determined that he had been carried away by the goblins; and there were not wanting some very credible witnesses who had distinctly seen him whisked through the air on the back of a chestnut horse blind of one eye, with the hind-quarters of a lion, and the tail of a bear. At length all this was devoutly believed; and the new sexton used to exhibit to the curious, for a trifling emolument,[18] a good-sized piece of the church weathercock[19] which had been accidentally kicked off by the aforesaid horse in his aerial flight, and picked up by himself in the churchyard, a year or two afterwards.

Unfortunately, these stories were somewhat disturbed by the unlooked-for reappearance of Gabriel Grub himself, some ten years afterwards, a ragged, contented, rheumatic old man. He told his story to the clergyman, and also to the mayor; and in course of time it began to be received as a matter of history, in which form it has continued down to this very day. The believers in the weathercock tale, having misplaced their confidence once, were not easily prevailed upon to part with it again, so they looked as wise as they could, shrugged their shoulders, touched their foreheads, and murmured something about Gabriel Grub having drunk all the Hollands, and then fallen asleep on the flat tombstone; and they affected to explain what he supposed he had witnessed in the goblin's cavern, by saying that he had seen the world, and grown wiser. But this opinion, which was by no means a popular one at any time, gradually died off; and be the matter how it may, as Gabriel Grub was afflicted with rheumatism to the end of his days, this story has at least one moral, if it teach no better one—and that is, that if a man turn sulky and drink by himself at Christmas time, he may make up his mind to be not a

---

18. Fee or charge.
19. Weathervane—a mechanical device for showing which way the wind is blowing.

bit the better for it: let the spirits be never so good, or let them be even as many degrees beyond proof, as those which Gabriel Grub saw in the goblin's cavern.

THE ROMANCE
OF A CHRISTMAS CARD
KATE DOUGLAS WIGGIN

The Romance of the Christmas Card *was published as a book in 1916. It is therefore really a novella rather than a short story. It is the longest reading in this collection, but it is broken into chapters so it can be read in stages. It is a light and happy tale of several different stories that all converge on one moonlit, snow-covered Christmas Eve. One thread is about Dick Larrabee. He grew up in the village of Beulah where everyone knows everyone—and has an opinion about them. Dick was a mischievous boy. He was, however, also a preacher's kid and therefore the dignified people of Beulah thought he should be especially well-behaved. Their harsh disproval of his antics drove him away. The American author Kate Douglas Wiggin (1856–1923) was also an educator. Her other yuletide tale,* The Birds' Christmas Carol (1888), *follows the holiday plans of the children of two large families.* Rebecca of Sunnybrook Farm (1903) *was so popular that it was turned into a Hollywood film starring the famous child actor Shirley Temple.*

THE ROMANCE OF A CHRISTMAS CARD

KATE DOUGLAS WIGGIN

CHAPTER 1

It was Christmas Eve and a Saturday night when Mrs. Larrabee, the Beulah minister's wife, opened the door of the study where her husband was deep in the revision of his next day's sermon, and thrust in her comely head framed in a knitted rigolette.[1]

"Luther, I'm going to run down to Letty's. We think the twins are going to have measles; it's the only thing they haven't had, and Letty's spirits are not up to concert pitch. You look like a blessed old prophet tonight, my dear! What's the text?"

The minister pushed back his spectacles and ruffled his gray hair.

"Isaiah VI, 8: 'And I heard the voice of the Lord, saying whom shall I send? . . . Then said I, Here am I, send me!'"

"It doesn't sound a bit like Christmas, somehow."

"It has the spirit, if it hasn't the sound," said the minister. "There is always so little spare money in the village that we get less and less

---

1. A scarf worn as a head covering.

accustomed to sharing what we have with others. I want to remind the people that there are different ways of giving, and that the bestowing of one's self in service and good deeds can be the best of all gifts. Letty Boynton won't need the sermon!—Don't be late, Reba."

"Of course not. When was I ever late? It has just struck seven and I'll be back by eight to choose the hymns. And oh! Luther, I have some fresh ideas for Christmas cards and I am going to try my luck with them in the marts of trade. There are hundreds of thousands of such things sold now-adays; and if the 'Boston Banner' likes my verses well enough to send me the paper regularly, why shouldn't the people who make cards like them too, especially when I can draw and paint my own pictures?"

"I've no doubt they'll like them; who wouldn't? If the parish knew what a ready pen you have, they'd suspect that you help me in my ser-mons! The question is, will the publishers send you a check, or only a copy of your card?"

"I should relish a check, I confess; but oh! I should like almost as well a beautifully colored card, Luther, with a picture of my own inventing on it, my own verse, and R. L. in tiny letters somewhere in the corner! It would make such a lovely Christmas present! And I should be so proud; inside of course, not outside! I would cover my halo with my hat so that nobody in the congregation would ever notice it!"

The minister laughed.

"Consult Letty, my dear. David used to be in some sort of picture business in Boston. She will know, perhaps, where to offer your card!"

At the introduction of a new theme into the conversation Mrs. Larra-bee slipped into a chair by the door, her lantern swinging in her hand.

"David can't be as near as Boston or we should hear of him sometimes. A pretty sort of brother to be meandering foot-loose over the earth, and Letty working her fingers to the bone to support his children—twins at that! It was just like David Gilman to have twins! Doesn't it seem incredible that

244

he can let Christmas go by without a message? I dare say he doesn't even remember that his babies were born on Christmas Eve. To be sure he is only Letty's half-brother, but after all they grew up together and are nearly the same age."

"You always judged David a little severely, Reba. Don't despair of reforming any man till you see the grass growing over his bare bones. I always have a soft spot in my heart for him when I remember his friendship for my Dick; but that was before your time—Oh! These boys, these boys!" The minister's voice quavered. "We give them our very life-blood. We love them, cherish them, pray over them, do our best to guide them, yet they take the path that leads from home. In some way, God knows how, we fail to call out the return love, or even the filial duty and respect!—Well, we won't talk about it, Reba; my business is to breathe the breath of life into my text: 'Here am I, Lord, send me!' Letty certainly continues to say it heroically, whatever her troubles."

"Yes, Letty is so ready for service that she will always be sent, till the end of time; but if David ever has an interview with his Creator I can hear him say: 'Here am I, Lord; send Letty!'"

The minister laughed again. He laughed freely and easily nowadays. His first wife had been a sort of understudy for a saint, and after a brief but depressing connubial[2] experience she had died, leaving him with a boy of six; a boy who already, at that tender age, seemed to cherish a passionate aversion to virtue in any form—the result, perhaps, of daily doses of the catechism administered by an abnormally pious mother.

The minister had struggled valiantly with his paternal and parochial cares[3] for twelve lonely years when he met, wooed, and won (very much to his astonishment and exaltation) Reba Crosby. There never was a better bargain driven! She was forty-five by the family Bible[4] but twenty-five

---

2. Marriage.
3. Church; caring for his congregation.
4. It was a tradition to write important events such as birth dates in the family Bible.

in face, heart, and mind, while he would have been printed as sixty in "Who's Who in New Hampshire" although he was far older in patience and experience and wisdom. The minister was spiritual, frail, and a trifle prone to self-depreciation; the minister's new wife was spirited, vigorous, courageous, and clever. She was also Western-born, college-bred, good as gold, and invincibly, incurably gay.[5] The minister grew younger every year, for Reba doubled his joys and halved his burdens, tossing them from one of her fine shoulders to the other as if they were feathers. She swept into the quiet village life of Beulah like a salt sea breeze. She infused a new spirit into the bleak church "sociables" and made them positively agreeable functions. The choir ceased from wrangling, the Sunday School plucked up courage and flourished like a green bay tree. She managed the deacons, she braced up the missionary societies, she captivated the parish, she cheered the depressed and depressing old ladies and cracked jokes with the invalids.

"Ain't she a little mite too jolly for a minister's wife?" questioned Mrs. Ossian Popham, who was a professional pessimist.

"If this world is a place of want, woe, wantonness, an' wickedness, same as you claim, Maria, I don't see how a minister's wife *can* be too jolly!" was her husband's cheerful reply. "Look how she's melted up the ice in both congregations, so't the other church is most willin' we should prosper, so long as Mis' Larrabee stays here an' we don't get too fur ahead of 'em in attendance. Me for the smiles, Maria!"

And Osh Popham was right; for Reba Larrabee convinced the members of the rival church (the rivalry between the two being in rigidity of creed, not in persistency in good works) that there was room in heaven for at least two denominations; and said that if they couldn't unite in this world, perhaps they'd get round to it in the next. Finally, she saved Letitia

---

5. Cheerful.

Boynton's soul alive by giving her a warm, understanding friendship, and she even contracted to win back the minister's absent son some time or other, and convince him of the error of his ways.

"Let Dick alone a little longer, Luther," she would say; "don't hurry him, for he won't come home so long as he's a failure; it would please the village too much, and Dick hates the village. He doesn't accept our point of view, that we must love our enemies and bless them that despitefully use us. The village did despitefully use Dick, and for that matter, David Gilman too. They were criticized, gossiped about, judged without mercy. Nobody believed in them, nobody ever praised them—and what is that about praise being the fructifying sun in which our virtues ripen, or something like that? I'm not quoting it right, but I wish I'd said it. They were called wild when most of their wildness was exuberant vitality; their mistakes were magnified, their mad pranks exaggerated. If I'd been married to you, my dear, while Dick was growing up, I wouldn't have let you keep him here in this little backwater of life; he needed more room, more movement. They wouldn't have been so down on him in Racine, Wisconsin!"

Mrs. Larrabee lighted her lantern, closed the door behind her, and walked briskly down the lonely road that led from the parsonage[6] at Beulah Corner to Letitia Boynton's house. It was bright moonlight and the ground was covered with light-fallen snow, but the lantern habit was a fixed one among Beulah ladies, who, even when they were not widows or spinsters, made their evening calls mostly without escort. The light of a lantern not only enabled one to pick the better side of a bad road, but would illuminate the face of any male stranger who might be of a burglarious or murderous disposition. Reba Larrabee was not a timid person; indeed, she was wont to say that men were so scarce in Beulah that unless they were out-and-out ruffians[7] it would be an inspiration to meet a few,

6. A house that a church owns for its minister to live in.
7. Criminals or brutes.

even if it were only to pass them in the middle of the road.

There was a light in the meeting-house as she passed, and then there was a long stretch of shining white silence unmarked by any human habitation till she came to the tumble-down black cottage inhabited by "Door-Button" Davis, as the little old man was called in the village. In the distance she could see Osh Popham's two-story house brilliantly illuminated by kerosene lamps, and as she drew nearer she even descried Ossian himself, seated at the cabinet organ in his shirt-sleeves, practicing the Christmas anthem, his daughter holding a candle to the page while she struggled to adjust a circuitous alto to her father's tenor. On the hither side of the Popham house, and quite obscured by it, stood Letitia Boynton's one-story gray cottage. It had a clump of tall cedar trees for background and the bare branches of the elms in front were hung lightly with snow garlands. As Mrs. Larrabee came closer, she set down her lantern and looked fixedly at the familiar house as if something new arrested her gaze.

"It looks like a little night-light!" she thought. "And how queer[8] of Letty to be sitting at the open window!"

Nearer still she crept, yet not so near as to startle her friend. A tall brass candlestick, with a lighted tallow[9] candle in it, stood on the table in the parlor window; but the room in which Letty sat was unlighted save by the fire on the hearth, which gleamed brightly behind the quaint andirons— Hessian soldiers of iron, painted in gay colors.[10] Over the mantel hung the portrait of Letty's mother, a benign figure clad in black silk, the handsome head topped by a snowy muslin[11] cap with floating strings. Just round the corner of the fireplace was a half-open door leading into a tiny bedroom,

---

8. Odd.
9. A cheaper kind of candle made from fat rather than beeswax.
10. Andirons are metal stands in a fireplace for stacking the wood upon. These ones are ornamentally designed to look like Hessian soldiers. Hesse is a region of Germany. It was once a sovereign, independent state and so had its own military with its own style of uniforms.
11. A cotton fabric.

and the flickering flame lighted the heads of two sleeping children, arms interlocked, bright tangled curls flowing over one pillow.

Letty herself sat in a low chair by the open window wrapped in an old cape of ruddy brown homespun, from the folds of which her delicate head rose like a flower in a bouquet of autumn leaves. One elbow rested on the table; her chin in the cup of her hand. Her head was turned away a little so that one could see only the knot of bronze hair, the curve of a cheek, and the sweep of an eyelash.

"What a picture!" thought Reba. "The very thing for my Christmas card! It would do almost without a change, if only she is willing to let me use her."

"Wake up, Letty!" she called. "Come and let me in!—Why, your front door isn't closed!"

"The fire smoked a little when I first lighted it," said Letty, rising when her friend entered, and then softly shutting the bedroom door that the children might not waken. "The night is so mild and the room so warm, I couldn't help opening the window to look at the moon on the snow. Sit down, Reba! How good of you to come when you've been rehearsing for the Christmas Tree exercises all the afternoon."

Chapter 2

"It's never 'good' of me to come to talk with you, Letty!" And the minister's wife sank into a comfortable seat and took off her rigolette. "Enough virtue has gone out of me to-day to Christianize an entire heathen nation! Oh! how I wish Luther would go and preach to a tribe of cannibals somewhere, and make me superintendent of the Sabbath-School! How I should like to deal, just for a change, with some simple problem like the undesirability and indigestibility involved in devouring your next-door neighbor! Now I pass my life in saying, 'Love your neighbor as yourself'; which is far more difficult than to say, 'Don't *eat* your neighbor, it's such a disgusting habit—and wrong besides—though I dare say they do it half the time because the market is bad. The first thing I'd do would be to get my cannibals to raise sheep. If they ate more mutton, they wouldn't eat so many missionaries.'"

Letty laughed. "You're so funny, Reba dear, and I was so sad before you came in. Don't let the minister take you to the cannibals until after I die!"

"No danger!—Letty, do you remember I told you I'd been trying my hand on some verses for a Christmas card?"

"Yes; have you sent them anywhere?"

"Not yet. I couldn't think of the right decoration and color scheme and was afraid to trust it all to the publishers. Now I've found just what I need for one of them, and you gave it to me, Letty!"

"I?"

"Yes, you; to-night, as I came down the road. The house looked so quaint, backed by the dark cedars, and the moon and the snow made everything dazzling. I could see the firelight through the open window, the Hessian soldier andirons, your mother's portrait, the children asleep in the next room, and you, wrapped in your cape waiting or watching for something or somebody."

"I wasn't watching or waiting! I was dreaming," said Letty hurriedly.

"You looked as if you were watching, anyway, and I thought if I were painting the picture I would call it 'Expectancy,' or 'The Vigil,' or 'Sentry Duty.'[12] However, when I make you into a card, Letty, nobody will know what the figure at the window means, till they read my verses."

"I'll give you the house, the room, the andirons, and even mother's portrait, but you don't mean that you want to put *me* on the card?" And Letty turned like a startled deer as she rose and brushed a spark from the hearth-rug.

---

12. A sentry is a soldier who has been assigned to keep watch on guard duty.

"No, not the whole of you, of course, though I'm not clever enough to get a likeness even if I wished. I merely want to make a color sketch of your red-brown cape, your hair that matches it, your ear, an inch of cheek, and the eyelashes of one eye, if you please, ma'am."

"That doesn't sound quite so terrifying." And Letty looked more manageable.

"Nobody'll ever know that a real person sat at a real window and that I saw her there; but when I send the card with a finished picture, and my verses beautifully lettered on it, the printing people will be more likely to accept it."

"And if they do, shall I have a dozen to give to my Bible-class?" asked Letty in a wheedling voice.

"You shall have more than that! I'm willing to divide my magnificent profits with you. You will have furnished the picture and I the verses. It's wonderful, Letty—it's providential! You just *are* a Christmas card to-night! It seems so strange that you even put the lighted candle in the window when you never heard my verse. The candle caught my eye first, and I remembered the Christmas customs we studied for the church festival—the light to guide the Christ Child as he walks through the dark streets on the Eve of Mary."[13]

"Yes, I thought of that," said Letty, flushing a little. "I put the candle there first so that the house shouldn't be all dark when the Pophams went by to choir-meeting, and just then I—I remembered, and was glad I did it!"

"These are my verses, Letty." And Reba's voice was soft as she turned her face away and looked at the flames mounting upward in the chimney—

---

13. "Eve of Mary" is a traditional way to refer to Christmas Eve—the night before Mary gives birth to Jesus. It is still an expression used on the Isle of Man where in the Manx language Eve of Mary is "Oie'l Verrey." The tradition being referred to is from countries where, instead of St. Nicholas or Santa Claus, *Christkind* (the Christ child) is said to be the mysterious gift-bearer on Christmas Eve.

My door is on the latch to-night,
    The hearth fire is aglow.
I seem to hear swift passing feet—
    The Christ Child in the snow.
My heart is open wide to-night
    For stranger, kith or kin.
I would not bar a single door
    Where Love might enter in!

There was a moment's silence and Letty broke it. "It means the sort of love the Christ Child brings, with peace and good-will in it. I'm glad to be a part of that card, Reba, so long as nobody knows me, and—"

Here she made an impetuous movement and, covering her eyes with her hands, burst into a despairing flood of confidence, the words crowding each other and tumbling out of her mouth as if they feared to be stopped.

"After I put the candle on the table . . . I could not rest for thinking . . . I wasn't ready in my soul to light the Christ Child on his way . . . I was bitter and unresigned. . . . It is three years to-night since the children were born . . . and each year I have hoped and waited and waited and hoped, thinking that David might remember. David! my brother, their father! Then the fire on the hearth, the moon and the snow quieted me, and I felt that I wanted to open the door, just a little. No one will notice that it's ajar, I thought, but there's a touch of welcome in it, anyway. And after a few minutes I said to myself: 'It's no use, David won't come; but I'm glad the firelight shines on mother's picture, for he loved mother, and if she hadn't died when he was scarcely more than a boy, things might have been different. . . . The reason I opened the bedroom door—something I never do when the babies are asleep—was because I needed a sight of their faces to reconcile me to my duty and take the resentment out of my heart . . . and it did flow out, Reba—out into the stillness. It is so dazzling white outside, I couldn't bear my heart to be shrouded in gloom!"

"Poor Letty!" And Mrs. Larrabee furtively wiped away a tear. "How long since you have heard? I didn't dare ask."

"Not a word, not a line for nearly three months, and for the half-year before that it was nothing but a note, sometimes with a five-dollar bill enclosed. David seems to think it the natural thing for me to look after his children; as if there could be no question of any life of my own."

"You began wrong, Letty. You were born a prop and you've been propping somebody ever since."

"I've done nothing but my plain duty. When my mother died there was my stepfather to nurse, but I was young and strong; I didn't mind; and he wasn't a burden long, poor father. Then, after four years came the shock of David's reckless marriage. When he asked if he might bring that girl here until her time of trial was over, it seemed to me I could never endure it! But there were only two of us left, David and I; I thought of mother and said yes."

"I remember, Letty; I had come to Beulah then."

"Yes, and you know what Eva was. How David, how anybody, could have loved her, I cannot think! Well, he brought her, and you know how it turned out. David never saw her alive again, nor ever saw his babies after they were three days old. Still, what can you expect of a father who is barely twenty-one?"

"If he's old enough to have children, he's old enough to notice them," said Mrs. Larrabee with her accustomed spirit. "Somebody ought to jog his sense of responsibility. It's wrong for women to assume men's burdens beyond a certain point; it only makes them more selfish. If you only knew where David is, you ought to bundle the children up and express them to his address. Not a word of explanation or apology; simply tie a tag on them, saying, 'Here's your Twins!'"

"But I love the babies," said Letty smiling through her tears, "and David may not be in a position to keep them."

"Then he shouldn't have had them," retorted Reba promptly; "especially not two of them. There's such a thing as a man's being too lavish with babies when he has no intention of doing anything for them but bring them into the world. If you had a living income, it would be one thing, but it makes me burn to have you stitching on coats to feed and clothe your half-brother's children!"

"Perhaps it doesn't make any difference—now!" sighed Letty, pushing back her hair with an abstracted gesture. "I gave up a good deal for the darlings once, but that's past and gone. Now, after all, they're the only life I have, and I'd rather make coats for them than for myself."

Letty Boynton had never said so much as this to Mrs. Larrabee in the three years of their friendship, and on her way back to the parsonage, the minister's wife puzzled a little over the look in Letty's face when she said, "David seemed to think there could be no question of any life of my own"; and again, "I gave up a good deal for the darlings once!"

"Luther," she said to the minister, when the hymns had been chosen, the sermon pronounced excellent, and they were toasting their toes over the sitting-room fire,—"Luther, do you suppose there ever was anything between Letty Boynton and your Dick?"

"No," he answered reflectively, "I don't think so. Dick always admired Letty and went to the house a great deal, but I imagine that was chiefly for David's sake, for they were as like as peas in a pod in the matter of mischief. If there had been more than friendship between Dick and Letty, Dick would never have gone away from Beulah, or if he had gone, he surely would have come back to see how Letty fared. A fellow yearns for news of the girl he loves even when he is content to let silence reign between him and his old father—What makes you think there was anything particular, Reba?"

"What makes anybody think anything!—I wonder why some people are born props, and others leaners or twiners? I believe the very nursing-bottle leaned heavily against Letty when she lay on her infant pillow. I didn't know her when she was a child, but I believe that when she was eight all the other children of three and five in the village looked to her for support and guidance!"

"It's a great vocation—that of being a prop," smiled the minister, as he peeled a red Baldwin apple, carefully preserving the spiral and eating it first.

"I suppose the wobbly vine thinks it's grand to be a stout trellis when it needs one to climb on, but doesn't the trellis ever want to twine, I wonder?" And Reba's tone was doubtful.

"Even the trellis leans against the house, Reba."

"Well, Letty never gets a chance either to lean or to twine! Her family, her friends, her acquaintances, even the stranger within her gates, will pass trees, barber poles, telephone and telegraph poles, convenient corners of buildings, fence posts, ladders, and lightning rods for the sake of winding their weakness around her strength. When she sits down from sheer exhaustion, they come and prop themselves against her back. If she goes to bed, they climb up on the footboard, hang a drooping head, and look her wistfully in the eye for sympathy. Prop on, prop ever, seems to be the underlying law of the universe!"

"Poor Reba! She is talking of Letty and thinking of herself!" And the minister's eye twinkled.

"Well, a little!" admitted his wife; "but I'm only a village prop, not a family one. Where you are concerned"—and she administered an affectionate pat to his cheek as she rose from her chair—"I'm a trellis that leans against a rock!"

Chapter 3

Letitia Boynton's life had been rather a drab one as seen through other people's eyes, but it had never seemed so to her till within the last few years. Her own father had been the village doctor, but of him she had no memory. Her mother's second marriage to a venerable country lawyer, John Gilman, had brought a kindly, inefficient stepfather into the family, a man who speedily became an invalid needing constant nursing. The birth of David when Letty was three years old, brought a new interest into the household, and the two children grew to be fast friends; but when Mrs. Gilman died, and Letty found herself at eighteen the mistress of the house, the nurse of her aged stepfather, and the only guardian of a boy of fifteen, life became difficult. More difficult still it became when the old lawyer died, for he at least had been a sort of fictitious head of the family and his mere existence kept David within bounds.

David was a lively, harum-scarum,[14] handsome youth, good at his lessons, popular with his companions, always in a scrape, into which he was generally drawn by the minister's son, so the neighbors thought. At any rate, Dick Larrabee, as David's senior, received the lion's share of the blame when mischief was abroad. If Parson Larrabee's boy couldn't behave any better than an unbelieving black-smith's, a Methodist farmer's, or a Baptist storekeeper's, what was the use of claiming superior efficacy for the Congregational form of belief?

"Dick's father's never succeeded in bringing him into the church, though he's worked on him from the time he was knee-high to a toad," said Mrs. Popham.

"P'raps his mother kind o' vaccinated him with religion 'stid o' leavin' him to take it the natural way, as the ol' sayin' is," was her husband's response. "The first Mis' Larrabee was as good as gold, but she may have

---

14. Reckless, rash.

overdone the trick a little mite, mebbe; and what's more, I kind o' suspicion the parson thinks so himself. He ain't never been quite the same sence Dick left home, 'cept in preaching'; an' I tell you, Maria, his high-water mark there is higher 'n ever. Abel Dunn o' Boston walked home from meetin' with me Thanksgivin', an', says he, takin' off his hat an' moppin' his forehead, 'Osh,' says he, 'does your minister preach like that every Sunday?' 'No,' says I, 'he don't. If he did we couldn't stan' it! He preaches like that about once a month, an' we don't care what he says the rest o' the time.'"

"Well, so far as boys are concerned, preachin' ain't so reliable, for behavin' purposes, as a good young alder switch,"[15] was the opinion of Mrs. Popham, her children being of the comatose kind, whose minds had never been illuminated by the dazzling idea of disobedience.

"Land sakes, Maria! There ain't alders enough on the river-bank to switch religion into a boy like Dick Larrabee. It's got to come like a thief in the night, as the ol' sayin' is, but I guess I don't mean thief, I guess I mean star: it's got to come kind o' like a star in a dark night. If the whole village, 'generate an' onregenerate,[16] hadn't 'a' kep' on naggin' an' hectorin' an' criticizin' them two boys, Dick an' Dave—carryin' tales an' multiplyin' of 'em by two, *ong root* as the ol' sayin' is—I dare say they'd 'a' both been here yet; 'stid o' roamin' roun' the earth seekin' whom they may devour."

There was considerable truth in Ossian Popham's remark, as Letty could have testified; for the conduct of the Boynton-Gilman household, as well as that of the minister, had been continually under inspection and discussion.

Nothing could remain long hidden in Beulah. Nobody spied, nobody pried, nobody listened at doors or windows, nobody owned a microscope, nobody took any particular notice of events, or if they did they preserved

---

15. A light branch for an alder tree (with which to whip them as a punishment).
16. Regenerate and unregenerate. That is, both those who have been saved and those who have not.

an attitude of profound indifference while doing it—yet everything was known sooner or later. The amount of the fish and meat bill, the precise extent of credit, the number of letters in the post, the amount of fuel burned, the number of absences from church and prayer-meeting, the calls or visits made and received, the hours of arrival or departure, the source of all incomes—these details were the common property of the village. It even took cognizance of more subtle things; for it observed and recorded the fluctuations of all love affairs, and the fluctuations also in the religious experiences of various persons not always in spiritual equilibrium; for the soul was an object of scrutiny in Beulah, as well as mind, body, and estate.

Letty Boynton used to feel that nothing was exclusively her own; that she belonged to Beulah part and parcel; but Dick Larrabee was far more restive under the village espionage than were she and David.

It was natural that David should want to leave Beulah and make his way in the world, and his sister did not oppose it. Dick's circumstances were different. He had inherited a small house and farm from his mother, had enjoyed a college education, and had been offered a share in a good business in a city twelve miles away. He left Beulah because he hated it. He left because he could not endure his father's gentle remonstrances or the bewilderment in his stepmother's eyes. She was a newcomer in the household and her glance seemed to say: "Why on earth do you behave so badly to your father when you're such a delightful chap?" He left because Deacon Todd had prayed for him publicly at a Christian Endeavor meeting;[17] because Mrs. Popham had circulated a wholly baseless scandal about him; and finally because in his young misery the only being who could have comforted him by joining her hapless fortunes to his had refused to do so. He didn't know why. He had always counted on Letty when the time should come to speak the word. He had shown his heart in

---

17. A Christian youth organization.

everything but words; what more did a girl want? Of course, if any one preferred a purely fantastic duty to a man's love, and allowed a scapegrace brother to foist two red-faced, squalling babies on her, there was nothing to be said. So, in this frame of mind he had had one flaming, passionate, wrong-headed scene with his father, and strode out of Beulah with dramatic gestures of shaking its dust off his feet. His father, roused for once from his lifelong patience, had been rather terrible in that last scene; so terrible that he had never forgiven himself, or really believed himself fully forgiven by God, though his son had alienated half the village and nearly rent the parish in twain by his conduct.

As for Letty, she held her peace. She could only hope that the minister and his wife suspected nothing, and she was sure of Beulah's point of view. That a girl would never give up a suitor, if she had any hope of tying him to her for life, was a popular form of belief in the community; and strangely enough it was chiefly the women, not the men, who made it current. Now and then a soft-hearted and chivalrous male would observe indulgently of some village beauty, "I shouldn't wonder a mite if she could 'a' had Bill for the askin'"; but this opinion would be met by such a chorus of feminine incredulity that its author generally withdrew it as unsound and untenable.

It was then, when Dick had gone away, that the days had grown drab and long, but the twins kept Letty's inexperienced hands busy, though in the first year she had the help of old Miss Clarissa Perry, a childless expert in the bringing-up of babies.

The friendship of Reba Larrabee, so bright and cheery and comprehending, was a never-ending solace. There was nothing of the martyr about Letty. She was not wholly resigned to her lot, and to tell the truth she did not intend to be, for a good many years yet.

"I'm not a minister, but I'm the wife of a minister, which is the next best thing," Mrs. Larrabee used to say. "I tell you, Letty, there's no use in human creatures being resigned till their bodies are fairly worn out with fighting. When you can't think of another mortal thing to do, be resigned; but I'm convinced that the Lord is ashamed of us when we fold our hands too soon!"

"You were born courageous, Reba!" And Letty would look admiringly at the rosy cheeks and bright eyes of her friend.

"My blood circulates freely; that helps me a lot. Everybody's blood circulates in Racine, Wisconsin."—And the minister's wife laughed genially. "Yours, hereabouts, freezes up in your six months of cold weather, and when it begins to thaw out the snow is ready to fall again. That sort of thing induces depression, although no mere climate would account for Mrs. Popham—Ossian said to Luther the other day: 'Maria ain't hardly to blame, parson. She come from a gloomy stock. The Ladds was all gloomy, root and branch. They say that the Ladd babies was always discouraged two days after they was born.'"

The cause of Letty's chief heartache, the one that she could reveal to nobody, was that her brother should leave her nowadays so completely to her own resources. She recalled the time when he came home from Boston, pale, haggard, ashamed, and told her of his marriage, months before. She could read in his lack-lustre eyes, and hear in his voice, the absence of love, the fear of the future. That was bad enough, but presently he said: "Letty, there's more to tell. I've no money, and no place to put my wife, but there's a child coming. Can I bring her here till—afterwards? You won't like her, but she's so ailing and despondent just now that I think she'll behave herself, and I'll take her away as soon as she's able to travel. She would never stay here in the country, anyway; you couldn't hire her to do it."

She came: black-haired, sullen-faced Eva, with a vulgar beauty of her own, much damaged by bad temper, discontent, and illness. Oh, those terrible weeks for Letty, hiding her own misery, putting on a brave face with the neighbors, keeping the unwelcome sister-in-law in the background.

It was bitterly cold, and Eva raged against the climate, the house, the lack of a servant, the absence of gayety, and above all at the prospect of motherhood. Her resentment against David, for some reason unknown to Letty, was deep and profound and she made no secret of it; until the out-raged Letty, goaded into speech one day, said: "Listen, Eva! David brought you here because his sister's house was the proper place for you just now. I don't know why you married each other, but you did, and it's evidently a failure. I'm going to stand by David and see you through this trouble, but while you're under my roof you'll have to speak respectfully of my brother; not so much because he's my brother, but because he's your hus-band and the father of the child that's coming—do you understand?"

Letty had a good deal of red in her bronze hair and her brown eyes were as capable of flashing fire as Eva's black ones; so the girl not only refrained from venting her spleen upon the absent David, but ceased to talk altogether, and the gloom in the house was as black as if Mrs. Popham and all her despondent ancestors were living under its roof.

The good doctor called often and did his best, shrugging his shoul-ders and lifting his eyebrows as he said: "Let her work out her own salva-tion.[18] I doubt if she can, but we'll give her the chance. If the problem can be solved, the child will do it."

CHAPTER 4

Well, the problem never was solved, never in this world, at least; and those who were in the sitting-room chamber when Eva was shown her two babies lying side by side on a pillow, never forgot the quick glance of horri-fied incredulity, or the shriek of aversion with which she greeted them.

Letty had a sense of humor, and it must be confessed that when the scorned and discarded babies were returned to her, and she sat by the

---

18. "Work out your own salvation with fear and trembling" (Phil. 2:12 KJV).

kitchen stove trying to plan a second bottle, a second cradle, and see how far the expected baby could divide its modest outfit with the unexpected one, she burst into a fit of hysterical laughter mingled with an outpour of tears.

The doctor came in from the sick-room puzzled and crestfallen from his interview with an entirely new specimen of woman-kind. He had brought Letty and David into the world and soothed the last days of all her family, and now in this tragedy—for tragedy it was—he was her only confidant and adviser.

Letty looked at him, the tears streaming from her eyes.

"Oh, Doctor Lee, Doctor Lee! If an overruling Providence could smile, wouldn't He smile now? David and Eva never wanted to marry each other, I'm sure of it, and the last thing they desired was a child. Now there are two of them. Their father is away, their mother won't look at them! What will become of me until Eva gets well and behaves like a human being? I never promised to be an aunt to twins; I never did like twins; I think they're downright vulgar!"

"Waly waly! bairns are bonny:

One's enough and twa's ower mony,"[19]

quoted the doctor. "It's worse even than you think, my poor Letty, for the girl can't get well, because she won't! She has gritted her teeth, turned her face to the wall, and refused her food. It's the beginning of the end. You are far likelier to be a foster mother than an aunt!"

Letty's face changed and softened and her color rose. She leaned over the two pink, crumpled creatures, still twitching nervously with the amazement and discomfort of being alive.

"Come to your Aunt Letty then and be mothered!" she sobbed, lifting the pillow and taking it, with its double burden, into her arms. "You shan't suffer, poor innocent darlings, even if those who brought you into the

---

19. This is a traditional Scottish proverb given in a Scottish dialect. My free translation is: "Alas, alas! babies are beautiful: One's enough and two's too many."

world turn away from you! Come to your Aunt Letty and be mothered!"

"That's right, that's right," said the doctor over a lump in his throat. "We mustn't let the babies pay the penalty of their parents' sins; and there's one thing that may soften your anger a little, Letty: Eva's not right; she's not quite responsible. There are cases where motherhood, that should be a joy, brings nothing but mental torture and perversion of instinct.[20] Try and remember that, if it helps you any. I'll drop in every two or three hours and I'll write David to come at once. He must take his share of the burden."

Well, David came, but Eva was in her coffin. He was grave and silent, and it could not be said that he showed a trace of fatherly pride. He was very young, it is true, thoroughly ashamed of himself, very unhappy, and anxious about his new cares; but Letty could not help thinking that he regarded the twins as a sort of personal insult—perhaps not on their own part, nor on Eva's, but as an accident that might have been prevented by a competent Providence. At any rate, he carried himself as a man with a grievance, and when he looked at his offspring, which was seldom, it seemed to Letty that he regarded the second one as an unnecessary intruder and cherished a secret resentment at its audacity in coming to this planet uninvited. He went back to his work in Boston without its having crossed his mind that anybody but his sister could take care of his children. He didn't really regard them as children or human beings; it takes a woman's vision to make that sort of leap into the future. Until a new-born baby can show some personal beauty, evince some intellect, stop squirming and squealing, and exhibit enough self-control to let people sleep at night, it is not, as a rule, *persona grata*[21] to any one but its mother.

David did say vaguely to Letty when he was leaving, that he hoped

---

20. To translate his thought into today's terms, he is saying that it is possible she is suffering from postnatal depression.
21. A person you are glad to welcome.

"they would be good," the screams that rent the air at the precise moment of farewell rather giving the lie to his hopes.

Letty was struggling to end the interview without breaking down, for she was worn out nervously as well as physically, and thought if she could only be alone with her problems and her cares she would rather write to David than tell him her mind face to face.

Brother and sister held each other tightly for a moment, kissed each other good-bye, and then Letty watched Osh Popham's sleigh slipping off with David into the snowy distance, the merry tinkle of the bells adding to the sadness in her dreary heart. Dick gone yesterday, Dave to-day; Beulah without Dick and Dave! The two joys of her life were missing and in their places two unknown babies whose digestive systems were going to need constant watching, according to Dr. Lee. Then she went about with set lips, doing the last sordid things that death brings in its wake; doing them as she had seen her mother do before her. She threw away the husks in Eva's under mattress and put fresh ones in; she emptied the feathers from the feather bed and pillows and aired them in the sun while she washed the ticking; she scrubbed the paint in the sick-room, and in between her tasks learned from Clarissa Perry the whole process of bringing up babies by hand.

That was three years ago. At first David had sent ten dollars a month from his slender earnings, never omitting it save for urgent reasons. He evidently thought of the twins as "company" for his sister and their care a pleasant occupation, since she had "almost" a living income; taking in a few coats to make, just to add an occasional luxury to the bare necessities of life provided by her mother's will.

His letters were brief, dispirited, and infrequent, but they had not ceased altogether till within the last few months, during which Letty's to him had been returned from Boston with "Not found" scribbled on the envelopes.

The firm in whose care Letty had latterly addressed him simply wrote, in answer to her inquiries, that Mr. Gilman had not been in their employ for some time and they had no idea of his whereabouts.

The rest was silence.

CHAPTER 5

A good deal of water had run under Beulah Bridge since Letty Boynton had sat at her window on a December evening unconsciously furnishing copy and illustration for a Christmas card; yet there had been very few outward changes in the village. Winter had melted into spring, burst into summer, faded into autumn, lapsed into winter again—the same old, ever-recurring pageant in the world of Nature, and the same procession of incidents in the neighborhood life.

The harvest moon and the hunter's moon had come and gone; the first frost, the family dinners and reunions at Thanksgiving, the first snowfall; and now, as Christmas approached, the same holiday spirit was abroad in the air, slightly modified as it passed by Mrs. Popham's mournful visage.

One or two babies had swelled the census, giving the minister hope of a larger Sunday-School; one or two of the very aged neighbors had passed into the beyond; and a few romantic and enterprising young farmers had espoused wives, among them Osh Popham's son.

The manner of their choice was not entirely to the liking of the village. Digby Popham had married into the rival church and as his betrothed was a masterful young lady it was feared that Digby would leave Mr. Larrabee's flock to worship with his wife. Another had married without visible means of support, a proceeding always to be regretted by thoroughly prudent persons over fifty; and the third, Deacon Todd's eldest son, had somehow or other met a siren[22] from Vermont and insisted on wedding her when there were plenty of marriageable girls in Beulah.

---

22. A beguiling woman.

"I've no patience with such actions!" grumbled Mrs. Popham. "Young folks are so full of notions nowadays that they look for change and excite-ment everywheres. I s'pose James Todd thinks it's a decent, respectable way of actin', to turn his back on the girls he's been brought up an' gone to school with, and court somebody he never laid eyes on till a year ago. It's a free country, but I must say I don't think it's very refined for a man to go clear off somewheres and marry a perfect stranger!"

Births, marriages, and deaths, however, paled into insignificance compared with the spectacular debut of the minister's wife as a writer and embellisher of Christmas cards, two at least having been seen at the local milliner's store.[23] How many she had composed, and how many of them (said Mrs. Popham) might have been rejected, nobody knew, though there was much speculation; and more than one citizen remarked on the size of the daily package of mail matter handed out by the rural delivery man at the parsonage gate.

No one but Mrs. Larrabee and Letty Boynton were in possession of all the thrilling details attending the public appearance of these works of art; the words and letters of appreciation, the commendation, and the occasional blows to pride that attended their acceptance and publication.

Mrs. Larrabee's first attempt, with the sketch of Letty at the window on Christmas Eve, her hearth-fire aglow, her heart and her door open that Love might enter in if the Christ Child came down the snowy street—this went to the Excelsior Card Company in a large Western city, and the fol-lowing correspondence ensued:

---

23. A store that sells apparel for women, especially hats.

MRS. LUTHER LARRABEE,

Beulah, N.H.

DEAR MADAM:—

Your letter bears a well-known postmark, for my father and
my grandfather were born and lived in New Hampshire, "up
Beulah way." I accept your verses because of the beauty of
the picture that accompanied them, and because Christmas
means more than holly and plum pudding and gift-laden trees
to me, for I am a religious man—a ministerial father and
three family deacons saw to that, though it doesn't always
work that way!—Frankly, I do not expect your card to have a
wide appeal, so I offer you only five dollars.

A Christmas card, my dear madam, must have a greeting, and
yours has none. If the pictured room were a real room, and
some one who had seen or lived in it should recognize it, it
would attract his eye, but we cannot manufacture cards to
meet such romantic improbabilities. I am emboldened to ask
you (because you live in Beulah) if you will not paint the
outside of some lonely, little New Hampshire cottage, as
humble as you like, and make me some more verses; something,
say, about "the folks back home."

Sincerely yours,

REUBEN SMALL.

BEULAH, N.H.

DEAR MR. SMALL:—

I accept your offer of five dollars for my maiden[24] effort in
Christmas cards with thanks, and will try my hand at

---

24. First.

something more popular. I am not above liking to make a "wide appeal," but the subject you propose is rather a staggering one, because you accompany it with a phrase lacking rhythm, and difficult to rhyme. You will at once see, by running through the alphabet, that "roam" is the only serviceable rhyme for "*home*," but the union of the two suggests jingle or doggerel. I defy any minor poet when furnished with such a phrase, to refrain from bursting at once into:—

No matter where you travel, no matter where you roam,
You'll never dum-di-dum-di-dee[25]

The folks back home.

Sincerely yours,

REBA LARRABEE.

P.S. On second thought I believe James Whitcomb Riley[26] could do it and overcome the difficulties, but alas! I have not his touch!

DEAR MRS. LARRABEE:—

We never refuse verses because they are too good for the public. Nothing is too good for the public, but the public must be the judge of what pleases it.

"The folks back home" is a phrase that will strike the eye and ear of thousands of wandering sons and daughters. They will choose that card from the heaped-up masses on the counters and send it to every State in the Union. If you will glance at your first card you will see that though

---

25. These are just filler syllables to indicate that some words would need to be thought up for this part.
26. James Whitcomb Riley (1849–1916) was a popular American poet.

people may read it they will always leave it on the counter. I want my cards on counters, by the thousand, but I don't intend that they should be left there!

Make an effort, dear Mrs. Larrabee! I could get "the folks back home" done here in the office in half an hour, but I'm giving you the chance because you live in Beulah, New Hampshire, and because you make beautiful pictures.

Sincerely yours,

REUBEN SMALL.

DEAR MR. SMALL:—

I enclose a colored sketch of the outside of the cottage whose living-room I used in my first card. I chose it because I love the person who lives in it; because it always looks beautiful in the snow, and because the tree is so picturesque. The fact that it is gray for lack of paint may remind a casual wanderer that there is something to do, now and then, for the "folks back home." The verse is just as bad as I thought it would be. It seems incredible that any one should buy it, but ours is a big country and there are many kinds of people living in it, so who knows? Why don't you accept my picture and then you write the card? I could not put my initials on this! They are unknown, to be sure, and I should want them to be, if you use it!

Sincerely yours,

REBA LARRABEE.

Now here's a Christmas greeting
    To the "folks back home."
It comes to you across the space,
    Dear folks back home!

I've searched the wide world over,
But no matter where I roam,
No friends are like the old friends,
No folks like those back home!

DEAR MRS. LARRABEE:—

I gave you five dollars for the first picture and verses,
which you, as a writer, regard more highly than I, who am
merely a manufacturer. Please accept twenty dollars for "The
Folks Back Home," on which I hope to make up my loss on the
first card! I insist on signing the despised verse with your
initials. In case R. L. should later come to mean
something, you will be glad that a few thousand people have
seen it.

Sincerely,
REUBEN SMALL.

The Hessian soldier andirons, the portrait over the Boynton mantel, and even Letty Boynton's cape were identified on the first card, sooner or later, but it was obvious that Mrs. Larrabee had to have a picture for her verses and couldn't be supposed to make one up "out of her head"; though Osh Popham declared it had been done again and again in other parts of the world. Also it was agreed that, as Letty's face was not distinguishable, nobody outside of Beulah could recognize her by her cape; and that any-how it couldn't make much difference, for if anybody wanted to spend fifteen cents on a card he would certainly buy the one about "the folks back home." The popularity of this was established by the fact that it was selling, not only in Beulah and Greentown, but in Boston, and in Racine, Wisconsin, and, it was rumored, even in Chicago. The village milliner in Beulah had disposed of twenty-seven copies in thirteen days and the minister's wife was universally conceded to be the most celebrated person in the State of New Hampshire.

Letty Boynton had an uncomfortable moment when she saw the first card, but common sense assured her that outside of a handful of neighbors no one would identify her home surroundings; meantime she was proud of Reba's financial and artistic triumph in "The Folks Back Home" and generously glad that she had no share in it.

Twice during the autumn David had broken his silence, but only to send her a postal from some Western town, telling her that he should have no regular address for a time; that he was traveling for a publishing firm and felt ill-adapted to the business. He hoped that she and the children were well, for he himself was not; etc., etc.

The twins had been photographed by Osh Popham, who was Jack of all trades and master of many, and a sight of their dimpled charms, curly heads, and straight little bodies would have gladdened any father's heart, Letty thought. However, she scorned to win David back by any such specious means. If he didn't care to know whether his children were hump-backed, bow-legged, cross-eyed, club-footed, or feeble-minded, why should she enlighten him? This was her usual frame of mind, but in these last days of the year how she longed to pop the bewitching photographs and Reba's Christmas cards into an envelope and send them to David.

But where? No word at all for weeks and weeks, and then only a postal from St. Joseph,[27] saying that he had given up his position on account of poor health. Nothing in all this to keep Christmas on, thought Letty, and she knitted and crocheted and sewed with extra ardor that the twins' stockings might be filled with bright things of her own making.

---

27. A town on the western side of Missouri.

Chapter 6

On the afternoon before Christmas of that year, the North Station in Boston was filled with hurrying throngs on the way home for the holidays. Everybody looked tired and excited, but most of them had happy faces, and men and women alike had as many bundles as they could carry; bundles and boxes quite unlike the brown paper ones with which commuters are laden on ordinary days. These were white packages, beribboned and beflowered and behollied and bemistletoed, to be gently carried and protected from crushing.

The train was filled to overflowing and many stood in the aisles until Latham Junction was reached and the overflow alighted to change cars for Greentown and way stations.

Among the crowd were two men with suit-cases who hurried into the way train and, entering the smoking car from opposite ends, met in the middle of the aisle, dropped their encumbrances, stretched out a hand and ejaculated in the same breath:

"Dick Larrabee, upon my word!"

"Dave Gilman, by all that's great!—Here, let's turn over a seat for our baggage and sit together. Going home, I s'pose?"

The men had not met for some years, but each knew something of the other's circumstances and hoped that the other didn't know too much. They scanned each other's faces, Dick thinking that David looked pinched and pale, David half-heartedly registering the quick impression that Dick was prosperous.

"Yes," David answered; "I'm going home for a couple of days. It's such a confounded journey to that one-horse village that a business man can't get there but once in a generation!"

"Awful hole!"[28] confirmed Dick. "Simply awful hole! I didn't get it out of my system for years."

"Married?" asked David.

"No; rather think I'm not the marrying kind, though the fact is I've had no time for love affairs—too busy. Let's see, you have a child, haven't you?"

"Yes; Letty has seen to all that business for me since my wife died." (Wild horses couldn't have dragged the information from him that the "child" was "twins," and Dick didn't need it anyway, for he had heard the news the morning he left Beulah.) "Wonder if there have been many changes in the village?"

"Don't know; there never used to be! Mrs. Popham has been ailing for years—she couldn't die; and Deacon Todd wouldn't!" Dick's old animosities still lingered faintly in his memory, though his laughing voice and the twinkle in his eyes showed plainly that no bitterness was left. "How's business with you, David?"

"Only so-so. I've had the devil's own luck lately. Can't get anything that suits me or that pays a decent income. I formed a new connection the other day, but I can't say yet what there is in it. I'm just out of hospital; operation; they cut out the wrong thing first, I believe, sewed me up absent-mindedly, then remembered it was the other thing, and did it over again. At any rate, that's the only way I can account for their mewing[29] me up there for two months."

"Well, well, that is hard luck! I'm sorry, old boy! Things didn't begin to go my way either till within the last few months. I've always made a fair living and saved a little money, but never gained any real headway. Now I've got a first-rate start and the future looks pretty favorable, and best of all, pretty safe—No trouble at home calls you back to Beulah? I hope Letty is all

---

28. A slang way to say that it is a small nothing of a place—more like a hole in the ground that animals would live in than civilization.
29. Confining—shutting him up in that place.

right?" Dick cast an anxious side glance at David, though he spoke carelessly.

"Oh, no! Everything's serene, so far as I know. I'm a poor correspon-dent, especially when I've no good news to tell; and anyway, the mere sight of a pen ties my tongue. I'm just running down to surprise Letty."

Dick looked at David again. He began to think he didn't like him. He used to, when they were boys, but when he brought that unaccount-able wife home and foisted her and her babies on Letty, he rather turned against him. David was younger than himself, four or five years younger, but he looked as if he hadn't grown up. Surely his boyhood chum hadn't used to be so pale and thin-chested or his mouth so ladylike and pretty. A good face, though; straight and clean, with honest eyes and a likable smile. Lack of will, perhaps, or a persistent run of ill luck. Letty had always kept him stiffened up in the old days. Dick recalled one of his father's phrases to the effect that Dave Gilman would spin on a very small biscuit,[30] and wondered if it were still true.

"And you, Dick? Your father's still living? You see I haven't kept up with Beulah lately."

"Keeping up with Beulah! It sounds like the title of a novel, but the hero would have to be a snail or he'd pass Beulah in the first chapter!— Yes, father's hale and hearty, I believe."

"You come home every Christmas, I s'pose?" inquired David.

"No; as a matter of fact this is my first visit since I left for good."

"That's about my case." And David, hung his head a little, uncon-sciously.

"That so? Well, I was a hot-headed fool when I said good-bye to Beulah, and it's taken me all this time to cool off and make up my mind to apologize to the dad. There's—there's rather a queer coincidence about my visit just at this time."

---

30. In other words, he would easily lose his sense of direction or purpose in life. He lacks fixed resolution.

"Speaking of coincidences," said David, "I can beat yours, whatever it is. If the thought of your father brought you back, my mother drew me—this way!" And he took something from his inside coat pocket—"Do you see that?"

Dick regarded the object blankly, then with a quick gesture dived into his pocket and brought forth another of the same general character. "How about this?" he asked.

Each had one of Reba Larrabee's Christmas cards but David had the first unsuccessful one and Dick the popular one with the lonely little gray house and the verse about the folks back home.

The men looked at each other in astonishment and Dick gave a low whistle. Then they bent over the cards together.

"It was mother's picture that pulled me back to Beulah, I don't mind telling you," said David, his mouth twitching. "Don't you see it?"

"Oh! Is that your mother?" And Dick scanned the card closely.

"Don't you remember her portrait that always hung there after she died?"

"Yes, of course!" And Dick's tone was apologetic. "You see the face is so small I didn't notice it, but I recognize it now and remember the portrait."

"Then the old sitting-room!" exclaimed David. "Look at the rag carpet and the blessed old andirons! Gracious! I've crawled round those Hessian soldiers, burned my fingers and cracked my skull on 'em, often enough when I was a kid! When I'd studied the card five minutes, I bought a ticket and started for home."

David's eyes were suffused[31] and his lip trembled.

"I don't wonder," said Dick. "I recognize the dear old room right enough, and of course I should know Letty."

"It didn't occur to me that it *was* Letty for some time," said her

---

31. Tearful.

brother. "There's just the glimpse of a face shown, and no real likeness."

"Perhaps not," agreed Dick. "A stranger wouldn't have known it for Letty, but if it had been only that cape I should have guessed. It's as familiar as Mrs. Popham's bugle bonnet, and much prettier. She wore it every winter, skating, you know—and it's just the color of her hair."

"Letty has a good-shaped head," said David judicially. "It shows, even in the card."

"And a remarkable ear," added Dick, "so small and so close to her head."

"I never notice people's ears," confessed David.

"Don't you? I do, and eyelashes, too. Mother's got Letty's eyelashes down fine—She's changed, Dave, Letty has! That hurts me. She was always so gay and chirpy. In this picture she has a sad, far-away, listening look, but mother may have put that in just to make it interesting."

"Or perhaps I've had something to do with the change of expression!" thought David. "What attracted me first," he added, "was your mother's verses. She always had a knack of being pious without cramming piety down your throat. I liked that open door. It meant welcome, no matter how little you'd deserved it."

"Where'd you get your card, Dave?" asked Dick. "It's prettier than mine."

"A nurse brought it to me in the hospital just because she took a fancy to it. She didn't know it would mean anything to me, but it did—a relapse!" And David laughed shamefacedly. "I guess she'll confine herself to beef tea[32] after this!—Where'd you get yours?"

"Picked it up on a dentist's mantelpiece when I was waiting for an appointment. I was traveling round the room, hands in my pockets, when suddenly I saw this card standing up against an hour-glass. The color caught me. I took it to the window, and at first I was puzzled. It certainly was Letty's house. The door's open you see and there's somebody in the

---

32. Like giving broth to drink to someone who is too ill for solid food or making a hot drink with a bouillon cube.

window. I knew it was Letty, but how could any card publisher have found the way to Beulah? Then I discovered mother's initials snarled up in holly, and remembered that she was always painting and illuminating."

"Queer job, life is!" said David, putting his card back in his pocket and wishing there were a little more time, or that he had a little more cour-age, so that he might confide in Dick Larrabee. He felt a desire to tell him some of the wretchedness he had lived through. It would be a comfort just to hint that his unhappiness had made him a coward, so that the very responsibilities that serve as a spur to some men had left him until now cold, unstirred, unvitalized.

"You're right!" Dick answered. "Life is a queer job and it doesn't do to shirk it. And just as queer as anything in life is the way that mother's Christmas cards brought us back to Beulah! They acted as a sort of magic, didn't they?—Jiminy![33] I believe the next station is Beulah. I hope the depot team will be hitched up."[34]

"Yes, here we are; seven o'clock and the train only thirty-five minutes late. It always made a point of that on holidays!"

"Never mind!" And Dick's tone was as gay as David's was sober. "The bean-pot will have gone back to the cellarway and the doughnuts to the crock, but the 'folks back home' 'll get 'em out for us, and a mince pie, too, and a cut of sage cheese."

"There won't be any 'folks back home,' we're so late, I'm thinking. There's always a Christmas Eve festival at the church, you know. They never change—in Beulah."

"Then, by George, they can have me for Santa Claus!" said Dick as they stepped out on the platform. "Why, it doesn't seem cold at all; yet look at the ice on the river! What skating, and what a moon! My blood's

---

33. "Jiminy" is a made-up word used to express surprise like "golly" or "wowza."
34. Depot is a word for the train station. He hopes that the horses there are already hitched to the carriage so that they can get a ride home without delay.

up,[35] and if I find the parsonage closed, I'll follow on to the church and make my peace with the members. There's a kind of spell on me! For the first time in years I feel as though I could shake hands with Deacon Todd."

"Well, Merry Christmas to you, Dick—I'm going to walk. Good gracious! Have you come to spend the winter?" For various bags and parcels were being flung out on the platform with that indifference and irresponsibility that bespeak the touch of the seasoned baggage-handler.

"You didn't suppose I was coming back to Beulah empty-handed, on Christmas Eve, did you? If I'm in time for the tree, I'm going to give those blue-nosed, frost-bitten little youngsters something to remember! Jump in, Dave, and ride as far as the turn of the road."

In a few minutes the tottering old sign-board that marked the way to Beulah Center hove[36] in sight, and David jumped from the sleigh to take his homeward path.

"Merry Christmas again, Dick!" he waved.

"Same to you, Dave! I'll come myself to say it to Letty the first minute I see smoke coming from your chimney to-morrow morning. Tell her you met me, will you, and that my visit is partly for her, only that father had to have his turn first. She'll know why. Tell her mother's card had Christmas magic in it, tell—"

"Say, tell her the rest yourself, will you, Dick?" And Dave broke into a run down the hill road that led to Letty.

"I will, indeed!" breathed Dick into his muffler.[37]

CHAPTER 7

Repeating history, Letty was again at her open window. She had been half-ashamed to reproduce the card, as it were, but something impelled her.

---

35. In other words, he's excited.
36. That is, rose up into sight.
37. Scarf.

She was safe from scrutiny, too, for everybody had gone to the tree—the Pophams, Mr. Davis, Clarissa Perry, everybody for a quarter of a mile up and down the street, and by now the company would be gathered and the tree lighted. She could keep watch alone, the only sound being that of the children's soft breathing in the next room.

Letty had longed to go to the festival herself, but old Clarissa Perry, who cared for the twins now and then in Letty's few absences, had a niece who was going to "speak a piece,"[38] and she yearned to be present and share in the glory; so Letty was kept at home as she had been numberless other times during the three years of her vicarious motherhood.

The night was mild again, as in the year before. The snow lay like white powder on the hard earth; the moon was full, and the street was a length of dazzling silence. The lighted candle was in the parlor window, shining toward the meeting-house, the fire burned brightly on the hearth, the front door was ajar. Letty wrapped her old cape round her shoulders, drew her hood over her head, and seating herself at the window repeated under her breath—

"My door is on the latch to-night,
    The hearth-fire is aglow.
  I seem to hear swift passing feet,
    The Christ Child in the snow.
  My heart is open wide to-night
    For stranger, kith, or kin;
  I would not bar a single door
    Where Love might enter in!"

And then a footstep, drawing ever nearer, sounded crunch, crunch, in the snow. Letty pushed her chair back into the shadow. The footstep

---

38. She has memorized something (such as a poem) to recite as part of the program.

halted at the gate, came falteringly up the path, turned aside, and came nearer the window. Then a voice said: "Don't be frightened Letty, it's David! Can I come in? I haven't any right to, except that it's Christmas Eve."

That, indeed, was the magic, the all-comprehending phrase that swept the past out of mind with one swift stroke: the acknowledgment of unworthiness, the child-like claim on the forgiving love that should be in every heart on such a night as this. Resentment melted away like mist before the sun. Her deep grievance—where had it gone? How could she speak anything but welcome? For what was the window open, the fire lighted, the door ajar, the guiding candle-flame, but that Love, and David, might enter in?

There were few words at first; nothing but close-locked hands and wet cheeks pressed together. Then Letty sent David into the children's room by himself. If the twins were bewitching when awake, they were nothing short of angelic when asleep.

David came out a little later, his eyes reddened with tears, his hair rumpled, his face flushed. He seemed like a man awed by an entirely new experience. He could not speak, he could only stammer brokenly—

"As God is my witness, Letty, there's been something wrong with me up to this moment. I never thought of them as my children before, and I can't believe that such as they can belong to me. They were never wanted, and I've never had any interest in them. I owe them to you, Letty; you've made them what they are; you, and no one else."

"If there hadn't been something there to build on, my love and care wouldn't have counted for much. They're just like dear mother's people for good looks and brains and pretty manners: they're pure Shirley all the way through, the twinnies are."

"It's lucky for me that they are!" said David humbly. "You see, Letty, I married Eva to keep my promise. If I was old enough to make it, I was old enough to keep it, so I thought. She never loved me, and when she found out that I didn't love her any longer she turned against me. Our life together was awful, from beginning to end, but she's in her grave, and no-body'll ever hear my side, now that she can't tell hers. When I looked at those two babies the day I left you, I thought of them only as retribution; and the vision of them—ugly, wrinkled, writhing little creatures—has been in my mind ever since."

"They were compensation, not retribution, David. I ought to have told you how clever and beautiful they were, but you never asked and my pride was up in arms. A man should stand by his own flesh and blood, even if it isn't attractive; that's what I believe."

"I know, I know! But I've had no feeling for three years. I've been like a frozen man, just drifting, trying to make both ends meet, my heart dead and my body full of pain. I'm just out of a hospital—two months in all."

"David! Why didn't you let me know, or send for me?"

"Oh, it was way out in Missouri. I was taken ill very suddenly at the hotel in St. Joseph and they moved me at once. There were two operations first and last, and I didn't know enough to feed myself most of the time."

"Poor, poor Buddy! Did you have good care?"

"The best. I had more than care. Ruth Bentley, the nurse that brought me back to life, made me see what a useless creature I was."

Some woman's instinct stirred in Letty at a new note in her brother's voice and a new look in his face. She braced herself for his next words, sure that they would open a fresh chapter. The door and the window were closed now, the shades pulled down, the fire low; the hour was ripe for confidences.

"You see, Letty,"—and David cleared his throat nervously, and looked at the coals gleaming behind the Hessian soldiers—"it's a time for a thor-ough housecleaning, body, mind, and soul, a long illness is; and Miss Bentley knew well enough that all was wrong with me. I mentioned my unhappy marriage and told her all about you, but I said nothing about the children."

"Why should you?" asked Letty, although her mind had leaped to the reason already.

"Well, I was a poor patient in one of the cheapest rooms; broken in health, without any present means of support. I wanted to stand well with her, she had been so good to me, and I thought if she knew about the twins she wouldn't believe I could ever make a living for three."

"Still less for *four!*" put in Letty, with an irrepressible note of teasing in her tone.

She had broken the ice. Like a torrent set free, David dashed into the story of the last two months and Ruth Bentley's wonderful influence. How she had recreated him within as well as without. How she was the best and noblest of women, willing to take a pauper by the hand and brace him up for a new battle with life.

"Strength appeals to me," confessed David. "Perhaps it's because I am weak; for I'm afraid I am, a little!"

"Be careful, Davy! Eva was strong!"

David shuddered. He remembered a strength that lashed and buffeted and struck and overpowered.

"Ruth is different," he said. "'Out of the strong came forth sweet-ness'[39] used to be one of Parson Larrabee's texts. That's Ruth's kind of strength—Can I—will you let me bring her here to see you, Letty—say for New Year's? It's all so different from the last time I asked you. Then I knew I was bringing you nothing but sorrow and pain, but Ruth carries her welcome in her face."

The prop inside of Letty wavered unsteadily for a moment and then stood in its accustomed upright position.

"Why not?" she asked. "It's the right thing to do; but you must tell her about the children first."

---

39. Judges 14:14.

"Oh! I did that long ago, after I found out that she cared. It was only at first that I didn't dare. I haven't told you, but she went out for her daily walk and brought me home a Christmas card, the prettiest one she could find, she said. I was propped up on pillows, as weak as a kitten. I looked at it and looked at it, and when I saw that it was this room, the old fireplace and mother's picture, and the Hessian soldier andirons, when I realized there was a face at the window and that the door was ajar—everything just swam before me and I fainted dead away. I had a relapse, and when I was better again I told her everything. She's fond of children. It didn't make any difference, except for her to say that the more she had to do for me, the more she wanted to do it."

"Well," said Letty with a break in her voice, "that's love, so far as I can see, and if you've been lucky enough to win it, take it and be thankful, and above all, nurse and keep it—So one of Reba's cards, the one the publisher thought would never sell, found you and brought you back! How wonderful! We little thought of that, Reba and I!"

"Reba's work didn't stop there, Letty! There was so much that had to be said between you and me, just now, that I couldn't let another subject creep in till it was finished and we were friends—but Dick Larrabee saw Reba's card about 'the folks back home' in Chicago and he bought a ticket for Beulah just as I did. We met in the train and compared notes."

"Dick Larrabee home?"

The blood started in Letty's heart and sped hither and thither, warming her from head to foot.

"Yes, looking as fit as a fiddle; the way a man looks when things are coming his way."

"But what did the card mean to him? Did he seem to like Reba's verses?"

"Yes, but I guess the card just spelled home to him; and he recognized this house in a minute, of course. I showed him my card and he said:

283

'That's Letty fast enough: I know the cape.' He recognized you in a minute, he said."

He knew the cape! Yes, the old cape had been close to his shoulder many a time. He liked it and said it matched her hair.

"He was awfully funny about your ear, too! I told him I never noticed women's ears, and he said he did, when they were pretty, and their eyelashes, too—Anything remarkable about your eyelashes, Letty?"

"Nothing that I'm aware of!" said Letty laughingly, although she was fibbing and she knew it.

"And he said he'd call and say 'Merry Christmas' to you the first thing to-morrow; that he would have been here to-night but you'd know his father had to come first. You don't mind being second to the parson, do you?"

No, Letty didn't mind. Her heart was unaccountably light and glad, like a girl's heart. It was the Eve of Mary when all women are blest because of one. The Wise Men brought gifts to the Child; Letty had often brought hers timidly, devoutly, trustfully, and perhaps to-night they were coming back to her!

Chapter 8

"Put the things down on the front steps," said Dick to the driver as he neared the parsonage. "If there's nobody at home I'll go on up to the church after I've got this stuff inside."

"Got a key?"

"No, don't need one. I've picked all the locks with a penknife many a time. Besides, the key is sure to be under the doormat. Yes, here it is! Of all the unaccountable customs I ever knew, that's the most laughable!"

"Works all right for you!"

"Yes, and for all the other tramps,"—and Dick opened the door and lifted in his belongings. "Good-night," he called to the driver; "I'll walk up to the church after I've found out whether mother keeps the mince pie and cider apple sauce in the same old place."

A few minutes later, his hunger partially stayed, Dick Larrabee locked the parsonage door and took the well-trodden path across the church common. It was his father's feet, he knew, that had worn the shoveled path so smooth; his kind, faithful feet that had sped to and fro on errands of mercy, never faltering in all the years.

It was nearly eight o'clock. The sound of the melodeon,[40] with children's voices, floated out from the white-painted meeting-house, all ablaze with light; or as much ablaze as a kerosene chandelier and six side lamps could make it. The horse sheds were crowded with teams of various sorts, the horses well blanketed and standing comfortably in straw; and the last straggler was entering the right-hand door of the church as Dick neared the steps. Simultaneously the left-hand door opened, and on the background of the light inside appeared the figure of Mrs. Todd, the wife of his ancient enemy, the senior deacon. Dick could see that a sort of dressing-room had been curtained off in the little entry, as it had often been in former times of tableaux[41] and concerts and what not. Valor, not discretion, was the better policy, and walking boldly up to the steps Dick took off his fur cap and said, "Good-evening, Mrs. Todd!"

"Good gracious me! Where under the canopy did you hail from, Dick Larrabee? Was your folks lookin' for you? They ain't breathed a word to none of us."

"No, I'm a surprise, Mrs. Todd."

"Well, I know you've given me one! Will you wait a spell till the recitations is over? You'd scare the children so, if you go in now, that they'd

---

40. A kind of small organ (a keyboard instrument).
41. A form of entertainment in which people are arranged on a stage to create a still-life scene. For instance, the nativity with Mary, Joseph, Jesus, and the shepherds, or Washington crossing the Delaware.

forget their pieces more'n they gen'ally do."

"I can endure the loss of the 'pieces,'" said Dick with a twinkle in his eye.

At which Mrs. Todd laughed comprehendingly, and said: "Isaac'll get a stool or a box or something; there ain't a vacant seat in the church. I wish we could say the same o' Sundays!—Isaac! Isaac! Come out and see who's here," she called under her breath. "He won't be long. He's tendin' John Trimble in the dressin'-room. He was the only one in the village that was willin' to be Santa Claus an' he wa'n't over-willin'. Now he's et something for supper that disagrees with him awfully and he's all doubled up with colic.[42] We can't have the tree till the exercises is over, but that won't be mor'n fifteen minutes, so I sent Isaac home to make a mustard plaster.[43] He's puttin' it on John now. John's dreadful solemn and unamusin' when he's well, and I can't think how he'll act when he's all crumpled up with stomach-ache, an' the mustard plaster drawin' like fire."

Dick threw back his head and laughed. He had forgotten just how unexpected Beulah's point of view always was.

Deacon Todd now came out cautiously.

"I've got it on him, mother, tho' he's terrible unresigned to it; an' I've given him a stiff dose o' Jamaica Ginger.[44] We can tell pretty soon whether he can take his part."

"Here's Dick Larrabee come back, Isaac, just when we thought he had given up Beulah for good an' all!" said Mrs. Todd.

The Deacon stood on the top step, his gaunt, grizzled face peering above the collar of his great coat; not a man to eat his words very often, Deacon Isaac Todd.

---

42. Stomachache.
43. A medical treatment in which a bandage that has a mustard-based ointment on it is placed on a sore or injured part of the body. While it was believed to do long-term good, it brought additional, immediate irritation and discomfort.
44. An over-the-counter medicine.

"Well, young man," he said, "you've found your way home, have you? It's about time, if you want to see your father alive!"

"If it hadn't been for you and others like you, men who had forgotten what it was to be young, I should never have gone away," said Dick hotly. "What had I done worse than a dozen others, only that I happened to be the minister's son?"

"That's just it; you were bringin' trouble on the parish, makin' talk that reflected on your father. Folks said if he couldn't control his own son, he wa'n't fit to manage a church. You played cards, you danced, you drove a fast horse."

"I never did a thing I'm ashamed of but one,"—and Dick's voice was firm. "My misdeeds were nothing but boyish nonsense, but the village never gave me credit for a single virtue. I ought to have remembered father's position, but whatever I was or whatever I did, you had no right to pray for me openly for full five minutes at a public meeting. That galled me worse than anything!"

"Now, Isaac," interrupted Mrs. Todd. "I hope you'll believe me! I've told you once a week, on an average, these last three years, that you might have chastened Dick some other way besides prayin' for him in meetin'!"

The Deacon smiled grimly. "You both talk as if prayin' was one of the seven deadly sins," he said.

"I'm not objecting to your prayers," agreed Dick, "but there were plenty of closets in your house where you might have gone and told the Lord your opinion of me;[45] only that wasn't good enough for you; you must needs tell the whole village!"

"There, father, that's what I always said," agreed Mrs. Todd.

"Well, I ain't one that can't yield when the majority's against me," said the Deacon, "particularly when I'm treatin' John Trimble for the colic.

---

45. "But thou, when thou prayest, enter into thy closet, and when thou hast shut thy door, pray to thy Father which is in secret" (Matt. 6:6 KJV).

If you'll stop actin' so you threaten to split the church, Dick Larrabee, I'll stop prayin' for you. The Lord knows how I feel about it now, so I needn't keep on remindin' Him."

Chapter 9

"That's a bargain and here's my hand on it," cried Dick. "Now, what do you say to letting me be Santa Claus? Come on in and let's look at John Trimble. He'd make a splendid Job or Jeremiah,[46] but I wouldn't let him spoil a Christmas festival!"

"Do let Dick take the part, father,"—and Mrs. Todd's tone was most ingratiating. "John's terrible dull and bashful anyway, an' mebbe he'd have a pain he couldn't stan' jest when he's givin' out the presents. An' Dick is always so amusin'.'"

Deacon Todd led the way into the improvised dressing-room. He had removed John's gala costume in order to apply the mustard faithfully and he lay in a crumpled heap in the corner. The plaster itself adorned a stool near by.

"Now, John! John! That plaster won't do you no good on the stool. It ain't the stool that needs drawin'; it's your stomach," argued Mrs. Todd.

"I'm drawed pretty nigh to death a'ready," moaned John. "I'm rore,[47] that's what I am—rore! An' I won't be Santa Claus neither. I want to go home."

"Wrop him up and get him into your sleigh, father, and take him home; then come right back. Bed's the place for him. Keep that hot flat-iron on his stomach, if he'd rather have it than the mustard. Men-folks are such cowards. I'll dress Dick while you're gone. Mebbe it's a Providence!"

On the whole, Dick agreed with Mrs. Todd as he stood ready to

---

46. Biblical characters known for the suffering they endured.
47. "Sore" said in his accent or the way he sounds because he is in pain.

make his entrance. The School Committee was in the church and he had had much to do with its members in former days. The Select-men[48] of the village were present, and he had made their acquaintance once, in an executive session. The deacons were all there and the pillars of the church and the choir and the organist—a spinster who had actively disapproved when he had put beans in the melodeon one Sunday. Yes, it was best to meet them in a body on a festive occasion like this, when the rigors of the village point of view were relaxed. It would relieve him of several dozen private visits of apology, and altogether he felt that his courage would have wavered had he not been disguised as another person altogether: a popular favorite; a fat jolly, rollicking dispenser of bounties to the general public. When he finally discarded his costume, would it not be easier, too, to meet his father first before the church full of people and have the solemn hour with him alone, later at night? Yes, as Mrs. Todd said, "Mebbe 'twas a Providence!"

* * *

There was never such a merry Christmas festival in the Orthodox[49] church of Beulah; everybody was of one mind as to that. There was a momentary fear that John Trimble, a pillar of prohibition,[50] might have imbibed hard cider; so gay, so nimble, so mirth-provoking was Santa Claus. When was John Trimble ever known to unbend sufficiently to romp up the side aisle jingling his sleigh bells, and leap over a front pew stuffed with presents, to gain the vantage-ground he needed for the distribution of his pack? The wing pews on one side of the pulpit had been floored over and the Christmas Tree stood there, triumphant in

---

48. Those who had been elected to the local government board.
49. Orthodox means "right doctrine." This is not being used as a denominational name (it is a Congregational church), but merely as a way of emphasizing that they think they are right about doctrine in contrast to the other church in town.
50. He thinks alcoholic drinks should be banned.

beauty, while the gifts strewed the green-covered platform at its feet.

How gay, how audacious, how witty was Santa Claus! How the village had always misjudged John Trimble, and how completely had John Trimble hitherto obscured his light under a bushel.[51] In his own proper person children avoided him, but they crowded about this Santa Claus, encircling his legs, gurgling with joy when they were lifted to his shoulder, their laughter ringing through the church at his droll[52] antics. A sense of mystery grew when he opened a pack on the pulpit stairs, a pack unfamiliar in its outward aspect to the Committee on Entertainment. Every girl had a little doll dressed in fashionable attire, and every boy a brilliantly colored, splendidly noisy, tin trumpet; but hanging to every toy by a red ribbon was Mrs. Larrabee's Christmas card; her despised one about the "folks back home."

The publishers' check to the minister's wife had been accompanied by a dozen complimentary copies, but these had been sent to Reba's Western friends and relations; and although the card was on many a marble-topped table in Beulah, it had not been bought by all the inhabitants, by any means. Fifteen cents would purchase something useful, and Beulah did not contain many Croesuses.[53] Still, here the cards were—enough of them for everybody—with a linen handkerchief for every woman and every man in the meeting-house, and a dozen more sticking out of the pack, as the people in the front pews could plainly see. Modest gifts, but plenty of them, and nobody knew from whence they came! There was a buzzing in the church, a buzzing that grew louder and more persistent when Santa Claus threw a lace scarf around Mrs. Larrabee's shoulders and approached her husband with a fine beaver collar in his hands: hands

---

51. "Neither do men light a candle, and put it under a bushel, but on a candlestick; and it giveth light unto all that are in the house" (Matt. 5:15 KJV).
52. Amusing.
53. Rich people. Croesus was an ancient king of Lydia famous for his wealth.

that trembled, as everybody could see, when he buttoned the piece of fur around the old minister's neck.

And the minister? He had been half in, and half out of, a puzzling dream for ten minutes, and when those hands of Santa Claus touched him, his flesh quivered. They reminded him of baby fingers that had crept around his neck years ago when he patiently walked the parsonage floor at night with his ailing child in his arms. Every drop of blood in his veins called out for answer. He looked above the white cotton beard and mustache to a pair of dark eyes; merry, mischievous, yet tender and soft; at a brown wavy lock escaping from the home-made wig. Then those who were near heard a weak voice say, "My son!" and those who were far away observed Santa Claus tear off his wig and beard, heard him cry, "Father!"— and, as Mrs. Todd said afterwards, saw him "fall on to the minister's neck right there before the whole caboodle,[54] an' cling to him for all the world like an engaged couple, only they wouldn't 'a' made so free in public."

No ice but would have thawed in such an atmosphere! Grown-up Beulah forgot how much trouble Dick Larrabee had caused in other days, and the children had found a friend for all time. The extraordinary number of dolls, trumpets, handkerchiefs, and Christmas cards circulating in the meeting-house raised the temperature considerably, and induced a general feeling that if Dick Larrabee had really ever been a bit wild and reckless, he had evidently reformed, and prospered, besides.

Yes, no one but a kind and omniscient Providence could have so beautifully arranged Dick Larrabee's homecoming, and so wisely superintended his complete reinstatement in the good graces of Beulah village. A few maiden ladies felt that he had been a trifle immodest in embracing, and especially in kissing, his father in front of the congregation; venturing the conviction that kissing, an indecorous custom in any event, was especially lamentable in public.

---

54. The whole lot of them.

"Pity Letty Boynton missed this evenin'," said Mrs. Todd. "Her an' Dick allers had a fancy for each other, so I've heard, though I don't know how true. Clarissa Perry might jest as well have stayed with the twins as not, for her niece that spoke a piece forgot 'bout half of it an' Clarissa was in a cold sweat every minute. Then the niece had a fit o' cryin', she was so ashamed at failin', an' Clarissa had to take her home. So they both missed the tree, an' Letty might 'a' been here as well as not an' got her handker-chief an' her card. I sent John Trimble's to him by the doctor, but he didn't take no notice, Isaac said, for the doctor was liftin' off the hot flat-iron an' puttin' turpentine[55] on the spot where I'd had my mustard—Anyway, if John had to have the colic he couldn't 'a' chosen a better time, an' if he gets over it, I shall be real glad he had it; for nobody ever seen sech a Santa Claus as Dick Larrabee made, an' there never was, an' never will be, sech a lively, an' amusin' an' free-an'-easy evenin' in the Orthodox church."

CHAPTER 10

"Bless the card!" sighed David thankfully as he sat down to smoke a good-night pipe and propped his feet contentedly against the little Hessian sol-diers. The blaze of the logs on his own family hearth-stone, after many months of steam heaters in the hall bedrooms of cheap hotels, how it soothed his tired heart and gave it visions of happiness to come! The card was on his knee, where he could look from its pictured scene to the real one of which he was again a glad and grateful part.

"Bless the card!" whispered Letty Boynton to herself as she went to her moonlit bedroom. Her eyes searched the snowy landscape and found the parsonage, "over the hills and far away."[56] Then her heart flew like a bird across the distance and beat its wings in gladness, for a faint light

---

55. A powerful oil.
56. The name of a traditional folk song.

streamed from the parson's study windows and she knew that father and son were together. That, in itself, was enough, with David sleeping under the home roof; but to-morrow was coming and to-morrow might be hers— her very own!

"Bless the card!" said Reba Larrabee, the tears shining in her eyes as she left the minister alone with his son. "Bless everybody and everything! Above all, bless God, 'from whom all blessings flow.'"[57]

"Bless the card," said Dick Larrabee when he went up the narrow parsonage stairs to the room of his boyhood and found everything as it had been years ago. He leaned the little piece of paper magic against the mantel clock, threw it a kiss, and then, opening his pocket-book, he went nearer to the lamp and took out the faded tintype of a brown-haired girl in a brown cape. "Bless the card!" he said again, with a new note in his voice: "Bless the girl! And bless to-morrow if it brings me what I want most in all the world!"

---

57. Words from the Doxology hymn written by Thomas Ken (1637–1711).

THE GIFT OF THE MAGI
O. HENRY

"The Gift of the Magi" is the most famous Christmas story in this collection. Though it is quite short, it has a plot twist that has kept people thinking about it—and coming back to it—for generations. Della and Jim are struggling on in a cheap, crumbling apartment with barely enough money to live on. In such circumstances, who could think of buying Christmas presents? "The Gift of the Magi" is an endearing celebration of the love that binds a married couple together. It was first published in the New York Sunday World in 1905. It has been made into a movie multiple times, and many other films and episodes of television shows have borrowed its plot. O. Henry was the penname of the American writer William Sydney Porter (1862–1910). While many other authors in this collection are primarily known for their novels, Henry was a master of the short story. He so excelled in this genre that a prestigious literary prize for outstanding short stories is called the O. Henry Award. In "The Caballero's Way" (1907), he introduced a character that would take on a life of its own in American cinema and culture—the Western desperado, the Cisco Kid. One of his greatest stories is about a bank robber on the run, "A Retrieved Reformation" (1903).

The Gift of the Magi

O. Henry

One dollar and eighty-seven cents. That was all. And sixty cents of it was in pennies. Pennies saved one and two at a time by bulldozing the grocer and the vegetable man and the butcher until one's cheeks burned with the silent imputation of parsimony that such close dealing implied.[1] Three times Della counted it. One dollar and eighty-seven cents. And the next day would be Christmas.

There was clearly nothing left to do but flop down on the shabby little couch and howl. So Della did it. Which instigates the moral reflection that life is made up of sobs, sniffles, and smiles, with sniffles predominating.

While the mistress of the home is gradually subsiding from the first stage to the second, take a look at the home. A furnished flat at $8 per week. It did not exactly beggar description, but it certainly had that word on the look-out for the mendicancy[2] squad.

In the vestibule below was a letter-box into which no letter would go, and an electric button from which no mortal finger could coax a ring. Also appertaining thereunto was a card bearing the name "Mr. James Dillingham Young."

---

1. "Parsimony" means thriftiness or frugality. She is so in need of money that she tries to negotiate a slightly lower price on every little thing she has to buy.
2. Being a beggar.

The "Dillingham" had been flung to the breeze during a former period of prosperity when its possessor was being paid $30 per week. Now, when the income was shrunk to $20, the letters of "Dillingham" looked blurred, as though they were thinking seriously of contracting to a modest and unassuming D. But whenever Mr. James Dillingham Young came home and reached his flat above he was called "Jim" and greatly hugged by Mrs. James Dillingham Young, already introduced to you as Della. Which is all very good.

Della finished her cry and attended to her cheeks with the powder rag.[3] She stood by the window and looked out dully at a grey cat walking a grey fence in a grey backyard. To-morrow would be Christmas Day, and she had only $1.87 with which to buy Jim a present. She had been saving every penny she could for months, with this result. Twenty dollars a week doesn't go far. Expenses had been greater than she had calculated. They always are. Only $1.87 to buy a present for Jim. Her Jim. Many a happy hour she had spent planning for something nice for him. Something fine and rare and sterling—something just a little bit near to being worthy of the honour of being owned by Jim.

There was a pier-glass[4] between the windows of the room. Perhaps you have seen a pier-glass in an $8 flat. A very thin and very agile person may, by observing his reflection in a rapid sequence of longitudinal strips, obtain a fairly accurate conception of his looks. Della, being slender, had mastered the art.

Suddenly she whirled from the window and stood before the glass. Her eyes were shining brilliantly, but her face had lost its colour within twenty seconds. Rapidly she pulled down her hair and let it fall to its full length.

Now, there were two possessions of the James Dillingham Youngs in which they both took a mighty pride. One was Jim's gold watch that had

3. She is putting on makeup.
4. A mirror.

been his father's and his grandfather's. The other was Della's hair. Had the Queen of Sheba lived in the flat across the airshaft, Della would have let her hair hang out of the window some day to dry just to depreciate Her Majesty's jewels and gifts. Had King Solomon been the janitor, with all his treasures piled up in the basement, Jim would have pulled out his watch every time he passed, just to see him pluck at his beard from envy.

So now Della's beautiful hair fell about her, rippling and shining like a cascade of brown waters. It reached below her knee and made itself almost a garment for her. And then she did it up again nervously and quickly. Once she faltered for a minute and stood still while a tear or two splashed on the worn red carpet.

On went her old brown jacket; on went her old brown hat. With a whirl of skirts and with the brilliant sparkle still in her eyes, she cluttered out of the door and down the stairs to the street.

Where she stopped the sign read: "Mme⁵ Sofronie. Hair Goods of All Kinds." One flight up Della ran, and collected herself, panting. Madame, large, too white, chilly, hardly looked the "Sofronie."⁶

"Will you buy my hair?" asked Della.

"I buy hair," said Madame. "Take yer hat off and let's have a sight at the looks of it."

Down rippled the brown cascade.

"Twenty dollars," said Madame, lifting the mass with a practised hand.

"Give it to me quick," said Della.

Oh, and the next two hours tripped by on rosy wings. Forget the hashed metaphor. She was ransacking the stores for Jim's present.

She found it at last. It surely had been made for Jim and no one else.

---

5. An abbreviation for Madame—a title of respect for a married woman which is used in various foreign lands.

6. Della suspects that the shopkeeper does not really have a right to the name "Madame Sofronie," but is just an ordinary, American woman who is pretending to be foreign in order to appear more sophisticated.

There was no other like it in any of the stores, and she had turned all of them inside out. It was a platinum fob chain[7] simple and chaste in design, properly proclaiming its value by substance alone and not by meretricious ornamentation—as all good things should do. It was even worthy of The Watch. As soon as she saw it she knew that it must be Jim's. It was like him. Quietness and value—the description applied to both. Twenty-one dollars they took from her for it, and she hurried home with the 87 cents. With that chain on his watch Jim might be properly anxious about the time in any company. Grand as the watch was, he sometimes looked at it on the sly on account of the old leather strap that he used in place of a chain.

When Della reached home her intoxication gave way a little to prudence and reason. She got out her curling irons and lighted the gas and went to work repairing the ravages made by generosity added to love. Which is always a tremendous task dear friends—a mammoth task.

Within forty minutes her head was covered with tiny, close-lying curls that made her look wonderfully like a truant schoolboy. She looked at her reflection in the mirror long, carefully, and critically.

"If Jim doesn't kill me," she said to herself, "before he takes a second look at me, he'll say I look like a Coney Island chorus girl. But what could I do—oh! what could I do with a dollar and eighty-seven cents?"

At 7 o'clock the coffee was made and the frying-pan was on the back of the stove hot and ready to cook the chops.

Jim was never late. Della doubled the fob chain in her hand and sat on the corner of the table near the door that he always entered. Then she heard his step on the stair away down on the first flight, and she turned white for just a moment. She had a habit of saying little silent prayers about the simplest everyday things, and now she whispered: "Please, God, make him think I am still pretty."

---

7. A "fob" is a small pocket. A fob chain is for securing something kept in that pocket—in this case, a pocket watch.

The door opened and Jim stepped in and closed it. He looked thin and very serious. Poor fellow, he was only twenty-two—and to be burdened with a family! He needed a new overcoat and he was without gloves.

Jim stepped inside the door, as immovable as a setter at the scent of quail. His eyes were fixed upon Della, and there was an expression in them that she could not read, and it terrified her. It was not anger, nor surprise, nor disapproval, nor horror, nor any of the sentiments that she had been prepared for. He simply stared at her fixedly with that peculiar expression on his face.

Della wriggled off the table and went for him.

"Jim, darling," she cried, "don't look at me that way. I had my hair cut off and sold it because I couldn't have lived through Christmas without giving you a present. It'll grow out again—you won't mind, will you? I just had to do it. My hair grows awfully fast. Say 'Merry Christmas!' Jim, and let's be happy. You don't know what a nice—what a beautiful, nice gift I've got for you."

"You've cut off your hair?" asked Jim, laboriously, as if he had not arrived at that patent fact yet, even after the hardest mental labor.

"Cut it off and sold it," said Della. "Don't you like me just as well, anyhow? I'm me without my hair, ain't I?"

Jim looked about the room curiously.

"You say your hair is gone?" he said, with an air almost of idiocy.

"You needn't look for it," said Della. "It's sold, I tell you—sold and gone, too. It's Christmas Eve, boy. Be good to me, for it went for you. Maybe the hairs of my head were numbered," she went on with a sudden serious sweetness, "but nobody could ever count my love for you. Shall I put the chops on, Jim?"

Out of his trance Jim seemed quickly to wake. He enfolded his Della. For ten seconds let us regard with discreet scrutiny some inconsequential object in the other direction. Eight dollars a week or a million a year—what is the difference? A mathematician or a wit would give you the wrong answer. The magi brought valuable gifts, but that was not among them. This dark assertion will be illuminated later on.

Jim drew a package from his overcoat pocket and threw it upon the table.

"Don't make any mistake, Dell," he said, "about me. I don't think there's anything in the way of a haircut or a shave or a shampoo that could make me like my girl any less. But if you'll unwrap that package you may see why you had me going a while at first."

White fingers and nimble tore at the string and paper. And then an ecstatic scream of joy; and then, alas! a quick feminine change to hysterical tears and wails, necessitating the immediate employment of all the comforting powers of the lord of the flat.

For there lay The Combs—the set of combs, side and back, that Della had worshipped for long in a Broadway window. Beautiful combs, pure tortoise-shell, with jewelled rims—just the shade to wear in the beautiful vanished hair. They were expensive combs, she knew, and her heart had simply craved and yearned over them without the least hope of possession. And now, they were hers, but the tresses that should have adorned the coveted adornments were gone.

But she hugged them to her bosom, and at length she was able to look up with dim eyes and a smile and say: "My hair grows so fast, Jim!"

And then Della leaped up like a little singed cat and cried, "Oh, oh!"

Jim had not yet seen his beautiful present. She held it out to him eagerly upon her open palm. The dull precious metal seemed to flash with a reflection of her bright and ardent spirit.

"Isn't it a dandy, Jim? I hunted all over town to find it. You'll have to look at the time a hundred times a day now. Give me your watch. I want to see how it looks on it."

Instead of obeying, Jim tumbled down on the couch and put his hands under the back of his head and smiled.

"Dell," said he, "let's put our Christmas presents away and keep 'em a while. They're too nice to use just at present. I sold the watch to get the money to buy your combs. And now suppose you put the chops on."

The magi, as you know, were wise men—wonderfully wise men—who brought gifts to the Babe in the manger. They invented the art of giving Christmas presents. Being wise, their gifts were no doubt wise ones, possibly bearing the privilege of exchange in case of duplication. And here I have lamely related to you the uneventful chronicle of two foolish children in a flat who most unwisely sacrificed for each other the greatest treasures of their house. But in a last word to the wise of these days let it be said that of all who give gifts these two were the wisest. Of all who give and receive gifts, such as they are wisest. Everywhere they are wisest. They are the magi.

IS CHRISTMAS UNBIBLICAL AND PAGAN?

A Christian Affirmation of Yuletide Joy and Celebrations

While almost all Christians in America participate in Christmas celebrations, sometimes they can feel a little uneasy about it or uncertain how to respond when they are challenged with the claim that certain aspects of it—or even the entire holiday—are pagan or unbiblical. It is not uncommon for polemical unbelievers to tweak believers by making these claims. This book participates heartily and joyfully in a Christian celebration of Christmas, and therefore this essay has been included to dispel any such worries or anxieties. It can be a truly, fully Christian thing to celebrate Christmas—gifts, feasting, decorated trees, lights, wreaths, and more. Let me explain why this is so.

Christmas is the celebration of the birth of Jesus Christ, of God becoming incarnate and entering our world as a baby to live a human life, die on the cross for our sins, and be raised to life again as King of kings and Lord of lords. In other words, Christmas is a time to remember and rejoice over some deeply Christian themes that are key parts of salvation history as revealed in the Bible. These themes had been already announced in the Old Testament by the prophets. The prophet Isaiah foresaw that a child would come who would be Mighty God in the flesh:

> The people walking in darkness have seen a great light; on those living in the land of deep darkness a light has dawned. . . . For to us a child is born, to us a son is given, and the government will be on his shoulders. And he will be called Wonderful Counselor, Mighty God, Everlasting Father, Prince of Peace. Of the increase of his government and peace there will be no end. He will reign on David's throne and over his kingdom, establishing and upholding it with justice and righteousness from that time on and forever. (Isa. 9:2, 6–7)

Another example is a prophecy of Micah that predicts that someone from Bethlehem will arise as a ruler—a figure who is not just a newborn like everyone else, but who is really coming out of the realm of the Eternal: "But you, Bethlehem Ephrathah, though you are small among the clans of Judah, one of you will come to me one who will be ruler over Israel, whose origins are from of old, from ancient times" (Mic. 5:2).

In the New Testament, John's gospel begins by announcing the good news of the incarnation: "The Word became flesh and made his dwelling among us. We have seen his glory, the glory of the one and only Son, who came from the Father, full of grace and truth" (John 1:14). The first two chapters of Matthew's gospel are focused on the story of Christ's birth, including the account of the magi coming to see the Christ child:

> After they had heard the king, they went on their way, and the star they had seen when it rose went ahead of them until it stopped over the place where the child was. When they saw the star, they were overjoyed. On coming to the house, they saw the child with his mother Mary, and they bowed and worshiped him. Then they

opened their treasures and presented him with gifts of gold, frankincense and myrrh. (Matt. 2:9–11)

Most beloved of all is the account of Christ's nativity in the first two chapters of Luke's gospel. It includes the account of the announcement to the shepherds:

And there were shepherds living out in the fields nearby, keeping watch over their flocks at night. An angel of the Lord appeared to them, and the glory of the Lord shone around them, and they were terrified. But the angel said to them, "Do not be afraid. I bring you good news of great joy that will be for all the people. Today in the town of David a Savior has been born to you; he is the Messiah, the Lord. This will be a sign to you: You will find a baby wrapped in cloths and lying in a manger." (Luke 2:8–12)

In the apostle Paul's letter to the Philippians, we even have what seems to be the lyrics of an early Christian hymn proclaiming the good news of Christ's incarnation and atoning death on the cross:

Who, being in the very nature God, did not consider equality with God something to be used to his own advantage; rather he made himself nothing by taking the very nature of a servant, being made in human likeness. And being found in appearance as a man, he humbled himself by becoming obedient to death—even death on a cross! (Phil. 2:6–8)

So the story that is celebrated at Christmas is a profoundly biblical one. Is the Christmas holiday itself, however, somehow unbiblical or pagan? Christians celebrated Christmas for well over a thousand years without such a concern troubling them. We know for sure that the church was celebrating Christmas by around AD 350, and as there are few church records from before then that have survived, we can only wonder how much earlier the practice might have started. In the sixteenth century, however, some Protestants were concerned enough to give up on Christmas altogether, especially those from the Reformed and Anabaptist wings of the Reformation. It might mischievously be said that the reformer John Calvin was the Grinch who stole Christmas. In the seventeenth century, Calvinist pastors in Scotland would go door-to-door throughout their parish on December 25th making sure that nobody was having a good time. In America, the Puritan governor of the Plymouth Colony, William Bradford, tried to forbid anyone—even those who were self-employed—from taking a day off work on December 25th. This concern about Christmas being unbiblical continued for around three centuries (that is, starting in the early sixteenth century and going to the early nineteenth century) before even most of these very same Protestant groups—including Presbyterians, Baptists, and Congregationalists—changed their minds again and decided that celebrating Christmas was a Christian thing to do after all. Nevertheless, because we still have the cultural memory of those three centuries when certain prominent Protestant groups rejected Christmas, some people are still a bit uneasy, wondering if those Reformers and Puritans were right in their rejection of the holiday and the current practice might be wrong after all. The unbiblical and the pagan criticisms are entwined in various ways, which mean that they cannot totally be separated, but I will focus on the unbiblical one first, and then address the pagan one. The end of it all, however, will be that we can celebrate Christmas in full delight and joy.

UNBIBLICAL

The unbiblical charge rests on two points. The first reason is that the Bible does not tell us the date of Jesus' birthday. In other words, although Scripture does give us a full and fascinating account of Jesus' birth, no specific date is mentioned. December 25th is not a date provided in Scripture.

The second reason is that nowhere in the Bible are Christians commanded to celebrate Christ's birth, nor is there an example of or reference to the church doing so anywhere in the New Testament.

These objections are only valid, however, if one takes a rather strict view of what is called the Regulative Principle in formal theology. The Regulative Principle asserts that anything that does not have explicit warrant in the New Testament is prohibited in Christian worship. Many Protestants groups have never accepted the Regulative Principle as a valid principle at all. For those who do, there then is a question of how strictly to apply it. The strictest version includes the claim that it is wrong to use musical instruments in worship because there is no clear New Testament warrant to do so. For example, a branch of the Churches of Christ denomination—helpfully often distinguished in its very name as "noninstrumental"—takes that view. In general, however, even churches that affirm the Regulative Principle such as Presbyterians and Reformed Baptists do not apply it so strictly—Christians can use organs, pianos, and guitars in our corporate worship in good conscience. In the end, most of these denominations would likewise decide that, although the Regulative Principle is valid, evoking it to forbid the celebration of Christmas was an example of an unduly strict application.

Some Puritans in the seventeenth century were so opposed to Christmas that they would try to thwart anyone celebrating the holiday by declaring December 25th to be an official, mandatory Fast Day. That effort, however, shows that their supposed biblical objection was not a valid one, for if the church cannot declare a Feast Day on December 25th because the Bible does not name that specific date, then the same logic would say that the church cannot declare a Fast Day on December 25th because the Bible does not name the date. Or, to put it positively, if the church is free to declare a fast on any day that seems good to it, then the church is also free to declare a feast or celebration on any day that seems good to it.

Moreover, as I have said, many Protestants have never accepted the Regulative Principle as a valid principle at all. They follow instead the Normative Principle, which says that if Scripture does not forbid something, then the church is free to decide that it would be a profitable addition to its worship and to make use of it as seems most prudent and best. Martin Luther followed the Normative Principle. If you asked Luther, "Where in the New Testament does it tell us to use musical instruments in worship?" he would have replied: "Where in the New Testament does it say that we are forbidden to use musical instruments in worship?" If the Bible does not forbid it, then we are free to decide whether or not it would be a helpful, wholesome, and edifying practice to do it. Luther was convinced that remembering Christ's birth every year on December 25th was an edifying practice that was good for Christian discipleship. Indeed, Luther heartily loved Christmas. He preached numerous Christmas sermons that have survived, and also penned Christmas carols. Here is a passage from one of Luther's Christmas sermons:

> She "wrapped him in swaddling clothes, and laid him in a manger." Why not in a cradle, on a bench? Because they had no cradle, bench, table, board, nor anything whatever except the manger of the oxen. That was the first throne of this King. There in a stable, without man or maid, lay the Creator of the world. And there was the maid of fifteen years bringing forth her first-born without fire or pan, a sight for tears! What Mary and Joseph did next, nobody knows. They must have marveled that this Child was the Son of God. He was also a real human being. Those who say that Mary was not a real mother lose all the joy. He was a true Baby, with flesh, blood, hands and legs. He slept, cried, and did everything else that a baby does only without sin.

I have preached a different Christmas sermon from a different biblical passage (or pulling out different points to expound from the same passage) in my home church for twenty years now. I could keep going for as many years and decades as God will give me because Scripture is inexhaustible, and the gospel is inexhaustible. The story of Christ's birth and the doctrine of the incarnation as given in numerous Scriptures are themes which we can return to with great spiritual profit year after year after year for as long as we live.

Here is the truth of the matter: Christmas is extrabiblical, but not unbiblical. Extrabiblical just means that it is based on choices that godly people are free to make rather than on details specifically given in the Bible. It is not unbiblical in the sense of something that is wrong to do if you want to be faithful to the Bible. Much of church life is extrabiblical in this way. If asked, "Where in the New Testament does it say that there should be a Wednesday night prayer meeting?" the answer is simply, "The Bible tells us to pray, and if it is perfectly fine for us to decide that Wednesday evenings are a desirable time to do it." The same is true of Christmas: the Bible calls us to teach our children and new believers the doctrine of the incarnation, that Jesus was actually God made flesh, and the biblical story of Christ's nativity and to rejoice in these great truths, and if December 25th is deemed to be a desirable time to do it, then we are free to do it. Given that even the federal government makes provision for us to have a day off work so we can celebrate on December 25th, it would seem pointlessly obstinate and stubborn to refuse to take advantage of this traditional day for remembering the birth of Jesus.

In fact, I want to draw your attention to a text in the Bible that is not in any way associated with Christmas to help you think about why it is not unbiblical. It is from the book of Esther:

> Mordecai recorded these events, and he sent letters to all the Jews throughout the provinces of King Xerxes, near and far, to have them celebrate annually the fourteenth and fifteenth days of the month of

Adar as the time when the Jews got relief from their enemies, and as a month when their sorrow was turned into joy and their mourning into a day of celebration. He wrote them to observe the days as days of feasting and joy and giving presents of food to one another and gifts to the poor.

So the Jews agreed to continue the celebration they had begun, doing what Mordecai had written to them. For Haman son of Hammedatha, the Agagite, the enemy of all the Jews, had plotted against the Jews to destroy them and had cast the *pur* (that is, the lot) for their ruin and destruction. But when the plot came to the king's attention, he issued written orders that the evil scheme Haman had devised against the Jews should come back onto his own head, and that he and his sons should be impaled on poles. (Therefore these days were called Purim, from the word *pur*.) Because of everything written in this letter and because of what they had seen and what had happened to them, the Jews took it on themselves to establish the custom that they and their descendants and all who join them should without fail observe these two days ever year, in the way prescribed and at the time appointed. These days should be remembered and observed in every generation by every family, and in every province and in every city. And these days of Purim should never cease to be celebrated by the Jews, nor should the memory of them die out among their descendants. (Est. 9:20–28)

Are you worried that December 25th is not named in the Bible as the day on which we are to celebrate Christ's birth? If so, I am here to put any such troubled consciences at ease.

Good Christian men and women, rejoice! What we see here in Esther is that Mordecai originally had the idea for this sacred holiday, the Feast of Purim, and the others agreed. Here again are the last verses from that passage:

The Jews *took it on themselves* to establish the custom that they and their descendants and all who join them should without fail observe these two days ever year, in the way prescribed and at the time appointed. These days should be remembered and observed in every generation by every family, and in every province and in every city. And these days of Purim should never cease to be celebrated by the Jews, nor should the memory of them die out among their descendants.

What I want you to notice is that, according to the text, this is a completely "man-made" holiday. God does not tell them to do it. In fact, God is not mentioned at all in the entire book of Esther. Mordecai and the Jews are not obeying a word from the Lord; they did not receive a message from God from an angel or in a vision or a dream or through a prophet; they just decided to create this sacred day and told all believers to observe it faithfully forevermore. In fact, Jesus himself would have observed the sacred feast of Purim every year as part of his devout practice of a life of faith and worship.

Esther chapter 8 seems to be smoothing over a problem that arose of customs in different regions regarding whether Purim should be celebrated on the 14th or 15th day of the month of Adar. The genius solution to this problem devised in the Bible is to declare both days to be holidays. The wisdom of the church is actually that December 25th is the first day of the Twelve Days of Christmas celebration. Twelve days of feasting! Most of us are not able to party as hard and as long as the church desires. We give up and start in with diets and New Year's resolutions, but the church invites you to hold off on such discipline and restraint until after Epiphany on January 6th.

Furthermore, this text in the book of Esther gives us a biblical model for how to keep a sacred day such as Christmas. This is presented in verse 22: "He wrote them to observe the days as days of feasting and joy and giving presents of food to one another and gifts to the poor."

Here is a list of four components of the biblical way to celebrate a sacred day:

1. WITH FEASTING. The biblical way to celebrate a sacred day is with food and drink of better quality and of greater quantity than usual. We are embodied beings. The Bible understands that the way to make a sacred truth a reality to us is for us to experience the delight of it in our bodies. Christians sometimes talked about Christ-mas being worldly because it involves indulgence, but the biblical model is that there is a time to fast and a time to feast. Earlier in the book of Esther they called for fasting because they were in a crisis, and once God delivered them, they then called for a feast. Feasting is a biblical way to celebrate. Many of us have traditions of foods which we only have or make during the holiday season. All kinds of things appear that we don't otherwise have—eggnog, candy canes, chestnuts, yule log cakes, mince pies, cranberry sauce, sage stuffing, gingerbread, and so on. I always roast a goose for Christmas—and never at any other time of year. These holiday traditions are a way to signal that one is feasting—that something heightening and special is happening to our culinary experience. Again, that is a biblical way to celebrate.

2. WITH JOY. Ecclesiastes makes it clear that there is *a time to rejoice*. Christmas is an annual time for rejoicing. Even in a hard year, even when many things have not gone our way, this is the right time to rejoice. The Christmas season is a time when we remind ourselves of things worth celebrating and endeavor to feel the joy of them— and to express our joy to others. In Charles Dickens's *A Christmas Carol*, part of what makes Ebenezer Scrooge so repulsive is not just

that he is a miser who treats others badly—especially when it comes to money—but that he lives a joyless life. He does not know how to rejoice. He eats meager, awful meals. Christmas comes but once a year, Scrooge is reminded, but he cannot find joy even on one of the few days of the year that is most set apart as a day of rejoicing. Let us not allow our cares and worries and never-ending list of things to do rob us of our Christmas joy. Rejoice!

3. WITH GIVING PRESENTS TO ONE ANOTHER. The "one another" in the text is emphasizing our own social circle—our family and friends, and perhaps coworkers and neighbors—the people that are a part of our social lives. We give them gifts as an expression of our joy because it can help create joy in us, and because it can bring joy to others. People find giving Christmas gifts a pressure because it takes time and effort and it is not easy to get right. But it is thrilling to know that you understand someone well enough to have found a gift that is just right for them. Gift-giving is a way of making the people around us feel seen and known and appreciated. It is the opposite of taking them for granted. It says you are special to me and I want to take the time and effort to acknowledge that. The text mentions food in particular. The Hebrew word used has the connotation of delicacies or fine or choice foods. In other words, a particularly biblical thing to do to mark a sacred feast is to give people high-quality baked goods!

4. WITH GIFTS TO THE POOR. Jesus was particularly critical of well-off people who just exchange gifts with each other and host dinner parties for each other and don't find a way for their giving to flow out to people in greater need than themselves and their own social circle. If it is all just a selfish, little world, it might be called

celebrating, but it is really soulless and joyless. Our own joy is increased when we find ways to be generous to those who really need our help. Christmas is rightly a time to give donations to charities and to find ways to help or bless people who are less well-off than we are. We tend to think of the commercialism and consumerism of Christmas, but we forget that Christmas is also the time of year when charities often raise the most money and are able to do the most good. Numerous charities have plans to help people specifically during the Christmas season. I have been a member of a church that focused its Christmas giving around Prison Fellowship's Angel Tree campaign, and another one that did so with Samaritan Purse's Operation Christmas Child. My current church raises money every Christmas season to pay the school fees for children in Uganda in the upcoming year. The Salvation Army, which is also a Christian denomination, is particularly known for raising money at Christmas time with its red kettles and for helping people in need out during the holiday season.

Celebrating Christmas with feasting, presents, giving, and joy is a deeply Christian thing to do.

PAGAN

We have now made it to the second accusation. Is Christmas really pagan? This charge is based on concerns that the celebration of Christmas is really a continuation of pagan celebrations or ways of celebrating—specifically, that it is based in the pagan celebration of the winter solstice or other Roman, pagan holidays from around that time of year; and that Christmas symbols such as Christmas trees, mistletoe, and evergreens are actually pagan symbols and pagan ways of celebrating.

The first thing to say about this is that it is an example of a logical fallacy that philosophers call the Genetic Fallacy—the fallacy that something is right or wrong because of its origins. Things change their meaning over time and what they meant to someone else in the past does not determine what they mean to us now. We all know that words or gestures that were once innocent can become rude over time and vice versa—again, what matters is what they mean to the people using them, not to someone else in another time or place or culture. We can think of examples of this even for things with pagan origins. For instance, the name of the month of March was originally a reference to the Roman god Mars, and the day of the week Thursday was a reference to the Nordic god Thor, yet it is simply not true that if I were to say to you: "Let's have lunch on the first Thursday in March," I would somehow be reverencing pagan gods. Such a claim would be to commit the Genetic Fallacy. The meaning of words or customs for us today is not determined by what they might have meant to someone else a long time ago. To observe that some people might have once lit a candle in winter to honor a pagan god does not mean that when I light a candle in winter I am honoring a pagan god—I might be honoring Jesus Christ, the Light of the World, who came into the darkness and whom the darkness could not overcome.

Second, whenever a new faith or ideology or way of life emerges, it inevitably expresses itself through the cultural resources to hand, which are therefore derived from preexisting ones. This is so self-evident it is hard even to imagine what the alternative might be. In other words, a clear, direct case of cultural borrowing does not necessarily tell us anything about something's meaning in its new context. Take, for instance, a holiday that we observe in the United States: Independence Day on the Fourth of July. An informed observer could notice innumerable cultural borrowings. For example, the use of red, white, and blue as the national colors is obviously simply adopted from Great Britain. Hearing the song "America (My Country, 'Tis of Thee)," one might immediately recognize the melody as that of the British national anthem ("God Save the King"). The fireworks might remind one of celebrations of the British monarchy, famously evoked just a couple decades before the American War of Independence in Handel's Music for the Royal Fireworks (1749). Our observer might be baffled by the claim that serving apple pie—a very common, traditional English dish—is somehow distinctively American, let alone imagining that the United States invented motherhood ("as American as motherhood and apple pie"). Again, what all this goes to show is that Great Britain preceded the United States and that new cultures arise by using the resources that are available to them. It would be absurd, however, to use these facts to claim that in their Fourth of July celebrations Americans are somehow *really* honoring the British monarchy and expressing their loyalty to the British nation and that if they want to be *truly* American they therefore must forsake the red, white, and blue, and the apple pie, and all the rest. It is no less absurd to claim that when Christians put up a Christmas tree to remember the birth of Christ they are somehow really honoring pagan gods from the past and all such fallacious reasoning.

Third, the Genetic Fallacy is even more ridiculous than usual in the case we are discussing because so many aspects of the celebration of Christmas are what the author Dorothy L. Sayers and the anthropologist Mary Douglas and other scholars have referred to as "Natural Symbols"—connections that are so obvious to make that they are likely to occur to many different cultures independently. No one has a copyright, for instance, on the symbolic significance of light coming into the darkness—it certainly does not somehow belong to pagans celebrating the winter solstice. It belongs just as much to Jews celebrating Hanukkah, Hindus celebrating Diwali, Christians celebrating Christmas, and a wide range of other cultures and traditions from across time and around the world. Cultures across the globe and the centuries have kept time by the course of the sun and the moon. Solstices have marked time for peoples across the planet from time immemorial, however much their religions and cultures have differed from each other. Likewise, no one has proprietary claims over the spiritual or cultural significance of the display of evergreen trees and plant decorations during winter—these are Natural Symbols. They speak symbolically of life even in a time of death, darkness, and decay. A common way to celebrate across the centuries and the globe has likewise been with feasting and gift-giving. None of these things belong to pagans; they belong to humanity.

Fourth, things that are said to be pagan are often no less rooted in the teaching and example given to us as Christians in the Old Testament. As the Bible reveals, the sacred festivals are often tied to solar and lunar cycles (Passover, for instance, to the spring equinox). Genesis 1:14 even declares that one of the very reasons why God created the sun and the moon was in order "to mark out the sacred seasons" (Moffatt translation). The same is true for using plants in celebrations. Moses himself established the sacred festival, the Festival of Ingathering, which is the Harvest Festival in Judaism. This is recorded, for instance, in the book of Numbers chapter 29. Here is the account in the book of Nehemiah of the people beginning to celebrate the Festival of Ingathering again after the exile:

> And in the law they found it written how the Lord had given orders through Moses that the Israelites were to live in booths on the festival of the seventh month. On hearing this, they issued a proclamation throughout all their towns and throughout Jerusalem: "Go to the hill country and bring in branches of olive, myrtle, palm, and evergreens to make booths as prescribed." (Neh. 8:14–15 Moffatt)

How is the sacred Festival of Ingathering to be celebrated? City dwellers and town folk go out into the countryside and gather evergreens and bring them back. Again, to claim that pagans also sometimes go out into the countryside and gather evergreens to celebrate their festivals does not somehow make a Jewish festival pagan. Nor does it make a Christian festival pagan.

Finally, it turns out that a lot of the claims regarding pagan connections to Christianity are not true—some of them were even deliberately made up in modern times. As I have said, it is ridiculous to think of the winter solstice as inherently pagan. All ancient cultures marked time by the sun and the moon—in fact, we still mark time by the sun and the moon—with the year being one cycle of the earth around the sun and a month being one cycle of the moon around the earth. In the ancient world, people were generally not literate—many entire cultures lacked any alphabet or written language—and thus the only way you could have a date for an annual festival was to agree on a day marked by the cycles of the sun or the moon.

The reason why Christians decided on December 25th for the celebration of Christmas is unclear. I know some very bright people who believe that it is the true date for Christ's birthday and that this information was handed down from Mary to the apostle John to later Christians. Although that is possible, I don't think it is very likely. I assume that Christians probably chose December 25th (which was the date of the winter solstice in the Julian calendar) for *theological reasons*—the winter solstice means that from that point on in the annual cycle there is more and more light and less and less darkness. Christ has come. He is the Light of the World: **"The light shines in the darkness, and the darkness has not overcome it"** (John 1:5). That is the spiritual meaning, for Christians, of the winter solstice.

We are also very used to celebrating something on a date that seems right for reasons other than historical accuracy. Most years, Martin Luther King, Jr Day does not fall on his actual birthday. Although it is often referred to as Presidents' Day, our federal holiday in February is officially called Washington's Birthday—yet it rarely falls on Washington's actual birthday. Even the king or queen of Britain has an official birthday that is celebrated every year and which is not even in the same month as his or her true birthday. In other words, we should be well used to the idea that something can be celebrated on a different day from the one of the historical event it marks.

Most of what passes for ancient pagan ritual and practices today are just modern inventions. If you go to the ancient site of Stonehenge in England for a solstice there will be all kinds of people in costumes and masks with all kinds of staffs and torches engaged in all kinds of rituals that they want you to imagine is a continuation of ancient pagan practices, but they have just made it all up. They claim that Christians are doing things that are taken from the ancient pagans, but even the modern pagans themselves aren't doing things taken from ancient pagans because we just don't have records of the rituals and practices of ancient pagans—everyone is almost always just guessing. All that Stonehenge tells you is that ancient people understood the cycle of the sun and created a meeting place that lined up with it. Again, all human cultures, whatever their beliefs—not least ancient Israel—have always paid attention to the cycle of the sun and the moon and planned their festivals accordingly.

I would like now to do a bit of a diversion on Washington Irving, America's first celebrity author. He was born in Manhattan in 1783 and died in 1859. He is credited with making writing into a profession—of being the first fiction writer to make a living by his pen. He was also the first American writer to be popular in Europe. Some of the terms he used are still popular today. He spoke of New York City as "Gotham." He invented the phrase "the Almighty dollar." And some of his stories have gone deep into the American imagination, including "Rip Van Winkle" and "The Legend of Sleepy Hollow." Irving's writings about Christmas significantly shaped how people think about the holiday. For example, he is a key early source for the developing legend of Santa Claus. First published in 1809, and later added to, Irving wrote *A History of New-York from the Beginning of the World to the End of the Dutch Dynasty, by Diedrich Knickerbocker*. In it, supposedly presenting traditionally Dutch views but actually adding in material of his own creation, Irving depicted St. Nicholas flying over the city in a wagon and climbing down chimneys to deliver presents. Though the book irritated the descendants of the Dutch colonists, the *Knicker-bocker History* was read widely in the United States and Europe, making its author a famous man and adding details to the legend of St. Nicholas as well as turning St. Nicholas into at least an honorary American.

In 1820, Washington Irving published a collection of stories called *The Sketchbook of Geoffrey Crayon, Gentleman*. It contained several stories that are about Christmas in England (three chapters of which are included in this collection), which are written as if they are the eyewitness account of a traveler. There are two ways to write fiction. One way is with what is called an omniscient narrator. This means that the story can follow several different characters and tell you what they are doing even when they are alone. It can even tell you what they all are thinking and feeling. The other way is for it to be an account by someone that is thus limited to what that narrator thinks and feels and witnesses and overhears. This latter way of writing fiction makes it particularly seem like it is a true account. Daniel Defoe's *Robinson Crusoe* was a pioneering novel, and because it was written as if it was Crusoe's own account in this way, many readers mistook it for a true story.

These Christmas chapters by Washington Irving were written in that way and therefore they often left an impression on people's minds that they were learning about people who actually existed and things they actually said and did and believed. These early chapters include an account in which the alleged author, Geoffrey Crayon, visits a manor hall in

England where the squire is keeping up all the old Christmas customs. In other words, many people read it as a true account of what people do and think in regard to keeping an old-fashioned Christmas in England. Irving helped people to cherish Christmas and thus was part of the holiday's rise in prominence and importance in the nineteenth century. Here is an early passage in these chapters:

> Of all the old festivals, however, that of Christmas awakens the strongest and most heartfelt associations. There is a tone of solemn and sacred feeling that blends with our conviviality, and lifts the spirit to a state of hallowed and elevated enjoyment. The services are extremely tender and inspiring. They dwell on the beautiful story of the origin of our faith, and the pastoral scenes that accompanied its announcement.

To return, however, to the question we are exploring regarding the alleged paganism behind Christmas, here is a bit of Irving's account of their going to church on Christmas Day:

> On reaching the church-porch, we found the parson rebuking the gray-headed sexton for having used mistletoe among the greens with which the church was decorated. It was, he observed, an unholy plant, profaned by having been used by the Druids in their mystic ceremonies; and though it might be innocently employed in the festive ornamenting of halls and kitchens, yet it has been deemed by the Fathers of the Church as unhallowed, and totally unfit for sacred purposes.

Irving just made this up to try to make his novel more entertaining. In Christian thought, there is, of course, no such thing as an "unholy plant." There were no church fathers who condemned mistletoe. In fact, we know that mistletoe was a standard expense itemized in church records when it came to decorating the church for Christmas and had been for centuries before Irving imagined some pagan concern about it.

A similar thing has happened with the Christmas tree. In the nineteenth century, a German author, Johannes Marbach, asserted without any evidence that the Christmas tree was a custom that came from the ancient, pagan, Teutonic past. This was quickly picked up on by other authors. German Nationalists pushed the idea as they saw it as a way to make Christmas a distinctly German holiday, one that would unify the German peoples.

Sometimes the true origins of things are the exact opposite of what is imagined. In Northumberland in England, there is a holiday season tradition called the Allendale Fire Festival. It involves an outdoor procession with barrels of fire. Many people today believe that it is an ancient, pagan rite that has been handed down from time immemorial. In truth, however, it is both modern and Christian. It arose in 1858 from the local Methodist church including in its holiday services an all-night prayer meeting that included a procession.

Scholars who have tried to trace the origin of the Christmas tree now usually find it in a distinctly Christian practice from the Middle Ages. During the Christmas season, the church would put on sacred mystery plays that told the biblical story of salvation history. These would begin with the account of the creation and fall, starting in the garden of Eden. What the audience would see on the stage was a decorated tree representing the Tree of Life. Thus, Christmas became associated with decorated trees, and eventually people wanted to keep the festooned tree up as a decoration in the town; then people started creating their own in their homes as well to add to the celebration. The Christmas tree is a Christian reminder that God's original plan for human beings was that they would enjoy the Tree of Life, a plan that—through Christ's birth, ministry, death, and resurrection—has been joyfully and triumphantly restored to us once again (Rev. 22).

As I have been trying to show throughout this essay, people like to insist—often on the basis of made-up evidence—that Christmas is built upon paganism, but those same critics ignore the much more obvious and indisputable ways that Christmas is built upon Judaism. Yet the narrative of the nativity of Christ in the New Testament is clearly foreshadowed by the glorious birth accounts of certain major figures in the Old Testament. Indeed, the parallels between Hannah giving birth to Samuel and Mary giving birth to Jesus extend all the way to the songs of the two mothers—Mary's Magnificat being noticeably influenced by Hannah's prayer (1 Sam. 2:1–10; Luke 1:46–55). That is unquestionably a borrowing from the past. As has been noted already, Christians continued the Jewish practice of dating their major religious feasts based on the stations of the sun and the phases of the moon. And again, as we have seen, even some of the seemingly merely cultural (as opposed to overtly spiritual) aspects of Christmas likewise can be seen as directly derived from ancient Israel's approach to a sacred day. To quote Esther 9:22 again, the biblical way to celebrate is to have a holiday; that they should "observe the days as days of feasting and joy and giving presents of food to one another and gifts to the poor." Because Christians are generally quite comfortable with the Jewish roots of their faith, these connections somehow become not worth pointing out to people, as the critics are only looking for evidence that will seem to discredit Christian practices.

So many of the words and phrases that are used to describe the Christmas season are wielded as indictments. Consumerism and commercialism are obvious examples. Those words can express real critiques of real problems. Gift-giving, however, is a way of fostering social bonds that has always existed across all human cultures, and thus it is bizarre indeed to try to make people who do wish to give presents feel ashamed simply for engaging in a beneficial and universal custom of social life.

Christmas is what you make of it. If you want to celebrate it as a

Christian holiday that honors Jesus Christ, then you can. No one can rightly tell you that by celebrating Christmas you are doing something inherently unbiblical or pagan or worldly. Decorate a tree if you like. Give gifts. Have a feast. Read aloud a classic Christmas story. Rejoice that a Savior has been born. Worship the Lord with gladness of heart. Good Christian Men, Women, and Children, Rejoice!

● ● ●

Those who are interested in the sources and scholarship behind the information provided in this appendix should consult Timothy Larsen (ed.), *The Oxford Handbook of Christmas* (Oxford: Oxford University Press, 2020). It has 45 chapters and each one has not only citations but also a "References and Further Reading" section at the end. Chapters especially relevant to this discussion include "The Dating of Christmas: The Early Church," "The Middle Ages," "The Reformation and Early Modern Periods," "The Nineteenth Century," "Reformed and Dissenting Protestants," "The Winter Solstice and Other Celebrations of the Season," and "Trees and Decorations."

ACKNOWLEDGMENTS

Special thanks go to my dear wife, Jane, who heroically read numerous Christmas stories aloud to me and offered valuable, initial feedback on which ones should go into this collection; to my editor at Moody Publishers, Catherine Parks, who immediately had a vision for this book, and who worked on it so diligently, cheerfully, and perceptively; and to Connor Rowe, who was my graduate student research assistant during a key stage of this project. I am also grateful to Dr. Blair Waddell and his congregation, Providence Baptist Church, Huntsville, Alabama, who invited me to give a series of church history lectures on the holiday and therefore prompted me to write, "Is Christmas Unbiblical and Pagan?"

I have worked hard to obtain a copy of a first or early edition of these tales. Therefore, almost all of the stories are presented here word-for-word as they originally appeared. In a few of them, however, a small deletion or substitution has been made of material that is likely to be too distracting for family reading aloud. We have inclined toward retaining the original spelling and punctuation unless it was likely to confuse readers today.

Twelve Classic Christmas Stories is dedicated to families that love to read. Some bookish families who enrich my life include Jim, Brita, James, and Arne Beitler; Drew, Emily, Beckett, Helena, Rosie, and MJ Bratcher; Rick, Alison, Charlotte, and Andrew Gibson; David, Elaine, Abbey, and Sam Hooker; Brian, Marissa, Hannah, Sam, and Ben Sabio Howell; Mark, Mary, Olivia, Ruby, Leah, Sena, and Sadie Lewis; Matt, Denise, Polly, and Peter Milliner; Shawn, Dorthy, Eva, and Corinne Okpebholo; and Dan,

Amy, and Anna Black Treier. The Larsens, too, are a family that loves to read, and thus I joyfully include in this list Jane and our three highly impressive children, all now adults: Lucia, Theo, and Amelia. As Lucia Holly is our Advent baby—and as she reads aloud to our family during Christmastide—this book is also dedicated to her. I love you, Lucia! Happy Christmas!

You finished reading!

Did this book help you in some way? If so, please consider writing an honest review wherever you purchase your books. Your review gets this book into the hands of more readers and helps us continue to create biblically faithful resources.

Moody Publishers books help fund the training of students for ministry around the world.

The **Moody Bible Institute** is one of the most well-known Christian institutions in the world, training thousands of young people to faithfully serve Christ wherever He calls them. And when you buy and read a book from Moody Publishers, you're helping make that vital ministry training possible.

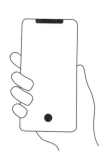

Continue to dive into the Word, *anytime, anywhere.*

Find what you need to take your next step in your walk with Christ: from uplifting music to sound preaching, our programs are designed to help you right when you need it.

Download the **Moody Radio App** and start listening today!

 MOODY Publishers    MOODY Bible Institute   MOODY Radio

Enjoy Charles Dickens's beloved masterpiece, freshly imagined within an enchanting woodland realm.

It may be because I am silly, but I rather think that . . .
I enjoy Christmas more than I did when I was a child.
My faith demands that such be the case. The more mature I
become the more I need to embrace the joys of the incarnation.
The more mature I become, the more I need to be but a child.

– G. K. Chesterton

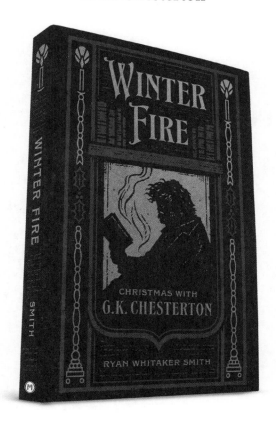

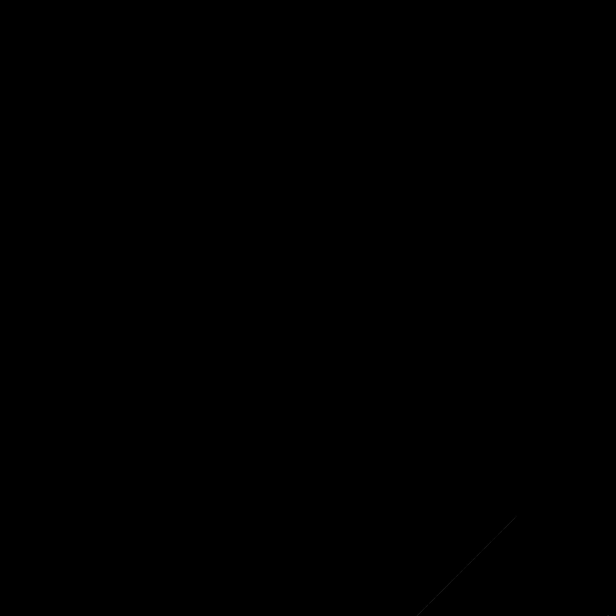